T0265684

LOST
WORLDS
&
MYTHOLOGICAL
KINGDOMS

ALSO EDITED BY JOHN JOSEPH ADAMS

* With Hugh Howey | ** With Hugh Howey & Christie Yant |
† With Douglas Cohen | ‡ With Daniel H. Wilson | § With Victor LaValle

LOST
WORLDS
&
MYTHOLOGICAL
KINGDOMS

EDITED BY

JOHN JOSEPH ADAMS

GRIM OAK PRESS
SEATTLE, WA

LOST WORLDS & MYTHOLOGICAL KINGDOMS
Compilation copyright © 2021 by John Joseph Adams.
All rights reserved.

"Introduction" by John Joseph Adams. © 2021 by John Joseph Adams.
"The Light Long Lost at Sea" by An Owomoyela. © 2021 by An Owomoyela.
"The Cleft of Bones" by Kate Elliott. © 2021 by Katrina Elliott.
"The Voyage of Brenya" by Carrie Vaughn. © 2021 by Carrie Vaughn, LLC.
"Comfort Lodge, Enigma Valley" by Charles Yu. © 2021 by
MSD Imaginary Machines, Inc.
"The Expedition Stops for the Evening at the Foot of the Mountain Pass"
by Genevieve Valentine. © 2021 by Genevieve Valentine.
"Down in the Dim Kingdoms" by Tobias S. Buckell. © 2021 by Tobias S. Buckell.
"Those Who Have Gone" by C.C. Finlay. © 2021 by C.C. Finlay.
"An Account, by Dr. Inge Kühn, of the Summer Expedition and Its Discoveries"
by E. Lily Yu. © 2021 by E. Lily Yu.
"Out of the Dark" by James L. Cambias. © 2021 by James L. Cambias.
"Endosymbiosis" by Darcie Little Badger. © 2021 by Darcie Little Badger.
"The Orpheus Gate" by Jonathan Maberry. © 2021 by
Jonathan Maberry Productions, LLC.
"Hotel Motel Holiday Inn" by Dexter Palmer. © 2021 by Dexter Palmer.
"On the Cold Hill Side" by Seanan McGuire. © 2021 by Seanan McGuire.
"The Return of Grace Malfrey" by Jeffrey Ford. © 2021 by Jeffrey Ford.
"The Tomb Ship" by Becky Chambers. © 2021 by Becky Chambers.
"Pellargonia: A Letter to the *Journal of Imaginary Anthropology*" by Theodora Goss.
© 2021 by Theodora Goss.
"There, She Didn't Need Air to Fill Her Lungs" by Cadwell Turnbull.
© 2021 by Cadwell Turnbull.
All works herein appear for the first time in this volume.

Dust jacket artwork by Allen Morris
Book design and composition by REview Design

Trade Hardcover Edition ISBN 978-1-944145-79-8
Signed, Limited Edition ISBN 978-1-944145-80-4
eBook ISBN 978-1-944145-82-8

First Edition, December 2021
2 4 6 8 9 7 5 3 1
Printed in China

Grim Oak Press
Battle Ground, WA 98604
www.grimoakpress.com

CONTENTS

INTRODUCTION

by John Joseph Adams

HERE BE DRAGONS.

That's what maps used to say when you reached the end of the known world.[1] It's a phrase that's fired humanity's imagination for hundreds of years: What lies beyond the edge of the unknown?

One of those things we imagined might lie in that distant beyond were so-called lost worlds or mythological kingdoms. Even if you're not familiar with those exact terms, you likely have heard legends of such fantastical places that were once thought to be real: Atlantis, Shambhala, El Dorado, Shangri-La, the kingdom of Prester John. This evocative idea was often explored in fiction as well, particularly in the late nineteenth and early twentieth centuries, in such classics as *The Lost World* by Arthur Conan Doyle, *Herland* by Charlotte Perkins Gilman, *The Land That Time Forgot* by Edgar Rice Burroughs, *King Solomon's Mines* by H. Rider Haggard, and *Erewhon* by Samuel Butler.

The abovementioned novels were all published more than a hundred years ago, and relatively few modern writers have turned

---

1 Or so many of us have been led to believe. A 2013 article in *The Atlantic*, however, casts doubt on that "truth," which seems likely to be apocryphal. In his research, the author, Robinson Meyer, found no ancient maps that bore that phrase, though it is found on the Hunt-Lenox Globe (from 1510).

their attention to this trope in contemporary times. In the present day, of course, there's very little of our world that can be said to be unexplored. To discover a lost world or mythological kingdom today would be a truly stunning event. And so, is it even possible to tell such stories in the modern era?

That was the challenge I put to the writers in this volume, and their response was an enthusiastic and convincing "Yes!"—as was mine when I read their stories. These tales are chock-full of the kind of sense of wonder we come looking for when we find our way to the science fiction/fantasy genre . . . and made me believe even more strongly that though the world is no longer a mystery, there's no need for the lost world trope to be lost to the sands of time.

Read these stories, and I think you'll agree. So come along with me—your tour guide if you will—as we travel through these magical, fascinating—and extremely perilous—journeys of the imagination.

John Joseph Adams, Editor
January 2021

LOST WORLDS & MYTHOLOGICAL KINGDOMS

An Owomoyela

The Light Long Lost at Sea

An Owomoyela

She saw Jaque again at the station, stepping down off the train with her brow furrowed, then turning back to offer a hand to someone in her awkward, courteous way. It brought a smile to Faville's face, no matter that she remembered when *she* would have been the one taking Jaque's hand, *she* would have been the one to receive that earnest courtesy. But time and distance had finished what circumstance had started, and now they stood on opposite sides of the platform.

Faville herself had changed, true. But it was always easier to count the changes on others. Jaque no longer wore the Peacekeeper uniform, though the slate-blue stitching of her jacket recalled it. Her hair was still corralled into braids, though the braids now curled across her head like windswept waves; her dark skin, if possible, seemed even darker.

Her boots were brown leather, riveted and stamped. She looked around the platform as though the crowds she'd once been inured to now overwhelmed her. And the soft coastal light lit on her like a train arriving or a ship docking: like the dawn, too, were a visitor coming to foreign land.

Jaque looked like a frontierswoman.

Faville crossed the platform to her and saw Jaque see her: a moment of wariness, quickly smoothed into the civil mask she'd practiced, practiced, practiced. But still, she let Faville speak first and set the tone.

It took no practice to make that tone warm.

"Jaque," Faville said, and reached across to clasp her hands. "I can't thank you enough for coming. It's been too long."

A fractional easing in Jaque's shoulders, there. And her small answering smile was, Faville thought, genuine. "It's good to see you," she said. Then, turning, "Please, may I present to you . . ."

Jaque hesitated with the name on her tongue.

Fortunately, her companion was more at ease. She stepped forward, offering her hands. "Bel," she said, and Faville clasped hands to greet her. "I've heard about you."

Faville laughed. What Jaque had shared, no doubt, would make something for the two of them to gossip over: not for any detail, but for the lack of it. "I've heard about you too," she said. Not *much*, but the quick amusement in Bel's eye suggested she understood. A fine pair, them: two women, united by happening to love the strange, difficult creature Jaque was.

"We shouldn't talk on the platform," Jaque said. Direct, as always. "You said . . . we haven't made arrangements for a room. Should . . . ?"

"Of course, as long as we're in town, you'll stay at my villa. Of *course*," Faville said. "But I thought you would want to go directly to the site. Do you? We've a boat already engaged." She glanced at Bel. "Of course, they're paid on retainer, and if you'd rather relax a while, they'll wait."

"I'd rather go to the boat," Jaque said, then frowned and seemed to remind herself of something. She looked to Bel, and said, "Sorry. Would you rather . . . ?"

"I'll follow you," Bel said. Her hand darted out to take Jaque's. "Always."

Perhaps for another woman, that might have merited more discussion, or perhaps elicited some overt token of affection returned. But Jaque, with her hidden, uncertain fluster, turned back to Faville and said, "You have your carriage?"

"This way," Faville said, and flashed her own smile as she led them toward the street.

No matter what had changed, Faville thought, no matter what she'd been through on the frontier, Jaque was still Jaque, at the end of it. If not still *her* Jaque, then still very much the same.

～

Bel, it turned out, was diversion enough for both of them.

Late spring had polished away the last of winter's rains, and the clear days of summer laid their mantle across the city. Robin's-egg skies would turn a more radiant blue as the day matured, and the fresh golden light lent an almost aching beauty to the whitewashed walls in this rich city district. Their carriage rolled northward and westward along the streets, farther from the wealthy neighborhoods and the Claimant's Terrace where Faville kept her villa, but Bel didn't seem to mind how . . . *common* the rest of the city was. She leaned out the window and exclaimed at shops and cafés, and shot a knowing look at Jaque once as they passed a modest building—scarcely larger than a house—which proclaimed itself the Water-Aster Baths. She seemed entranced by the open-air hawkers, and let out a cry of amazement when a white gull swooped down and lit on a streetlamp just as they passed under it.

"You've never been to the coast?" Faville asked, smiling. It was easy to play host to so enthusiastic a guest.

Bel turned back to her, a wide grin making her features generous. "Not the northern coast, no," she said.

That caught Jaque's attention, and she turned to her partner with all indication that she'd never thought to ask. "The Capitol?"

"South of that, even," Bel said. She reached for Jaque's hand again. "I grew up there. Didn't I tell you?"

Jaque looked away. Curious, Faville leaned forward. "What city?"

"New Corundum," Bel said. "Warm Mountain." The historians' name followed by that of the resettlers'. "Of course, it was half a day from the mountain, by horse. I never went up the slopes. I was mostly in the middle-city: no slopes, no shore."

Faville saw, but didn't comment upon, Bel's hand tightening on Jaque's. She elected not to pursue that small-talk further.

"One of my uncle's clippers is waiting for us at Garinrock," she said. "We'll take the ferry there and then go out to sea."

"*Garinrock,*" Jaque muttered, with the tone of someone who'd heard more than she ever wanted to about the place. Granted, that was the tone most everyone who'd spent time in Marematre took of Garinrock.

Marematre was a thriving city, settled after the Old Empire had collapsed. The land it sat on had been hardscrabble hills and forests before the collapse's various catastrophes had carved out the Sound beside it. Garinrock, called New Monscanus by some harder-headed traditionalists, still had the bones of the old city that had ruled this territory, and indeed the bones were still visible here and there: in the arcades and colonnades; in the segments of the raised aqueduct which had once brought water coastward from the fresh inland rivers; in the dome roof of the Old Temple, preserved against all reason on weatherbeaten columns like knobby legs. Even the stones of its streets—many of them, anyway—were vast Imperial things: slabs a horselength on each side, carved from some distant quarry by magic, transported by magic, and only lately, as stones counted it, with their magical protections failing such that ruts could be worn by feet and carriage wheels.

But the old city, Monscanus, had been shredded. The land under it had been shattered and scored into islands and the inlets, canals, bays, and straits that made up the North Sound. The old bones had been in ruins for generations, scattered over the islands, and the men and women who'd settled there and decided to become so proud of its history were not, for the most part, the descendants of old Monscanus. Garinrock was a younger city than Marematre itself, for all Garinrock's pride of place.

The ferry, though—smoothly bridging those rivalries—was a pleasant ride. At least Bel seemed to think so, once they were through the Marematre passenger port and into the little vessel's cabin. She was more than half entranced by the islands as they ambled past them, the waters of the Sound slapping the ferry's side and sending up seaweed-scented spray.

"I've never seen the open water," Bel said. "Not close."

"Bad business, the ocean," Jaque muttered.

Faville glanced at her, wondering where that sentiment had come from. It was a common enough superstition, yes, but out of place in a mouth which had never been prone to spouting superstitions before.

"People think it's a bad business because they think nothing's out there," Faville said. "Just saltwater, fish, and eventually the Barrier. You can't build on it, there's nothing left to explore, and there are enough fishermen." She grimaced around the words, recognizing how many of them—choice and cadence—came directly from her uncle. "But it's not any more soaked in ill luck than the rest of our little world."

"Which is bad enough," Jaque muttered back. She turned her head—not quite back to the mainland, but enough that Faville could see, in profile, some condemnation of the whole nation behind them. And the land around, beyond, in the cracks of the nation; and all the debris the Empire had left behind. "And you've found something exceptional out there."

Jaque's tone suggested that *exceptional* carried the heavy suspicion of *worse*, in her mind. Faville folded her hands: the quickest expedient she knew to keep from making any flustered gesture. "Men in my uncle's employ found it," she said. "He's got this fantastic idea to loop a rail line out to sea, in sight of the coast—finally complete a Marematre-Deires line." And connecting the northernmost great coastal city with the southernmost was the kind of feat of engineering a businessman could build a legacy on, if not a dynasty. Years of maniacal rail-building overland hadn't managed it yet, for his company nor any other. "He says that depending on the lay of the ocean floor, it might be cheaper to build a trestle offshore than to carve through all the mountains and whatnot. Not to mention the spectacle."

"And his scouts ran into some remnant magic that might upset his plans," Bel guessed.

"No," Faville said. "They ran into a spectacle."

Jaque fixed her with a searching look. Faville leaned forward.

"Not just transit, but *tourism*," she said. "That's Uncle's thinking. As the spot's near Marematre, he's asked me to round up someone—discreetly—to look at it. And an official surveyor is discreet enough, I suppose, but . . ." She trailed off. "I *know* you."

"Hmm," Jaque said. Coming from her, it really was consideration, not doubt.

"Wait until you see it," Faville said. "It's quite something."

"I'm sure," Jaque said, distantly.

Bel glanced to her. And Faville could swear she saw sadness crimp her eyes.

~

Old Imperial murals and mosaics aside, it was rare to see many ships on the water. The fishermen, of course, setting out their nets or hauling them in, and a few wide barges that shipped goods up and down the coast, staying as near to land as possible. A few hardy souls or eccentrics maintained pleasure craft, as well; some even dared sail out to the coruscating Barrier that had billowed up around the Empire when it fell.

Some foolhardy adventurers had even tried to cross it. Those had not returned.

But Faville's uncle's clipper was not quite any of those things. Rather, it was a callback to an earlier age, when messages, messengers, and small luxuries went more swiftly by water than they did down the coast's mountainous terrain. It was a beauty of speed and efficiency. Its draft was deep enough to force them away from the coastal shallows to which the barges kept, and its sails seemed to catch any flicker of wind.

The last time Faville had set foot on this vessel, she'd been a child, visiting her uncle in the Capitol. They'd used it as a glorified pleasure boat back then—sailed out to watch the sunset over open waters and sailed back under the glittering stars.

The ship had seen some refurbishing, since.

For one thing, it had a wireless telegraph now. This rather put the lie to maintaining it as any sort of courier vessel, but people didn't tend to argue with her uncle about any of his capital goods.

A small crew of sailors—none known to Faville beyond courtesies—was waiting on deck, and the captain bowed her and her guests aboard with an air of distracted command. Faville had no sooner completed greetings and introductions than the captain was dismissing his crew back to their duties, snapping out orders to make them ready to sail.

Hardly before any of them were out of earshot, Jaque turned to Faville. "These people have seen the site?"

"Some of them," Faville said.

"I'd like to talk to the ones who have."

A Peacekeeper's decisiveness, Faville thought. "I'm sure that can be arranged once we're on the water."

"Hmm," Jaque said, and glanced to Bel. Then to Faville. "Would you excuse me," she said, neutrally.

She took herself off in the direction of the ship's captain.

Bel watched her go with an expression of bemusement. "Was she always so direct?"

"As long as I've known her," Faville said. "I thought her impolite, at first."

"Oh. I just thought her exotic," Bel confessed. "Dangerous."

She said the word fondly.

Faville hesitated a moment, wondering what Jaque had seemed, in that distant posting. Oh, she knew the allure of young Peacekeepers, but that allure usually turned on the neatness of their uniforms, the promise of training and discipline and solid employment. And authority. She hadn't considered that one might go courting *danger*.

"I'd like to watch us sail," Bel said, before Faville had worked out a response. Bel waved her hand at the view over the deck rail— mostly green vegetation on broken rock, still, laced through with the gray waters of the Strait leading sea-ward from the Sound. Faville nodded, and the two of them found an out-of-the-way place to watch the world go by. Obligingly, the ship pulled from its dock.

After a time, with her attention still mostly on the waters and the coastlands, Bel asked, "How long did you know her, before she came to Tagamonti?"

"Years," Faville said. She wondered if she should mention the fact that they'd been all but betrothed, but somehow, she couldn't see Jaque hiding that from Bel. "She was stationed nearby, for some time."

"You know what she did, out east?"

Now, that was a sticking point. And had been. "No," Faville admitted. "I know hardly anything."

And *out east* was its own mystery. Tagamonti Territory was so far removed from the lands near Marematre that it could have been the far side of the world, not just the far side of the bowl that had become their world after the Empire's collapse. Faville didn't know what customs ruled there. What food they ate—surely not the fish and berries and cresses that thrived along the coast. If their roads were paved; if their houses were painted. Jaque had complained, in her letters, about the baths she'd found in the towns near where she was stationed.

In those simple reports, her work had been treated with a notable silence.

"She and my brother were close, I think," Bel said. "Before he died."

Ah, Faville thought. That was . . . something. "I'm sorry."

Bel shrugged, though the sadness pulling the corners of her eyes wasn't nearly so casual. "It was magic," she said. "*Imperial* magic."

And here Faville had called her back, over the breadth of the nation, to give her opinion on Imperial magic.

At least Jaque could safely stuff all her feelings on the matter into a sturdy chest, and then leave that chest under a bunk. Not that Faville would wish her to. She frowned, and cast an eye toward Jaque's trail. "Should I apologize, do you think?"

"No," Bel said, slowly. "I don't think she'd want you to. She doesn't like to talk about it."

And yet, here it was, in the air between them. "But you don't mind?"

"I hate what happened. I hate that it *had* to happen. But I can talk about it." Bel glanced, sidelong, at Faville. "But is that really what you want to know?"

Maybe not. *What were they to each other?* and *How close were they?* interested her more. Jaque's letters had mentioned Bel, often enough. Never . . . she didn't even know Bel's brother's name.

Bel didn't wait for her to form a diplomatic question. "He . . ." Bel grimaced. Her eyes traced the deck and fetched up at the hatch belowdecks, where Jaque had vanished. Faville wondered what would happen if Jaque were to reappear. Would Bel find comfort in that? Be bolstered? Would she swallow her words?

What *had* happened to Jaque, out on her eastern assignment?

"My brother swore fealty to someone who thought old Imperial magics were going to solve all our problems," Bel said. "They didn't. Obviously."

Faville sought something to say to that. She wanted to inquire into that closeness; the Jaque she'd known hadn't found it easy to get close to anyone. But she didn't want to prod that wound. "Swore fealty," she settled on. That was a question, of its own. "I thought—forgive me."

"You thought ruffians from the heath wouldn't hold to things like that?" Bel asked, a wry note in her voice.

Faville swallowed chagrin. "I didn't think Tagamonti was the heath—"

"There are a few old notions of civilization we held to," Bel said. "Were. There *were*."

In Marematre, on the well-civilized western coast, the only people who bothered with notions of fealty were the Peacekeepers and the older, more conservative political and business families. Even Faville's relations, stuffy as they were, didn't hold to that custom.

"You know, M—" Bel bit off the word. The name? "This *man*. Our . . . liege. He had one of those long wraps, carted it halfway across the continent in a chest—edged in purple and everything—

he'd do *salutationes* on weekends. Sit there on a camp stool in fifty pounds of cloth, drinking wine, having all of us come up to chit-chat with him, one after another, in turn . . ."

Faville had been looking at her increasingly askance, as she'd gone on. Somehow, the notion of camp stools and some remarkable number that could be folded into a phrase like *all of us* hadn't figured in her imaginings.

Bel caught her eye and cleared her throat. "Anyway," she said, and that was as good as saying *Maybe I shouldn't have said that.* With a touch of *I don't think I'll explain* on the side. "I think he wanted us to be our own little Old Empire. It didn't work out."

"I had the impression that it 'didn't work out' rather spectacularly," Faville said.

The last of Bel's levity drained. "That impression is quite correct."

Silence settled between them, metered out by the slapping waves.

At length, Faville said, "I'm glad you were able to come with Jaque. And it's such a fine day; if you've never been on the water before, I think we can make a good showing."

As peace offerings went, it was at least diverting. Bel gave her an odd look, too knowing, but they talked about nothing more treacherous than native coastal plants and the railway business until Jaque returned, caught Bel's eye, and offered one hand in a shrug; she didn't seem to have found anything from the sailors that she wanted to share.

Of course, Jaque had always needed some coaxing.

Faville cleared her throat. "Bel," she said, "If you'd permit me to speak with your beloved? Unchaperoned?"

Bel looked at her, and Faville didn't think she was assessing a threat. Then the woman walked to Jaque—each footstep deliberate on the rocking deck—and drew her in for a kiss. That kiss, unless Faville missed her guess, had more of care in it than possessiveness.

Whenever Jaque had kissed Faville, her eyes had been open

when they pulled apart. Always searching her face, looking for confirmation, asking without asking *Was that right? Could I have done better? Did I satisfy you?* It was . . . strange, to watch her with Bel; she still kissed as though she were returning to the instructions in her head. But when Bel left her, Jaque's eyes remained closed, and there was almost pain in her expression. Like a woman trying to hold the scent of a flower which had been brought and borne away on the breeze.

"I think I'll make myself pleasant to the sailors," Bel said, and swatted Jaque's hip.

Faville looked away.

Jaque came up to the railing beside her. Here, framed against the water and the sea, she looked just as striking as that youth in uniform Faville had become fond of. But older. Wiser?

And why had Faville brought Jaque out, anyway? Because she might know something, certainly, but . . . she might have hired a surveyor, for that. And true, a surveyor might be tempted to go and sell this extraordinary information to another buyer, but the most reputable ones had to be inured to such temptations. It was their *job*.

Maybe she ought to admit that she'd called the woman here, across half a continent, for the sake of a lingering affection, though not one which had lingered unchanged.

And Jaque had come with her new sweetheart by her side. Faville had invited the both of them.

Faville had shaped this at its beginning. She couldn't hide from that truth. With her own hands she'd held the paper and swept the pen. She hadn't sent Jaque to Tagamonti, but she'd sent her off into the heath of a foreign love just the same. She'd relinquished any claim on Jaque, of her own free will, before it could fray and fall away from her.

But perhaps . . . friendship. She could hope for friendship, again; she missed it. An intimate friendship was surely not beyond

14

them; the kind of intimacy that was known to flourish, now and again, even where a former courtship had been.

So she'd go on as she'd begun. She'd asked Jaque out for business. Business it would be, until they had their footing.

"You're not a Peacekeeper anymore," Faville said. "Do you still keep their secrets?"

"I've been released from service," Jaque said. "Not from my oaths."

There was a thriving trade in ex-Peacekeeper consulting, which the Peacekeepers despised but were never quite able to stamp out. But if that were known to Jaque, she seemed not to have recognized it as an option.

Not that Jaque hadn't been subtle, in her own ways. She certainly had secrets of her *own* she'd carried, and even now Faville could only guess the shape of them. "You know about magic, don't you?"

Leaving aside secrets, professional or personal, Jaque had still always been . . . a cipher, strange in her postures and expressions, but a cipher which could be read, given time and familiarity. Faville once had both. But this stillness was something she hadn't encountered before; something which Jaque must have learned in the Peacekeepers and declined to bring home to Faville's lap. Jaque considered the water as they cut through it, and only at length said, "Some."

"Was it something you saw often, in Tagamonti?"

Jaque's eyes cut across to Faville. Her expression was still unreadable.

"One hears all sorts of things," Faville said. "And Tagamonti borders Cruenlacus . . ."

The dead territory, the Red Basin, one of the other great, cataclysmic reminders of the Empire. The stories about the heath—*not*, Faville reminded herself, that Tagamonti was quite *heath*—were bracing. The stories about the Red Basin were horrifying.

15

"I've been through there," Jaque remarked.

Faville startled so violently that Jaque grabbed her elbow, snake-fast. Faville wondered if she'd looked about to topple over the edge.

After a moment, when Jaque judged her steady on her feet, she let go. "I was lost there. A few days, I think." She frowned, as though the memory was unclear.

"That—you—" A few false starts finally gave way to some coherent question: "How did you get *out*?"

"A friend fetched me," Jaque said, which only raised more questions in its place. "He knew the . . . Basin."

It sounded like some other word should have been there. Cautiously, Faville asked, "Bel's brother?"

Jaque cut her another glance. "No," she said. "But *his* friend first."

And this friend, who knew the Red Basin and could fetch lost Peacekeepers from its desolation, had been unable, or unwilling, or unavailable, to help Bel's brother against whatever Imperial magic he'd run afoul of. Faville was, at once, deeply curious, and extremely wary of learning more.

"I suppose," she said, "after that, the magic that's left here on the coast must not seem like much. We've nearly cleared it all up, I understand." Or learned where not to tread.

Some hidden humor quirked the corner of Jaque's mouth, and vanished. "I think," she said, "if that were true, you wouldn't have written me."

Ah, Faville thought, and turned to the waters. "The coast, I think, is very unlike the sea."

~

Even on their fast clipper, the sun had risen, hung at the peak of the sky, and began to ease its way downward before they came to the site.

From a distance, it was nothing: a shimmer on the water—which might have been any reflected glint of sunlight or cloud. At night, perhaps, it would call more attention—that was a possibility her uncle had considered, muttering about rail timetables for this prospective water route—but even sailors did their best to avoid the sea at night when they could help it.

It was a minor miracle that this site had ever been noticed at all.

Faville wondered what other secrets—gems, or traps—lay unknown beneath the surface of the water.

The sailors brought them up to the edge of the gleam, and at a word from Faville, eased the ship into the illuminated water. Jaque and Bel fetched up at the deck railing without Faville needing to summon them.

As though in response to Jaque's presence, the glow rose to meet them.

Like a living thing.

Faville had sailed out here. Only once. She'd gazed into the water from the deck, and then peered through the waterscope the sailors had carried out.

When she had come, the water had not gone still as glass. The light had not burgeoned like dawn.

Bel stared down in wonder. Jaque simply stood, watching, as though this strange welcome was nothing unexpected. She spread her hands over the water, like a woman testing the warmth of a fire.

"What . . . ?" Faville breathed.

Jaque glanced at her, one eyebrow crooked in inquiry.

Faville looked into the water. Now, it was like a glass roof; now, it was clearer than any glass roof she'd ever seen. She could see, extending beneath them, some patch of world—whether blurred at the edges or fading under the waves, she wasn't certain.

Boulevards and fora—the perfect forms which Garinrock mocked in ruins. People, *people* moving about, in the effortless decadence of their draping robes. Slaves in loincloths—surely, in the Old Empire, they would have been slaves?—with baskets upon their heads, laden with fruit and fish and bolts of cloth.

None of them looked up toward the surface of the water, their sky, where Jaque stood watching them.

"I needed a waterscope to see, last time," Faville said. "How did you *do* this?" The sight was even more of a spectacle, now. Even without the rail to Deires, people would pay to witness this.

Jaque flicked her fingers, as though Faville's question were an insect that had tried to land on her. "I've seen this sort of residue before," she said.

Faville made a choked noise, as the questions *You've seen this?* and *Residue?* and *Where? How? How came you by such wonders?* all clogged her tongue.

She had expected . . . Jaque's amazement. Expected that Jaque would eventually offer the name of a more knowledgeable authority—some Peacekeepers contractor or bank surveyor or *someone* who might be brought out to view this place, in turn, and make formal recommendations.

She hadn't expected Jaque to narrow her eyes in thought, and then proclaim—with every evidence of expertise: "This is an echo."

Shocked, Faville could do little but repeat the words. "An echo?"

"Of the Empire," Jaque said. "They were soaked in magic, then, and the magic's drifted here, and kept their shape."

Faville shuddered. "Like a ghost."

"No." Jaque returned her hands to the railing. "A ghost is a human spirit, too tethered by magic to disappear. This is magic, which kept the form of its container. There's nothing human here."

Below, a dog—the shape of a dog—bounded into a pavilion as they coasted over it. A boy followed it, striking a rolling ball with a stick so that it rolled into a knot of people and the dog bounded after it.

Faville watched them all: the irritation of the men and women about their tasks; the dog as it wove its russet body around their legs; the boy, laughing. But Bel was the one who said the words. "They look human."

The iron that closed over Jaque's face startled both of them. "So does a corpse," she said, and stepped away.

Faville reached out her hand. Bel caught Jaque's arm first. "Love—"

Jaque's shoulder twitched, but she didn't quite throw off Bel's touch. She looked at Faville. "Stay away from the Empire's remnant magics," she said. "Tell your uncle to build the rail closer to shore. Or don't build over water. Nothing good will come of being so near to this."

Then she did walk away, leaving Bel and Faville to stare after her.

Faville looked at Bel. But Bel's face, too, closed up. She started after Jaque and made it half a step before apparently deciding better of it; the only expression she gave back to Faville was apology.

Apology for . . . what? For Jaque, and her brusqueness? For the advice?

No, Faville thought. That hadn't been advice. That had been directive.

If Faville trusted her, she'd hew to that directive.

Of course, there were two questions: Did she trust Jaque? And even if she did, would that matter to her uncle?

Faville turned back to the water. With Jaque gone, waves were beginning to ripple over the surface again; a few of the sailors, their voices not quite below her hearing, were beginning to mutter. A problem there, likely, but hopefully they were professional enough to save their complaints for her uncle.

Staring down into that light—that echo—let questions rise and crest and lap down into her mind like the waves which carried their ship. She couldn't grasp any of them long enough to address them. Not but that the one she'd ask questions of hadn't walked away.

At length, she managed, "It's beautiful."

Bel's gaze on the water was uneasy. "A lot of deadly things are."

~

Faville would have turned the clipper around and sailed home to Marematre. So, she suspected, would the captain—but it was her uncle who paid the captain, and apparently he'd left his own orders. So they remained at sea while telegraphs went wirelessly back to shore, downcoast to the Capitol, and their night was spent by the glow of the Empire's echo.

She and her guests shared a ship's breakfast at the captain's table: porridge with huckleberries, coffee, dried fish—though why the fish was *dried* was beyond Faville. Maybe the sailors were all too busy to fish their provisions fresh. Or maybe no one trusted fish pulled up from waters that shone with their own light.

Before they had quite cleared their plates, someone knocked at the cabin door and handed through a folded paper. The captain took one look at it and handed it over to Faville with a muttered "Ma'am." It didn't have the neat printing of a telegram office, but the ship's wireless officer had handwriting legible enough to serve.

The message was clipped, even though Faville's uncle owned the telegram office he sent from, and they would hardly charge *him* by the word.

> Mirage - no danger - good sport. Secure for survey.
> Fine opportunity for tourist line.

She read it twice over, to be sure.

Her uncle was a man of formidable good humor and an opportunistic obstinance he called optimism. He could invite someone to his desk and share tea and fruits and cordial conversation for an hour while they worked out that he wasn't agreeing with them, and never would, and that they had to come around to his way of thinking or be crushed under the wheels of his business.

And when he left the room, he would shake their hand, and call them *my friend*, and smile, and mean it. And be no less immovable for the fact.

By the third time she read the message, the whole table had fallen silent, their eyes on her. Expecting bad news, probably. And did this count?

She met Jaque's eyes. "My uncle has decided to go ahead and develop the route."

She expected a protest along the lines of *That's a bad idea*. Perhaps, *Tell him he shouldn't*. Not Jaque's spine stiffening, her eyes narrowing, and her voice like steel: "No."

"No?" Faville sat up straighter. "Jaque, love, it isn't *my* decision—"

Jaque's lips had drawn back, her teeth bared like an animal's. Bel's eyes widened.

"Jaque," Bel ventured, "we'll be on the other side of the nation from any mistakes they make here—"

"These mistakes are not so small that the breadth of a *nation* would protect us from them," Jaque growled, and shoved herself away from the table.

Faville startled backward as Jaque stormed out. She looked at Bel, and the woman looked stricken; more afraid than a tantrum should have occasioned.

It was enough for Faville to make hasty apologies to the captain and rush after Jaque. Bel followed on her heels, and the captain did as well; any disruption on his ship being, after all, his concern.

By the time Faville reached the deck, Jaque was already there, at the rail, staring down into the ancient city's echo-glow. The sight stopped Faville cold.

She'd seen Jaque confused, frustrated, irritated. She'd seen her brooding, and pondering, and focused intently on problems before her.

She'd never seen Jaque *angry*. Or—as her eyes suggested now—caught on the lip of some volcanic rage.

She was so arrested by the threat written in Jaque's every line that until the man stepped past her, Faville hadn't noticed the stranger on deck with them.

Tall and lean, with an Imperial hawk-nose; black hair with a loose wave tied tightly at his nape. Dressed in hides and home-spuns, in a style that seemed not so much *classical* or *Imperial* as . . . *ancient*. And dark, not as Jaque was dark, but as though he stood in a shadow cast by nothing.

Jaque brought her hands over the railing, though she no longer looked like she was warming her palms by a fire. Now she looked like she was conjuring one. "It shouldn't be here," she said.

The man glanced down into the water, his face all cool detachment. "Should, shouldn't," he said. His voice was dismissive. "You know how little that means."

Jaque's lips contorted. Faville watched, frozen; she'd seen Jaque struggle for words, before. Never like this. *"I don't want it"* was what burst from Jaque's mouth when her internal war was settled. She tore her eyes from the echo below and fixed them on this . . . stranger. "Help me."

He nodded, shortly, and reached over and covered her hand with his.

Beneath them, something flashed like dynamite. The mirage, the echo, the glimpse into the great Imperial past they'd built their dreams upon . . . *burst*. The light writhed and twisted beneath the water like a fire; Faville had been to mine openings and ground-breakings at her uncle's elbow, but never witnessed something like *this*—

The water surged.

Faville shouted. She wasn't the only one. Now the crew was rushing up to see what was happening; a sailor caught her around the waist and drew her back toward belowdecks. Another ran toward Jaque across the heaving deck, and stumbled to a halt when she raised her hands, fingers curling to fists. *Marionette,*

Faville thought, inanely. Her mind didn't seem to be working quite right. Refused to make sense of what she was seeing.

Magic... wasn't *like* this. Magic was something the Old Empire had raised, and built grandly of, and abused, and left in shards for their descendants to worry about. Magic in the present day was a thing of rumor and disappointment: perhaps some secret Peacekeeper asset could conjure light or move without sound; perhaps some heathlander could enrapture rabbits or dowse water.

No one could make the sea convulse with wildfire.

Jaque should not make the sea convulse with wildfire.

And yet. The sea was convulsing.

Another shouting voice: a woman's shouting voice. Bel, slipping out from the grip of another sailor, running toward Jaque. The man, the stranger, turning to watch her, head tilting like a carrion bird. Jaque's face a bitter rictus.

Bel putting her hand on Jaque's forearm. Stepping closer. Wrapping her arms around Jaque's chest.

And Jaque's eyes closed, and her face tilted up, and the sunlight caught such a look of anguish that Faville couldn't bear to watch. She closed her eyes.

But slowly, the ship's lurching slowed, and the angry slap of the water quieted.

When she managed to look again, Faville saw Jaque's arms wrapped around Bel, her face buried in Bel's dark hair, and her shoulders shaking.

The stranger, whoever he was, was nowhere to be seen.

~

It was Bel who came down to Faville's cabin after the sailors had ushered her belowdecks and hastened the clipper away from the scene. The sea had returned to its usual . . . not placidity, but natural disruption; the waves were as they were elsewhere on the water, and the color was the deep gray-green-blue that was lit only

23

by the sun above. And while the ship had been no more rocked than by a common squall, Faville doubted the sailors would let Jaque near their ship again.

Recalling the look in Jaque's eyes, Faville doubted Jaque cared one bit.

"What *was* that?" she asked. Her voice sounded small, even in the close cabin. "*Who* was that? Do you—do you know?"

Bel shook her head, and said, "My brother's friend, I think. He doesn't talk to me." She spread her hands, helplessly. "None of them told *me* about . . . they've been dabbling with magic for—I don't know!" Her hands returned to her lap, and twisted in her skirts. "We knew my . . . my brother had magic in him. It saved our asses—sorry; sorry, saved *us*. More than once. But how, and why, and by who . . . it wasn't something we talked about."

Language, Faville's reflexes urged her to say, while curiosity voted for *What did you need saving from?* and *What kind of magic?* and *How could you not talk about* that? But she knew. There were things one *didn't talk about,* because they weren't civil. And what was this nation of theirs but a wave of civility, civilization, spreading out to tame all the chaos the Empire had left in its wake? From west to east, to the north and the south, the rolling hills to the bitter Red Basin, the Barrier to the shining sea?

"Was that the magic of the lost Empire?" she asked.

Bel stared at Faville, her eyes as hollow as the ocean. For that moment, Faville thought the both of them shared the same expression; two souls lost in a kindred misery, a common fear.

"I don't know," Bel admitted. "She doesn't talk about it. But I don't think so." She shook her head. "I think it's . . . wild magic. The magic that was here before the Empire shaped it. Magic that's come around again. Older than the Empire."

"Older," Faville said, and tasted the word on her tongue. Not like dust; no, dust seemed a thing of civilized lands. Dust was a thing to be cleared off banisters and shelves. This was *older,* like leaf litter, like loam, like wide gray rivers, like the fogs that gathered over Marematre each winter as though each winter fog was just an echo, ringing back, back, from the dawn of time.

They'd built a nation on the Old Empire's bones. And the Old Empire, which Faville had always thought of as some *first* thing, had built itself on something older yet.

And Jaque, and Bel's brother, and whoever that man was who'd appeared from nowhere and vanished back, they all had some tangled history with it. And Faville, and Bel, crept to the edge of that tangle and saw . . . what? Hints, vague shapes, shadows?

Ruins?

A light, and an echo, under the obfuscating waves?

Shivery thought, that. What uncharted territory was *Jaque*, now? What lay hidden under those surfaces Faville had thought she'd known?

"I should speak to her," Faville said, vaguely, and didn't move. After a moment, she realized she was afraid.

Bel, hesitantly, said, "Maybe."

Maybe admitted space for doubt. That felt reassuring, though it was a craven kind of reassurance. Faville set her jaw, gathered her courage, and rose from her seat.

She found Jaque on the deck, near the prow, neatly avoided by the sailors going about their business. Her face was angled toward the mainland, though her eyes didn't seem to see it.

Faville and Bel drew up to her, and Bel settled down on the wood beside her. None of the three of them spoke, for some time.

Then Jaque lowered her head, and said, "I'm sorry."

That human admission seemed strange, after the day. Faville made a little, negating noise, and a weak gesture of one hand.

"I don't think you should call on me again," Jaque said.

Let the past be the past. What they'd had between them was history, too, if only a small, prosaic kind. And yet, against all propriety, Faville heard herself say, "I love you."

A familiar crease appeared between Jaque's brows. Cruel of her, Faville thought, to give Jaque such a difficult gift. But Jaque said, "I love you," and her hand closed on Bel's hand. "I love Bel. I owe Bel. We have debts to pay."

I don't, Faville thought. She lived in a villa, in Marematre, jewel of the civilized coast, second only to the Capitol. She'd never touched this world of desperation and fealty and magic that Jaque seemed to be immured in.

She didn't know what to say to that. She stepped away.

Not that there was anywhere to go. Their world was bounded by the hull of the ship, until they arrived in Garinrock. Where they would be let back into another world, with a larger bound.

Worlds in worlds. Histories atop histories. Her next task would be to explain this to her uncle, somehow, when she didn't understand it herself—and then to put it behind her.

She looked out over the surface of the water, cool and enigmatic and fathomlessly deep. Then turned herself back toward the mainland and the new cities growing there.

KATE ELLIOTT

The Cleft of Bones

Kate Elliott

Every morning Ula woke before dawn. After so many years in the dolos quarters, she could have commanded one of the tiny alcoves allotted for the most senior of the slaves. Instead she chose to sleep in the women's barracks. Most nights one of the young ones would come to her, crying, and she would offer what comfort she could. She would not abandon them. She remembered those evil days too well, when she had suffered what they were suffering.

This day, restless dreams woke her, although as soon as her eyes opened she could not recall anything except a woman with a feathered crest and a snake's tongue. Was it an omen? Agitation curdled in her gut. Not even a rooster crowed. Was she dead and not yet aware of dying? Had her body been stripped of its simple tunic and dropped into the Cleft of Bones?

Did she *want* to be dead? She contemplated the pain in her right hip and the usual morning ache in her head. Footsteps shuffled past as people yawned and murmured around her. One wept quietly.

"Naiya, is that you?" she said softly. "Come here."

The girl sat, huddling against her. She was at the cusp of marriageable age and had arrived a month ago on an imperial trading ship, cargo from a distant land. Ula knew a few words of her crooked language, and she coaxed the girl to take in a little courage, enough to meet this one day, then sent her outside.

No, she wasn't ready to descend into the Cleft of Bones.

She rose with joints popping and muscles tight. Outside, she took her turn at the latrines and wash basin in the hazy predawn gray. Those who cleaned and supplied the sacred mount must not stink, so unlike the dirt-stained farm dolos who toiled on the outer island, and the harbor dolos who reeked of fish and brine, the temple dolos were allowed the luxury of washing and of possessing two work tunics.

Around her, the other dolos took their turns to wash. Old Uncle—eldest of all—gave each person a round of yesterday's flatbread with a dollop of cold porridge ladled on top, the only food they would eat until dusk halted their labors. They gathered at the locked gate of the dolos quarter, lined up in columns, an old tradition to make sure no one overslept and got punished. This month the count was two hundred and eight women and ninety-seven men.

As eldest woman, Ula had the responsibility of ringing the summoning bell to let the guards know all were accounted for and ready to go. She rang it once, then twice, then the required third time. A jolt shifted the ground, as if the island had yawned and, after a moment's consideration, settled back asleep.

The newer slaves murmured with worry, but she thought nothing of the mild shift. Earth tremors happened every year or two, whenever the world snake shifted in its dreaming slumber. Such quakes were much weaker than the brutal storms, monstrous spawn of the howl and the fury, that blasted through the islands during the rainy season. Naiya took a place at the back. Ula caught her gaze and nodded, but the girl was too frightened and exhausted to do more than stare at her with hopeless eyes.

Guards unlocked the gate from the outside, letting them onto the dolos road, the walled path slaves used to get around the island. As temple dolos, they held first rank among slaves, which besides water to bathe meant a little extra sleep each day. The gates to the farm dolos quarter and the harbor dolos quarter were already open, their inhabitants sent out to labor before sunrise.

The dolos quarters were in a compact compound built on one side of the wide causeway that connected the sacred mount to the big outer island called the Sickle. To get to the harbor and the fields, the slaves would turn left, heading to the island, while she led the temple slaves to the right toward the mount. Above them, a road paved in marble linked island and mount. Her feet had never touched and would never touch that road.

Water slapped at the wall. Here, the sea stank of urine and feces because the currents washed refuse into the curve of this shore. To avoid the stink, the main harbor was situated on the other side of the causeway.

Their path ended in a locked gate at the base of the sacred mount. This hill-like cone of an island had once been separated from the Sickle by a shallow ford. When the first kings arrived, they built the causeway to bind the sacred mount to the main island, and constructed wharves and dug channels to create a safe harbor alongside. The conical hill had been built as a series of wide terraces, each tier smaller than the one below. On the mount's flat summit rose the airship spires and their floating piers as well as a temple and archives dedicated to the ten founding kings of the archipelago.

Again Ula rang a summoning bell. A guard opened the gate. As a group, the dolos headed up a set of walled stairs, pausing at each of its tiers.

"May it be a peaceful day," she said as she rang the dolos

bell at the gate into the lowest tier, that of the war-wagers' barracks and their training grounds. The gate was opened from the inside and the slaves who served on that tier allowed to enter. The war-wagers risked their lives that all might live in peace, so the echelon taught, and thus could take payment as they wished. She had herself begun as a cleaner in the barracks. Even after all these years, a pain stabbed deep in her heart as she watched Naiya and the others file through the gate, their heads bowed and shoulders slumped and despairing.

"May you have the strength you need," she said to the porters who filed into the warehouse tier, from which they would haul up and down all day from the town and the docks to fetch luxuries and desirables for the higher tiers and the airship trade.

"May you forage wisely without being caught," she said to those who hurried into the garden terrace, with its busy kitchens preparing generous meals for the war-wagers and elaborate delicacies for the echelons.

She wished patience, levelheadedness, and caution for those serving in the three residential tiers of the echelons. Free workers looked upon the dolos as creatures who had lost the favor of the gods and thus lacked honor. In the eyes of the highborn echelons, the dolos could scarcely be called people at all.

She kept climbing past the highest residential tier. The dolos stair went all the way to a closed gate at the top, where porters would haul their laden baskets, heavy bags, and awkward chests to the priests and the airship crews. She turned aside before she reached that gate.

A narrow opening in the wall let onto a path that led around to the bay-facing side of the mount. Here the tiers had collapsed into jagged cliffs stacked one below the next all the way to the fissure known as the Cleft of Bones. The bodies of temple slaves who had the presumption to die on the sacred mount were consigned to this lightless crevice. Some said their souls were consumed

by ghosts and bodiless demons, and that the priests threw them
there to keep the underworld fed. Ula had believed this once too,
a long time ago. Not anymore.

The trail cut like a goat path across this steep and dangerous
slope. Foam-capped waves broke on rocks far below. The danger
was matched by the beauty. From up here she had a grand if perilous view of the circular bay created by the protective curve of the
great sickle-shaped island. Pine trees, olive groves, and assiduously
tended vineyards lent stretches of green to the stony land. A second island, called the Sheaf, lay athwart the bay's wide opening
onto the ocean. Its rocky slopes added further shelter from the
fury of the deep. On either side of the Sheaf, channels allowed for
ship traffic. This was the safest harbor in all the archipelago realm
of the ten kings.

The holy archives were part of the temple compound on the
summit. The trail she walked, however, wound beneath the summit to the archive's lower level. She entered through an ancient,
abandoned guard tower whose forward edge thrust precariously
over the cliff's edge. The tower's roof was half fallen in, and
beneath the remaining patchwork of tile and timber hung a summoning bell.

A dolos bell had no real use up here. She kept it oiled because
that was the tradition handed down across the generations since
the first echelons wrested the island out of the hands of the snake-
tongued monsters who had roamed the archipelago before the
arrival of civilized people.

The upper level of the archive overlooked the beautiful calm
water of the caldera bay. The feet of dolos were not allowed to sully
the marble pavement of the building where scholars and council-
ors met, so she only knew of it by description. For thirty years she
had swept, dusted, and organized the two lower chambers, carved
into the rock, that held the contents of the archive.

A stub of a path led from the ruined guard tower to a door set into the cliff face. She went inside, latched the door shut behind her, and pulled on her work smock. As always, she first checked the shelf at the top of the long flight of stone steps that linked the two levels. In a basket on the shelf, scholars left notes asking for specific scrolls to be brought up, along with returned scrolls that needed to be put away in the rooms below. Since a heavy curtain separated the stairs from the upper level, cutting off all light, she had to count by touch: nine returned scrolls today; no requests.

As she carried the basket down the stairs, she paused, hearing voices speaking above her, from beyond the curtain.

"I reject that theory entirely," a man was saying in the snappish, impatient accent of the highest echelon. "It is a fashion of bored students to pretend there was a civilization in this archipelago before the kings of blessed memory led our fleets here."

"Think you so? Is there not a tract that details the history of the first ships and how they fought flesh-eating savages who sharpened human bones to make weapons?"

"An outrageous tale to entertain credulous menials and illiterate farmers."

"I heard the old prince speak of an ancient chronicle written into a crumbling old scroll. He said it included a script no one had deciphered. And strange, frightening tales told by the last savages to the kings' archivists of that day. Of women with snake tongues, and wolf-headed warriors who devoured the hearts of their enemies."

"He said all those things when he was ill and raving, at the end. Ranting about a terrible doom soon to fall upon our illustrious kingdom because of our ancient crimes. You know how dying people are."

At the end? Had the prince died? Her palms went clammy, succeeded by a hot sweat prickling on her face and neck.

"He seemed so strict and rational before his health failed. I didn't know he secretly savored superstitious lore. Let's go down and look, Seos. Please. Don't you find it odd the lower archives have been off-limits to us all these years?" The second speaker had a lighter voice, probably a woman. "Or do you fear we'll meet one of the flesh-eaters the students delight in describing?"

"It's dark down there," protested Seos.

"Dark! I think you fear the scuff and patter of their hooves! Or was it mandibles? Ha! I am not afraid! The old prince can't scowl us into submission now, can he?"

Bells sewn to the curtain tinkled as it was shoved aside. Ula hurried into the main room below. The long, narrow chamber had three window slits, a table placed to get maximum light, and the shelving system with baskets and labels.

The voices grew louder as they argued over which of the ancient chronicles were true and which mere fabulisms. Since the stairs led directly into the front room, they'd spot her at once, so she crept as soundlessly as possible through a carved opening into the lightless back room.

"Is there no lamp, Seos?" asked the second speaker.

"Give your eyes a moment."

"Oh, I see. It isn't so bad once the eyes adjust. This orderly precision is a surprise! The labels clear and readable, even in this bad light. I thought the new head archivist was useless!"

"This isn't his doing. He's only been head archivist for ten days."

Ten days! Ula had not seen the prince since the last new moon, but as he often journeyed by airship to other islands, and was sometimes gone for months at a time, she'd had no way of knowing he'd been ill. For him to be dead! And with no warning, no chance for her to make plans. As if that would matter.

Seos was still talking. "He'll have plenty of chances to ruin the prince's work in the days and months to come. They say he wants to sell the old scrolls. Although who would buy these dusty old relics?"

"Don't you find this place odd?"

"How so?"

"Who keeps everything tidy and organized? Didn't the old man used to keep a pornai down here? They say he liked to dabble his toes in the sewer."

"Don't be crude. He was of the royal lineage of Atlas the Founder. He would never stoop so low. Let's find that history scroll you're looking for and get out. The air is bad. The novices say there are noises down here when there shouldn't be."

"Should we have brought our knives? I told you there were monsters."

"Not so loud!" warned Seos. "Here is history. It *is* well arranged. Very clear."

"What's back here?" said the lighter-voiced speaker. Footsteps approached the archway. "Another chamber?"

The back chamber was little more than a long, wide passageway carved into the rock, with shelves built on either side. A space used to store the least valuable items of the archive. If the speakers brought a lamp, they'd see her. She sidled deeper into the darkness. One cleft wide enough to fit a body opened under the rock into which the steps had been carved. She wedged herself in backward until the cleft grew too narrow, then turned sideways and eased farther, praying silently to the goddess to conceal her. Her heel scraped at a rim and hovered over a gap of air. A breeze drifted upward from a rift that cut into the mount, one of the many cracks and cavities in the rock.

Years and years ago, when he'd been trying to earn her trust, the prince had told her that the sacred mount was riddled with rifts and crevices, of which the Cleft of Bones was only the most visible. When she'd asked about ghosts and bodiless demons, he laughed and told her that what others called ghosts and demons was the sound of the wind. That exchange had changed something deep for her, made her realize the echelons understood the world no better than others did. It was only that they need not

36

fear what they could not see, because they lived at the top, while others crouched below and would be first to be eaten.

"It's so black!" exclaimed the light-voiced one. "I can't see a thing. Why is there no oil in this lamp? How does anyone find anything here? You know, if he took up with his pornai as a young man, she'd be an old woman now. Maybe he hid her bones here so no one would know of his shame."

From the front chamber, an exclamation. "I found it. *An Account of the Western Migration of the Blessed Kings and the Settling of the Five Isles Beyond the Pillars of the World.* Let's go up, Vesa. This place makes my skin crawl."

They left.

After a while, when the ache in her chest eased, Ula squeezed out of the cleft. The light in the front chamber seemed particularly bright, even sparkling, but maybe the sparkling was tears in her eyes.

She hadn't loved him. A dolos like her, seen and desired by a prince come to congratulate the war-wagers on a victory, could not say no. He'd brought her to the archives for his own pleasure. As time passed, he'd taught her to read and write and allowed her to organize the jumble of old, discarded scrolls he cared little for. The office of head archivist was passed down in the royal line to younger sons; it was nothing he'd asked for. But she read and read and read. Stories were a form of strength. Late at night, when her brethren in the quarter wished for entertainment or could not sleep for the fears eating at their hearts and bodies, she told them stories she had read from the archives. She knew every scroll like a comrade. She loved them all.

Her chest felt squeezed and breathless as she set down the basket of scrolls on the table. When would the new head archivist descend the steps to inspect the lower depths of his domain? What would happen to her then? Would she be buried alive in the prince's tomb according to the laws of the old days, when the echelons demanded slaves attend them in the afterlife? Would she be executed for impiety, even though it was the prince who had placed her here, and it had been impossible for her to say no? Would she be cast, still living, into the Cleft of Bones?

Light cut across the polished grain of the wood, illuminating the nine scrolls. She had to put them away, then dust and sweep, then repair a few scrolls that had been torn or mishandled. Then there'd be time for herself, to read or to copy a scroll she might trade to a merchant for silphium to prevent pregnancy and medicinals for the many ailments suffered by those who must work without enough rest or food or dignity.

She'd learned to measure the days with thanks for small mercies and sparks of beauty. To live in the space of what waited before her right now was the only way to survive. What might happen, or might not, what she feared or hoped for, was a burden she had learned to set aside.

She set out the scrolls, read the labels she had painstakingly created over the years, a blend of writing for the highborn and ribbons of different lengths and textures so she could find and return scrolls in the darkness. Once she had developed the system of ribbons, she'd been able to save most of the lamp oil the prince had delivered for her use. This oil she bartered for small items to make the lives of the others in the dolos quarters a trifle easier. They were the only family she had. She gave them what she could.

A double tap sounded on the outer door, the sound making her jump with a spike of fright. A thrust of memory. But the first double tap was followed by two more, the pattern used by the porters to announce deliveries. Ink, reeds, papyrus, and oil. She leaned on the edge of the table, waiting for her breathing to steady. She had to go open the guard tower's door for them.

A strange sighing sound caught at her ear. The garden birds

had stopped singing. The wind had ceased. She looked out the leftmost window.

Its view framed the harbor and the prosperous city built along the lower slopes and shore of the Sickle. Beyond the docks lay the great caldera bay. Anchored ships dotted gemlike waters. From this window she could see out through one of the wide channels to the ocean. It was a view she often savored for its beauty, although the horizon was as bitter as it was sweet. As a girl, she'd been brought across the ocean to this harbor as a prize of war.

The scene she saw now made her soul quaver and her heart shrink with a disquieting premonition of something very bad, something worse even than the news of the prince's death. A strange and precautionary tale she had read in an ancient scroll, an account the prince had called the embellishment of an undisciplined mind. *After the sea's fall, the monster out of the deep will devour all the land in a threefold wave rushing in without mercy.*

The water was receding from the shorelines, as if in the unseen distance a monstrous leviathan was swallowing all the ocean into its fathomless gullet. Ships at anchor settled onto the seabed. Fish flopped, exposed to air and sun. Strange pits like beehive holes riddled the steep sea floor, now exposed. Exactly as the old scroll had described.

From above, a man's voice said, "Will you look at that? We can go fishing with our hands."

A strange grinding noise, as of a massive door opening, reverberated through the chamber, shaking her out of her stupor.

She hurried out the door and along the short path to the old guard tower. It took her several tries fumbling with the outer latch before she unhooked it. When she flung open the door, two porters gaped at her, baskets at their feet: Temi and Kewa, who came every day.

"Run down to the lowest tier as fast as you can. Ring the bell at every gate. Tell them to start climbing. You climb too. Don't get caught below."

"That's not allowed," said Kewa, the older of the two lads. "We'll be punished."

"The waters will return in a great wall and drown the shore and lower slopes. It is written by the ancient sages. It happened before. *Go!*"

She poured all her will into the word. She was eldest. She had survived.

They raced away. She set her hand to the bellpull, rang the bell three times, and again, and again. And prayed to the goddess, *Let them hear and listen. Let them climb.*

On the height she waited, observing the scene with an eerie, detached view like that of a bird. Far below, people ran to aid sailors thrown to the sea floor when their ships toppled sideways as the receding water left them on dry ground. Folk carried baskets to scoop up fish. Children poked sticks into exposed holes, sliding on slippery rocks. From the building above she heard laughter as more priests and archivists crowded to the crown's edge to get a view of the marvel.

Three figures in the calf-length tunics worn by dolos women came hurrying along the path and crowded into the guard tower beside her. The eldest, a stubborn woman called Dorra, spoke.

"Aunt, why did you call us? We aren't allowed up here. They'll kill us."

"A great wave is coming that will drown the city and the lower tiers. Hide in the inner chamber. There's oil and a lamp in the chest to the right. You'll see the way."

They hesitated, hearing the laughter from above.

Then Dorra said to the others, "Do as she says."

More arrived in twos and threes. No one had the courage to make the ascent alone, and no dolos on the sacred mount was allowed to congregate with more than two of their brethren, so groups kept their distance from each other. So far no one in the temple above had taken notice. The stairs were hidden by walls, and anyway, the echelons paid no attention to their slaves except to punish them for wrongdoing.

She counted as each individual passed her in the tower and went inside. How many would make it up here? How many would be lost below? Twelve. Twenty-nine. Thirty-eight. All dolos who worked on the residential tiers. Then three from the garden tier, followed by three more and three more and three more.

A shout rang out: "Halt! Halt!" A scream cut through the air. She stepped outside the guard tower's cracked gate.

Halfway between the dolos stair and the guard tower, two young war-wagers stood cursing, each grasping the hair of a dolos. One was Naiya, panting, eyes wild, blood on her knuckles from being dragged over stones. The man holding her looked ready to heave her off the path, to cast her into the Cleft of Bones. But he and the other one looked up, startled, as Ula strode to them. The only old women they saw were their aunts and grandmothers, so her age and tone of authority gave them pause.

"What means this? Do you mean to sully the holy archive with dolos blood? I serve the high archivist. It is he who has called these dolos here to clean."

"Death is the punishment for any dolos who sets foot on the seventh tier," said the shorter of the two.

"Then kill me first and answer to the high archivist, if you're so eager." When the man hesitated, she knew she'd won. "Hadn't you better go down to the port and stop people from looting cargoes? Many of those ships have not been unloaded. Make sure the king's tithe isn't stolen!"

War-wagers were trained to take orders; no one would walk willingly into the bloody jaws of death otherwise. They released the girls but gave Ula a look, a promise of punishment if she proved a liar.

She said, "Take the echelon stairs to get to the harbor faster."

They hurried off. They were young, too, not knowledgeable enough to see the flaws in her explanation. She was sending them to their deaths, but that was two fewer war-wagers to threaten her people.

Naiya collapsed to the ground and clung to Ula's legs, sobbing. The other dolos sank to her knees to pray in a loud wail.

"Hush! Go inside."

"What's that noise?" whispered Naiya.

The wind had shifted direction. A distant groan turned into a sucking sound.

On the crest of the mount, the airships lashed to spires began to sway and pull as wind gusted. The laughter of the archivists and priests broke off to become shouts of alarm. A rising rumble pitched over the islands.

Ula pushed the girls toward the door. "Hurry."

Past the wide channels on either side of the Sheaf rose a strange silver-gray cloud topped with foam, like a great storm cloud rolling in. More dolos staggered past her as she retreated to the guard tower. Eight. Eleven. Seventeen.

Handsome young Achlu, who served on the war-wager tier, lurched to a halt beside her, gripping her arm in fear. "May the Small Mother protect us," he gasped. "The ocean has turned into a wall."

"Go! All of you, go!"

Another five, nine, eleven, hurried past her as the storm swept in, slow but inexorable. Three more, then two, then two. The hazy curtain resolved into a moving wall of water. Thundering, it crashed in white spouts of foam, scouring clean the slopes of the Sheaf and the headlands of the Sickle. The water tore trees, buildings, animals, people and churned them into a wild unstoppable force.

On the sea floor, amid the ships, by the piers, in the town, screams rose like smoke. The scramble began, people running for the shore, but it would be too late.

More dolos arrived, pouring past Ula until she could not understand how they could all fit in the lower level. She gave up counting. Still they came, as winds ripped at the height, as anything not tied down on the terraces below lifted into the air as chaff. The water roared with the howl and the fury of a roused monster come only to wreak havoc. The piers and port were inundated with murky water that rampaged over the empty dolos quarters, that surged up to the war-wagers' terrace in a rush of waves boiling across the bay in a whirlpool of destruction. And still the waves washed higher.

New screams, from closer at hand, yanked her attention away from the horror below. More war-wagers had come, spilling out from the dolos steps. Swords out, they cut down from behind the group of porters frantically running toward her on the path.

First to arrive was Kewa, the one she'd first sent down. His face was flushed with exertion. He shoved her rudely to the tower door. "Barricade it behind you, Aunt! Keep them safe who are already inside."

She stumbled across the threshold, but by now her arms were too numbed by shock to shift the door. The youths were strong but had no weapons except desperation. At Kewa's shout they turned and charged bladeless into the pursuers. Some grappled the war-wagers off the path, falling with them down the deadly cliff. One porter put himself in the path of a sword strike so others could wrestle the war-wager down and batter him with rocks. Blood spilled red. For a slow, calm space she heard men shouting on the summit above to board the airships, while on the path the fighting swirled and stopped. The few surviving dolos limped to the door.

"How many?" Kewa's arm was cut to the bone, blood dripping like rain from his skin. "How many made it?"

More shouts, from both above and below. Had the priests and airship crews seen them?

"If they come down the steps from the upper level we'll be trapped," she said. "Everyone in. We can block the inner chamber with overturned tables. That will hold for a while."

Then they would all die.

But hadn't they already died once? Taken in war, shorn of their freedom, and sent to serve implacable masters?

They went in. As the porters shifted the furniture and a heavy cabinet, she followed the murmur of voices and the stink of fear into the inner chamber. The oil and lamp were gone, but even without light to see she felt there were not as many as she expected. Had so few made it up here? Hadn't one hundred and fifty at least been salvaged? Yet that many could not fit inside the narrow space.

She trod in their wake, sensing a motion at work like an eddy drawing her in. The people were moving into the cleft where she had hidden. Were they leaping to their deaths? Was this the mercy they believed she had promised them? To choose their own time of dying in the Cleft of Bones?

A hammering began at the guard tower's latched door, punctuated by the angry shouts of war-wagers come to wreak vengeance.

Kewa came up behind her. "We'll stay behind, Aunt. Hold them off."

"No need, we can all go together," she said. She had held off death and despair all these years for the sake of the others, and because she could still find joy in the scraps she had, but what was left to them now? The dolos were dead below, or would be killed. Those of the echelon who survived would hoard the food that remained, or escape on the airships.

Choosing death on your own terms was itself a victory.

She reached the cleft and squeezed in. But it didn't feel the way it had earlier. Now an echo wafted up, the breath of tens, of a hundred. She knew the lower level as intimately as her own hands. When she reached the gap of air where she'd halted before, the person in front of her kept walking.

The empty pit was gone, miraculously replaced by a steep ramp that descended into the heart of the hill. A faint lamplight gleamed far below like the will-o-wisps of her childhood on a lost lakeshore.

This was unknown territory. She thought of the legend of the savages whom the civilized had driven out of these islands. But there was no going back.

Behind her, Kewa whispered, "What is this place, Aunt?"

"It is all that is left to us."

She started down, steadying herself with a hand on the rock face.

Shapes were carved into the rock, reliefs creating hollows and ridges as she descended. Here, a spiral. There, a face with eyes, an angled nose, a slit for a mouth. Far in the distance the howl and the fury raged. Runnels of water ran like tears through the grooves and dripped onto the worn steps. The air took on a new scent, musty and spicy together. The lamplight grew larger as the ceiling fell away to become a large space whose walls could not be seen within the dim aura. The stairs ended. People crowded against each other, but they parted to let her through.

When she reached Dorra, she saw why the woman had stopped. The raised lamp illuminated the stern but kindly face of a feather-capped woman whose parted lips revealed a snake's forked tongue. In her hands she displayed a basket of eggs. At first Ula was stricken that they had intruded where they were not allowed, and she hastily bowed as to a prince.

Then she realized the woman was a statue. Beside her stood a stone consort, a jackal-headed male figure, bare-chested and with a knee-length wrap covering belly and thighs. Crossed spears jutted out from behind his back, but he too carried a basket, this one laden with fish, as though inviting them to a feast.

"They welcome us," said Ula into the breathing silence. "Open your hands to show we are come without violence in our hearts. We beg you, lady and lord, protect us. In turn, we will protect you. If we survive, we will honor you. Dorra, put out the lamp to save the oil."

Dorra pinched out the flame. They stood shoulder to shoulder without speaking for a long time. Dolos knew how to wield their silence as a shield.

A wash of water swept along the floor, swirling around their feet, and fell away, receding back to where it had come from. Wind wailed, heard through a hundred cracks in the rock. A surging pound of surf thundered below as if trapped in a deep chamber at the root of the world. Moisture pattered down from the unseen ceiling.

Again water spilled across the cavern floor and again it receded. Ula waited, aware of the presence of the statues although she could not see them. But eyes weren't the only way to know the world. The ancient ones had waited down here for a long time, closed away in their hidden cavern, turned into rumors of ghosts and demons.

A third time the water came, more of a thin skin that quickly patched into random puddles. Three waves.

"Keep the lamp," she said to Dorra. "I'll go see."

"Aunt, you mustn't go up."

"It is I who must go."

They could not argue with her, because she was eldest. In their eyes, she had discovered this refuge, sent them to it, even though she knew it was no doing of hers but rather of the ancient ones who had waited here. Maybe they had been waiting for generations for just this moment, to welcome the lost and the forgotten.

In darkness her people made a path for her, returning her by touch and with murmurs of thanks until she reached the ramp. She had wondered if the magic that made the crevice open—something to do with pressure and water, she guessed—would close it again, but the ramp was still there. The way was still open.

Kewa caught her arm; she knew him by his hoarse, pained voice and the sticky scent of blood on his fingers from his wound. "Aunt, let me go first."

"No. This is my journey."

Ascent was harder. She grew winded and had to pause partway up, listening for the shouts of the war-wagers or the laughter of the priests. All she heard was the wind.

The steps let into the widened crevice. The crevice into the inner chamber, smelling of salt, water pooling where stone was worn by the tread of generations of feet. The light in the outer chamber seemed stark. The tables were all a jumble. She could not get out the door into the guard tower nor see what lay beyond there. Branches had gotten stuck in the narrow windows, blocking her view. She had to go up, to the temple, where no dolos was allowed to walk.

She crept one cautious step at a time. The curtain was askew. Past the curtain she halted in a kind of entryway. From here she looked across the open summit. All but one of the airship piers had broken in the wind. People crowded at the remaining pier's base, although no airship moored there, as if waiting for rescue to come now, soon, at their command.

To her right lay the open rooms of the archive, each a sheltered spacious terrace looking over the harbor, the city, and the bay. She went to a railing and stared. The waves had swept the harbor clean. Wreckage bobbed in the water. Corpses floated. A barrel rocked. The city looked like a rake had torn through it, tumbling roofs and walls, scoring trenches in the streets, tossing refuse everywhere. Not a creature moved, not in the distant streets nor on the wave-breached terraces of the sacred mount, with crumbling walls and bodies flung into corners where they'd lodged and drowned.

The only places on the islands that looked untouched were the high fields where dolos labored. There she glimpsed figures moving, running, seeking. How many were slaves and how many those who guarded the slaves? Even if they fought for their freedom and gained it, how long would that freedom last? Were the other islands of the archipelago stricken as well? When would the echelons and their war-wagers return in force?

To live in the space of what waited before her right now was the only way to survive. What might happen, or might not, what she feared or hoped for, was a burden she had learned to set aside. Choosing life on your own terms was itself a victory.

She returned to the lower level. She called down into the Cleft of Bones where the ancient ones had sheltered them. They came up from the darkness into what future they could not know.

CARRIE VAUGHN

The Voyage of Brenya

Carrie Vaughn

After raiders from the north burned three villages to the ground, Brenya decided to take drastic measures and call on the gods for help.

Which was not to say her folk hadn't already been calling on the gods: at dawn and dusk, wailing prayers and slitting the throats of lambs over altar stones, begging for succor and safety. But still the raiders came because the gods had left this land ages ago, crossed the sea to their own holy realm in the West, abandoning the mortal world. Brenya figured that someone ought to go and tell them they were needed and ask for their return.

"Brenya, you cannot do this." Parrick, her brother, had recently been anointed as a holy acolyte and took himself rather too seriously.

Ignoring him, she continued checking her overturned currach for leaks. The pitch-coated leather was sound; she was sure the little boat would carry her far. She'd carved charms of whales and seabirds out of seal bone and tied them to the wicker frame to ensure that the blessings of those seaborne creatures followed her.

"Please don't go." He begged, but he would not come down on the sand and risk soiling his bleached tunic, the sign of his rank. He stayed up on the grassy hillock, hands clenched at his side.

"Someone must go," she said, taking hold of the currach's edge and heaving it over.

"No, you're wrong! We must stay here and defend ourselves. Why do you think there's any help to be had across the sea?"

"If the gods will not hear our prayers from here, then someone must go and shout at them close by."

"Brenya—"

Difficult, packing for a journey when you didn't know how long you were going to be away. A week or two at least, she thought. She brought skins for rainwater, sinew line and bone hooks to catch fish. She had two spears and a couple of extra spearheads. She was a good hunter and could fend for herself as long as she needed to. A wool cloak, leather shoes.

"Brenya. You cannot go and find the gods. No one can."

She straightened from her task and faced him. "Why not? Has anyone tried?"

"Brenya." As if her name were a spell he could cast to change her mind.

She marched up the strand to face him. "Why not? The gods live in the West, correct?"

"Well yes, of course—"

"Why should I not go and tell them what's been happening here?"

"Because the journey is impossible. You'll die." Anguish wracked his voice.

She shook her head. "It's not impossible. I'm good with a boat. I can do this."

"It's not that, it's . . ." He trailed off because he could not say the words.

Brenya could. "Do you believe the gods already know what is happening here, have already heard our prayers and simply do not care? Or that there are no gods at all?" The newly made acolyte's mouth stayed closed. He'd become an acolyte for the status, not out of faith. At least he wouldn't make himself a hypocrite out loud. She swept her arm. "Look around; every day we walk past the circle of stones twice as tall as any man, planted to give us a doorway to midsummer. Cairns as big as hills. Standing stones with the signs of the gods carved all over them that have stood for a thousand years. This was a land of giants once, to have such stones and monuments all around us. The gods walked here, you cannot deny it!"

"The gods are not for us to know," he said.

"You say that when you have dedicated your life to them?"

"Even if you reached their land in the West, they will strike you down for presuming."

"Then tell me, holy Parrick, what must I do? Let the raiders destroy everything we have and kill us or take us all for slaves?"

He looked away, wincing. "These troubles cannot last forever."

"No, they will end when none of us are left. Or . . . I can go get help."

"Brenya . . ." Her name again, spoken like a prayer.

"I will be back as soon as I can. I will bring help." She would bring the gods who had built the lichen-covered monuments that stood as evidence of what the world had once been. Returning to her preparations, she put the oar in the boat and pulled on her cloak, wrapping the ends over her shoulders.

"Wait," he said. "Just . . . to a count of thirty. Wait. And count slow!"

"What for?"

He ran, disappearing around the hillock. This would be a perfect time to shove her currach into the water. She could row past the breakers before Parrick returned with yet another lecture. But she dutifully counted.

At twenty-five, he came back over the hillock carrying a hide bag. "Here. A few more things for you." This time, he came out on the sand, his sandaled feet slipping, to give her the gift. The bag held wrapped flatbread, a square of cheese, some flint, a knife. Odds and ends, but all would be useful. And a charm: a stone with a carving, the stylized roundel of an oak tree, its branches reaching up and its roots reaching down. It had been passed down in their family for ages. It was said to be from the same time as the stone circle and the giants' cairns, when the gods walked the land.

"So the gods will know you as one of their own," Parrick said. "And so you will remember to come back to us."

"Thank you," she whispered.

The stone talisman had a hole with a leather thong through it. She put the thong over her neck. Blinking back tears, she embraced him, and he was not too proud to hug her back.

"All will be well," she said. "You'll see, all will be well."

"Remember to keep watch of the north star. Follow the constellations home. Come home, Brenya."

"Yes, of course I will." She smiled.

He helped her push the little boat into the water, their feet splashing. The surf tried to push it back, but only once before she swung over the edge and got hold of the oar. She rowed and rowed, past the breakers and into the swells, the distance between her and land growing wider.

She looked back once. Parrick stood there, his arm raised, forlorn, like a standing stone himself set to mark her journey. She waved back. He lowered his arm.

She didn't look back again.

~

Within not very much time at all, Brenya lost sight of land, even the outlying islands and small jutting rocks that held colonies of nesting seabirds. This should have terrified her. Away from land, the currents would catch her, there was no shelter at all, and she had to rely on the sun and moon and stars to steer by. A screeching, childish part of her screamed to turn back, she still had time to go home before she lost all sense of direction on the endless gray-and-silver field that now comprised her world.

Nonsense. The sun moved west. She rowed to the setting sun.

The first night, she did not sleep. She lit some peat in a clay bowl, rowed by its glowing orange light and faint warmth, slow and steady, imagining the beat of a drum to guide her, thumping in time to the draw of her breath, a long inhale and a long exhale. The bone talismans clacked lightly against the wicker frame, encouraging her. She didn't know how far she had to row; it wouldn't do to go too fast and wear herself out. The waves seemed to push her along, as if supporting her quest.

The second day, her arms felt like cracked mud, though the rhythm had become ingrained. She kept on, oar dipping to the left, then right, then left, even as she nodded off, then started awake, rowed for a time, then nodded off again. She didn't want to sleep and leave the boat unguided. She realized she had perhaps hoped too earnestly that the land of the gods wouldn't be so very far away after all. It would have been easy for gods and giants to go back and forth between lands. They made the world; they simply knew where everything was and the seas would part for them. A small human like her had to row.

Seabirds followed her, the sleek white ones with orange dagger bills and black helmets, the stumpy little black ones with the brightly painted bills. The terns glided over her, heads tilting this way and that, studying her with onyx-black eyes. The puffins skittered fast and low over the water and didn't pay her any mind except to squeak, as if put out that they had to change course around her boat, where they hadn't expected to find an obstacle.

At the end of the second day, the rain began. The change in weather had come in so slowly, no storm of wall-like clouds with thunder and lightning to give a warning. Just a building mist that turned the sky gray and, soon enough, poured down a constant drizzle. At least there wasn't wind, and the waves hadn't grown too fierce. She was merely soaked. *Everything* was soaked. She had to put down the oar and use a cup to scoop out water collecting on the bottom of the boat, after replenishing her waterskins.

With the sky shrouded, she saw no setting sun to row toward, no north star shining. Never mind—in the morning she would reorient herself. West would appear again, she wouldn't be too terribly far off course.

The only reason no one had successfully sailed west to find the dwelling of the gods was that no one had ever tried. She held Parrick's talisman and prayed. *Let me find you. Let me speak to you. You thought your children grown enough to take care of themselves, but we are not, we need help.*

When she got the boat mostly bailed out, she tried to make shelter, stringing her cloak around the edge, lashing it to the frame. Kept the rain off, but then the cloak became soaked and water dripped through. She shrugged her cloak, heavy and stinking with rain, over her head, then curled up. She thought she was too cold, was shivering too hard to sleep. But by that time, she was so exhausted she passed out immediately.

～

A fog came in so thick she could not see the sky. She could not see twenty paces beyond the edge of her boat. She did not know where she was. Water lapped against leather, and the boat's frame creaked. But it still floated.

This was harder than she thought it would be. She had known it would be hard; she'd been warned. Surely it would be hard, because if it were easy someone would have done it before. But all the stories, all the quests and adventures, the tales of gods and giants and the heroes who bested them in the songs—they'd all succeeded, hadn't they? It must be possible; at least, that was what she thought. But Parrick had warned her, hadn't he?

The gray mist paled, which meant it was day and there was sun, but it didn't show as even a veiled circle overhead. There was nothing. She didn't dare row, in case she got the direction wrong. But she had no choice. She had to row, or drift wherever the waves pushed her.

A cry rattled the fog, and she looked, hopeful. But it was the squealing cry of a bird, and a moment later a tern came to perch at the edge of her boat. It adjusted its stance, ruffled its wings as it settled, and tilted its head at her.

She stared. "I don't have any fish for you." She didn't know what else to say.

"Where do you think you're going?" the bird said. "We never see your kind this far out."

Well. This really was an adventure then, if birds were talking to her. Or . . . well no. She'd have noticed if she had died in the night. There'd have been some . . . announcement. Wouldn't there?

Of course there would have been. "I'm going to find the gods and ask for their help."

"Oh really? How goes the journey?"

She screwed up her face and looked around. "I'm a bit lost at the moment."

"Oh, I'm sorry. Can I help?"

"Maybe, if you can tell me which way is west?"

"I don't know what west is."

"But you go everywhere."

"We go north and south. We migrate according to the thrumming in our bones. But I don't know west."

"Then can you show me to the land of the gods?"

"I don't know what gods are."

"I thought talking animals on these adventures were supposed to be helpful."

The tern snapped its bill. "I thought you might like some company."

"Can you maybe . . . fly above the clouds and tell me which way the sun is moving?"

"How do you know the clouds don't go all the way up?"

"I don't, but I thought you might."

"I'll check."

When the bird was gone, Brenya regretted asking it to go. She wasn't sure it would come back, and she found she would, in fact, like some company.

She might as well put out a hook and line and try for some fish. The air stayed dank, everything she had was wet, and she was shivering. Her little bowl of peat had gone out. Everything was soaked and wouldn't dry.

Huddled in the middle of the boat, she shook the line and waited.

And waited. She had caught fish from the sea before, but that was close to shore, not out on the wide ocean. She had thought . . . or maybe she had hoped . . . that being out here would be similar enough to home that she could manage. But things were too different.

A bird plunged from the sky, struck the water, and popped back to the surface a moment later, a silvery fish wriggling in its beak. With a couple of jerks of its head it flipped the fish around and swallowed it whole. So, the problem wasn't that there were no fish, she thought sourly.

"You came back," Brenya said.

"Sorry," the tern said. "Had to go a lot farther than I thought. Then I was just *starving*—takes a lot of energy, flying that far up. But sun's out now. Any luck?" Bobbing on the waves, the tern nodded at her line.

"No." She scowled.

"Here, just a minute." With a flap of wings and a flicking of spray, the tern launched, rose up, circled for a moment, and once again dived straight down like a spear. It reemerged, floating on the surface with another twitching fish. This one, it tossed into the boat, where the fish flopped for a moment before lying still, gills gasping.

Brenya hated to sound ungrateful, but she wasn't sure she could eat the little thing. "Thank you, but did you find the sun? Can you tell which way is west?"

"I still don't know west. But the sun? The sun is up." The tern nodded, satisfied, then launched straight into the air and flew away.

Up. The sun was up. Well, then. Brenya began rowing again, to keep warm.

～

The mist thinned, and if the clouds didn't exactly part, they got so she could see the disk of light, like a circle of beaten gold. If she didn't grow warm, she at least didn't get any colder. As the disk moved, she found west again.

Squinting, she studied the horizon ahead, and all around, searching for the hazy shapes that would mean land. The more she stared, shading her eyes against the light, the more she thought she saw something. But no, what she thought was a spit of rock was just another wave; what she thought was a stretch of island was her own imagination.

Gripping the stone talisman around her neck, she whispered, "Please, Bran and Cor and Dana and Cerri, all the gods of earth and sky and sea and fire. Please guide me. Give me a sign and I will come to you."

She rowed until her arms felt like sticks of wood and her breath rasped in her lungs.

Ahead, so low that she almost missed it, appeared a spit of land that really was land and not a wave, not a shadow built out of mist and hope. She rowed for it, not believing this was the land of the gods, but to give herself a rest, to sleep with no fear of drifting off. Gray and uninviting, the hillock steamed wetly in a mist.

She had never seen a more desolate patch, worn smooth and shining. Not even birds came here, and only a few small barnacles clung to the surface along the water. The land seemed unmoored, rising and falling with passing waves. It made her uneasy. Nevertheless, she rowed the boat to the edge, hopped out, dragged it half out of the water, and considered. This was bleak. Another step and she'd be off on the other side of the spit, and it was only a few paces long. If she went to sleep here, she might find the whole of it had washed away in the night. Shading her eyes, she looked westward. Maybe this time the land of the gods would appear to her. But nothing did, just this strange piece of flotsam.

Which shifted, one end of it lifting, a spout of fish-stinking air erupting from a divot. An eye rolled to look back at her, and a great mouth, bigger than her little boat, parted.

"Why are you walking around on my back?" said a soft voice that rumbled like fingertips skittering over a drumhead.

Brenya screamed, and the land slipped out from under her. She fell, splashing. The boat rocked away on the sudden wave of movement. Madly, she paddled after it. If she lost the boat, she would drown. Water went up her nose and salt scratched down her throat; she choked and coughed. She reached and her hand hit the leather hull, which only pushed it away. She tried again, and the boat seemed to be fleeing from her. In one last effort she flung herself out of the water, or tried to. Kicked her legs and reached as far as she could to grab the edge of the frame. Didn't make it.

The whale—the spit of land was actually a whale—got its nose under her. Her bare feet slipped on its smooth skin, it tilted its head, and this time she got her footing and the whale lifted her until she fell over the side and onto the pile of wet wool in the middle of her boat.

She lay gasping. Her eyes stung, her skin shivered. She would never be warm again.

"Are you all right?" the low, calm voice asked.

"No." She gasped, caught her breath, wiped water from her eyes. "Yes. I don't know." Swinging round to lean over the side, she looked out, and found that giant island-shaped gray face looking back. "You're a whale."

"Yes."

"I've heard stories about this," she said. "Someone rows to an island and discovers it's actually a whale. But I didn't think it could really happen. I mean, surely I'd notice if I was walking on a *whale*—"

"When your kind have been at sea for a long time, without enough water and sleep, you start to hallucinate. You want to see land so badly everything starts to look like land. It happens more often than you might think."

"Really?"

"Well, not all that often. Mostly because you people don't come out here much. What are you doing this far out?"

"I'm going to find the gods and ask for their help to stop the raiders who've invaded our land."

"Oh." The whale sounded uncertain, unconvinced.

"What's wrong?"

"Just . . . that seems like a very big quest."

"It is, I suppose."

"I've not heard of anyone ever doing such a thing."

"But that doesn't mean it can't be done," she said. If she'd had to describe exactly how the whale shrugged, she wouldn't have been able to do it. It had no neck, no shoulders. Nevertheless, somehow, she knew that the whale shrugged. "You don't think I can."

It sank underwater, then broke the surface, a fountain of mist blowing from its blowhole, water sheeting from its smooth thick skin. "I didn't say that."

"But it *must* be possible."

"Why? Why must it be?"

"My home is filled with the impossible, cairns as large as villages, stones as large as whole houses that have been moved and tilted. No one mortal could have built those things, but there they all stand. So there must be gods and giants, and they must have walked upon the earth once. Where did they go? Our stories say they have a land far in the West at the edge of the world."

"Did you think that 'far' might mean something different to giants who can build with stones larger than a house than to a girl in a boat? Did you not think that the ocean might have no end?"

"I didn't know what else to do. There was nothing else I could do except wait for the raiders to kill us."

"So you row out to meet destruction instead?"

She hadn't thought about crying until that moment. With the wet and salt water, the tears didn't really show.

A flutter of feathers, a rustle of air, and the tern settled on the edge of the boat. The whale blew out a greeting, and the tern dipped its orange bill.

"Did she tell you?" the tern asked.

"She's going west."

"I don't even know what west is."

"It is an imprecise destination," the whale said.

Brenya hugged her knees, which set the boat to rocking, just a little. "I don't suppose either of you can tell me how to reach the land of the gods in the West."

The whale and tern exchanged a glance. The whale sighed a

fishy breath and said, "You must die to reach those lands. That's what those lands *are*."

"But then how will I get back home?"

Both the tern and the whale gave her chastising looks.

She had made a lot of assumptions before setting off on this journey, she realized. But . . . if she could reach the land of the gods, convince them to help, and if she saved her home and people . . . then the trip would be worth it even if she didn't return home. Yes, that was her purpose.

"Thank you for your help," she said. "You must understand, I have to try."

"How far will you go before you've gone too far to turn back?" the tern said. "I always know how far I can go before I need to return to the nest."

"I don't know," she said. "I should probably get rowing. Thank you, both."

"Good luck," the tern said, and flew.

The whale blew out a cloud of mist, dipped its head, and humped over into a dive, its great fanlike tail pausing above the water, then slipping under without a splash.

She was alone again, and she rowed.

~

Possibility one: the land of the gods existed and was in reach, she just had to go a little farther.

Possibility two: the land of the gods existed but was too far to find in a simple hide boat and she would fail.

Possibility three: the land of the gods did not exist.

Her gut lurched, because here, in the middle of an unconcerned ocean, she knew which of these was most likely. Finally, she knew. She stared at the oar in her hands as if it had betrayed her, as if she had not been the one using it to bring herself so far from home, for nothing.

What Parrick must think of her. He had known; he had begged. She should have listened. And now she was likely too far away to turn back, had drifted too far off course, even if she rowed to the rising sun until her food ran out—and what if the raiders had come and destroyed everything while she was gone?

What was she *doing*? Nothing. None of this would do any good.

She yanked the stone talisman Parrick had given her off her neck and threw it as hard as she could, toward the setting sun. It flew so far she didn't hear the splash when it hit the water. It vanished, and she was alone.

Right away she knew she shouldn't have done that. Her link to home, her proof of who she was—she shouldn't have thrown it away. Now she had nothing at all. She was too impulsive, Parrick would say. This whole journey proved it. However well she thought she had planned, in reality she'd known nothing at all.

She was a fool.

She curled up at the bottom of her boat, snugged up with her cloak, and found she was too tired to cry.

~

For a few hours, she slept. The sun was low when she woke, and she put off trying to decide what to do. She would drift regardless, and in another hour maybe something would change.

Insight, she needed insight.

Or maybe a miracle.

Because she might as well drink the last few drops from her waterskin, she raised it to her lips and—

And saw the land to the West.

The clouds parted and the sun shone on lush green hills, climbing gently up from a flat, inviting beach where white-capped waves slipped and came to rest. There were forests and meadows, stands of flowering heather pouring down from weathered stone,

64

all of it the most beautiful sight Brenya had ever seen.

All at once exhaustion and despair fell away and she rowed as hard as she could, until the tide caught her little boat and carried it on breaking waves up to the sand. She fell over the edge, managed one last heave to drag it up on the beach, then collapsed.

And slept.

When she woke again, the world was still in daylight. The sound of shushing, slipping waves calmed her. The sun warmed her, and yes she did feel warm again, and dry, finally dry. Her lips were cracked, her stomach growled, but she was on solid land and she was alive.

At least, she thought she was alive.

She stood, walked a little ways up the strand. This world seemed very much like home, quiet and verdant. She even heard bleating nearby, a flock of sheep grazing on the next hill maybe. But where were the gods and giants, and their houses of stone, their cairns and circles? From this section of beach, this land seemed deserted. *Maybe . . . ,* she thought, *maybe the gods stopped listening to prayers because they're . . . gone?*

That seemed unlikely. Impossible. Gods lived forever; that was what made them gods.

She retrieved her spear from the boat, pulled her pouch over her shoulder, and set off in the direction of the sheep. Maybe there would be people nearby, and if she could find people, she could find the dwelling places of the gods.

Following the call-and-response of throaty sheep, she left the sand and waves, crossed a grassy hill, which in turned opened to a meadow . . . and there they were, wool dirty and tangled, dotting the greenery with their heads to the grass. Shading her eyes in the diffuse light—a haze seemed to block the sun, she could not tell the time of day—she looked out. No walls, no fences. Still no cairns and stones. Not so much as a line of rising smoke to show where people might be.

"Hey! How'd you get here!"

The pasture lay at the edge of a forest, and from the shadows of the trees a man emerged, the shepherd, dressed in ratty torn skins and furs, carrying a gnarled staff. His soiled beard grew to his midriff, the hat he wore appeared to be made entirely of bark, and he stared at Brenya only for a moment before running away.

"Wait!" she called after him. He ran faster, and Brenya stopped, confused. The sheep bleated like nothing was wrong.

A moment later he returned, and a woman accompanied him. "What is it?" the woman was saying, and the ratty man pointed.

She was beautiful. The most beautiful woman Brenya had ever seen, with glistening raven-colored hair swept down her back, a clear far-seeing gaze, movements graceful as mist among the trees. She wore a leather tunic and a woven stole, bone ear-rings and beads around her neck. She leaned on a spear with a bronze point, much like Brenya's own. She could have been a hunter from any village along the coast back home.

She wasn't giant-sized; she didn't seem like she could lift great boulders to build a cairn. Except for how beautiful she was she seemed . . . ordinary. She gazed at Brenya, not as someone looking upon a great seawoman who had gone farther than any of her people ever had before and found the land of the gods. Rather, she had the look of a mother regarding a child who has done some mischief.

The woman came across the meadow toward Brenya. "You shouldn't be here."

Brenya wanted to fall at the woman's feet and apologize. That was how she knew that yes, this was a goddess, and she had reached the land in the West. Instead, she steeled herself and tried to explain.

"Yes, I know, I completely understand that now. But I've had a very difficult journey and I need help. I'm looking for those who built the great stone cairns and temples in the lands of the east.

66

Is this . . . is this the land in the West, the home of the gods?"

"Well, yes—"

Brenya grinned, then laughed. "I did it. *I did it!* Oh please, great Mother Dana, your children are in danger. We have no one else to turn to, you must return to your lands in the east and help protect us against the raiders—"

"Those aren't *my* lands." She didn't *quite* seem like she was laughing at Brenya.

"But . . . didn't you build the tombs and cairns and circles and standing stones, the monuments that mark out the land and tell the coming of the light and the turning of the seasons? You built them all, didn't you?"

She shook her head. "Your ancestors did that, all on their own. Built tombs to house the dead, to mark their place in the world so those who came after would remember."

But we don't remember, Brenya thought. If the standing stones and cairns were built by people, by her own ancestors—why did they stop building, and why did they tell stories of the gods? She had set out on this voyage based on that other world.

The woman continued. "Look around, do you see any tombs here? We have no need of them."

She had called the woman Dana, mother goddess of them all, and she hadn't denied it. She corrected the other point, but not that one. "I don't understand." Brenya had never felt more lost, even when she was in the middle of the ocean.

"I know. It's a lot to take in."

Brenya swallowed a lump in her throat and asked, "Am I dead?"

"Not really. Not quite yet. But this place is . . . strange. You probably shouldn't stay too long. Come with me." The woman walked off, back toward the sand and waves.

What could Brenya do but follow?

The ratty man had returned to the trees, leaning up against

a trunk and watching them closely. He might have been some forest god of earth and growing things. Of sheep and those who looked after them.

"We need help," Brenya said, running after Dana. "Raiders have come, and we pray and pray for help but no help comes. So I thought if I asked in person—"

The woman turned on her, flustered. "We cannot answer every single prayer that comes to us. We cannot change anything that you cannot change for yourself."

"But I thought if I came here—"

The woman held up her hand, and Brenya fell silent. They continued walking.

The little currach was on the beach where she left it, and Dana stared at it a moment. "You came here in *this?*" Brenya nodded. "Huh. I expect they'll make a story about you when you get back home."

"Oh, I hope not. This has all been . . . well. I don't feel very heroic right now." But she thrilled a little at those words. The goddess said she would return home . . .

"Never mind. The stories are out of our hands in the end. Oh, wait just a moment—"

She went into the surf, her bare toes squishing in wet sand. Plunged her arms into the water like she meant to catch a fish bare-handed. Shifted around, searching, and straightened with something clutched in her fist.

"I think this is yours." She held out a stone talisman on a leather thong.

Brenya took it from her. Yes, it was the same gray stone, with the ancient weathered carving, oak branches lifting up, roots reaching down. Her talisman. She clutched it to her chest and stared. "Could . . . could I have thrown it in the waves anytime and found you? Is that what I needed to do?"

Dana shook her head. "You needed to make a journey."

"I have so many questions."

"I know."

"I don't know what to do now."

"Go home, Brenya. I think I can help you get home a little faster than it took you to get here. The wind will be at your back this time." She went up to the thicket above the sand and began pulling down branches to cut.

Brenya looked back at the sea, back to the land, and didn't know where she was. "If I pray to you, will you listen?"

"Will you still pray to me, even if I don't answer?"

Brenya put the talisman over her neck and said, "Yes."

"Well then. Let's get you out of here before this place decides you really do belong here."

~

When Brenya returned home, she did so under sail, pushed by the western wind. With Dana's help she tied a mast to one side of the boat's frame, lashed another length of wicker across, and stretched a triangle of her cloak between them. She stuck the oar out the back as a rudder to steer the way, and instead of rowing she only had to hold the course. She passed flocks of terns and pods of whales, but couldn't tell if any of them were the ones who had spoken to her. They flew and swam off too quickly, as if they were on quests of their own.

Her only fear was not knowing what she would find when she returned home. Had the raiders come already, or did she have time to warn her people that the gods would not help them and they must prepare to defend themselves alone? And they could prepare—after all, their ancestors built the mighty cairns and circles of stones.

And she, Brenya, had rowed her boat all the way to the West. They could do this thing.

~

Finally, days later, Brenya reached another green-robed island. This one couldn't help but be a little dimmer and foggier than the last she had visited, but she recognized the rocky cliff with flocks of seabirds swooping and tumbling around it, the hills rolling to a rough-shaped bay, and toward this she steered.

A figure stood on the highest hill overlooking the bay; it spotted her and ran off. She was too far away to see who it was, a familiar face or an enemy. Might be that raiders had overrun the land and she'd be killed the minute she came ashore.

"Please, Dana, let everything be all right."

This felt like she'd sailed to her doom. In the shelter of the bay the wind died. She took down the sail, took up the oar, and rowed the rest of the way. Her boat was sturdy as ever—the leather a little worn, the pitch a little cracked. But it had been strong and faithful.

A whole group was waiting on the shore to meet her—the figure on the hill must have been a lookout who'd spread the word. And there, in the front, so familiar in his white tunic, was Parrick. His beard had gotten scruffier, but that didn't hide his smile.

"Parrick!" she called.

"Brenya!" He laughed and cried both, and the lot of them, all folk from her village, came down to help her drag the boat up onto the sand. She tumbled out and into Parrick's arms and for a long time stood there in the moment, on solid land and in safety. She didn't know how she was going to explain any of it. She didn't know what question to ask first about what had happened while she was gone.

Then Parrick shook her. "You did it, Brenya! I don't know what happened or how, but you did it! The raiders are gone, the land is safe! And you, you've returned with the wind at your call. We all saw you sliding across the waves like a fish!"

"It's a sail. We can put them on all the boats, I think," she said. "What do you mean, the raiders are gone? What happened?"

"But surely you know?"

"Tell me anyway."

"It was a plague." He shrugged, his arms flapping to his sides. "They began to sicken, and decided our land was cursed and left it. We've had peace all summer. It happened just after you left—it's all because of you!"

She was amazed. "But that . . . that isn't really how it happened."

Her brother seemed taken aback. "Well then, how did it happen?"

"It . . . it went very badly. As soon as the fog came in I couldn't see the sun or stars or anything, and then the tern tried to help but it didn't know which way west was and it tried to get me a fish, but . . . well. And then I thought a whale was an island, and it was very kind about it, but it couldn't help me either, and so I kept going because I'd gone too far to turn back, or so I thought, but I gave up. Parrick, I gave up, but then there it was, the land of the West and Mother Dana, and she said she couldn't help us, but she showed me how to build the sail for the boat and then sent me on my way, and . . . I wasn't even sure anything would be here when I returned."

None of that made sense, and everyone was looking at her like they didn't know what she was talking about. How could she ever hope to explain what had happened?

Parrick took her hand. "So it was you," he said. "You *did* reach the gods and they answered your call!"

"I . . ." *The stories are out of our hands . . .*

"We'll tell the story forever, Brenya, how you crossed the water to the edge of the world to ask the gods for their help, and saved us all!"

People wouldn't really remember. They wouldn't. In time it would all get twisted up; people would think her a giant who had built cairns of stone. She wouldn't be around to tell anyone otherwise. So, she supposed, there was no sense in worrying about it.

"Did you know that it was our ancestors who built the standing stones and circles and cairns?" she said. "It wasn't gods and giants at all."

Parrick smiled nervously. "But . . . how? How would they have done such a thing? Surely . . . surely they had the guidance of the gods." He seemed so happy—so relieved—to have his faith confirmed.

"Never mind," she said. "I'm just glad to be home." She took Parrick's hand, and they all walked back to their village where the villagers cooked a good hot dinner for her, and told stories far into the night.

CHARLES YU

Comfort Lodge, Enigma Valley

Charles Yu

1/12/19

We stayed here six years ago on our honeymoon so we stayed here again. Everything about this place is sooo great. Comfy bed, clean facilities, helpful and smiley staff and of course a variety of decent (my husband says more than decent) breakfast choices. The fitness room is basic and small but there are beautiful roads (and hills) to run on (or jog). Not that I jog since I hurt my knee, but I did see one or two joggers out there. Would definitely stay here again. Want to give it four and half stars but since half stars are not an option (they should be!) we will reluctantly give it four but you know what we mean. A little far from the energy vortex though.

Brent F. and Derek F.

Was this review . . . ?
- Useful
- Funny
- Cool

1/5/19

Nice place. From the noise and taped-off sections it looks like they are slowly updating the rooms. Ours was fairly nice although a bit weird. The room dimensions were long and skinny and seemed to change every time we entered or even when I went in the bathroom and came out a second later, the room felt like a different shape or something.

On one end of the room there is a kitchen counter with a sink and a fridge underneath. Nothing on the other counter, yet the console under the television had a microwave . . . just a really weird setup.

Also, in the bathroom, the faucet was barely over the sink so whenever I washed my hands, I got water all over the counter.

At night I was awoken (woken? awakened?) by flashing lights—or other psycho-visual phenomenon, based on internet research—from the bathroom and when I got up to investigate I was momentarily sucked into some kind of temporal anomaly which was annoying. The television reception was pretty bad also . . . doubt that was a coincidence if you know what I mean. But the staff was nice and rooms were clean so I give it four stars.

Cathy S.

> 1 person voted for this review
> • Useful (1)

12/31/18

This was the absolute worst Comfort Lodge I've ever stayed with—and I did it for two and a half days!!!

Wayyyy overdue for an update. Um hello the bathroom was the dirtiest I've ever seen in a hotel or motel or whatever you would call this.

Backstory (it's relevant): came here for New Year's with a group of friends from university (actually two groups who didn't quite get along back then, but are united through me as the common person of both groups and a lot of us now work in insurance or legal services).

Haven't seen these chuckleheads for years and was expecting to just kick it, tip back a few drinks by the pool, but what I was not expecting was to come away from this whole experience extremely disappointed and embarrassed (embarrassed because this was my idea).

For one thing, even though they advertise this place as being in *South* Enigma Valley (according to the website, just "minutes away from the heart of the mystery") in actuality it's NINE MILES. More like 9.2 miles, according to Google. Furthermore, the shuttle is hourly so if you miss it I guess you are just supposed to wait. Guess they don't have a lot of guests who bill their time by the hour. (I told my traveling companions that calling it Enigma Valley–adjacent would be more accurate, and they all agreed.)

My recommendation—not great value, especially for the amenities (or lack thereof).

And "P.S." Just FYI the nightly apparitions are not "charming" or part of the local color. They're terrifying.

Tyler K.

9/25/18

Came here with my husband and our new baby for our first getaway as a family. The night before we left, she was crying nonstop and none of us got any sleep so the whole drive we were fighting.

When we entered the lobby, we could feel it immediately. We didn't know it at the time, but that was the first sign of the Opening.

We checked in and got our key and as we entered the room, a chill went through me, to my core. The baby instantly fell into the best sleep she has ever had. My husband drank a tallboy and got a little frisky and I wasn't totally opposed to the idea but then we heard the whispers.

I liked that the place was walking distance to a few local restaurants and stores. Rooms were clean and it was quietish. Having a varied breakfast included was a nice bonus, I was appreciative of the potatoes and the to-go bags if you were rushing out early in the a.m.

When we woke up the next morning, it was over a year later and the baby was walking around the room. I had slept for almost four hundred nights. The Gates had Opened fully and the army of the inside had taken my husband a prisoner. I don't want to say I told you so, but "I told you so." How many times did I say to him we should do Reno, we should do Reno, but no, Mr. I Know How To Plan A Vacation For My Family had to go and get all fancy and now look what happens.

Denise L.

> Reply from Management (9/28/18):
>
> Dear Denise,
>
> Thank you for taking the time to let us know about your stay with us. I apologize that your experience was less than satisfactory. Although it is of course not going to make up for the disappointment in losing your husband and the father of your child, we can offer vouchers for a discounted stay at any of our properties nationwide. Please contact me if you would like to discuss further!
>
> Clarissa Pender
> Business Manager
> Comfort Lodge, Enigma Valley

9/12/18

I've read some of the bad reviews on here but I have to say that although they are not totally unfair I think some of them go a little too far in slamming this place. The staff all seem to be trying really hard and if you think it's so easy to run a business then you should try it yourself and see how you feel if/when people go online and start to bash you or slam your place of business.

That said, I have to say, one thing I do think is true is that Enigma can be a very expensive place to visit. Having said that, this place offers a reasonable alternative to the higher-priced resorts (which some of us can afford, just choose not to).

We were here for the annual Diamond Tier insurance brokers golf getaway (Regional Top 5%, two years running baby!) so we didn't have a chance to check out any of the excursions we heard so much about.

While we were there, someone apparently fell into the Chasm and was presumed dead but then three days later returned, saying she had been to "the other side."

Farrah A.

7/4/18

Sadly, I believe I'm going to have to give up on this hotel. It seems that every time I've stayed here over the past couple of years they have really let me down in one way or another.

During my most recent stay, I booked my reservations well in advance. My membership in the Loyalty program allowed me a free upgrade and a voucher for one free night, to any vacant rooms.

When I got to the hotel the girl at the desk told me my choice was just a suggestion and that she was assigning me a different room.

Initially, I believed this was not going to be a problem as it is a one-floor structure and most of the rooms are pretty much the same. Or so I thought. What she did not tell me, however, was this room she gave me had a door in the floor. You heard me right. What kind of place has a door in the floor? My bathroom was down there, subterranean, and when I called to complain they just said it is in the fine print of the program that I can be stuck with any room they choose. I had to pee a lot that night (my bladder has not been the same post-40th birthday) and it was so cold down there in the "dungeon" (as my traveling companion called it) that I could see my own breath. Not good.

As I had booked the room for two nights, the next morning I went down and told them that I would like a different room. The staff member informed me that they were fully booked and I would have to wait for them to see if a room may open up. This was obviously unacceptable. I checked out and moved my stay to the Marriott in West Enigma, which is connected to the shopping mall—super convenient.

I believe that this hotel really needs to take a long hard look at their operational practices and the way they are treating their guests. And, if you stay here and they assign you room 119, unless you can sleep through anything, ask for a different room.

Brie V.

11/11/17

I chose this location based on both price and the pool. I had planned to enjoy the warm weather on frequent occasions, which I did. This pool was often full of bugs and appeared to be in desperate need of some cleaning. I imagine it's hard to keep it clean constantly but it was not the ideal experience I had hoped for. The hot tub is nice and this is a great place to sit at night and watch the stars. When I dunked my head underwater, I encountered my greatest fears and lived a thousand lifetimes. The Gate has Opened, the army has advanced, a scout or "guide" had come here, into the jacuzzi, to show me the way to the Hidden Kingdom, but I was too afraid. Not following into that place is my greatest regret in life. And every time I drive by I always look at the motel and wonder what if.

(name withheld)

11/26/16

This is a pretty good hotel. I have stayed here a number of times over a span of many years. I travel a lot for work. I'm in sales. If you or your family are in need of life insurance, please contact [POST FLAGGED FOR VIOLATION OF TERMS AND CONDITIONS.]

Dan F.

3/25/15

There are crumbs everywhere!

Daniel F.

3/8/14

Great Wi-Fi signal and TV—especially the special channel for an education on all things Enigma. *And the Voice spoketh unto me, and sayeth the Voice for all time: the Gate has many apertures.* Ever since my stay, I sort of black out for a few moments here and there. My partner thinks it's stress, but our health insurance doesn't cover a lot and has a high deductible so I'm just trying to tough it out *the Hidden Kingdom awaits, do not delay, we await your arrival for the next phase of being* and the concierge guy said they had no more energy bars but he did give me a couple of those packages of animal crackers they have for kids sometimes *and then he turned to me and I followed it into the next realm where my heart was.* Plenty of parking. Free, tasty breakfast that varies a bit each morning. Gym is a little small, and all machines, no free weights.

(name withheld)

7/29/17

Few notable observations:

The place is located on a slanted platform. This means that when you turn into the building, each side of it is inclined and may require you to park and walk. Also, the incline goes up in every direction, which I believe is a spatial and logical paradox and also a pain in the frickin butt. Who designed this place, M. C. Escher?

There is free parking, and I found the area very easy to navigate.

The fitness center does not offer any free weights (dumbbells). There is a treadmill and two ellipticals, and a busted looking rowing machine. However, for the brave, one could easily take a step off the treadmill and onto a scenic hiking trail! I heard howling from that direction.

The art in the lobby is also kind of nice, which is weird for a Comfort Lodge. Local artists display here. It's so great when a place is connected to its surroundings, especially in this world of big corporate chains.

One could argue that the Comfort Lodge is the home of a central Vector-Point! .. but I digress . . .

Davy "D. D." D.

8/13/16

I'm normally a Starwood guy but a month ago I decided that it would be wise to build some status with another hotel chain. So one of the weeks that I needed to be in the area, I figured why not. I expected the same level of quality for roughly the same price. Boy was I wrong!

First of all when I arrived they were cleaning the carpets which is great but I would think there is a better time to do that than during peak check-in hours. Second of all whatever they used to clean the carpets was very strong-smelling and I have a sensitive nose and soft palate. Third of all every time I was in the lobby (or at least 75-80% of the time) during my trip it seemed like they were cleaning the carpets. I don't know what's going on with these carpets but that seems a little excessive!!

My room was also a connecting room which I specifically asked not to have so I called down to see if he could switch me. While I was on hold, the door opened and . . .

[REDACTED]

Which I am really not cool with.

P.S. The only thing that I personally liked about this hotel was the breakfast, as it was the usual breakfast that you find at most hotels. What the hell do they do to those *eggs*?!?!

Beth K.

8/22/15

Let me start by addressing the elephant in the room: yes, they do still have wine by the fireplace every night!

This location can use updating particularly in the tub area, as you can see by my photograph the tub had a large chip in it.

I have lost my family. But my new family awaits through the Gate.

(name withheld)

1/3/13

Thanks I find this location to offer good value and good location. The rooms are large and clean. Morning breakfast is adequate for the masses. But most of all the front staff (H/T to: Brianna and Ashleigh! Thanks for the extra soaps—shhh, your secret is safe with me!). and are top notch at guest services. Thanks for a relaxing and pleasant visit.

Breanna (a friend of Brianna)

5/21/12

My favorite part about staying at this particular location was the live music! There was a man who played music on his flute during breakfast and weekend nights. The melody matched the music nicely. He's a local musician, some kind of shaman, I think, who plays at different venues and selling CDs for a living. His name escapes me at the moment, Shepherd of Lost Children or something like that.

Greggg (not a typo)

8/16/11

I would give zero stars if it was an option. Beds were like rocks. Carpet was filthy. Dresser drawers were falling apart. We were told 2 queen beds but they were doubles. Air conditioner was noisy and did not cool the room.

Wrinkled and cold sausage. Eggs were surprisingly good.

Not A Fan

11/19/10

This hotel needs updating. It is dark, wallpaper is stained, and carpet is frayed. TV is bolted to cabinet so you can't turn it right or left. Rooms are noisy. Starting at 5 a.m. you hear the doors slamming. Don't know if it was just our room. Our room was second floor overlooking lobby. Apparitions were annoying. We got back a month ago and my son has not stopped crying.

Housekeeping did not leave toiletries and did not clean sink and toilet. (hair strands still in sink)

On last night heard music from lobby/breakfast area starting at 8 a.m. Glad it wasn't playing the other days. Went down to see where it was coming from and the Destruction of Glory had begun. Lobby smells weird.

(name withheld)

2/24/19   ***Updated review***

My husband came through the door, his beard was long. He had some kind of weapon when he entered, which he set down by the door. A sword, or something. I said since when do you use a sword and where have you been and did you bring diapers? He said shit, he forgot and turned to head back out, but before doing that he picked up the baby and kissed her then he kissed me and said that everything made sense now.

Denise L.

GENEVIEVE VALENTINE

The Expedition Stops for the Evening at the Foot of the Mountain Pass

Genevieve Valentine

"Oh come on, Cameron, how much longer will you be a fool?"

Peter's shout echoed off the rocks—ridiculously loud, Nanette thought; they were doomed to be taken hostage sooner or later, but practically begging for it before you'd even dropped into the chasm was quite another thing. According to the company notes, Gens Absconditae who lived under the mountains almost never had scouts aboveground, but Nanette would hardly blame them for sending some.

"Straight through to the end, probably," muttered Adam. She glanced at his flawless profile, outlined gently by the firelight as he sketched something. It was too faint for her to see what; they were too high on the mountain for his fountain pen to work, and he'd had to switch to charcoal, which had done his art no favors.

Above them at the mouth of the pass, Dr. Cameron, whose voice was also much too loud, was halfway through a little speech about human knowledge straight out of the diary entry he'd dictated to her when they'd made camp for the night. It had already sounded rehearsed then—flawlessly delivered, with pauses so he could look down and see whether she was moved.

("All those who came with us on this journey into the magnificent unknown, for the sake of knowledge alone—Is the rhyme too much? Yes, sorry, Miss Parker, let's go back—for the sake of pure science, we honor the work of all those who came with us and promise that these new discoveries—we'd better discover something very flashy to bring out of our pockets here, eh, Miss Parker? Let's hope Kellerman finds some nice minerals in time— will enlighten future generations, and solve our most enduring mysteries. Yes. Wonderful. You wouldn't mind if I went again just for myself, would you?")

He liked to practice these things, and it was her job to let him. He should sound good on camera. It would all be important later.

Dr. Kellerman, who was staring toward the peak as the argument bounced and faded upward into the stars, sighed into his pipe. He was the team's geologist, and by the end of the week he'd be dead.

Down the slope, around a fire that smelled like a much better dinner than anything their group had produced, the guides were drawing straws.

("Only one of them has to stay behind," Peter had told her that afternoon, in the tone he saved for when he was telling her something she wasn't meant to know, as they'd distributed sleeping bags to the tents. "It's why any of them ever sign the contract. Decent chances. The money's really very good, and the family gets paid whether or not the fellow comes back."

"Why do any of them have to stay? They don't know about whatever's at the bottom of the chasm."

Peter had glanced at her from over the top of his spectacles. "Well, they're paid to do a job. You have to have some pride in your work, don't you?")

Easy enough for Peter to say, she thought, watching the fire flicker and vanish into the dark. Peter was slated to survive.

Adam finished his sketch and held it up. "That should do it, Nanette, don't you think?"

"You're holding it away from the light, darling."

"But then it might catch fire!"

Dr. Kellerman said, "Good."

She shot him a look. He wasn't wrong—Dr. Kellerman hadn't been wrong about anything so far; she was going to miss him when he died—but Adam was harmless. Old Man Howard owned the company that had sponsored the expedition, partly hoping for the discovery of useful minerals and partly just wanting to get rid of his younger son. Adam had no skills except college-football stamina, but he listened pleasantly whenever Barrett shouted about extinct plants or Kellerman frowned at an arrowhead. Really, he was taking it all very well.

The sketch was terrible. A day's nearly-vertical climb up the jagged mountain, with an abyss of sky on either side, had been flattened into an unpleasant ice cream cone or an iffy morning on the stock market. Dr. Kellerman made a small, horrified noise.

"I think you've found a wonderful way to think about everything we've been through on this trip, darling," she said. Adam smiled, warm eyes and perfectly white teeth, and went to show Barrett.

Barrett had not quite realized how serious the company had been about the likely perils of the mission until they were packing at the base camp. He was by this point extremely inclined not to die, as if that made him very independent-thinking and above the rest of them; Adam called through the canvas about his sketch to no avail. Barrett was so determined not to play his part that he hadn't even asked Peter what he was meant to die doing, which Nanette thought was a fairly egregious oversight for a history professor.

She'd asked. It was classified, but Peter had cared less about that after a certain altitude. ("You've kept your head on pretty well," he'd told her a few days past base camp. "I hear some of the girls who agree to come out with these expeditions just go to pieces in the field.") Tomorrow morning, when Barrett finally lost his patience and tried to storm out the way the defecting guides had taken, and Cameron failed to reach Barrett before he slipped and was lost to the mountain, they would be the only two surprised.

Scrambling to rescue Barrett is how Cameron will find the chasm that leads them to their Gens Absconditum civilization—the only way, apparently, to guarantee the outcome. Sonar could tell you only so much; hired locals who never came home again could only get you so close; men like Peter could never dare explain how they knew where to look. For real discovery, you needed a sacrifice.

The wind picked up—nine of the guides down the slope paused their packing a moment, watching the veil of snow on the ground skitter up and over their bags. The one who wasn't packing lifted his head to the sky.

All day as they climbed, the wind had pulled at her; she'd been fighting it so hard, the mountain the only safe ground, that when they finally reached this little plateau she'd thought for a horrible moment she had overbalanced forward off the rock and into the endless sky. She'd scrambled back, Adam told her, trying to save herself; he'd had to grab her by the harness to keep her from falling.

Nanette huddled under her coat and shifted closer to the fire, nudging Adam's feet a little out of the way. It was unlikely she'd be any warmer for a while, and she wanted to be selfish while she still could. She'd seen reports from other Gens Absconditum expeditions; remarkable textiles in every one, none of which ever made it across a woman's navel.

A shutter clicked somewhere over Adam's shoulder.

"Charlie, for God's sake, I'm in pin curls."

92

"But we're losing the light!"

"Don't worry, we're closer to the sun here," Adam said. "It'll be light for longer."

"I wish I was the one dying first," muttered Dr. Kellerman.

"There won't be time for this in the morning," Charlie said, softer. "We should get the shot while the getting's good."

Nanette sighed, but he was right. Adam scrambled up to hover, holding out one wide palm for the pins she pulled out and smoothing the worst of the curls with his fingers. Together it took less than a minute.

"Thank you, darling," she said, and Adam beamed.

He was a darling. All their dates in the weeks leading up to the expedition had been unspeakably pleasant, except for the inevitable moments they had to let Dr. Cameron see them long enough to start getting jealous.

"It makes him work harder," Peter had explained in the briefing after she'd finally met Cameron, her fingers still clammy from Cameron's Ivy League handshake. Sad, she'd thought, but as strange as it was to watch Adam making excuses for dropping by the company on a Saturday evening, it was just as well Peter had planned things out this way. She wasn't sure if her regular charms worked seven thousand feet up a mountain with only one tube of lipstick and a dozen bobby pins, and the last thing she wanted was for America's great dreamer to get to the forgotten splendor of a world beneath the world and lose interest.

(Rare, the contract had explained, but not impossible. Leaders must be carefully handled—what they do is so very important, what they bring to the venture is paramount, no trouble is too great to make sure they get what they need—and if you falter in your duty of support, nothing will save you. You must do anything it takes, if you want to get out. You'll live, the contract said, just above the place you had to write out the names of who would get your money when you died.)

"Right, lovebirds in their places please and let's have this over with," said Dr. Kellerman, who'd packed his pipe again to get a dignified curl of smoke in the photograph. He was the kind of professor who liked to really look it. When he was working and had to keep his hands free, he wore his scarf like a cravat tucked smoothly into his coat. Adam had laughed about it once ("What for? No one's going to see."), but Nanette stopped him. Sometimes a photo came back, a fluke from a broken camera someone had managed to grab from the wedding feast as the team sacrificed their last expendable man so that the explorer and his right-hand man and the young lady of his choice could escape and bring back their report. Everyone had a right to be memorialized as they liked on the off chance that something survived.

Sometimes it was a feast of immortality they escaped from. There were lots of those, wherever they were going now.

Charlie took a few shots with his clunky newsboy's camera, angled carefully to avoid the guides who were very nearly packed for the journey home. Not a bad photographer, really, but the newspaper needed the company's advertising money more than it needed one more young man who could take serviceable pictures. At least he was truly excited about it all; Kellerman had stopped caring about rock about halfway up the mountain and Barrett had been squirrelly to start with, but Charlie couldn't stop talking about the photograph the company had showed him just before they'd all set out (blurry, something like a cavern but like a palace too), trying to make guesses about what kinds of places you could carve out of rock from within a mountain like this, so he could photograph it in a way that would look good in the papers.

"That's if we make it out," Adam said once, too intense, looking right at Charlie.

"Photographers die all the time doing dangerous things." Charlie cut little paths through his oatmeal with the spoon. "It's a lot more normal for us than for secretaries."

"Very true," said Dr. Kellerman, with a weighted look at Nanette, and after a moment she realized Charlie didn't know the order of expendability. The company wanted their pictures free of unconscious truths, if any pictures made it home, so nobody had told him. As far as Charlie knew, the future was wide open.

"Miss Parker," Charlie whispered, "if you could angle toward the camera a little, please."

"Oh, but I look so much more candid in profile," she said, smiling and tilting her chin up. She hadn't looked him in the eye the whole time they'd been on the mountain. If she looked, she would tell him. He'd spoken to Adam about it, apparently; how cold she was to him, how sorry he was for whatever he had done.

A little up the slope, Peter was saying vague, astonished things as Dr. Cameron talked about the scratch in the rock.

"Haven't you read the notes from the expedition in the Southern Hemisphere? It's uncanny how similar this is. Rocks don't get marks like this unless there's been a human hand involved, Peter. A human hand! By God, I was right! I was right, this is really it!"

Nanette had picked up those notes for him—some expedition from a few years ago down someplace hot, which Nanette couldn't fathom. She'd waited until a day Dr. Wallis was out at a lecture; Estelle Wallis had herded her into the kitchen rather than the parlor, poured coffee with hands that rattled the pot. "I hope you don't mind," she'd said. "I like the light here, and it's quiet."

The curtains in the front rooms were all nailed closed into the window frames. Nanette managed, "It's a lovely kitchen." The coffee steamed up toward her face as she leaned forward for the sugar. In true London fashion, the summer had abandoned being rainy just long enough to get stifling, and that morning had been so hot that the collar of her blouse was stuck to her neck. She'd wished Estelle, who was wearing the largest sweater Nanette had ever seen, had thought about lemonade instead.

"Marry him," Estelle had said, hardly visible behind the

door as she ushered Nanette out. She hadn't spoken since coffee; Nanette startled and began to object, but Estelle kept going— "Make the captain do it, first boat you get on. They can make you go somewhere else, otherwise. None of our business. Marry at once."

(Nanette read the notes on a park bench four blocks from the house. Classified, she'd been told, but she was skilled by now at looking blank, and the men at the company had yet to catch on.

It was like all the others; discovery, disruption, collapse. Barbarian places, the notes always said, alongside whatever meager plunder they had managed, and a list of the company dead.

She wanted to burn them and run. She wanted to be on the mountain already, before anything was terrible yet, looking up at stars that people kept telling her were there and she had never seen. She wanted to be falling from something high up.

The heat was too heavy to walk in. She paid four pence for the bus back home to the studio flat she shared with Betty from the secretarial pool; the company didn't pay their girls enough to live alone—it was meant to encourage them to marry—and her expedition money wouldn't come through until she came home again or died.

"Never sign their excursion contract," she told Betty, and then locked herself in the washroom until it was dark.)

Inside his tent—the smallest one, where he slept alone so that he would get restless faster and be ready to run—Barrett was crying. It sounded like the wind, if you didn't listen very hard.

"We should all just go home," Nanette said, just to see how it sounded. Watching the nine guides pack to get the hell out of here had made her fingers itch. She fought the urge to stand up and bolt.

Adam looked up at Kellerman, one hand already on the ground, ready to launch as soon as he gave the sign.

"I have a family," said Dr. Kellerman. "Shall I break my contract and let the company repossess them? Do you have so little to lose, Miss Parker?"

She had a mother whose health was poor and getting poorer, and a brother who couldn't find work any more now that everything was drying up. The company had never asked about her family, but her mother had called to wish her luck before she ever left for the mountains, and told Nanette the company had sent her a copy of the contract, and to be careful on her trip.

"A good secretary makes luck," Nanette had said lightly, the old joke so that her mother would laugh, and so that she wouldn't ask how the company had known where her mother lived, and so that she wouldn't falter and ask her mother what she meant by Careful.

Dr. Cameron came back to the fire, boots crunching heavily through the snow. His hood was down. The cold probably made him work harder, she thought, as he glanced at Adam's fistful of bobby pins and back up to Nanette's hair, being slowly tugged into knots by the wind.

"Don't you worry, Miss Parker," he said. His hand on her shoulder weighed thirty pounds. "We're exactly where we need to be, and tomorrow, we'll know more about this civilization than anyone ever has." Forty pounds. "This is the brink of a whole new world."

"Cameron!" Peter called from up the slope. "What do you make of this? Before tonight I'd have sworn it was just a fissure, but since you pointed it out . . ."

Dr. Cameron, glint in his eye, snatched up Adam's lantern and clomped back toward the narrow pass. Nanette massaged her shoulder.

"That's three times today," Adam said. "Kellerman, you owe me five bucks. Or, pounds. Whatever you've got."

"I only saw one other time!" Kellerman cried, looking to Nanette.

"Oh no, it was three—this afternoon, after Peter cut our field radio loose and it fell down the mountain, he clapped the other shoulder and told me to buck up."

"Dammit. It shouldn't count unless I can see it."

"Very geologist thing to say," Nanette said, and Dr. Kellerman snorted.

"Come on, old man," Adam said, smiling but not really, "you won't have need of it much longer. Pay up."

"And what are you going to spend it on," Kellerman muttered as he handed over a damp, half-crumbled bill to Adam, who was frowning into the fire. "Ice cream on the journey home?"

Nanette murmured, "Steven."

There was a little quiet.

"Sorry there, Howard," Dr. Kellerman mumbled. Adam nodded but didn't look up, smoothing the bill and tucking it carefully into the inner pocket of his coat.

It really was too bad about Adam. The rest of them had at least signed a contract first. Adam hadn't even heard about the expedition until his father invited her over to the Howard family home for tea and explained what Adam was expected to do.

He'd met all expectations (strange that his father didn't think he was fit for business; he could certainly keep to a brief). He'd only wept the once, after a particularly long day up the mountain back when they were low enough that there were birds, low enough that on your breaks you could see the country spreading out beneath you, like there was still a way back. He'd clung to her when she held him.

She was never marrying Cameron. She'd jump off the mountain first.

Kellerman stood up and stretched. "Right," he said, casting a look around at nothing in particular. "It sounds like Barrett's cried himself to sleep, and there's nothing else to do until he makes a run for it in the morning, so I'm going to see if I can actually go into this thing rested."

Nanette set her hand on Adam's knee to keep him quiet until Kellerman was out of hearing. They were upwind of him, it felt like; she waited until the tent flaps closed, just to be safe.

"I'm sorry," Adam sighed. "I get so angry whenever I see Cameron, and I'm sorry I take it out on the rest of you but I can't–I can't stand it, Nan, I really can't. I thought Peter was the devil, but it's worse with Cameron! All this goddamn coddling." He raked a hand through his hair. "How can he not see what's going on?"

An expedition leader worth the name would have noticed that something was terribly wrong with everyone on his crew. None of the expedition leaders ever had.

"You know, *I* didn't sign a contract," Adam said darkly. "Nothing's stopping me from telling him the truth. I could go tell him right now, right in front of Peter. Stop it all."

Her hand tightened on his knee, a little spasm going through her.

"You could," she said. "But it's a risk. And I don't know if it would work. There's no way you'd be the first to snap his leash, and no other expedition has ever come home like that."

"Not worth it, then?"

She hadn't said that. She didn't say it.

"I'm worried about you," Adam said, quietly, like he was already thinking better of admitting it. He smoothed a hand over her hair as the wind whipped at it. "I really am. What will you do?"

Send Cameron straight down the chasm after Barrett. Get Peter in the heart with an arrowhead. Try to get poisoned the first night, when everyone still had an excuse to look foolish and she could be free of the whole affair. Get Cameron poisoned—everyone said expedition leaders had incredible luck, but secretaries make luck. Grab Adam's hand instead, at the temple feast, and run.

"I'll stay up for a little while longer," she answered, uncurling his fist to take the pins out before he could draw blood. "It's early yet, the moon's barely risen. No, Adam, darling, please don't ask."

It was quiet, after that. Peter had managed to wrangle Cameron into their tent without another round of dictation. Whatever noises Barrett made were quiet enough for the wind to take them. If she didn't think about it, the tents looked like snowdrifts pressed up against the rock; if she didn't think too much about it, this was her fire, and she was here all alone.

Betty had signed up for a submarine expedition just before Nanette left for the mountains. "I wanted to be a marine biologist," she explained, "so it's not even how much I need the money, it's that whatever happens down there is as close as I'm likely to get," like she wanted Nanette to understand why she hadn't listened, like Betty needed to worry about what anyone thought any more except Captain James Derwent—the company hadn't arranged a fiancé for poor Betty, who was going to have to ingratiate herself with pluck alone if she wanted to make it out of whatever Atlantis the man was hunting for. Nanette had gone straight to the boat and made Adam order enough champagne to knock her out until they were far enough from shore that it was too late to think of swimming back.

(Rare, the company had said, but not impossible. You'll live, said the company, if you really want to. For real discovery, you needed a sacrifice.)

The mountain blocked out the moon, but the air was clear and empty all around her, and if she looked straight up, there were stars and stars and stars.

When her neck hurt, before her fingers were too cold to be of any use, she took hold of a curl and started to pin. Tomorrow would be busy, and she'd need to look her best.

TOBIAS S. BUCKELL

Down in the Dim Kingdoms

Tobias S. Buckell

The airship's spotlights played off the vast rocky sides of the shaft that plunged deep into the Earth's core through the lithosphere and eventually to our destination: the Center of the Earth!

I yawned.

We fell so slowly, the sides of the shaft several hundred feet away, and it had been a long, boring day of this. There'd been a boy, earlier, that caught my eye. But now he was talking to Bridgette with the French accent and the big chest. Laughing at anything she said like it was the cleverest thing in the entire world.

Or below it.

I wondered how long it would take for Bridgette to reach Mashu if I pushed her off the side. The tour guide had told us how far down the Earth's crust really stretched before the hollow core began, and then how much farther down the land of Mashu was from even that.

For a second, I started to work the math. Three thousand

miles down, and terminal velocity being about two hundred miles an hour.

"Good grief, that's hours of falling," I said out loud.

It was a bit delicious, really, now that I thought about it.

"What's that, Kia?" my mother asked. "Who's falling?"

Mother, one Patricia Baker, her face tan from a week in San Marino, peered over the tour brochure to look at me. I scowled at her. "Nothing. I wasn't talking to you."

God. Wasn't this the worst? I could almost reach out to touch any one of the fifteen people crammed into the observation gallery, including Bridgette and the cute boy mooning over her.

I kicked the back of her chair.

"Sorry!" I pretended to look flustered and apologetic.

The Boy (because now that's how I thought of him) looked positively thankful at getting to see Bridgette jostled about.

How pathetic.

I could go back to my room, but my brother, Anthony, had been eating everything the dining room had to offer. His flatulence clung to the walls. Just thinking of his smell made me move over to the edge of the gallery for even more fresh air.

Grandpa Taylor clung to the railings there, looking down into the darkness with a toothy grin. "The first time I descended we didn't know how far this all went. We kept expecting to hit the bottom, so we dropped even slower than this. It took a whole week!"

His knuckles looked like they might puncture his thin, splotchy skin at any moment. I looked over at him, and his bushy eyebrows, then back down into the never-ending darkness.

"I ought to jump off just to speed it all up. I don't know if I could bear this being any longer," I said with a sigh.

Grandpa Taylor grunted. He wanted to say something, but bit it back. I could tell he wanted to call me impatient or ungrateful, but we were still all at the honeymoon stage at the start of a family vacation where everyone was in good spirits and pretending to like each other.

"I miss Ryan," Grandpa Taylor finally said, moving the conversation somewhere else. "All this would have left him lost for words."

"Who?"

"Ryan! Ryan. My partner." Grandpa looked at me like I was something he'd found moldering in the fridge. "We were the first ones to descend. To find that the Earth really was hollow. Ryan St. Claire."

"Oh." *That* Ryan.

The truth was I could give a shit. It was all ancient history. I'd been forced to come along during the holidays instead of going to Mallorca like I'd wanted because Mother wanted to reconcile with Grandpa Taylor. She'd been written out of the will—for what, I had no clue, earthly or unearthly. For Mother this was an apology tour, a period of groveling and emulating the actions of an actual doting, caring, real daughter.

I was to be Best Supporting Actor to her leading role.

"If we stay cut out, there's no more Mallorca, no more private school, no more personal driver," she'd hissed at me on the flight to Iceland. "You'll be of age soon, you'll need his legacy if you're to live well. Or at least to marry well. There isn't much time: his health is failing. That's why he's taking this last nostalgia trip."

To Mashu, the land in the Center of the Earth.

I huffed in annoyance. You couldn't get a tan by going where the sun doesn't shine, and a tan was all the rage in those new Hollywood pictures. My holiday was going to be ruined by this.

~

In the summer of 1774 the Schiehallion experiment took place on an isolated, almost symmetrical mountain in Scotland. Apparently it involved some tweedy scientists and a pendulum.

They swung the pendulum, measuring the length of its swing against stars and took hundreds of measurements near the mountain to verify that, yes, the mountain did indeed slightly deflect the pendulum's swing. Gravity *worked*.

Surveyors then measured the mountain to determine its mass.

Once they had that, if they added the amount the pendulum bobbled compared to a normal swing on Earth, they could run the math and figure out how dense the Earth was.

So, you can imagine, the brochure I had in my hands said, *that it was quite a shock when Mashu was discovered in 1930.*

My eyes glazed over as I got to the part about *extra dense exotic material* that *interfered with measurements*. I crumpled the brochure up and threw it over the railing when the dinner bell rang.

All thirty passengers poured out of our rooms or meandered over from the observation galley. We pulled out the aluminum chairs from the brushed aluminum table to sit. The captain of the airship hosted one of the tables and the navigator the other.

Now came my utterly favorite part: the ant-people.

They swarmed around us, bigger than dogs, but smaller than llamas. Their big, expressionless eyes glittered in the lamplight as they poured drinks from pitchers held in their many hands.

"Scubbies!" Grandpa said, delighted. He'd taken his meals in his room until today, not feeling well due to the changes in air pressure as we descended through the Earth.

"They prefer to be called—"

Grandpa cut the navigator off with a wave of his hand. "When we landed on the first day they swarmed the craft, chewing up our helium tanks and destroying the rigging until I fired a warning shot. Poor creatures had never seen a gun before. They tried to attack, but I put lead right between those big eyes and they backed off awful quick when they saw what happened to their friend."

"A different time, before the accords," the captain said diplomatically.

"Now they're crawling your rigging and serving us drinks, different times indeed, Captain," Grandpa agreed. He held up a cup. "More wine, my old buddies!"

The navigator and captain looked uncomfortable, about what, I couldn't say. Sometimes people got a bit starstruck around Grandpa. He was the discoverer of Mashu, the man who'd changed the entire world's understanding of, well, *the entire world*.

"Oh." The captain looked up from his pocket watch. "It's time."

With a nod from him, the ant-people stepped to the side of the dining room and dimmed the interior lights. At the same time, more exterior spotlights blazed into life. It looked like daylight thrown onto all the walls around us.

"Would you look at that!" a passenger next to me breathed.

The walls crawled with ant-people, moving small metal girders into place. Welding torches flickered, and rock drills nattered away like woodpeckers.

"This is to be the trans-surface elevator," the captain announced grandly. "Capable of taking hundreds of people per car on seven different tracks to the surface of Iceland, and down to the interior of the Earth all the way to Mashu. Soon anyone will be able to buy a ticket to the Center."

"It'll ruin the whole place," Grandpa muttered. "It'll change it all."

To which I could only think, *good*. I really didn't want to travel down to some barbaric world hidden away in the middle of the Earth. I wanted room service, those fancy new air-conditioning systems, and maybe to sneak a few rum punches.

Who was I kidding: there was no *maybe* when it came to rum punches and vacation.

None of that existed in Mashu right now, according to the

guides. No, it was all thatch huts and ant-people hives. Dim stretches of land lit only by the phosphorescent burning of the cavern's ceiling. Droves of weird animals that had survived the descent somehow.

It was a dreadful place to go on vacation.

But, as Mother said, *needs must.*

The things one did for family . . .

Bridgette caught my eye over a roll that she nibbled at with all the grace of a chipmunk. The Boy pushed his long dark hair out of his eyes and offered to butter another roll for her.

"Oh, I just couldn't eat anything more," Bridgette chirped.

She'd only eaten that single roll, and it had been a delicate ten minutes. I wanted to stuff the whole chicken the ant-person was carving for my parents down her throat.

I raised a fork, and left my middle finger in the air as I took a big bite of the steak I'd opted for.

"I saw that," whined Anthony.

I kicked my brother under the table, hard enough that he coughed up a piece of chicken.

"Anthony!" Mother hissed.

"It wasn't my fault!"

"That's not how we behave at the table."

Seeing my brother choke on that piece of chicken brightened my day up somewhat.

Metaphorically speaking.

~

We burst out of the roof of the world's interior the next morning, the phosphorescent sky dazzling the airship's cabins with a hot light that woke us all, a welcome change from the perpetual gloom we'd been descending in.

The airship edged away from the massive elevator that now

hung in the air like a line of silver thread that connected the roof of rock far over Mashu and the ground below.

Eventually, though, the novelty wore off and people stopped hanging on to the railings in the observation room to return to the dining car or their own rooms.

By night, I was alone except for the navigator. Only down here "night" was just more of the constant dim glow that would be our companion for the week ahead, as there was never really any dark in Mashu, its only natural illumination being the faint light from its vast phosphorescent ceiling.

"So many of them are clambering around on the outside," I said to the navigator as I peered over at the elevator works from the observation railing. I liked the fresh air; the cabins got stuffy and Anthony whined if I opened the portholes. "Isn't it dangerous?"

The navigator, Mr. Kelly, stood upright in his uniform. It had been starched so severely that it made him something of a statue. He had kind of a silver fox, "cute old guy" thing going for him, and I'd been pestering him with questions since The Boy still had shown no inclination to dislodge himself from Bridgette's gravitational pull.

"Mashu doesn't have a lot of resources like above-worlders," Mr. Kelly informed me gravely. "And what they did have, they lost to the first adventurers who traded information and technology to them in return for precious metals. The Mashunites work wherever they can find it."

First adventurers. Like Grandpa Taylor.

"We were like the goddamned conquistadors," he'd growled at a recent "family dinner" Mother forced us to throw for the first time in ages in a weak attempt to try and make up to him. "We blew through their kingdoms, with thousands of scubbies behind us carrying our spoils back to our ship. We were like gods."

He spent a lot of time talking about the good old days when

he'd dropped down into the dim kingdoms like a ravaging plague.

Sometimes I felt like being back on the surface depressed him. I wondered why he didn't just go back down and live there.

I tried to flirt with Mr. Kelly. Nothing could come of it, my parents would be more than scandalized. Plus, where could we even retreat to get into trouble together? The airship's cabin, swinging precariously under all the rigging, had few nooks and crannies.

Well, maybe Mr. Kelly would know of some.

But he wouldn't say. He was as stiff as his uniform and brushed off my hints and advances with all the excitement of a decrepit pensioner's doddering *harrumph*. As he walked away, closing the door to the crew quarters and mechanical rooms, I made a note to write a damning letter about him to his company.

It would insinuate that he had pressed himself on me, a young waif, unwise to the ways of more seasoned and traveled men. Why, it was conduct unbecoming—

The Boy passed by me on the walkway to the passenger rooms.

"Hi!" I said, as brightly and eagerly as Bridgette ever had. I touched his shoulder and smiled. I looked deeply into his eyes.

He rushed away from me, contracting in on himself like a turtle as he did so.

"But what's your name?" I shouted at the empty space.

He'd been interested enough in *my* neckline that first day we motored out over the Atlantic toward Iceland. I'd cornered him near the door to the dining room when everyone had gone to the observation deck.

Apparently he'd *not* spent time in France, as he'd said, because when my tongue found his he'd coughed, fought me off, and run right into the arms of Bridgette a day later. Bridgette with the French name, but who was so dreadfully Anglian.

Her parents had airs.

Bridgette.

I'd spent a lot of the trip wondering what she whispered into The Boy's ears about me. He looked so ashen whenever he saw me. Then they would turn away and whisper to each other.

What were they saying?

I hated that she'd taken him away from me.

What was his name?

I just wanted his name.

Then I saw her, alone, standing by the rail of the observation deck. She was eating a piece of chicken like a savage, and throwing the bones over the side.

Too delicate to eat in front of anyone at dinner, but here I found the real Bridgette. The faker.

"Bridgette," I snarled.

She jumped, like a half-startled cat caught on the counter, as I pressed close to her plain face.

"You," she said. "You."

"Why'd you do it?" I asked.

"Do what?"

Her insouciance lit a fire deep within me. Like a trans-Atlantic steamer coming up to full boil, the coal all stoked.

"Why did you take The Boy?"

"Andrew?" She wiped smeared lipstick and grease. "I didn't take him. You repulsed him. Sticking your tongue down his throat like that. We know who you are. We know who your whole family is."

I controlled my anger. I remained cool.

I rushed forward and shoved her over the rail without even a hint of hesitation. One moment, I just wanted to wipe that smile away, and in the other, a flurry of petticoats slapped the other side of the railing as Bridgette exhaled in tight surprise: "Oh?"

And then, a split second later, as she fell, she began to scream.

At the same moment, I heard a footstep near the rooms, and the door slam.

~

I once saw a play where the actor, Reginald Gorby, threw himself so into the role of bereaved father that he cried real tears right on the stage before us all at the matinee. I remember being so impressed by his utter command of the stage. I'd set out at once to become an actress, and learn everything I'd seen Gorby do.

My mother eventually had our butler, Mr. Edsby, whip that plan of becoming an actress right out of me. But now those days of staring at myself in a mirror willing those tears to form came back to me with all the speed of a door slam.

"My God!" I shrieked. "My God! She's fallen from the rail!"

Reginald Gorby never threw himself into a role so deeply as I threw myself into the part of Ms. Kia Taylor, stunned at the horror of seeing her fellow passenger fall to her death.

I wept. I screamed. People woke up and rushed to the gallery in their nightclothes. They even had to wrestle me down as I leapt up onto the railing, as if to jump off after Bridgette.

A doctor joined my parents in our room and gave me a dose of something that made my whole body prickle and warm up as I began to fall asleep.

Rarely had I ever felt so deeply satisfied as when I laid there, listening to everyone speak in hushed, sympathetic tones around me.

Maybe now The Boy would pay some attention to me. I'd been through a horrible trauma, hadn't I?

That was a thought I wrapped around myself like a blanket as I floated on opioid dreams until I opened my eyes and saw Grandpa Taylor sitting on a chair alone with me, his fingers crossed with each other, staring intently at me.

"I saw what you did," he said in a soft, curious voice.

I played dumb, but Grandpa shook his head.

"Don't. Don't do that." His firm growl stripped decades away from the frail old man. I saw, in the shadows of the room, the man who had descended down into the heart of the Earth to force strange new empires to bow at his feet and give him their gold.

I swallowed hard.

How to describe the fear that rose inside of me like a horrid flood? The storm that churned within my chest?

"Do you want to know why I dropped all my children from the will?" Grandpa asked, pulling the chair closer to me.

I stared at the silver hair jutting out of his ears so that I didn't have to meet his piercing eyes.

"I did it because they are weak," Grandpa hissed. Clear hatred curled his lips. "Cushy, soft people in comfortable lives. They create nothing, do little, and are no better than vampires sucking at my generosity. But I was wrong about you. I thought you were like your aunts and uncles. But you're not."

I barely dared breathe.

He leaned closer until our noses almost touched. "Do you know the truth about explorers? We talk about conquistadors and Columbus as if they were bold adventurers. But have you read about the things they had to do? They were willing to kill. Rape. Murder. They did what they *had* to do. Those gunslingers in the American West? The soft and rotten pretend to be them, want to be them, but they're just vagabond murderers as well. Ill-fitted for city life."

His voice cracked, and so did the knuckles of his hands as he massaged them together.

"Grandfather . . ." I had never been scared of him before. His eyes gleamed with such excitement as he talked about rape and murder.

"They call me an adventurer. Ryan too. But they always gloss over the things we had to do. Building empires, changing the world like I did, it requires a lack of patience with soft civilization."

He stood up with a groan and hobbled over to the porthole to look down at the patchworks of farms, the dark splotches of wild forests, and the shimmering sea in the distance where he'd once told me giant squid waited to pull Mashunite ships down under the surface.

"It used to be a hard place down there," Grandpa said. "A place that forged you. Where only the strongest could exert their will. I came back to feel it again, before civilization tamed it. But here I see it came to show me something else. It has revealed your true self to me. You're a *colonizer*. You're an *empress*. Oh, the granite skipped a generation, but I see it's finally resurfaced—in you. You might be just a girl, but I could put a pith helmet on you and send you to the darkest jungle. I know it, now. I feel a fool that I didn't see this earlier. But I saw it in you when you pushed that annoying girl over the side of the ship."

I sat up, groggy no longer. "Please. Grandfather. You won't tell anyone?"

"No, my child." He reached into his jacket and pulled out a fresh, crisp sheet of parchment. "I am the last creature that would dare such a thing."

He handed me his last will and testament. Signed. Witnessed by the very doctor who had treated me just hours ago and the captain of the airship. An unimpeachable duo of co-signatures. The thing my mother had so long quested fruitlessly for.

"What is this?" My fingers trembled.

"Everything. It's yours. Not your mother's, not anyone else in this family. Because I can see that only you have the fire to grasp what you want. You'll do something interesting with it, whereas, everyone else would only *spend* it."

Grandpa Taylor laughed and hugged me, his cologne stinking of alcohol and cedar, and for the first time in my life, he planted a dry kiss on my forehead.

The man was damn *proud* of me.

"The scubbies might try to kill me when we land," he said.

Startled, I pulled away from his embrace. "What?"

"They blame me for their ills, instead of their own shortcomings. Ever since we made contact, they act as if I personally did everything horrible that ever happened to them. They refuse to take responsibility! I see the murder in their compound eyes. The crew can barely stand to walk past me. I will stand against them and find my measure when they come for me."

"And when will that be, do you think?" I asked politely, and with a genuine interest, looking down at the will in my hands.

~

It was a horrible thing when Mr. Kelly, the navigator, found Grandpa Taylor's body staked to the ground outside the landing mast a day later.

"A savage business," he said. And though he had spoken in favor of the Mashunites, the whole business had him quite rattled.

The way poor Grandpa Taylor had been slashed at and mutilated, it put everyone right off continuing the vacation. And without our family patriarch to force us all to continue on, we really had no choice but to demand the captain take us back on the very next airship.

I certainly demanded it, through terrified tears.

"We should have an investigation," one of the passengers said. "We don't know what happened or who's responsible."

That sentence made my stomach twist in a slight bit of fear.

But this wasn't London. There was no Scotland Yard to come sniffing around for fingerprints. And if they did come, by airship, their arrival would still be days away.

So Grandpa's body was preserved in alcohol for us to bring home, and we were soon back on the stuffy old airship, climbing for the shaft in the sky that would take us back to the old world above.

"The Mashunites are terrified that this incident will be in the papers," the captain mournfully told us over dinner. "They have put everything into this project with Grand Oceanic Travels to build the elevator. Their entire country will go bankrupt if this fails and no one wants to come here."

Everyone made sympathetic noises about the poor ant-people as the very creatures served us our roast beef and pudding.

It was a dreary country to be visiting anyway, I thought. And Grandpa said it was a hard place. Things like this happened in tough places. Though, I'd expected him to fight back harder than just scratching up my arms as I'd gagged him and staked him to the ground. He'd looked so shocked when I stepped back to consider exactly how to slash his body up in a way that would look like the ant-people had done it.

It was tiring work and I couldn't wait to get back up to the surface and put this emotionally taxing experience behind me.

Because I had things to look forward to. The Boy's parents had panicked about how dangerous Mashu was and were returning with us.

He saw me staring at him across the table, and he looked down, nervous.

Yes, my little rabbit. Soon I would have you too.

Because, I thought as I watched a flock of graceful pterodactyls skim the clouds we rose into, I would take what I wanted, damn the consequences, destroy anything, full steam ahead. I was the granite, the explorer, the adventurer.

C.C. FINLAY

Those Who Have Gone

C.C. *Finlay*

Trish clung to the back of the 2-up ATV as Dustin jounced it across the Arizona desert; by the end of the second hour, she was sure he planned to kill her. Use the camp shovel in the pack tied on behind her to dig a shallow grave. Use the extra canister of gas to burn her body.

Or maybe he'll just leave my body for the coyotes.

Somehow, that seemed worse.

Dustin knew she was thinking about splitting up with him. Last week, when she mentioned taking a break for a while, he'd gotten jealous. Asked her if she had a different boyfriend. (She didn't.) Then he'd gotten angry. Said he couldn't stand the idea of any other man with her.

So she had stayed. She didn't want a confrontation right then. She didn't like confrontation.

And now he's taking me out into the middle of the desert, as far from civilization as it's possible to get. Why else would he come this far? She had seen something on the news once about officials finding dead bodies somewhere around here. Maybe just people coming across the border who didn't make it. Or maybe this was a place where someone killed people, dumped the bodies, and got away with it.

Scanning the landscape for possible sources of help didn't turn up any options, but that's how she spotted the sign that said, in bright red letters, DANGER UNEXPLODED ORDNANCE DO NOT ENTER, and beneath that, PELIGRO MUNICIONES VIVAS NO ENTRES, for anyone who might be approaching from the south. They must be on the bombing range where Dustin used to work.

He pointed to the sign a split second later and offered a quick thumbs-up, like he was giving her a present. She smiled brightly, even though she was sitting behind him so there was no way he could see her. She felt disgusted at herself, and then the disgust made her angry. Angry at Dustin, for being a jacked-up twenty-seven-year-old guy just out of the Air Force with a lot of big, expensive toys. Angry at herself for being a dumb eighteen-year-old girl who fell for a guy just because he had big, expensive toys.

A low, sawtoothed ridge of mountains cut across the southwestern sky. He aimed straight for it. As every jolt and bump of the ATV rocked through her bones, she retraced their path in her head, looking for a way back.

On Thursday night, Dustin had come into the Culver's restaurant during Trish's shift, which he did a lot. He ordered a value basket with a mushroom-and-swiss Butterburger, upgraded the side to onion rings, and got a large soda pop. He stood there sipping on his soda and, in between customers, asked her if she wanted to go camping this weekend.

"My mom's up in Vegas this weekend with Jim." Jim was her mom's current boyfriend. They'd been dating for about six months. Not even half as long as her and Dustin. "Let's stay at my house and watch movies."

"I thought you liked camping."

Sure, she liked camping . . . when her mom was home. Her mom didn't like Dustin, and Trish didn't like Dustin's creepy roommate, so where else were they going to go to chill together? But there was no time to explain that to him: a family with five small, indecisive kids jammed up her line, and she needed to get Dustin out of the way before her manager yelled at her. So she said yes to camping just because it was easier than saying no.

But then they didn't go to the usual campground, where she knew some of the other campers. Dustin drove out toward Organ Pipe Cactus National Park instead, said he had a surprise for her. He was acting weird. More quiet than normal. More serious. She let herself feel excited because she'd never been there and *organ pipes* made it sound really pretty. Then they passed a sign that said they were entering the Cabeza Prieta Wilderness. That seemed more like the kind of place they would go camping. After a while they left the road for a dirt track and left Dustin's truck behind, locking it up and rolling the ATV down the ramp off the back. All the camping gear was rolled up in a pack strapped on the back. They rode the ATV down the dirt road until it turned into a trail. Now even that had disappeared. They were off the map as far as she could tell, out in the middle of the desert on some kind of bombing range where nobody was supposed to go.

And nobody knows I'm out here. Nobody knows I'm with Dustin this weekend.

She would have to find some way to help herself.

If she waited until the ATV slowed down to cross a dry wash or climb some hill, maybe she could jump off. But what would she do after that? Run twenty miles on foot back over the desert to reach some empty road? Dustin would just turn around and run her down before she got twenty yards.

She pulled out her phone and thought about calling 911. No

signal. Of course there was no signal. Who needs cell service in the middle of a bombing range?

In with the camping gear, strapped down behind her, she knew there was a gun. Dustin never went anywhere without a gun, and he didn't have a holster strapped to his belt. It was probably his Desert Eagle .357. On their second date, he had taken her out to a shooting range to show off that particular weapon. She was pretty sure he loved that gun more than her. After all, he sometimes went to bed without her but he never went to bed without *it*.

No matter how far she twisted in her seat, there was no way to search the gear as long as they were moving. The ATV bounced around so much that her head constantly snapped from side to side, making it impossible to get a good look at anything.

So she clung on tightly and waited for another opportunity.

They crossed a small valley. Pale green palo verde trees, creosote shrubs, and silvered brittlebush grew in clumps along the sandy washes and on the gravelly slopes. A cluster of tiny fighter jets zipped across the wide blue sky and then curved away toward the horizon. Ahead of them, the mountains ran from south to north, all rock and sharp edges with the parched green fringe of winter growth lining the seams between angular ridges. Trish figured she had until they reached the mountains to come up with a plan. Right now her plan was to put off the bad things for as long as she could.

Her heart jumped when Dustin slowed the ATV and circled back toward a dry wash they had just crossed.

He turned off the engine and she tensed, balling her hands into fists. In the silence, he muttered, "Holy shit."

"What is it, baby?" she asked.

"Stay right here, I'll be back in a minute," he said, climbing off the ATV.

"I'm going to get a snack," she said. She always asked him for permission before she messed with his gear. Not that she was going to wait on his permission this time, but it might buy her an extra minute or so. He wouldn't run to stop her and do things for her *the right way* the moment he saw her in their pack.

"Sure," he answered absentmindedly as he started to wander off.

Permission granted. She exhaled with relief, jumped down, and tore frantically into their gear, looking for his gun. If she got that, she could hold it on him. Make him drive her back to the road. Drive off and leave him here. Shoot him if she had to. But hopefully it wouldn't come to that. He had taken her to the shooting range several times now, so she figured he would take her seriously when she pointed the gun at him.

The moment her fingers closed on the small, hard box, she froze. Her hands trembled as she pulled it out of the pocket. It fit neatly in her palm.

"Holy shit," she whispered, echoing him.

She glanced over her shoulder before opening it.

A diamond ring. The one she'd tried on at Costco. Well, the small one she'd tried on at Costco. Definitely not the big, pretty one she'd loved.

But that was just a joke!

He wasn't planning to kill her.

He was planning to *propose.*

"Hey, Trish! Trish, come here! You got to see this!"

His voice snapped her out of the deer-in-the-headlights moment. Heart pounding, she shoved the ring box deep into the pack and quickly stuffed everything else into place. "Coming!"

As she got close, he held out his arm protectively to stop her, like a crossing guard. "You see it?"

She expected a pile of bones or some weird bird or any of the thousand things you find in the desert, the sort of things he usually liked to show her. *But not a diamond ring. Not that.* What she spied instead, thirty yards away, on the lip of the wash, was a distinctive pile of stones, smaller ones piled on top of larger ones like a primitive pyramid.

"Who do you think made it?" she asked.

Dustin snorted, laughing at her, which made her feel young and foolish. "Whoever works at the bomb factory, I guess."

Then she saw what he saw, at the bottom of the dry creek bed. A long, rusted cylinder with fins, nose sticking into the ground. Like a barrel cactus, with one awful flower.

"That's from before I was in the Air Force," Dustin said enthusiastically, eyes glinting. "Maybe all the way back to the Vietnam War."

"But it's a dud, right? That's what they call them? So it's not dangerous?"

Peligro municiones vivas no entres.

"No, it's more dangerous than ever," he said. "It didn't go off when it hit. That happens sometimes. It could sit safe like that for a hundred years or it could explode a minute from now. You just never know. Whatever you do, don't kick it."

Like she was going to kick it. "But we're safe here, right?"

"Not if it goes off. See how it sits just below the landscape. You could be a hundred yards away and unless you went down into the wash you'd never see it. I just wanted to record the GPS coordinates so I can tell the guys at the bombing range where it is when I get back."

She thought about pointing out the pyramid of rocks. Someone had been out here and seen the bomb. But she didn't say anything.

"We should get going," he said, grabbing her wrist and pulling her back toward the ATV. Her first impulse was to jerk her arm free of his grip, but she decided against it. "Hey, why'd you tear up the bag?"

"I was looking for something to snack on."

"It's right here in the side pocket, where it always is."

"I forgot. It's the sun. Makes me drowsy." She smiled, letting her arms and head tilt listlessly like she was just a dumb, helpless girl.

"Next time just ask me where it is," he said, his forehead creased in anger while he checked the pack. "Here you go." He handed her a protein bar and zipped everything up again before climbing back onto the ATV. "Get on. We've got a long way to go before we stop for the night."

"Sounds great." She climbed back on behind him. *What else am I going to do?*

The ring didn't matter. Not if she trusted her instincts about him.

It could be safe for a hundred years or it could explode a minute from now.

Don't kick the bomb.

She figured she still had until they reached the mountains to come up with a plan.

~

They were still riding at 5:00 p.m. when her phone vibrated its daily reminder to take her birth control pill. A year ago, the reminder had its own ringtone—the hook for "Bury a Friend," which was cheesy as hell and she didn't care—but she changed it when Dustin started making a big deal out of it. She didn't know whether he didn't like the song or didn't like that she was a seventeen-year-old high school girl taking birth control or if it was something else that bothered him. But he had told her several times that she wouldn't always need to be on the pill.

As far as she was concerned, she definitely needed to be on the pill. Her mom had gotten pregnant at nineteen, and based on the way she partied and carried on now, it seemed like she resented missing out on the good times in her twenties. But Trish wanted to make Dustin happy, so she got rid of the ringtone. As long as she didn't rub the pill in his face, he couldn't be upset about it. She'd just have to remember to take it once they stopped.

The pale skin of the sky was starting to bleed red along the rough edge of the mountains. Dustin stopped twice, doubled back once. They had to be getting close to wherever it was he was taking them. As the ATV slogged up the side of a mountain, they startled a herd of bighorn sheep eating scrub along a mostly vertical slope. They turned their heads, confused at the engine-rumble of the ATV's approach, then scattered as it got closer.

"It's just up ahead," Dustin said, bringing the ATV to a slow stop. She could hear the relief in his voice. "Leave the gear here. We'll come back for it in a little bit."

She climbed off the back and quickly stretched her sore muscles, then got into her bag and popped the pill out of its pack while Dustin was trying to get something out of his own gear without letting her see him. The ring, no doubt.

We all have secrets. She put the pill on her tongue and swallowed it without water, so she wouldn't have to ask him for a bottle. *But how secret are they, really?*

"Follow me," he said, waving her after him, and when she did, she saw he had the Desert Eagle tucked in the back of his waistband.

The trail, such as it was, twisted up a crease in the eastern slope of the mountain. On the left hand, there was a mostly dry creek bed filled with polished stones that were damp here and there, probably from the recent rain. They passed one standing pool of water about an inch deep, where they startled some black-tailed deer who bounded away downslope.

If you're planning to kill someone, this is the perfect place to do it. They'll never find the body.

"Have you ever been to Yellowstone?" Dustin asked, as he reached back to help her climb over a boulder that jutted awkwardly across the path.

"No," Trish answered. "But I'd like to go, someday."

"We'll go! I'll take you there." He dusted his hands off on his jeans. "The thing is, it's probably the most famous national park in the United States. Everybody thought it was all mapped out, that we knew every square inch of it. There were fifty waterfalls in it, and they all had names, and were marked on the trails so people could find them."

"Uh-huh," Trish said, not sure where this was going.

"But a few years ago, there were these three guys who weren't so sure. So they went off the trails, made their own paths, and they found over two hundred more waterfalls in the park. *Two hundred.* Nobody had ever seen them before. There were no pictures, nobody had named them. These guys, they wrote a book about it, and—shhh! Wait a second."

He held up a hand and gestured for her to stop. When he didn't move or say anything, she whispered, "What? What is it?"

"I thought I heard something, maybe a rattlesnake. Keep an eye out, okay."

"Sure."

The trail grew steeper as they went. "Anyway, the point is, we think the whole continent is mapped, but it isn't. And we're smack in the middle of the biggest, emptiest part of it. There's an Indian reservation east of here that covers four thousand square miles, and barely has anyone living in it. It's all desert. And then next to that is Organ Pipe Cactus National Monument—that's another five hundred square miles, and nobody lives there. Then the Cabeza Prieta Wildlife Refuge is connected to that—"

"We drove through part of it this morning."

"Right! That's, like, I don't know, another fifteen hundred square miles. As big as Rhode Island, one of the rangers told me, and nobody lives there either. And then that's connected to the Goldwater Air Force Range, where I was stationed, and that's close to another three thousand square miles, that basically nobody lives in. All total, it's over eight thousand square miles.

Eight thousand. That's bigger than the country of Israel. Five hundred years ago, there was a trail that cut through here called El Camino del Diablo, the Devil's Highway. The conquistadors used it to travel across the desert from Mexico to California, and now there's nothing . . . Ah, here we are."

He stood there, with his fists on his hips, looking up at a curved wall of rock. Water trickled over the edge some thirty feet up, flowed down the face in a wet streak, and collected in a shallow pool at the base. When the pool overflowed, it fed the streambed they had followed to reach here. The setting sun squeezed through a crack in the ridge, turning the stone a pale yellow and the flowing water into liquid gold. The pool at the bottom sat in shadow, and it gleamed silver-blue, reflecting a bit of the sky overhead. It was so shallow that in another week or so it would probably be dry again.

"Okay, that's really beautiful," she admitted.

Dustin grinned at her with the pride of a small boy. "And it's all ours. Only ours."

Technically, it's the U.S. government's. But she didn't say that aloud.

"A couple years ago, when I was still in the Air Force, I was stationed out here, and I got sent out to do ordinance retrieval, like that bomb we saw earlier. Just after a rain, like this week. It went faster than expected, and my buddy and I killed some time by exploring up into these mountains. I figured I might be the first human being to ever see this particular waterfall."

If there was a highway here used by conquistadors, chances are you aren't the first human being to ever see this. People always find the water in the desert. There was no point in saying so. Dustin was the center of his own universe, and she couldn't say anything to him that would ever make him think otherwise.

He got down on one knee.

Oh, shit. This is it. He's going to do it.

"When I found this spot, I knew it was a special place, just like

I knew you were special the moment I found you. Out here, we might as well be the only two people in the world. And I brought you out here to ask you the most important question of our lives. Because that's what I want us to be. Together, for the rest of our lives. The only two people in the world who matter."

She didn't want to get married. Not now. And not to Dustin, not ever. She'd just graduated high school five months ago, and she had a job, and that seemed like enough for now. She wasn't sure what she wanted to do with her life yet. Maybe join the army or maybe become a cop. She liked shooting guns. But here she was, out here in the middle of nowhere with Dustin. *Like we're the only two people in the world.*

He reached into his pocket and pulled out the small black box from Costco.

"Trish, will you marry me?"

She had a plan. It was the only plan, really. Given the circumstances.

"Yes, yes, of course I will," she blurted out, and then she pulled him up to his feet, before he could put that cheap little ring on her finger, and she started to kiss him so he wouldn't look at her face and see how she really felt, and then she half undressed him in a hurry, and then herself, and they fucked in a frantic rush right there on the flat rock beside the silver pool of water so that he would be happy and she could get home again.

Twenty minutes later they were hiking back down toward the ATV in the twilight, and she saw flashes of white just ahead, in the shadow of an overhang. They must have walked right past it on the climb up. "What's that?"

"Huh. It looks like a cross."

That's exactly what it was. The kind of cross that people put up by the side of the road where someone died in a car accident. Sitting next to it were a couple gallon jugs of water and a plastic grocery bag full of protein bars.

"That's thoughtful," she said. "Maybe somebody passed away nearby, and their friends put this up to remember them and help anyone else who gets lost out this way."

"Nobody out this way but illegals, crossing the desert from Mexico into the U.S.," Dustin said. "The wall never got built the way it should have and there's still no fence along big stretches of the border. The desert would be barrier enough if it wasn't for shit like this. Stand back."

He pulled the gun out of his waistband, aimed, and squeezed the trigger twice. The jugs exploded like water balloons, splashing Trish. The shots echoed off the mountainside and her ears rang.

She went very still and quiet.

"Serves those fuckers right," Dustin said as he kicked the contents of the bag down into cracks in the rocks where they'd be difficult to reach.

She didn't say a word the rest of the way back to the ATV, but she spun the diamond round and round on her finger.

~

A couple hours later, after the last twilight faded and the sky above them transformed into a lace of stars, Trish sat at the campfire, happily sated on rare steak and more happily buzzed on her third beer from Dustin's cooler.

She had options to consider. Dustin had problems—he dated high school girls, for one thing—but maybe that was okay. She could drag things out with him. In a few more years, he probably wouldn't be interested in her anyway.

"I've got to go pee," she said, standing up.

"Don't go too far," he said.

"Don't go anywhere at all," said a third voice.

Trish froze. Three shadowy figures came out of the dark, two men and a woman, carrying old hunting rifles. The woman stood close to Trish. Aimed the rifle at her. She was the one who'd spoken. Dark hair framed a light brown face a lot like Trish's but older, thinner, with more hard edges. She wore a crocheted granny sweater over a charcoal-colored sweatshirt and faded blue jeans over decent boots. The two men flanked Dustin, rifles pointed at his chest. At a glance, they looked like father and son, with similar height and features, dressed to do some work in their backyard: work shirts over faded tees, a Diamondbacks tee for the old man and a Captain America shield for the younger one, with blue jeans and sneakers. The older man's face was creased with anger, exaggerated by the shadows from the firelight, and the younger one looked patient and resigned, which was the reverse of what Trish usually saw at the restaurant when fifty-year-old men came in with their twenty-year-old sons.

"What the *fuck*?" Dustin said.

"We've been watching you all day," the woman said. "You made so much noise, you were hard not to notice. We were just going to let you come and go, and ignore you, right? But then you had to go and shoot up the supplies. People's lives depend on those supplies."

"Eres un pendejo," said the older man in the Diamondbacks shirt.

"This is America," Dustin snapped. "Speak American."

"I am American, so anything I say is American, *asshole*," the man said. "Is that *American* enough for you? My family's been here way longer than yours."

"Just give us the rest of your water and whatever food you have, to replace the supplies you destroyed, and we'll call it even," the woman said. "First thing in the morning, you ride out of here and we won't shoot at you from wherever we happen to be hiding."

"Just do it, Dustin," Trish said. To the woman, she added, "We could head out of here tonight. Right now."

She was relieved to have an excuse to go.

"*Fuck* that," Dustin said. His hands pressed against the ground, closing into fists. That wasn't a good sign. His gun was sitting on a rock, just out of reach, or he probably would have grabbed for it already.

"It's okay, baby," Trish said. "They just want to replace some supplies. You heard them—people's lives depend on those supplies." *Maybe our lives depend on those supplies, Dustin. Aren't you paying attention?* "It's not worth fighting about."

The woman jabbed the gun in Trish's direction. "Why don't you just go ahead and get them for us?"

"Okay, sure," Trish said, turning toward their bags.

"Don't do it," Dustin growled.

"Shut up," the man said.

"Go on." The woman prodded her with the rifle.

Trish could feel her emotions shutting down and the calculator in her brain ramping up, just like they did when her stepdad Clarence used to get drunk and lose his temper. She focused completely on the tasks at hand, which were, first, to get these people whatever they wanted so they would go on their way, and second, to keep Dustin from doing anything stupid.

Dustin had other plans. As Trish started walking toward their gear, he flung two fistfuls of gravel at the faces of the men. The woman lifted her rifle into the air and shot. Trish flinched from the flash and the blast, covering her ears. Dustin flopped over sideways to grab for his gun as the man in the Diamondbacks shirt hit his head with the butt of the rifle. The Desert Eagle went off in Dustin's hand, another bright burst of orange and a double crack from the shot and a boulder a few feet away. The younger man kicked Dustin in the ribs, then kicked the gun out of his hand and jumped beyond his reach. Trish felt her legs begin to wobble. *That's weird,* she thought. *I feel way too calm for that to happen.* Then her left knee buckled and she fell to the ground.

"Shit," the woman said. "This one's been shot."

"You're such an asshole," the older man told Dustin. "Shooting your own girlfriend."

Dustin had a hand on the side of his head. Blood flowed out of a gash in his scalp, covering half his face like a garish mask in the flickering campfire light. "Trish? Trish? You okay?"

"I'm fine," she said. Pushing herself to her knees and forcing herself to stand up again. "I'm fine, I wasn't shot. I saw it hit something over there. Let's just give them what they want, baby. Nobody has to get hurt."

There was silence and the smell of gunpowder. The fire crackled and sent up a flare of sparks. Four faces watched her.

"Your leg," the woman said softly, breaking the silence. "Ricochet."

Trish looked down. Her left leg. There was a big hole ripped in the calf of her jeans. Everything from her knee down was soaked in blood.

Her head spun dizzily. The woman's hand on her shoulder pushed her down. "Sit, okay." Trish sat. To the other two men, she said, "Tie him up while I look at this real quick."

"Tie him up with *what?*" the older man asked.

"I'll check their gear," the younger one said, and started rummaging through their bags. He would find rope. Dustin always traveled with plenty of practical supplies.

"Jesus Christ, you bastards," Dustin squealed. "Look at what you made me do to her! You're fucking going to jail for this if I don't do something about it first."

"Shut up, Dustin," Trish said.

"What?" He sounded confused.

"This is all going to be okay, but you just have to shut up." She'd been shot. It had a totally unexpected clarifying effect on her thoughts. If they were going to get through this—*if I'm going to get through this*—Dustin needed to shut the hell up and stop making things worse.

The younger man yanked Dustin's arms behind him and began tying his hands together while Dustin babbled a useless stream of protest. The woman grabbed Trish's hand and made her push it on a spot just behind her knee. It hurt. "Keep pressure there, as hard as you can," the woman said.

She ran over to their gear and came back, tearing Trish's extra shirt in half. After squatting and slicing off the leg of Trish's jeans with a pocketknife, she examined the wound.

"Your first aid kit is shit," she said, as she tied a bandage just below Trish's knee.

"It's not mine, it's Dustin's," Trish said, wincing at the sharp pain. She thought about it for a second, relishing the way her thoughts felt so clear even if her sense of balance was spinning. "What's he need a first aid kit for anyway? He's invulnerable."

The woman snorted as she pressed fingers to Trish's neck and checked her pulse.

"She going to be all right?" the young man in the Captain America tee asked.

The woman glanced up and gave sort of a half shrug, which was not at all reassuring. "You got a sewing kit?" she asked Trish.

"You mean, like here or back at home?" Like it mattered where. Like she had a sewing kit.

"Here."

"No."

The woman crouched on her haunches and wiped her bloody palms on her thighs. She took a deep breath and sighed. "I've got to take her back."

There was a moment of silence. *Back where?* Trish thought.

"It was a ricochet," the woman said. "The slug was flattened and it took out a chunk of her calf. Like a shrapnel wound. I've got to sew her up or she could keep bleeding."

"If you guys hurt her, I will seriously—" Dustin started, but the rest of his threat was cut off by the barrel of the old man's gun poking at his head. An altogether more effective threat.

"You know we can't do that," the younger man said.

"How about we just shoot him in the leg too, then take their stuff and leave them out here," the older man said. "Let them walk until they find their own help."

The woman stared at Trish, looked her up and down. "This one didn't do anything wrong, not really. I think I can fix her up in about fifteen minutes, but I need my gear to do it right."

"It's not your fault, and it's not your responsibility," Diamondbacks said.

"What happens if you don't?" Captain America asked.

"Wait, how bad is it?" Trish stared at her leg and the fresh bloodstain spreading on her bandage.

"Even if we went and called in help for them, a helicopter rescue is probably two hours away," the woman told the men. "If we put them on the ATV and aim them for the closest road, it's even longer. But if I take her and the ATV, it's about an hour, then fifteen minutes to patch her up, and then an hour back. We take their water and supplies and we all go our separate ways."

"How bad is it?" Trish repeated.

The older man in the Diamondbacks tee shook his head.

"I'll blindfold her," the woman said.

The older man shook his head a second time.

The younger man seemed deflated. "I told you this was a terrible idea. We could have just replaced those supplies with some of our own water."

"It's the principle of the thing," Diamondbacks snapped.

"Okay, then, I'm taking her," the woman said, as if they'd had a discussion and come to a consensus. Neither man argued with her. She stood up and helped Trish to her feet. They hopped over to the ATV and she helped Trish sit on the back.

"Wait, you can't just take her away," Dustin said.

The woman ripped another shirt in half, one of Dustin's, and tossed a piece to the older man. "Gag him if you want."

He grunted in a way that made it sound like some form of

agreement. Dustin struggled as they bound up his mouth. Trish wished she could say that she'd never seen him that angry before, but she remembered what he had been like when she talked about taking a break from dating.

The woman apologized as she tied the blindfold around Trish's eyes. "Sorry I have to do this."

"Are you going to kill me?" Trish asked.

"I'm trying to save your life." She climbed onto the front of the ATV—it was strange to feel it but not see it. "How much fuel is in this?"

"A full tank," Trish said. "Dustin filled it up from the spare gas can before he made camp."

"Good. Hold on."

~

Trish wrapped her arms around the woman's waist. Whatever trail they were on wasn't very smooth: the ATV bucked and bumped like it was trying to throw Trish off the back. She held on tighter and leaned against the woman's back. The air had cooled to the point of being chilly—nighttime in the desert—but the woman's body felt warm, even through the sweater and hoodie. Trish closed her eyes and tried to rest. She suddenly felt very tired.

The woman jostled her. "Hey, wake up, stay awake." Then she shouted, "Talk to me. What's your name?"

But I'm so sleepy. That probably wasn't a good sign.

"Trish." It came out as a whisper so she shouted it. "Trish!"

"Trish what? See, the idea is that you keep talking. To stay awake."

"Patricia," she shouted. "Patricia Velez." She paused. "My mom says she can't remember why they picked that name." Another pause. *I'm supposed to keep talking.* "I think my dad picked it. But he left my mom when I was a baby. Or she left him. It was too late to change it. So she only calls me Trish."

"That sounds hard, Trish. You get along with your mom?"

"She's all right. She's in Vegas. With Jim." She fell silent again.

"How's Jim?"

Trish was still trying to answer the first question. The ATV was climbing upward at an angle now, and it took more concentration not to fall off. "My mom's got her own shit to deal with. But she does her best. I know she loves me." Another long pause. "I need to get out of that house." Another pause. "Jim's okay. He's better than Clarence was." Pause. "I'm so tired." It came out as a whisper, so she shouted it. "I'm so tired!"

"That's okay. But stay awake for me, okay, Trish. We're almost there. Tell me about Clarence."

Trish didn't feel like talking about Clarence. He was gone now. No point in thinking about him anymore, except as a point of reference. So she started talking about her mom again. She wasn't even sure what she was saying, but the woman told her several times to talk louder, so she shouted everything. The terrain changed, and they were headed down, and then after a short while, up again.

The ATV began to slow and then it came to a stop. The woman turned it off. "Trish? You still with me?"

"Right here."

"I need you to let go of my waist so I can stand up. I'll make sure you don't fall over."

"Okay." Trish let her arms flop down to the side. The woman twisted, held on to Trish, as she stood up.

"We're going to have to walk a little ways from here." She pulled Trish to her feet and eased the blindfold off her head. They were in another part of the mountains, but she couldn't tell where. "Put your arm over my shoulder. Let all your weight rest on me. Yeah, just like that. Okay. We're going this way. You ready?"

"Yeah." They took a few steps forward. "Am I going to die?"

"Someday, sure. But not today. We got this."

The land was rough. It didn't even seem like there was a trail. But Trish didn't spend much energy on looking around. She just focused on the next step, the next one-footed hop, as the woman helped her along. Then suddenly they were over a ridge of some sort and down into a narrow cleft between two steeper walls. A large courtyard occupied the center of the area, and there were smaller structures, some collapsed and in ruins, around the edges. It was all the same color as the rock. From the air, it was probably invisible. As they descended toward this village, they stepped across a narrow canal filled with water that flowed down toward a garden area filled with plants.

"What . . . what is this place?" Trish asked. "Some kind of lost city?"

"'Lost'?" The woman snorted. "Does it look like we misplaced it? Come, this way."

She led Trish to a low structure and helped her duck her head to get through the door. Trish stumbled as they stepped down into a pit—the building was half underground. It was dark inside until the woman turned on a battery-powered lantern. The artificial light was bright and jarring—Trish winced. A small wooden table occupied the middle of the room. In addition to the lantern, it held a navy-blue duffel bag emblazoned with a Banner Health logo, along with several bottles of water, three empty bowls and spoons, and a pan with cold beans in it. There were sleeping bags rolled up against the wall.

"I'm an ER nurse," the woman said. "Trauma certified." She lifted the bag and placed it on the floor. "I've got a lot of basic gear with me, so I just need you to lie down here and let me take a look at you."

Trish was so happy to lie down. The woman grabbed one of the sleeping bags and tucked it under her head, and she was even happier. Then she put the lantern on the ground right next to Trish's leg.

"What is this place?" Trish asked.

"This village has been here a thousand years." The woman opened her bag and arranged a set of tools as she spoke. "We come out here now to help people crossing the desert. They need food and water. Sometimes they need medical help. There might be a border between the United States and Mexico, but the O'odham people have their own nation that stretches from Arizona all the way down to the Gulf of California. For a thousand years, people have walked across the land, north and south, between work and families. Hold still now, I'm going to cut this off."

"No, I mean, what is this, like a pueblo, or—unh!" As the make-shift bandage fell away, blood flow returned suddenly to her leg, bringing with it a bright rush of pain.

"Shit." The woman started tearing open packets of gauze and pressing them against Trish's calf. "I need you to reach down and hold these right here while I cut some more of your jeans off so I can get a better look. Yeah, just like that. Good. Press harder. Good."

She used an odd pair of scissors, flat on one side, to get in and cut off Trish's jeans above the knee. She cleared the torn denim out of the way and put on a pair of disposable latex gloves. As she tore open packets that looked like wet wipes, a strong smell of rubbing alcohol filled the air.

"Keep pressing." She wiped the blood off the rest of Trish's leg, turning it gently from side to side to inspect it for other injuries. "No, this isn't a pueblo. Didn't you study the Huhugam in school?"

"The Hohokam?"

"That's the word archaeologists use. Like they're an object or something. We call them the Huhugam. The ancestors. Those who have gone. But the word implies that they still have a connection to the living." She moved Trish's hand off the gauze and replaced it with her own.

"Ouch!"

"Yeah, I'm not going to lie, Trish. The only painkiller I have on hand is ibuprofen, and I can't give it to you just yet because it works like a blood thinner. So this is going to hurt. You need to be strong. I'll be as quick as I can be. Are you ready?"

Trish nodded. *I can be so fucking strong. You have no idea how strong I am.* She could feel the tears welling up in her eyes. She quickly wiped them away on her sleeve so she could watch.

"Okay, here goes. What do you know about the so-called Hohokam?"

The woman pulled the gauze away and a fresh flow of blood bubbled up. She tore open a couple sterile packs with things that looked like tweezers or clamps. It was hard to tell. She pulled back the skin on Trish's leg and went fishing in with the cold tool. Trish gritted her teeth to ignore the pain and watched.

"Aha, here's the culprit," the woman said, holding up a bloody blob of metal. "A bullet fragment. I thought maybe that was it. Do you have any tattoos?"

"What? No." Her head swam. She was thinking about getting a tattoo, but Dustin didn't approve, so she was going to do it after she broke up with him. The little diamond ring felt suddenly heavy on her finger. She twisted it upside down and closed her fist on it. "Why?"

"Lots of people have them. I have a couple." She put a clamp on something and lifted a curved needle with black thread. "They're made with needles, kind of like this one. Sometimes it helps people to know they can handle that before I sew them up. I'm going to sew you up now. It will hurt, but just a little bit. I know you can handle it. What did you learn in school about the Hohokam, Trish? Talk to me."

"I don't know," Trish said, as she watched the little silver hook sink into her skin. "They lived here in Phoenix. Canals or something. It's like a big mystery. They just disappeared."

"The most urban civilization in North America. Cities with tens of thousands of people, great public spaces, sports arenas. And they were farmers, in the desert. Miles and miles of canals, expertly engineered. The only civilization in North America with irrigation, and on a massive scale. Then climate change happened. The desert got hotter. Their technology wasn't sufficient to keep their big cities working any longer."

She sewed quickly as she spoke, continually wiping the area clean as she went. The alcohol swabs hurt worse than the needle. Her tools sat at her right hand, and a pile of trash accumulated on her left.

"You need help in here?" A subdued voice from the doorway. Trish startled. A woman stood there, holding an infant. A man behind her. Mostly silhouettes, framed by the doorway, against the sky outside.

"No, we're fine," the nurse said. "We've got this."

The man nodded and they left.

"People live here?" Trish asked.

"People pass through here, on their way to somewhere else." Her face was a mask of concentration. The lines around her mouth tightened. "Kind of like you."

"What happened to them?"

"To who?"

"To the . . ." She wanted to use the word the nurse had used. ". . . Huhugam? Where did they go?"

The nurse tied off another knot, picked up the scissors, and clipped the thread. She leaned back and wiped her forehead on her arm. "Maybe they didn't go anywhere."

～

The nurse padded Trish's stitches with gauze and wrapped her leg with surgical tape. Trish drank a bottle of water and part of another. The hike back to the ATV went slowly. Her body felt drained, exhausted. The ride back to the camp took forever, but the pain was enough to keep her awake, even blindfolded.

The smell and sizzle of bacon greeted their return. The ATV rolled to a stop and the nurse asked "What's going on?" before she took off Trish's blindfold.

"They had food and coffee in their gear," Diamondbacks answered. "If they're leaving tonight, figured they won't need it. Shame to let it go to waste."

"I hope there's some coffee left," the nurse said.

"Here, have the rest of mine," Captain America said, offering his. "They only brought two cups."

Trish saw Dustin lying on his side, hands tied to his feet and half her shirt stuffed in his mouth. His eyes were wide and muffled words fought to get past the gag as he struggled against his bonds.

"I'm fine!" she shouted at him. "You shot me but now I'm fine! Just . . . don't do anything else! Don't do anything else and we'll be okay!"

Everyone fell quiet at the vehemence of her voice. Dustin went very still and just stared at her, his eyes even wider, if that was possible. The nurse held the cup of coffee to her mouth with both hands and watched Trish over the rim for a moment before tilting her head back and emptying it. Diamondbacks caught her eye and then turned away.

Trish sat down on a rock by the cooling campfire, exhausted.

Captain America shouldered a backpack full of gear and hoisted a gallon jug of water. "I've got the replacement supplies. We better get going."

"Yeah," said the nurse, putting the cup down with a weary sigh. She rested her hand on Trish's shoulder. "Wait at least an hour before you untie him. Hell, leave him here if you want. You should have enough gas left to get back to the road if you head straight out of here when you leave."

"Got it," Trish said. She was tempted to leave Dustin here, if that wouldn't count as murder.

"Go to a doctor and get that leg checked when you get home, okay?"

"Right." She wanted to laugh. Like she could afford a doctor. Like she could explain what happened.

The nurse paused, waiting until Trish looked up and met her eyes. She glanced down at the Costco ring. "You can do better."

Trish shrugged.

The nurse returned the gesture. The three of them gathered at the edge of camp. Captain America turned back last, held up his rifle, and tapped his wrist where a watch would be. Then they took ten steps and disappeared into the brush and shadows.

As soon as they were gone, Dustin grunted to get Trish's attention and started to struggle to get loose. She checked the time on her phone and waited while he struggled until he was red in the face and then just glared at her furiously.

When she finally untied him after an hour, he was too angry to speak to her. He just immediately started packing up all their gear and loading up the ATV. The work was sloppy, rushed, not like his usual tidiness. His first words to her were when he straddled the machine. "Get on," he said. "Let's go."

"We can't see a thing out there! Let's just wait until morning!"

"Like hell. By morning, this place is going to be swarming with Border Patrol and people from the Air Force. They are going to hunt down those fuckers and make them pay for what they did to you."

They saved my life when you shot me. "Okay, if that's what you want. I just don't want any more trouble."

"Get the fuck on the back and let's go."

Trish climbed on and wrapped her arms around him. The diamond felt heavy on her finger, despite its size. He sped away so quickly she almost fell off. She gripped tighter. All she had to do was make it back to Phoenix. That's all she had to do.

He checked some point of reference she didn't catch and then headed straight across the desert back the way they came. No meandering or following the naturally curving trails of the landscape this time—it was just a straight shot with minor deviations for obstacles too big to go over. Every time they crossed a wash it was too fast and she was nearly bucked off the ATV. Dustin grew more reckless as they went, pushing the machine faster and harder, and the bounces got rougher and higher. Shapes jumped in the lights, cactuses and clumps of brush emerging suddenly out of the dark.

And then, just ahead, a primitive pyramid of stones appeared on a ridge.

Dustin swerved to avoid it; Trish let go of Dustin and slipped off her seat. As she fell, she glimpsed a wash dropping away in front of them, and at the bottom, barely glimpsed in the starlight, a giant rusty metal cactus with three fins flowering on top.

Don't kick the . . .

There was a giant orange blossom of light and a sound wave that slapped her out of the air and into the ground.

~

A red haze, muddied voices, swirling lights, mechanical thunder, a red haze, a red haze of pain.

~

She woke up in an ER bed, stirred by a persistent beeping, surrounded by bright lights and numerous machines. She hurt all over.

A nurse came in, a short man with a shaved head and a calm demeanor. "You are a very lucky woman," he said, as he turned off the alarm and hung a new IV bag.

"Don' fil luckee."

"Someone had called in a trespassing complaint, and there was already a patrol coming out to investigate when they saw the explosion. They had a medflight helicopter out there in just over an hour." He paused. "We used your fingerprint to unlock your phone and call your mother. She's on her way back from Vegas." He paused again.

"Dus'in?"

He shook his head. "He . . . wasn't as lucky as you. I'm very sorry for your loss."

Trish nodded and covered her mouth with her hand, so he couldn't see her sense of relief. Suddenly she *did* feel lucky. She forced herself to imagine some sort of sadness for the loss of Dustin. The loss of the man she had thought he was when they first started dating. When she could feel that, she slowly lowered her hand. "Oh my god," she whispered.

He rested a hand on her shoulder for just a second. "Some officers are going to come in soon with questions for you."

She nodded again. By the time he left her room, she had retraced the day in her head and found a way forward. One that wouldn't endanger the people who'd tried to help her.

She would tell the truth. Mostly.

Dustin had taken her out there to propose. At this special waterfall he found. She didn't even know where they were going. He thought he heard a snake. When he shot his gun in the dark, a ricochet hit her leg. He'd sewed her up best he could and they were hurrying back toward town when they hit the old bomb.

If they had more questions, she could give them more answers. How they'd been dating over a year. How they'd left his truck back on one of the dirt roads—she could help them find it. How he used to be in the Air Force.

The authorities would believe her.

She would make them believe her.

There were no other people. There was no village hidden in the mountains. Only those who were already gone.

A gentle knock sounded at the door. An officer stood there. When she met his eyes, he took off his hat.

"Sorry to bother you," he said. "I have a few questions about how you and your boyfriend—"

"Fiancé," she said, choking on the word. She lifted her hand to show him, but it was empty. Of course—they'd removed her jewelry when they brought her into the hospital. "We . . . we were engaged to be married."

He seemed almost embarrassed by her show of emotion. "I tried to talk to you earlier, but, uh, you were still kind of fuzzy. If now's not a good time . . ."

"Now is good," she said. She sat up straighter in her bed and rubbed the empty spot on her finger where the engagement ring had been. "I can do better."

E. LILY YU

An Account, by Dr. Inge Kühn, of the Summer Expedition and Its Discoveries

E. Lily Yu

Amundsen-Scott-Klenova Polar Station—April 5, 2050

Arrived via helicopter from McMurdo two days ago with the Argentinian native Catalina Park and the American refugee Dom Sanchez to find the station in rough shape but still habitable after the winter. Modularity does wonders for one's age.

For the first time in human history, the Antarctic ice shelf is entirely melted. That means walking on glacial talus or wading through bacteria-rich mud (formerly permafrost) up to our knees. Neither fun. The whole continent plucked like a chicken, stripped of any loveliness or mystery, baking naked under the baleful solar eye.

It would be more bearable with clouds, but there haven't been clouds in years. Children point to them in pictures and ask what they are. Your birthright, I say. Cumulus, nimbostratus, cirrus. Which we sold for a mess of sweet crude.

The American does not find this observation funny and

informs me that German parenting is barbaric. My daughter is a well-adjusted adult, I tell him, as much as one can be in this world, and she calls me regularly. Does yours?

Amundsen-Scott-Klenova Polar Station—April 10

The other two scientists are decent company at mealtimes. They listen to me talk about Cherenkov detectors and neutrino flavors with polite attention and well-concealed yawns.

Park's doing a geological survey, as if there's anything of worth in this dead place besides pristine neutrino trails (and those are much less pristine now). Every morning, she sloshes out whistling "Perfidia." I can tell this will become a point of contention shortly, given the difficulty of sleep during this six-month day.

Sanchez much less obstreperous. He's that terrible anachronism, a climate scientist, and I suspect that he laughs to avoid crying. Park and I stick to English out of pity for him, rather than resorting to our translation implants.

Amundsen-Scott-Klenova Polar Station—April 12

Today Park returned to base early, trembling and agitated. She said she'd found a major geological feature not marked on any of our maps. Sanchez grabbed one of the old expeditionary packs from a locker and volunteered to go back with her to see. I, of course, finished setting up my new detector panels before following them to Park's coordinates, where I found them leaning over the edge of a hole about 2m across, of indeterminate depth.

It being afternoon, I proposed that we retire to the station, sleep, and investigate in twelve hours, fully equipped and with our faculties refreshed. Without giving my plan the slightest consideration, Sanchez hammered a couple of bolts into the rock, attached carabiners, and rappelled down.

Damn Americans.

Park hesitated. "We do need food and water. And longlights."

"I grabbed everything already!" came the reply from within the hole.

I was all for leaving him in there and returning to my neutrino sensors, but Park reminded me of my obligation to keep the German Republics involved in any groundbreaking discovery. This was a commitment I had accepted without second thought because I considered the South Pole a wasteland, scientifically speaking. But here, very literally, was broken ground.

"If I wanted to find Thule," I mumbled, "I'd have gone north."

"Sorry?"

We compromised. Sanchez would establish a route to the bottom of the hole while I retrieved ice gear, extra longlights, this log, and a sensible stock of supplies, and sat-called our plans and coordinates to McMurdo.

You'd best believe I took my time.

A geological anomaly, West Antarctica—April 14

We have been two days in the depths of what Park says is a lava tube, formed by one of the 154 known volcanoes of Antarctica. The rock is slick with icemelt. The stone walls around us are striated to the flow line, ropy and mazed above. On average the passage is 3m wide and 4m high, narrowing to 1-2m at points.

Every so often we encounter jagged heaps of rock, fallen from the ceiling, over which we must scramble with our equipment, banging into hard edges and bruising ourselves.

When we glance up, our headlamps shine on a ceiling speckled with white mold.

Sanchez says it reminds him of royal tombs in Egypt, their ceilings painted deep blue with silver stars. Or of the sight of the Milky Way from an Arizona camper. Or of Hawaii—

Park says we must be the first humans to see this place.

Though I have never found geology enthralling, her words sent a shiver down my spine.

Everywhere we can hear a wet, musical trickling, as the liquid remnants of the ice shelf sink down through the earth.

Every few hours Park logs a memo to her wristwatch, stating base time and estimated coordinates. I ask her about the possibility of sudden floods from above.

"Could we be swept away?" I say. "Or could our exit be plugged with sediment?"

She says, with less confidence than I'd like, "83% of the ice shelf went straight into the ocean. There shouldn't be any volume of water aboveground sufficient for a flood. Most likely, we'll find ourselves blocked by icemelt lower in the tube."

When we reach that waterline, we will retrace our steps to the base, and she will publish her data and astound the world. Or at least the little corner of the world occupied by geologists.

When I mention that I'm neglecting my own project for this expedition, Sanchez scoffs. Park observes that these tunnels provide an even cleaner environment for neutrino detection than my current laboratory, which I admit to be true. This provides some consolation.

A geological anomaly, West Antarctica—April 17

Sleeping and waking in total darkness is standard for any over-wintering Antarctic mission, given the South Pole's six-month night, but the stations themselves are brightly lit. I am not used to spending unvarying hours straining to see unevenness in the rocky floor. Our glowworm progress through the tunnel grows disorienting.

At one point I was certain that I imagined a faint breeze on my face, but then Sanchez whooped, pinwheeled his arms, and huffed in lungfuls of what he proclaimed to be fresh air.

An odd look on Park's face. She has become very quiet.

E. Lily Yu

A geological anomaly, West Antarctica—April 18
I could swear I heard a skittering among the rocks, but that is likely a side effect of prolonged sensory deprivation.

According to Park, we have descended to a depth of 1,000m below sea level, a total descent of approximately 4,000m.

A geological anomaly, West Antarctica—April 19
Two of the longlights have reached the end of their battery several days early, perhaps due to the pervasive damp, leaving us with two that we are alternating. Park's wristwatch flashes lunatic green numbers. She says the accelerometer needs servicing.

I pleaded for us to return to base.

Sanchez stared at me as if I had grown two heads. "To come this far and turn around?"

Park said simply that the longlights had geothermal chargers, and that if we descended another 500m, the ambient temperature should increase enough to charge all of our lights. I pointed out that our supplies were rapidly diminishing. As of today, we have only four days' calories left, barely enough for our return.

"You're welcome to go back yourself," Park said. "Take one of the working lights and your third of food and water. But I'm going on."

"I'm with her," Sanchez said. "You don't quit something like this."

No matter what I said about precautions, preparations, discretion in valor, and so on, neither would budge.

And so, fuming silently, I went on.

Subterranean West Antarctica—April 21
The events of the past two days beggar the scientific imagination.

As Park predicted, the air grew warmer on our way. Our remaining longlights' batteries drained more gradually.

As time went on, there came into the tunnel a faint blue-green light altogether different in source and quality from the

153

hard white beams of our longlights. I do not know if I noticed it first, or Park, or Sanchez, but none of us said anything.

And then the tunnel, which had been descending steeply, dropped away entirely. Our longlights, probing, found nothing but darkness, no apparent walls at all. Then we lowered the beam and discovered a ramp of broken basalt at our feet. Farther down, this sloped into a lake of meltwater.

As our eyes adjusted, we perceived ourselves to be standing in an aperture high in the wall of a cavern. The rock walls dripped and glimmered with a weak blue-green light. Once we turned off our longlights, this faint light was just enough for us to pick out reflections and half-submerged tumbles and towers of rock.

"Bioluminescent bacteria," Sanchez said, "containing luciferin."

"Or fungi," Park said.

I sat down and caught my breath in awe at the otherworldly beauty of the scene. With my next breath, I said, "This is all very nice, but we only have one day's rations left. We're at least eight days' travel from the surface. The math—"

Sanchez said, looking toward the lake, "That's not going to matter."

In that dimness, I did not at first distinguish the figure in the distance. It had a glowing oval for a face and glowing hands, and it moved across the water on an irregular raft.

Park shouted and flashed her longlight twice in its direction before I could knock the light from her hands. But it was too late. Her voice echoed across the water. The figure had seen and heard us. It paddled toward us with excruciating slowness, hands shining in the water.

Park scrambled down the slope of scree to the waterline and stood there, waving. It occurred to me, too late, that she was absolutely mad. This time Sanchez did not follow her. He picked up a heavy rock and weighed it thoughtfully in his hand.

Americans! Even after the cratering of their country, their first recourse remains violence.

Luminiferous face and hands aside, as the figure approached, it became recognizably human, if shorter than any adult I might encounter on Hermannstraße. The raft proved to be a roughly oblong piece of pumice, about 1m by 2m.

After a brief and far too excited exchange, Park beckoned us down. I descended with reluctance, Sanchez following, his makeshift missile in his hand.

To our surprise, the stranger spoke a pidgin derived from perhaps a dozen languages, including Spanish, Chinese, and Portuguese. Our implants translated approximately every other word, though not without warning beeps and chirps. Via our implants, Park described our need for food.

From the stranger's slow, unhurried response, we understood that we were to first apply the same phosphorescent paste that he wore on his face, because only thieves and deceivers kept their expressions obscured. So saying, he offered a barklike bucket of the stuff. It was cool and slimy to the touch, coated my fingers like oil, and smelled like a neglected attic.

One by one, he ferried us across the lake on his pumice raft, which rode alarmingly low in the water under the weight of two people and one bag of equipment. Once we had all crossed, getting variably wet in the process, he led us through a low and narrow passage showing the flakes and dimples of chisel work. I ducked my head to avoid bashing my skull on the rock and fixed my eyes on Sanchez's heels.

What we saw when we emerged at the other end—what my anthropologist daughter would have murdered me to see—I can only describe as a city.

To be more precise, I observed a series of interlocked bubbles carved into the walls of the cave we now stood in, every inch of stone illuminated by thick layers of bacteria. This bioluminescence was multiplied by crystal prisms, precious stones, and hammered metal mirrors, all of which magnified the bacterial glimmer to a kind of twilight sufficient to live in.

The forty-odd residents appeared healthy enough, if stunted in growth. They watched us as we passed. Beds of leathery mushrooms tended by children offered an obvious source of clothing fibers and protein. The rest of their diet, we were soon to learn, consisted of a gelatinous broth of bacterial cultures unappetizing in appearance.

We were served bowls of this jelly soup, which thankfully had no strong flavor or smell, as well as hot water that tasted of minerals. Then we were shown to pallets of dried mycofibers in what functioned as a spare room in our ferryman's burrow. Exhausted by novelty and by our long trek, we fell asleep at once.

I awoke to a bonelike creature, something like the skeleton of a small lizard, tapping at my forehead. Without thinking, I swatted it away. There was a giggle. A small child tugged at the strings attached to the creature: the lizard was a toy of some sort, it appeared.

The ferryman, hearing us, came in and shooed the child out, then offered me more of the broth I had yesterday.

My cochlear implant mangles his name. I will call him Pytheas. From him I learned that this city, called Blue, was one of ten, an entire underworld that none of us had known about. The denizens were descended from the survivors of sinkholes, earthquakes, tumbles into crevasses, and other such catastrophes: miners buried by collapsing tunnels who dug deeper and broke through; lost spelunkers; and unfortunate scientists such as ourselves.

Most died of injuries or starvation before discovering the sparse, edible patches of cave slime, or before they were rescued by those who'd come before. But some did survive. We three were the first to descend alive in several decades, by their reckoning.

"So you don't know about what happened to America," Sanchez said. He had been awake and eavesdropping all this time. "The nuclear war, and so on."

"Don't depress him with that," I said, but in vain. The mutual destruction of America, Russia, and Iran is a story dear to the heart of every refugee from those countries, told differently depending on the storyteller's nationality. I have heard thirteen variants by now, in addition to what I myself saw in the news, and will not waste words on what everyone knows. At the time of the war I was still young and did not fully understand. I was selfishly glad for the chance that the radioactive clouds of ash and smoke, wide as continents, might trigger a period of global cooling. As we now know, that prediction was inaccurate. But we were desperate for optimism then, before we became simply desperate.

When Park awoke, she waded into the conversation with an account of global ecological devastation, the melted ice caps, the rising sea, and the murderous perpetual heat. Sanchez interjected with technical (one wonders if translatable) details.

This history visibly discomfited our host. He took our empty bowls away to wash. In the corridor I saw him lift up the child and hold her tightly.

"If you'd like," he offered when he returned, "I could show you the city."

We agreed at once.

Here and there the tunnels that functioned as thoroughfares, bruisingly low for my height, opened up into enormous natural caverns. Their walls were daubed with blue-green bacteria, their spaces devoted to mycoculture or parklike forms of recreation.

In one of these caverns, we saw the dinosaurs.

They were the giant cousins to our host's daughter's toy. Incomplete skeletons of petrified bones, opalescent in the murk, shambled past us. Glow-faced riders drove their halting steps, pulling mycofiber sinews on pulley joints.

The lack of fauna this far underground, our host told us, was hard on the soul. These contraptions were like puppets or parade floats, mechanical and lifeless.

They looked lifelike enough to *me*.

I pointed to two mounds of brightly glowing bacteria, placed out of reach on a ledge and a stone pillar, that gave off far more light than the culture on the walls.

"How did you make those lanterns?" I asked. "Why aren't they everywhere?"

"Those are burials," Pytheas said. "After the last of their light, we'll move the remains to our mushroom beds. One cannot waste organic material at these depths."

Impatient, Park returned to metallurgy: where had the dinosaur's pulleys and the city's metal mirrors come from?

"Magma flows," Pytheas said. Certain bubbles in the stone were naturally heated, like ovens, and used for cooking and boiling water. Others, shielded by thin surrounding walls, were merely warm, until a metalworker drove through the floor to expose magma. The molten rock could be used for processing ores and for smithing.

"Extraordinary," Park said.

"But what about crime?" Sanchez asked. "How do you punish people? How do the human passions play out?"

"There isn't sufficient nourishment for such things," our host said. "We conserve our energy for work and for thinking, and make peace with each other as quickly as we can."

Sanchez said, "So you just—cooperate?"

"No one unreasonably withholds consent. Sometimes there is construction that we collectively agree is necessary. A new room, for example, or a street. Then those of us who are able and not needed elsewhere work in shifts until the project is complete."

Sanchez said, "Where's the mother of your children? Is she dead?"

There are days I don't regret the obliteration of American culture.

Pytheas said, "She prefers to live in another city. Food is more plentiful here, light more plentiful there. And her family is there as well. There is so little meaningful choice down here that we do our best to respect the decisions that people do make."

As we crossed the city, a handful of residents introduced themselves, inquiring about our health and well-being and how we liked the city. They evinced little interest in politics or current affairs.

One elder, a survivor of a caving expedition, proved fluent in a dialect of Spanish. She happily engaged Sanchez in a reminiscence about elotes and chilaquiles. But when he suggested taking her to the surface to eat them again, or else bringing them down for her (corn still grows in northern Canada), she fell abruptly silent and withdrew.

"You said you were a geologist," our host said, his eyes on Park. "You know what rock is breakable, what rock is strong—"

"Whereas climate science is useless without climate," Sanchez said. "Not to mention astrophysics without stars."

"Thanks," I said.

Our host said, "If you could look at our plans to preserve the icemelt as aquifers—"

Park said, "I'd be happy to."

They went off together, heads bowed. I wondered if the schematics were drawn in glowing lines of bacteria. Sanchez shied a pebble of white pumice through the eye socket of one of the park's dinosaurs. Its operator barely acknowledged us.

Sanchez said, "The dire lack of flavor and nutrition aside, you have to admit the situation has appeal."

"Does it."

"We could survive down here for a very long time. No ozone holes. No radiation. And some of the men look damn fine."

"As if you could tell."

Sanchez chuckled. "Oh, I can tell."

"You'd live like a bat."

"A few things could be improved," he said. "I have ideas. If you wanted to hear—"

"Go play with a dinosaur," I said.

"Good idea," Sanchez said. "But it's a pterosaur, and technically that's not—"

I flapped my blue-green hand at him, and he went to talk pulleys and strings with the operator.

That left me to pace the cavern's perimeter alone. I admired the bacteria-painted walls and the universal language of graffiti scratched into their blue-green glow: names, hearts, crude drawings. At a well-tended section, someone had drawn a simple diagram of the city, followed by a spoked wheel of what looked like other cities, their names incomprehensible to me.

A hollow clattering announced Sanchez's turn at the pterosaur. It pivoted, flapped, and collided with a boulder. Several bones came undone.

"I can fix it," Sanchez said.

The operator shrugged.

Eventually Pytheas returned with Park.

"She says the tunnel you came through connects to the surface," he said.

"Did she?" I said carefully.

Park was oblivious. "Of course it does."

Pytheas said, "We explored that tunnel before the lake formed. We didn't find an exit. Only solid rock and ice."

"All the ice in Antarctica's melted," Sanchez said. "Must have poured down through that tunnel. Made the lake."

"That's how we'll bring in the machines I told you about," Park said.

"I see," Pytheas said, rubbing the bridge of his nose.

Pytheas did not dine with us that evening, saying an urgent

matter required his attention. As we ate our bowls of bacterial jelly, Park chattered about ferrying down welders and scrap metal, rock corers and pickaxes, friends and family. The city could be enlarged to hold another hundred people without much difficulty, once they had the machines. Sanchez pontificated about spices, vanished and available, and mused on the shelf life of synthetic flavorings underground.

"None of that will be happening," I said.

Park said, "It certainly won't be easy. Especially the coring machine. But it's possible. Unlike Sanchez's imaginary limes."

"They're not going to let us leave," I told them. "The last thing they want is trouble from above."

"After decades down here, they must want to see the sun," Park said. "Plants, other humans, the stars—I know I would."

"Not after you went on and on about our nuclear wastelands and new and incurable diseases—"

"I think you're underestimating human curiosity," Sanchez said. "Eve, Pandora, Oppenheimer . . ."

I said, "You can stay. I can't stop you. But Helene is never going to forgive me if I don't tell her about this."

"Your logic is a bit strained," Sanchez said, fairly.

The blue-green paint on Park's face illuminated her doubt. "We only have three ration packs, and I haven't checked the longlights."

"I don't care," I said, regretting how much I sounded like Sanchez. "I'm leaving."

Sanchez said, "We'll see you topside soon. Don't scoop Park, okay?"

"I'm an *astrophysicist*," I said.

Blue City outskirts, Subterranean West Antarctica—April 22

That night, I lay down on my pallet like the others. I waited until I heard the mycofiber curtain part and swing back as Pytheas returned from wherever he'd been. Once I was sure Pytheas, Park, and Sanchez were all asleep, I arose, wiped the bioluminescence from my skin, and quietly packed the remaining rations. Earlier, I had left the longlights in one of the oven-like bubbles, and I was now gratified to see that they held full charge.

It was not difficult to retrace our path through the city. I slunk and hid, though nobody seemed to be awake, feeling naked and guilty without my paint.

When I reached the icemelt lake, I found Pytheas's raft tied to a boulder on the shore. I untied it and pushed off. The water was cold (a rare sensation) but not unpleasantly so. I dipped my unlit hands in it and paddled toward the far wall and the slope of scree.

The climb tore my gloves and scraped my hands raw. Rocks shifted beneath me and clacked downward. Some splashed into the water.

At the mouth of the lava tube I looked back, heart loud, fearing pursuit.

One figure stood upon the far shore. Its face was luminous but unidentifiable at this distance. It could as easily have been Park or Sanchez as Pytheas, or some other resident out for a midnight stroll.

It made no move to follow, if it even noticed me.

Out of an abundance of caution, I kept the longlights doused until I advanced some distance into the lava tube, far enough that I could no longer detect that fragile, algal, blue-green light.

Now I walk, conserving my rations, flicking on the longlights only when necessary. As much as I can, I proceed in the dark. Without Park's wristwatch I am blind and disoriented, uncertain of where I exist in space and time. I feel the weight of the rock overhead as much as if it pressed on me.

What I'm doing might be called abandonment. But one of us ought to tell the world. One of us ought to tell Helene.

E. Lily Yu

AP News, McMurdo, Antarctica—May 2, 2050

After a month of radio silence from the team at the Amundsen-Scott-Klenova Polar Station, a search and rescue team deployed on Saturday. Coordinates sent in the last outbound message led rescuers to a newly exposed lava tube, in which they found Dr. Inge Kühn in serious condition, dehydrated, starving, and vividly hallucinating the existence of an underground city. Some 50 meters on, the tunnel terminated in an apparent collapse, rendering further rescue attempts impossible. Entries in her log suggest these hallucinations have been ongoing for several weeks.

The other two scientists on assignment at the station, Dr. Catalina Park and Dr. Dom Sanchez, are presumed dead in the tunnel collapse.

Helene's home, Prenzlau—July 14, 2050

I am in my daughter's small flat, which she shares with her husband, two children, and three bounding dogs, to "get well," as they say. As if any of us could get well in these final days, as the sun burns us to hard tumors and fine ash. The room is hot. Every room is hot, everywhere, with no relief.

My own quiet quarters at the Max Planck Institute in Garching seem as distant and unreachable as a fever dream.

"Helene," I say. "You believe me, don't you?"

"I want to," she says as she shades the windows. "It's a wonderful story. But I can't. Because if I did, then what? No one believes you—it would drive me wild."

"It could be our secret," I say. "Just between you and me."

"Mama, no," she said.

She always was a well-reasoned girl.

I am not the only scientist in history to face the disbelief of the masses. Far from it. There is a bust of Boltzmann on my desk at the Institute. It is a lonely journey at the best of times, listening for the silent fall of neutrinos from a vast and unforgiving sky, and extrapolating from their passage the strangeness of other stars.

What is harder to bear is the grief of Sanchez's husband. Tell me the truth, he said to me, over and over, as if I wasn't. Every week or so he calls to ask again.

I miss Park and Sanchez to the point of dreaming about them. I imagine they will do well in their new home. Better than us above, certainly. Sanchez's last paper suggests we have at most thirty years before 97% of this planet's surface becomes uninhabitable.

Perhaps I should have stayed with them. But no. I had to tell Helene. Even her confusion, even her incredulity are precious to me. I did not tell her fairy tales when she was a child. The world seemed too far gone for stories of wonder, for tales of truth rewarded and kindness crowned. A lapse—an error of pessimism—on my part.

Helene turns off all the lights as she leaves, except for the lamp at my bedside. I switch that off myself, as I have every night. For a moment the room is perfectly dark, as dark as the depths of a lava tube.

Upon my arrival, my expedition boots were tossed into a corner of this room. If I look over at them, as I do every night, I can still see, on the left side of one heel, the faintest of blue-green glimmers, growing ever fainter and harder to discern.

JAMES L. CAMBIAS

Out of the Dark

James L. Cambias

"Relative velocity zero," said Agha from the pilot's seat. "Distance five hundred twenty meters."

"Plasma sail off," I said, and tapped the control. The haze of ionized gas around our ship dissipated as the electric field shut down. Agha and I could see our target clearly.

Langtar habitat was a big stubby cylinder looming half a kilometer behind us. It was a couple of kilometers across and about five kilometers long. The whole thing was rotating, oriented at right angles to its orbit so the docking hubs were at the north and south poles.

I took a look with the telescope, watching for a full minute as Langtar turned on its axis. "No obvious damage, no outgassing, no debris."

"What about heat?" Agha asked.

"Surface temperature's uniform across the day and night sides.

Energy budget shows a net positive. Something's generating power in there."

"Which means some kind of control system's still active. Maybe we should ping it again."

"Be my guest," I said.

"This is the ship *Bold Venture*, out of Okeola habitat, approaching Langtar habitat. Langtar, please respond." He set the comm system to repeat it, working through the whole spectrum from optical laser down to ten-meter radio.

I take no blame for the ship's stupid name. I wanted to call it the *Phoenix*. Okeola generated a random number to decide and Agha won.

"Still no response," I said after ten minutes.

"Looks like we've got salvage," said Agha. "Stick a transponder on it, claim this piece of junk for Okeola, and let's get out of here."

It was tempting. But Okeola had appointed me the mission commander, which made me responsible for doing everything properly. "Ignoring comms doesn't mean it's a derelict. We have to go inside and have a look."

Agha called up a big numerical display on the inside of our control bubble, counting down from sixty-two hours, nineteen minutes. "That's our window. If we're not in this ship with the engine burning when that hits zero, you and I are going off into the dark for the next couple of millennia."

"I'm aware," I said.

Our mission was simple: match orbits with Langtar and see if it was still a live habitat. If yes, say hello and leave. If no, claim it as salvage, then do a braking burn to swing our little ship onto a Jupiter intercept so that the big guy could sling us back into the Main Swarm. Refuel there and return to Okeola. Agha and I would hibernate most of the time, so the ship could be small and cheap. Simple.

Except, not so simple. For complicated reasons involving a

war with genocidal machines back in the Fourth Millennium, Langtar's builders put it on a steeply inclined two-thousand-year orbit, so it spent most of its time out in the Kuiper Belt, where the Sun was just a brighter-than-average star in the endless night. Our home hab Okeola had a similarly tilted orbit, but stayed sensibly inside the orbit of Venus. When Langtar came plummeting into the inner system, only Okeola was in position to launch a salvage mission.

The obvious plan would be for Okeola to install a fragment of her own mind in an unmanned spacecraft and fire it off. But she had another problem, and the name of that problem was "Agha and Eto."

There's vid of Agha and me as infants with the rest of that year's crop. It shows a mass of wiggly little bodies, some with fur, some with feathers, some hairless. You can spot the two of us immediately: we're the ones fighting over a toy bunny.

That set the tone for Agha and me over the next eighteen standard years. Every game became a grudge match. Every class became a competition. Every social event became a battle. Okeola just wasn't big enough to hold us both. When our home hab set up a competition to pick the crew of the Langtar salvage mission, Agha and I tied for first place, so Okeola stuffed us into a fragile little ship and shot us into space.

I picked the north pole docking hub. Agha did the piloting. He was actually very good, not that I would admit it to his face. As mission commander, I decided where the ship should go. He just executed my orders.

The docking hub looked like a little open cup sitting atop the curved end of the rotating habitat. But it was pretty big—a hundred meters across and twice that in length. With the plasma sail shut down and retracted, *Bold Venture* slipped inside like an arrow into an empty quiver.

Agha set us down on the inner surface of the hub. That close to the axis Langtar's spin only generated a twentieth of a g, so our spindly spaceship sat on the surface without harm.

We suited up and passed through the pressure membrane to the outside. The place was suspiciously tidy. An active dock would have equipment stowed outside, maybe a ship under repair and a couple of work pods ready for use, or at least some useful scrap. Langtar's north pole was utterly empty. The surface was covered by a fine layer of dust.

Six hatches were spaced around the habitat end of the docking hub, marked with the ancient bisected-square airlock glyph. We bounced over to the nearest and Agha tapped the surface with his gloved finger. Nothing.

Fortunately airlock design is a very conservative technology, strong on failure safety and backward compatibility. The manual latch was obvious and simple, and made to resist vacuum-welding. I gave it a two-handed tug and the hatch popped open.

Inside the displays were dark—but one light panel still glowed. Which meant some power was still available. I sealed the outer door and Agha found the manual fill valve.

"The moment of truth," he said, and gave it a tug. We were rewarded with a puff of visible vapor and a hissing sound that grew louder as the airlock filled. Agha took hold of the latch for the inner door. "Ready?"

"Wait." I checked my suit's tester. "Half a bar of pressure, oxygen thirty percent, nitrogen sixty-five. Two percent each carbon dioxide and water vapor. Traces of ammonia and methane, some complex organics. That's a little odd. Okay, open it up, but keep your suit sealed—we won't know about biohazards for a while yet."

"As you command, O great and wise leader." He gave a grunt as he turned the latch, then pushed the door open and the two of us looked into Langtar for the first time.

Langtar looked back at us, in the form of half a dozen angry chickens hovering in midair. They were scrawny roosters with puffed-up red combs, oversized wings, and wicked-looking claws. Behind them I could see a few dozen hens nesting on the floor and some chicks fluttering around in the low gravity like little yellow clouds.

My impression of Langtar's hub facility is just a blur of feathers, beaks, and ankle-deep composted chicken shit. Our suits were tough enough to shrug off strafing runs by angry roosters, but neither of us wanted to linger.

Three elevator shafts passed through the circular hub deck. Above, they met at the light tube, which ran down the axis of the habitat. Below, they stretched down into a layer of haze over a dark green surface.

When the elevator doors didn't open as we approached I stabbed frantically at any surface that might be a touch pad, but nothing happened. A rooster slammed into the back of my head and the fabric of my hood went rigid as it tried to peck my scalp.

"This way!" Agha yelled over the squawks and fluttering. He had spotted a service ladder on the side of the elevator shaft, and began climbing down. I would have preferred a more methodical approach, but the chickens outvoted me, so I followed Agha down the ladder.

Climbing down a kilometer-long ladder is quite a job. Thankfully we were on the spinward side of the elevator shaft, so Coriolis pushed us toward the ladder rather than trying to pull us off.

The ladder was graphene-coated titanium, which hadn't rusted even after six millennia. It was coated with moss and lichen, though, and the chickens obviously used it as a perch. Even with our gloves set to sticky, it was hard to keep a grip.

"I think I know why your tester found all that ammonia," said Agha, scraping chicken shit off his feet. "Hey, watch it!" he added as I did the same and spattered some onto his hood.

The builders put platforms every hundred meters along the ladders, where support struts reached to the habitat wall. We stopped at the first one to have a look around without poultry attacks.

"Not dead," said Agha.

Not dead at all. The interior of the hab was brilliant green. A lush tangle of forest covered the entire floor of the cylinder.

Completely. I could see no farms, no clearings, not even buildings. Just a thousand shades of green streaked with mist.

"The systems are obviously working," I said. "We have to find a control node." Stake our claim in the name of glorious Okeola, and all that.

"It could be anywhere," he pointed out.

I did a little mental math. Thirty square kilometers of floor, covered by thousands of years of jungle growth, divided by two people with no idea what they were even looking for . . . We could spend a year wandering around down there. I didn't say that out loud, of course. What I said was "Let's send out our eyes and have a look."

Each of us had a little fist-sized remote sensor drone. I sent mine to see what was at the bottom of the ladder. Its evasion program got a bit of a workout when a couple of hunting chickens tried to snatch it out of the air.

What I saw on my faceplate display was . . . trees. Lots and lots of trees, some of them immense. They were pretty, if you like trees, but I wanted to find proof that this hab still had some entity capable of maintaining minimal-standard technology—a power plant, a comm system, or a processor suitable for a Baseline-Equivalent intelligence. The light overhead meant a working power plant, but we had no evidence of anything else.

An empty hab was free for salvage. Okeola could sell the rights to someone willing to spend the delta-v to get to Langtar, or even keep them and send over a daughter colony in a couple of millennia. Habs take the long view.

"What do you see?" I asked Agha.

"Nothing much," he said. "I checked the axial fusion tube. Doesn't look like anyone's taking care of things. There are vines growing on the supports, and chicken colonies, and spiderwebs like you wouldn't believe."

"All right, let's go on."

"Fifty-nine hours," he said.

"I'm aware of that. Come on." I led the way down.

At the halfway mark Agha retracted his hood. "My tester doesn't show any germs, and I'm dying in here." His face was beaded with sweat.

"That was dumb," I told him. "Six hours is the minimum."

"Don't you ever get tired of following rules?"

"If you do things properly, you don't die. This isn't a game, Agha."

"I know!" he said, and laughed with delight.

Just before we started down again, he stopped. "Um, Eto, there's something I've been meaning to tell you. When we get to the Main Swarm to refuel . . . I'm leaving."

"Leaving?"

"That's what I said. You can go back to Okeola. You're mission commander, after all."

"You'll be all alone," I pointed out.

"Alone? I'll be with *everybody*! I won't be stuck inside Okeola, in a weird orbit, looking at the Swarm and knowing I can't reach it because it would cost too much energy. That's why I busted my ass to make sure I got on this mission. I'm getting off at the first place we dock, and I'm going to spend the rest of my life seeing the solar system."

"There's a billion worlds out there. Even if you spend all your time on ships you won't see more than a tiny fraction."

"That's more than I'll see if I stay in Okeola, isn't it?"

I started to answer, but stopped myself. It wasn't seemly for a mission commander to argue with a mere crewman, especially one who was planning to mutiny and jump ship.

Besides, Okeola and I would be better off without him.

～

Agha and I got down to the ground and looked around. Immediately to the north was the hab wall, covered with vines. In every other direction, jungle.

Except . . .

"Does that look like a building to you?" I pointed to spinward. Past a couple of trees and a thicket of some kind of ground cover with big floppy leaves was a vine-covered bulk. Beneath the tendrils and leaves I could barely make out the glint of sunlight on diamond windows.

We clambered over a huge fallen log and pushed the vines aside to reveal a mildew-covered diamond wall. Agha and I worked our way along the wall and around a corner before we found a door. It was a powered door, self-locking, but long ago some tiny vine tendrils had forced their way into the cracks around the door. The diamond pane was nearly unbreakable, but after years—centuries?—of slow growth the vines had simply popped the door out of its track.

Agha and I squeezed inside and turned on our suit lights. The interior smelled of animal urine, rotting leaves, and soot. The walls were charred and melted in spots, and the ceiling was simply gone, revealing blackened concrete panels of the floor above. Vines, both inside and outside, obscured the windows. The ground floor was all one open room, stripped bare. In the center a staircase spiraled up out of the muck.

He poked around the ground floor while I had a look upstairs. That was an even bigger mess than the ground floor. A couple of the windows were open, and the whole place had been invaded by

174

tree branches and vines. The floor was a foot deep in dead leaves and animal droppings.

But in one corner, the floor was swept clear, down to the concrete. A sturdy chunk of log supported a sheet of diamond windowpane, and I could see that one corner of the pane was broken off. On the floor below it shards and dust glittered. Off to one side was a little pile of diamond fragments.

My spine tingled as I realized what I was looking at. "Agha, get up here!"

He came up the stairs three at a time.

"Look what I found. Someone's been chipping bits off this windowpane."

"Like flint. Like the first humans on Earth."

"Only this is recent. Someone's still alive here."

"So much for salvage, then. Okeola's going to be disappointed."

"Maybe not," I pointed out. "If they're chipping old windowpanes for tools, that means they've lost the ability to run the hab."

"This wouldn't be the first colony to choose a low-tech lifestyle," said Agha. "There have been neo-primitive habs since the Third Millennium."

"But even those have someone aboard who's tech-capable. Support crew, or a caretaker system. That's the rule: any ship or hab has to have at least one intelligence on board which can maintain minimal-standard tech. If nobody in Langtar knows how to do that, Okeola can put in a rescue claim, which is almost as good as salvage."

~

Outside we headed south, away from the elevator shaft. You can't really get lost in a rotating hab—just bobbing your head a little is enough to stay oriented. We found the remnant of a road, which we followed until it dead-ended in a swamp. It looked like it had once been a farm section, but drainage had failed, leaving the whole section covered by a meter of dark-brown water and a thicket of reeds taller than I was. Little clumps of trees poked above the reeds here and there.

The swamp filled an irregular region about five kilometers across. Agha and I had to go around it, which meant more delay as we hunted for paths and had to backtrack every time we found ourselves up against the edge of the water yet again.

Finally we found a route leading along the length of the hab that wasn't flooded—though it was overgrown, and centuries had turned the pavement into a mass of loose graphene chunks mixed with compost.

As we went down the broken-up road through the jungle, I did take plant samples and feed them to my tester, hoping to discover some lost variety or valuable mutant. But the jungle was depressingly mundane—mostly food crops and ornamentals, all drifted away from their familiar forms. The plants were tall and spindly, their blossoms and fruit were small and drab, and the genomes didn't show anything exciting.

We could hear the local animal life: birds calling, insects buzzing and chirping, frogs peeping, lizards and small mammals scuttling around the undergrowth. Those last ones gave me a scare at first. It turns out a bushy-tailed little gray mammal scurrying through leaf litter makes as much noise as a monster the size of a cargo van.

I was about to propose a rest break when a new sound echoed through the forest. Human voices! We could hear them coming from up ahead, and they didn't sound happy. Agha gestured, and I followed him to the thicker foliage at the edge of the old roadway. We set our suits to green, then moved toward the sound, keeping our heads down and trying to be quiet.

We reached a circular clearing with the overgrown remains of more buildings around it. In the center of the space three people were doing some kind of weird dance. Two young men, holding thick tree branch segments, were circling around a young woman, who held a long bamboo pole tipped with something that sparkled brightly in the light. The men were making all the noise—a grating series of cries like birdcalls. All three wore very determined expressions and nothing else.

One of them darted at her, and she poked the sparkly tip of her pole at him. But as she did, the second one ran at her from the side and hit her on the shoulder with his piece of wood. She cried out in pain and tried to hit him with the other end of her pole.

It all snapped into focus for me. They weren't dancing. The two men were trying to kill her. The pieces of wood were clubs and the pole was a spear tipped with a shard of diamond.

Agha figured it out at the same time I did, but his reaction was to break from our hiding place and run at them, shouting, "Hey! Stop that!"

The two men looked at him, startled. Agha was bigger than they were, and had sealed up his suit and set it to rescue orange. Neither man looked more than a meter and a half tall, and they were wiry and lean rather than bulky. They had tangled hair, dull expressions, and were very dirty.

The sight of a garish faceless monster waving its arms startled the two men, and they backed off a few paces. One of them picked up a chunk of graphene and threw it at Agha. Of course the smart weave of Agha's suit went rigid at the point of impact so it bounced off harmlessly.

That really spooked them, so they withdrew to the cover of the woods, still shrieking. The young woman with the spear whirled and kept the point between her and Agha. Now that she wasn't fighting for her life, I could get a good look at her. She was small and skinny, with a massive braid of rust-colored hair, huge dark eyes, and pale skin striped with what looked like crushed algae and berry juice.

"Hello," said Agha, and raised his hand. "We're friends. We come in peace."

She just looked at him, then glanced in the direction the two men had gone before dropping to her knees and wailing.

That was when we noticed the body lying in the tall grass. It was a young man with hair like hers and the same paint stripes on his skin. She bent over him, murmuring and crying, and tried to pick him up.

He was utterly limp. His head lolled to one side and I could see that one side of it was all smashed in. I opened my own suit then and added about half a liter of assorted stomach contents to the local ecosystem.

Agha took a step forward to help her, but she snatched up the spear and brandished it at him, so he backed up a couple of meters and tried the same greeting as before in all the archaic languages his suit could translate: Saur, Altok, Ningen, Woshing, Rocasa, Al-Arabiyyah, and English. She just stared at him warily.

"They've had at least four thousand years of language drift," I told him. "You might as well be speaking in binary."

He retracted his hood and smiled at her, then tapped his chest. "I am Agha. I come from up there." He turned and pointed back up at the hub where we'd entered.

The young lady took that opportunity to bolt.

I sent my remote after her. She was really very graceful as she sprinted through the grass to spinward. At the edge of the swamp she climbed into a wood-and-hide canoe, then paddled away into the reeds. She kept looking back as she paddled.

I called back my remote and had it circle the clearing, watching for the men with clubs. Meanwhile I joined Agha, and we both stared at the dead body in the grass while we tried to figure out what to do.

"Seen enough?" he asked.

"I'm not sure," I said. "We still have no idea what's going on here."

"There's murder," he answered. "That's going on."

178

We looked at the dead body some more. Neither of us had ever seen one before.

"What happens when Okeola puts in a rescue claim?" Agha asked after a while.

"Same as salvage, mostly. She gets control of the hab, or can sell the rights to someone else. The only difference is that you have to evacuate the inhabitants before you scrap the habitat. Unless they really have gone post-sapient. Then they just get euthed. These people could easily be sub-baseline."

"*She* looked okay," he said, and looked off toward the flooded section.

"We've got about fifty hours left," I said. "We'll look around a little longer, then head back to the ship to sleep. Spend another day making recordings, plant the transponder, and then we're off to Jupiter."

That cheered him up. Not that I cared about Agha's moods, but a good commander should always pay attention to the crew's morale.

We set out south again, in the direction the two men with clubs had gone. I wasn't exactly thrilled about that, but the alternative was trying to go through a swamp without a boat. We moved cautiously in case they were waiting for us, and set our suits to safety green so that we'd blend in with the foliage.

The road emerged from the forest canopy at the edge of a wide transverse avenue, cracked and weedy but not yet gone to jungle. Beyond the avenue the road split to go around a hill—and then I realized that it wasn't a hill but a dome a couple of hundred meters across. Vines and weeds covered it completely, but the smooth graphene surface underneath looked unbroken.

"That looks important," said Agha.

I couldn't disagree. We walked up to the dome, searching for an entrance.

What happened next was my fault, I freely admit. Both of us were preoccupied with looking at the dome, rather than at the ground. I took a step—but the ground wasn't solid, just a scrim of branches covered with leaves. Agha saw me start to fall and grabbed my arm, with the result that both of us fell into the pit.

"Where are we?" I asked some time later, once I could breathe and think again.

"Some kind of tunnel," said Agha. His suit light showed graphene walls lined with pipes and conduits. Half a meter of dark, foul-smelling water covered the floor. Off to spinward the tunnel sloped down until the ceiling met the surface of the water. In the other direction it ran about ten meters to a barrier of diamond windowpanes, graphene panels, and rotting logs. Above us the pit was a neat rectangle of daylight, obviously an access shaft which someone had converted into a death trap.

"Can you stand?" he asked.

"Sure," I said—and then discovered that I couldn't. Something very bad had happened to my left knee. I activated the suit's built-in medical kit and then screamed as it straightened that leg before stiffening the fabric around my knee into a splint and injecting me with a painkiller.

"If you could climb up and throw down a vine or something," I suggested.

Agha's response was to stand at the bottom of the shaft and shout, "Hey!"

Four shaggy heads just like the men Agha had chased away earlier looked over the edge, and a moment later chunks of wood and broken graphene began to rain down on us. Agha helped me get out from under the shaft and we waited until their high-pitched shrieks died down.

We tried attacking the barrier on the uphill end of the tunnel, but even our shape-changing multitools couldn't do much against the sheer mass piled up. A prybar would have made all the difference, but we couldn't pull free anything strong enough to use—especially since I could barely stand.

Agha tugged and cut and pulled and strained at the barrier. Finally he just completely lost control and started kicking it, showering us both with graphene splinters but otherwise accomplishing nothing. Eventually, worn out, he slumped against the wall across from me.

"Forty-six hours. If we can't get out of here by then, we're stuck. Any orders, O great mission commander?"

"I don't know," I said. "Wait and see if they go away?"

"Not a great plan," he said. Then he gave the barrier another useless kick. "I can't believe I'm stuck here with *you*! I wanted to get away from Okeola and away from *you*, but now it looks like I'm going to be stuck with *you* even when we're both dead."

I didn't answer, even though I wanted to tell him how he was the one taking risks while I just wanted to complete the mission properly. But he was angry enough already, and the two of us were stuck in a pit, and my leg hurt. So I let it go.

We rested for a couple of hours, hoping that the four shriekers up on the surface would lose interest in us and wander off. I slept a bit; I don't know if he did.

"What's our welcoming committee up to?" I asked him when I woke again.

"No change. I sent up my remote. They're camped out right by the pit, eating some critter."

My own stomach gurgled, reminding me I hadn't eaten since we left the ship. "Do they have a fire?"

"Nope. They're eating everything raw."

"Definitely post-sapient," I said. Wishful thinking, I admit. Fair's fair—they were keeping me trapped in a pit to starve, I could imagine them getting euthed by whoever bought the salvage rights.

Just then everything went dark. Back home in Okeola the windows dim down to just enough to read by, but inside Langtar the light simply switched off with no warning and everything became utterly black.

"Now's my best chance," said Agha. "I'll climb up and try to get rid of those goons."

"There's four of them and only one of you."

"Maybe I can lure them off and double back, or knock them out, or something."

"Agha, don't—" I stopped. What I wanted to say was *don't leave me*, but my pride wouldn't allow it. So I said, "Don't do anything foolish."

"No promises," he said. Then he made his gloves and boots sticky and began climbing out as silently as he could manage.

From above I heard a sudden outburst of bird-shriek noises, and the sound of many running feet receding into the distance. Then silence.

I had a long time to sit and think. My eyes could see nothing but blackness, the only sound was the drip of water and the buzz of insects, and I couldn't do anything but lie on the tiny patch of dry floor next to the barricade and feel my knee throbbing.

I was going to die here, I realized. If the four shriekers didn't catch Agha and murder him, the logical course of action for him would be to make for the ladder, get back aboard *Bold Venture*, and get the hell away from Langtar and me. He could go off to one of the big habitats like Juren, or glittering Deimos itself, and spend another century telling about his thrilling adventure in the lost habitat.

No! Just the thought of being reduced to a supporting role in Agha's story made my heart pound with anger. If he thought he could go off and leave me, he was wrong, as always. I made my own suit sticky and began climbing out.

It was a hellish task. Even with sticky gloves I slipped back more than once. With one leg rigid, unable to bear my weight, I had to go very slowly. One hand up, then the other, then haul up the rest of me and anchor my one good foot, then repeat. I progressed by centimeters. In the utter darkness I couldn't tell how far I'd gone, and I didn't dare turn on my suit light for fear of attracting attention.

It took me about an hour to climb that thirty-meter shaft. The darkness above was so profound that I could only tell I had reached the surface because my hand felt the edge of the pit. I pulled myself up until I could rest my torso on the ground and roll away from the edge.

I wasn't sure if I could walk, and I didn't want to risk falling again, so I crawled. I waggled my head until I could tell which way was north, and then I just started crawling. I couldn't bend my bad leg, so I was dragging it along.

The suit protected me as well as it could. My hands and knees were bruised, but not scraped. My face was running with sweat inside my hood; eventually I gave up and retracted it. I might be picking up some unknown spore or virus, but the sensation of a cool night breeze on my face was worth it.

Besides, I figured I probably wouldn't make it to the elevator anyway. So why not be comfortable?

I stopped often to rest. I had no idea how far I'd gotten from the dome. The night was full of noises, and all of them sounded like enemies waiting to ambush me, or unknown monsters. I kept as quiet as I could, but inside my head I blamed Agha for getting me into this, and cursed him for leaving. I never cursed Okeola. I kept finding reasons to hope she would save me. After all, I was the good one, the loyal one, the one who followed instructions. Wouldn't she send a rescue party?

I think I slept once or twice, because the time sometimes passed awfully quickly. According to my timer there were thirty-two hours left in my launch window—assuming Agha and the ship weren't long gone already.

The lights came on exactly twelve hours after they went out, pitch dark to full light in just a second. I had to cover my eyes for a minute or two before I dared look around. The forest was suddenly loud with bird cries, startling me. For a moment I thought the club-wielding killers had found me. Then I realized it was actual birds, greeting the day with an earsplitting chorus.

I'd managed to drag myself about half a kilometer in the dark. I was on one side of the road going north, and at the moment nobody was around. My suit was still green, but if anybody wanted to follow me it wouldn't matter—there was a clear trail of flattened weeds and disturbed soil stretching back from my feet to that pit. Even a post-sapient could follow it.

I spotted a fallen branch amid the dead leaves and ground cover, and crawled over to it. A few cuts with my multipurpose tool and I had a makeshift staff. That let me haul myself to my feet, and I began hobbling north.

I hadn't gone far when I saw a shaggy figure stand up about twenty meters ahead of me. It was a man with long tangled hair and a matted beard. A badly healed scar ran across his chest. He'd been lying in the foliage next to the road. He didn't start shrieking, or raise his club. Instead he approached me, head cocked curiously. I didn't move, and held up my free hand, palm out.

When the scarred man got within about ten meters of where I stood, he made a reedy high-pitched sound. It didn't sound long or complex enough to be real communication, but he looked at me expectantly. I didn't reply, so he repeated it, a little louder and maybe a little angrily.

"It's okay," I said, keeping my voice even and nonthreatening. "I'm your friend. This is all a big misunderstanding."

The sound of my words enraged the man with the scar. He went from wary and curious to bared-teeth fury before I finished speaking. Brandishing his club at me, he gave a loud series of shrieks. From elsewhere in the jungle I heard answering cries coming closer.

I had no idea what to do. When I tried to hobble around the scarred man he moved to block me, but he didn't attack. He just kept up that endless, repetitive noise.

Soon three more emerged from the jungle and took up the cry. They circled me, angry but fearful. Finally one of the new arrivals took a swing at me with his club. More or less by reflex I blocked it with my walking stick, and he dropped back a couple of meters. Then my suit went rigid on my left shoulder as a blow from the one behind me sent me staggering.

I swung my stick around me and got my suit hood up and sealed. The four of them danced around me, never ceasing their monotonous chatter.

Then that jerk with the scar swung his club at my one good leg. My suit went rigid to protect me, but that threw me off balance and I toppled to the ground. In an instant they were on top of me, raining down blows. My suit could only blunt the impacts so much. They might not be able to smash my skull but they could rattle my brains around inside it.

I flailed with my stick, and felt it connect a couple of times. At least they'd have some bruises to remember me by. One of them got my stick away from me so I curled up as best I could as they pounded me.

And then it all stopped. The shrieks faded away into the distance.

I waited for a couple of seconds and then looked up. A band of people painted with stripes were hurrying toward me, armed with spears. And in the lead was Agha.

~

My next clear memory is of being spoon-fed broth by Niwa. That was the name of the girl we'd met earlier. Her uncle Mizhi was one of the leaders of the Shiig tribe, who stopped by to see me and make friendly gestures.

They spoke Woshing, sort of. The accent was very weird, and there were some changes in grammar. More importantly, they could *read and write* Woshing, so whenever Agha and I couldn't understand something we'd scrawl characters in the dirt and read Mizhi's answer.

"My folk have kept the old tongue," he told Agha and me. "We have books and tools, and try to keep the old works going—those which keep the world alive. All who become men and women must learn to read the manuals."

They didn't have any storage devices. The maintenance manuals were hand-inscribed on graphene sheets, which they kept in a diamond box in the home of the eldest member of the tribe. All the Shiig lived on an island in the middle of the flooded section. There were about a hundred of them, including children.

I said I needed to rest, and waited until Niwa and Mizhi left before speaking to Agha. "Why are you still here? There's only thirty hours left."

He looked genuinely surprised. "When I got away from the dome I saw a light. It was Niwa and her family, getting Gan's body. That's the dead guy, her brother Gan. They were scared, of course, but when I tried translating to Woshing, one of them caught a few words of what I was saying. I explained about you being stuck in the pit, and as soon as the lights came on, we came to get you. I'm pretty amazed you got out of the pit by yourself."

"It wasn't easy. I thought you had gone back to the ship."

He didn't say anything for maybe half a minute. "I thought about it," he said at last. "But, well, when Niwa asked about you I couldn't just lie to her. So I told them you were stuck, and they agreed to come help get you out."

There was something going on that I didn't quite grasp. But I was too tired and stressed to make sense of it all, so I tried to focus on the most important question. "When can we leave?"

"Oh, I thought we'd stay here overnight and head for the hub at first light tomorrow. Langtar's on a twenty-four-hour cycle, so there will be plenty of time for us to get to the ship. You're in no shape to go anywhere right now."

I tried to argue, but it's hard to convince someone you're fit to travel when you can't even sit up on your own. So I had broth, slept, slept some more, and finally felt strong enough to get up right around nightfall.

The Shiig tribe had a big communal dinner with a bonfire just after dark. I don't know if they did that every night or whether it was a special gala in our honor, but everyone seemed jolly enough.

At dinner I was on Mizhi's right and Agha was on his left, but Agha was definitely the center of attention. I was still too tired and banged-up to compete. I couldn't avoid noticing that Niwa stuck to him like a meteor patch the whole evening.

When everyone was done eating and the fire had burned out, the whole community went to bed—except for two of the young men, who stayed on watch with spears in case animals or enemies came in the night.

Agha and I bedded down on the ground next to the glowing coals of the fire. Niwa hung around for a while until her uncle rather sharply called her inside. Only then could Agha and I talk together.

"Eto, are you going to put in a salvage claim?"

"On Okeola's behalf, yes. It's pretty obvious there's nobody on board in control of Langtar's systems. These guys may be able to read the manuals but they're stuck in a swamp. By any definition this hab's a derelict."

"And what's she going to do with the claim?"

I shrugged, and then winced at the bruises and strained muscles the shrug revealed. "My guess is that she'll sell it. Okeola always needs foreign exchange cash. She can't export much. This would be a huge windfall."

"The purchaser would have to catch Langtar right away."

"I'd expect them to send a single replicator on a fast rocket. It could latch on, start converting Langtar's mass into more replicators and rockets, then use the atmosphere as propellant to shoot all the valuable bits back to the inner system."

"And the Shiig people get consumed along with everything else."

"Agha, there's a quadrillion humans in the solar system, and we're just baseline intellects. Who's going to care if a hundred people get misclassified as post-sapient?"

"There must be *something* we can do. We've got tools, we've got our own knowledge. We could change everything."

"We are going back to the *Bold Venture* as soon as it gets light, and then we are getting the hell out of this place forever." To reassure him, I added, "Besides, Langtar may be out of range of any salvage mission already. Even if Okeola does make a claim, it'll be a couple of millennia before anything happens."

I hesitated before adding, "There's something else to think about. Langtar's got magnetic scoops on the outside, made to sweep up hydrogen when it passes near the Sun. They didn't deploy this time. How long has it been since Langtar refueled itself? Someday the lights will go out and everybody will die. That could happen in a thousand years or it could happen tomorrow."

He nodded, looking glum. "I guess you're right. I'll try to explain it to Niwa."

The next morning he went out with her to spear fish and break the news. I didn't hear what he said to her, but I watched their conversation. They stood together at the water's edge, and she had one arm around him, looking proud and a little possessive. He turned and took her hands and they stood facing each other. He spoke, and then she went away crying.

I had an easier time with Niwa's uncle Mizhi. "Agha and I must go away again," I told him, and he nodded.

"I thought so," he said. "You wish to go home. That is best. Do you think either of you will come back?"

"I don't know. This place—Langtar—is heading away from the Sun. It will be hard to reach again."

"I am sad to hear you must go, but that will pass. Now all will know that the manuals are true, not fables. The others"—he gestured at the world beyond the swamp—"abandoned the wisdom of the manuals. They have grown dull-minded, and they fear and hate all who do not echo their calls. The tale of your visit will inspire the Shiig forever."

A dozen Shiig took us in canoes to the edge of the swamp. Even Niwa came along. She stayed at the back of one boat until Agha and I were saying goodbye to her uncle for the last time. Just before we turned to leave, she flung herself at Agha and gave him a kiss that must have lasted a full rotation.

We made good progress at first. The trail led to the old road, and we followed that straight toward the ancient elevator shaft rising out of the jungle ahead. I suppose we should have been more cautious.

Three of the "others" caught us by surprise, not far from the old building at the bottom of the shaft. They had spears and clubs, and kept quiet and hidden until we were just a few meters away. Then, with an eerie chorus of shrieks and birdcalls, they burst from cover and threw their spears.

Agha jumped in front of me, and one of the spears gashed his scalp above the right ear.

A second later they were on us. I got knocked down again, but Agha dodged aside and stayed on his feet. He picked up one of the spears they had thrown at us and jabbed it at the man battering at me with a club. It wasn't a sim, or a safe sporting weapon. He actually stuck the sharp diamond point of the spear into the man's body, and the man made a loud shriek and began to bleed bright red blood.

He scrambled off of me and away from Agha, and I got to my feet. The three of them hung back, looking at the two of us.

Most of their attention was on the sparkly diamond spearpoint, which Agha kept pointed at them. We backed away from them cautiously, and they didn't follow.

I felt so relieved I gave a whoop. We were free!

My mood lasted about five minutes—the time it took us to get through the jungle to the base of the elevator shaft. I spotted them first: four more men, all armed with diamond-tipped spears. They must have heard us because all four turned toward us right then.

We ducked behind a fallen tree. In our green suits we blended right in. But I could see the men craning their necks and moving from side to side, trying to spot us but not daring to leave their post. Behind us we could hear the calls of the men who'd ambushed us.

Then I heard someone moving through the woods. Agha and I went flat on the ground, letting the waist-high plants hide us. Two of the ones we'd met earlier passed by, scanning the ground as if looking for tracks. The one Agha had stabbed wasn't with them, but it hardly mattered. Six to two was pretty bad odds, even with our suits to protect us.

"Where's your spear?" I whispered to Agha.

"I threw it away."

"Why?"

"I didn't think I'd need it, okay? What can you see?"

I sent out my remote, keeping it high to avoid notice. The squad blocking our way had brought bundles of supplies with them. We'd get hungry before they did—and if we didn't get up that shaft before teatime, we'd never get away.

"I wonder how Niwa's people are doing," said Agha.

"They'll be fine."

"Maybe we should go back and check on them."

"They'll be *fine*. We should think about how to get rid of these guys."

We crouched in silence for a time, then Agha spoke again. "Okay, I know what to do. I'll draw them off so you can get to the ladder."

"But how will—" I stopped. "You're staying?"

He nodded.

"For *her?*"

"Not just for Niwa. I can *do* something here. Help her people, maybe even figure out how to activate the hab's control systems. I can do something that *matters.*"

"It's just one hab. There's a billion others."

He shrugged. "Go on. Go!" He got to his feet and set his suit to high-visibility orange. A moment later we heard the bird cries approaching, and Agha dashed off to the south, away from me and away from the ladder.

Five of the hunters went past but didn't spot me. The sixth stayed by their camp, but with my remote to watch him and my suit to hide me I was able to circle around to the other side, then I crept to the ladder and started climbing before he noticed me.

I climbed faster than I've ever climbed before, until I was sure I was out of reach of his spear. At the second platform I stopped to rest, and sent out my remote for one last sweep. I couldn't find Agha, or the hunters chasing him either. I guess he got away.

There's not much else to tell. I reached the hub and found my way back to the *Bold Venture*. I spent sixteen years in stasis and woke up in time to look down on the cloud tops of Jupiter's south pole, then used my last fuel reserve to dock at Juren. It took me another couple of years to get home to Okeola.

I never did plant a transponder on Langtar. After all, there was definitely one person inside it capable of operating minimal-standard tech. Okeola received my report without comment.

I'm back in Okeola now, and I hardly ever think about Agha anymore.

I wonder if he ever thinks of me?

DARCIE LITTLE BADGER

Endosymbiosis

Darcie Little Badger

There were fossils, minerals, and plaster dinosaur bones displayed in the grand entry of Smilodon Hall, remnants of a larger collection that had been scattered among museums after the university cut storage to install more offices in the Department of Earth Sciences. The building, with its vaulted ceilings, white limestone walls, and relics encased in glass, reminded Jul of a cathedral. She stood in front of the fossilized remains of two fifty-million-year-old fish. They were labeled with yellowing index cards:

(a) *Diplomystus*, Eocene Green River Formation. Cause of death: choking.

(b) *Diplomystus*, Eocene Green River Formation. Cause of death: being eaten.

That's a glass-half-full or glass-half-empty situation, ain't it? Jul thought. Either the fossil was a permanent reminder of the worst decision *Diplomystus* (a) ever made, or it was a tribute to the

195

strength of *Diplomystus* (b), an Eocene David that used its own dying body to take down Goliath.

There was a hint of movement in Jul's peripheral vision, and then the display-case glass reflected not one but two faces: Jul's round, plump, and brown face, and the long, gaunt, white face of Boris, another grad student in Professor Milligan's lab.

"Another late night for you?" Boris asked.

"I need to discuss something with Milligan," Jul explained. "What about you?"

"Going to the bar with the others. See you on the boat Tuesday."

Once, Boris might have invited Jul for drinks with him and the other grad students, but he no longer bothered. Logically, Jul knew why the invitations had stopped. Too many *no, thank yous*.

She did slightly miss the gesture though.

With that thought, Jul exited the mini museum in Smilodon Hall. First as an undergrad and then as a grad student, she'd known Milligan for seven years, yet Jul always felt nervous before she knocked on his office door. Like she was a saleswoman pushing a magazine subscription nobody wanted. Jul couldn't shake the feeling that, every time she had a meeting with Professor Milligan, she had to sell the idea that she belonged in a scientific lab.

"Come in," the professor shouted. Jul entered the office and, after closing the door behind her, sat in a plush faux leather chair in front of a heavy oak desk. The boxy room was windowless, but several paintings and photos of the sea hung on the walls, giving the illusion of space. As always, Jul found her attention drawn to a giclée print above Milligan's computer. The print depicted a lonely beach at sunset. In the impressionist style, an indistinct suggestion of a person was wading into the shallows. Something about the image simultaneously enthralled and troubled Jul. Perhaps it was the blankness of the bather's face; it resembled a mirage. Or maybe it was the wayward paint stroke at the edge of the horizon. A darkness that hinted at something approaching from the open ocean.

Something big.

"What's up, Julie?" Milligan asked, staring at a table of numbers on his computer screen. "Hmm. This model output is wonky." He was the kind of middle-aged professor who wore T-shirts, jeans, and Crocs to lectures, had a constant five-o'clock shadow, and was well-liked by most students, despite rigorous grading standards.

"I found something interesting," Jul said. "Confusing. Are you sure the Abyssal Pit is, well, old? Any chance it formed within the last twenty years?"

"That's really unlikely," Milligan said. "What's this about?"

"Just. Well. I was reviewing old reports, and in 1997, a NOAA survey vessel passed over the area—I mean, exact coordinates—where we identified the Abyssal Pit formation, and they didn't notice anything. Just typical flat topography. It's almost like . . ."

"Like it's possible for scientists to make mistakes?" He chuckled. "Don't stress. Maybe it's new. Maybe the old data is wrong. We'll know more next week. You know. When we visit the pit in a ship from the twenty-first century. But. You know what? Go ahead and write up a report about that NOAA stuff. I can review it over the weekend."

"Ah, sorry," Jul said. "I'm visiting family. Gotta drive home tonight."

Milligan put his hands up, as if surrendering to the bad-idea police. "No worries. Enjoy your time together. There won't be a chance for that when you're in the middle of the ocean. Oh! And Jul?"

"Yes?" she asked.

"Remember to pack a toothbrush. On my first oceanographic cruise, I had to rub soap on my teeth with a pipette-cleaning brush for two weeks. It was a safety violation, but you get desperate out there."

She smiled and promised, "I'll remember." Three tooth-brushes—a primary and two spares—were already tucked in the duffel bag she'd packed days ago.

It was eleven p.m. when Jul pulled into the driveway of her family home, but all the windows were bright. She wondered who'd waited up. Her parents? Her sister? Her brother-in-law? Her grandmother? Then, the high-pitched voice of her seven-year-old nephew, Reggie, called out, "She's here!" With a thud, the front door burst open, and Reggie ran across the porch, hopped down the steps, and jogged in place, lit by the beams of Jul's lights. He clutched a hammerhead shark plushie. The kid probably picked that toy from his menagerie of plushies just to make Auntie Julie the Oceanographer happy.

"Hey, Reg!" Jul stepped from her car and spread her arms; Reggie almost knocked her over with the enthusiasm of his hug.

"Why are you awake so late?" she asked.

From the doorway, Jul's twin sister—resplendent in a mois-turizing paper face mask and blue cotton robe—said, "He traded me a clean room for the chance to stay awake 'til you got here."

"Aw! You cleaned your room for me?"

Reggie shook the hammerhead up and down, making his toy nod its T-shaped, googly-eyed head.

"Come inside," Jul's sister said. "Grandma made you tamales."

Later, after a midnight supper, Jul volunteered to tell Reggie a bedtime story and tuck him in for the night, but all he wanted to talk about was, in his words, "Why do you have to go on a boat all month, and what are you studying, anyway?"

In his bedroom, Jul disentangled an oval loop of Hot Wheels racetracks from a twelve-gallon box of toys. "Where are the cars?" she asked. Reggie rolled his eyes to the ceiling and smiled with the edges of his lips turned down; she knew that expression.

"Reg, what did you do?"

In response, he crossed the room in four quick hops and knelt beside his bed. With a sweep of his arm, Reggie pushed a tangled mess of dirty clothes, cobwebs, and more toys—*god*, Jul thought, *there aren't enough Tupperware boxes in the county to hold all those*—into the light.

"Cleaned your room, huh?" she asked.

"It counts!"

"I won't tell." She filled the racetrack with cars, fitting them bumper to bumper until they resembled a ring-shaped train with no beginning or end. "Come here," Jul said. "What happens when I push one of these cars?"

Instead of answering aloud, Reggie sat cross-legged beside her and gently pushed a gray truck forward. The ring of Hot Wheels went round and round. After a couple loops, he concluded, "They all move."

"Something similar happens in the ocean. Water pushing water across the world. We call it the global conveyor belt."

"That's what you're studying?"

"Not really. Pretend that the empty space in the middle of the racetrack is a deep, twisted cave at the bottom of the ocean." She flicked a red race car off the tracks; it lay on its back, plastic wheels on rod-shaped axles spinning, slowing, and finally stopping. Jul pushed the gray truck again, and the ring of cars orbited the metaphorical cave. "See?" she asked. "The ocean keeps moving and changing, but anything stuck in that hole—like the red Corvette—is sorta protected. My boss used his machines to look at the Pacific floor, and under miles of water, he found . . . well, it's probably the deepest, most twisted cave on Earth, but we're not certain about anything yet. We call it the Pacific Abyssal Pit."

Reggie flicked another car off the tracks. "What's in the cave?" he asked.

"Ancient water!" She pantomimed widemouthed disbelief, because Reggie was grinning like she was joking. "I'm serious," Jul said. "The history of our planet is written in the composition of

199

old sea and stone." Reggie stared. She was losing him. A scientist's worst nightmare: civilian antipathy. If she could not inspire wonder in the heart of a precocious child, who could she inspire? "We may find life too!" she added. "Deep-sea crabs and worms and other, stranger things."

"Stranger how?" he asked.

"Well. There are these deep-sea tube worms with long white stalks ending in feathery red tufts. Kinda look like flowers. They grow from the deep-sea floor, where there's no sunlight. One day, scientists picked a tube worm and cut it open. It bled this bright red stuff made of hemoglobin, just like our blood!"

"Did they kill the worm?" Reggie asked. "Did it die?!"

"Um. Not sure," she lied. "Maybe they sewed it up and replanted it. That's what I'd do, anyway."

"Oh, good."

"The scientists went, 'What use is all this red stuff to a tube?' See, in humans, blood carries oxygen from the lungs to other parts of the body. The tube worm does something similar. In order to survive on the bottom of the ocean, this clever little guy invites special bacteria into its body. The bacteria grow and make carbon food for the tube worm, and in return, the tube worm 'breathes' through its red flowery parts and carries oxygen to the bacteria. The different species depend on each other. It's beautiful."

"Hmm." Reggie snatched the car from the center of the tracks and hugged it against his chest. "Be careful, Auntie."

"I will," she promised. "Now, time for bed."

～

Tuesday morning, Jul arrived at the docks in a maroon sweater over a T-shirt and khaki pants that could be converted into shorts with a couple of well-placed zippers. She double-checked that her spiral laboratory notebooks were secured in a waterproof bag and chased a pair of anti-nausea pills with a bottle of water.

Jul carried her luggage to the research vessel, the R/V *Orion*, at the end of the university dock. Gulf water sloshed gently against wooden pillars coated with barnacles and tunicates. The humid air was thick with a distinctive ocean scent that she knew to be dimethyl sulfide, a compound emitted by microscopic marine organisms. Every time she smelled it, she remembered her first encounter with the ocean. Seventeen. Returning home from a funeral with her parents and sister. One of her cousins had overdosed. For four hours, everybody traveled in silence, not even listening to the radio. Then, her father turned off the highway and drove along the edge of the Gulf. All that blue was the strangest thing Jul had ever witnessed. She rolled down her window and breathed deep. It felt like her first breath.

Later, when Jul's high school class read *The Odyssey*, she understood on an instinctual level the power of the siren's call. She felt it, a magnetic longing for all the knowledge in the ocean. She pulled all-nighters for the call. Went into student-loan debt for the call. Moved three hours away from her family and suffered from incurable homesickness for the call. Perhaps all oceanographers, to some extent, felt sirens beckoning.

Professor Milligan was already waiting at the end of the dock. He raised a hand, and as Jul nodded in acknowledgment, her cell phone rang. She paused, dropping her duffel bag to answer the call from her mother.

"Hi, Momma!" she said. Smiling in anticipation.

And then no longer smiling.

"Oh, God," Jul said.

She sat, crushing her duffel bag under her weight. Holding her phone against her ear as she bowed her head until her forehead was inches from her knees. "Reggie, Reggie, Reggie," she said, as if she could save him by repeating his name. One shouldn't say the names of the dead. Especially those lost early. Too early. Too violently. "What happened?" she asked. "Will he . . ."

Professor Milligan and Boris were now standing beside her, posing questions with their eyes. Ten minutes later, wilting further beneath their attention, Jul said, "Momma, I'll call back in a minute."

The professor didn't wait for her to hang up before he asked, "Is everything all right?"

"My nephew was in an accident." Her voice jumped an octave, pulled taut by fear. "He was leaving the school bus, and this car . . . it didn't even slow down."

"No," Boris hissed. "I'm so sorry. How bad are the injuries?"

According to her mother, Reggie had broken both his legs. A cracked hip. One ruptured kidney. Survivable, if there weren't complications, but he'd suffer.

"Bad, but . . . it could be much worse." She had to be with Reggie, her sister, her parents. Jul couldn't step on that ship.

"I need to leave," she said, resenting fate not only for hurting Reggie but also for stealing the accomplishment she'd worked so long and hard to achieve. Seven years of studying, research, and ramen noodle suppers had brought her to this dock. Another few hours, and she would have been beyond the reach of bad news. God, Jul felt monstrously selfish for mourning a dream when her little nephew was in pain.

It was what it was. Jul picked up her duffel bag and started walking back to the parking lot.

"You can't," Professor Milligan said.

She stopped. "What?"

Milligan jogged to her side, putting a hand on Jul's shoulder. "He's not dying, right?"

She shook her head. Nothing was certain, but nothing was ever certain. Hence gravity being considered a theory. She had to believe that Reggie would live like she had to believe that, if she jumped, the Earth would pull her down again.

"This is not an easy lesson," Milligan said, "but you need to understand that if you interrupt million-dollar research every time a second cousin or grandmother has a health crisis, zero science would get done. There's no time to replace you."

"Reggie needs me," she said.

"Do what you gotta do, then. It's your choice. But . . . look, I stuck my neck out for you, Jul. I turned down other students— postdocs—who applied for your spot on this journey."

Boris said nothing. Only looked away.

"This research will make your career," Professor Milligan continued, "but if you leave now, you'll have no thesis data." The implication was clear: *And no thesis advisor.* "Let the doctors help your nephew. He'll get excellent care. There's nothing you can do for him. But I—we—depend on you."

Now, Boris nodded in agreement.

Two hours later, Jul stood on the upper deck of the *Orion* and watched the continental edge recede with distance. She gripped the upper rail on the bulwark tight, clinging to the ship until the temptation to throw herself into the water and swim home was extinguished by the ultimate loss of the land to the sea.

~

Jul hadn't expected a Carnival cruise, but the ship was much smaller than she'd anticipated. Thirty-six scientists from five research groups shared two labs and one computer station on the R/V *Orion*. They tried to minimize crowding by working in shifts, but the internet-linked computers were rarely free.

Fortunately, because of time zone differences, Jul could Skype her family at night (middle-of-the-ocean time), when it was morning in Texas. That's what she was doing on day seven of the cruise, as the ship approached the Abyssal Pit. In spurts, footage of Reggie played across her computer screen. He was in a hospital bed, surrounded by plushies—mostly wolves and frogs, his favorite animals. And the hammerhead shark.

Reggie was trying to tell her a story about one of his teachers, but the slow connection garbled everything, making his animated hand gestures choppy and his voice robotic. She waited until he settled back against the pile of white hospital pillows to say, "You need rest. We can talk again tomorrow, okay, Reg? I love—"

A young woman, an intern from a French biology lab who'd been reviewing videos on the other side of the computer station, cried out. At the same time, the Skype call lost connection.

"Are you okay?" Jul asked, standing. Loane was a slight woman with dark-blond hair restrained in a messy bun. She slept under Jul's upper bunk in their shared cabin.

"I saw a person-shaped thing," Loane said, pointing at her computer screen. "It ran in front of the camera."

A few days before the cruise, the French group had sent a remotely operated vehicle—ROV—with a deep-sea camera to the region near the Abyssal Pit. They were interested in the crabs that lived around the hole. Unfortunately, the ROV could not venture into the pit itself. The machine might introduce contaminants and disturb any existing stratification. Plus, the shape of the pit was not fully resolved. That's where Jul's lab—and their mapping technology—came into play. Although they had a general concept of the formation's twisted shape, the details were still fuzzy, especially with depth.

"Can I see?" Jul asked, leaning over Loane's shoulder. The video currently showed a swath of brown sea floor and lots of nothing else. However, a hazy murk of sediments was suspended in the water, as if recently disturbed.

"Sure." Loane skipped the video back thirty seconds. The water was clear. The frame empty. A moment passed and then . . .

"Holy smokes," Jul whispered, her tone reverent, as if she meant it when she said "holy." In the distance, from right to left, a woman-like figure ran across the sea floor; she wore bright, billowing white, and her steps were rapid and smooth. The figure's indistinct head swayed from side to side as she moved, and her arms were tucked daintily against her chest, the same way Reggie tucked his arms when he pretended to hop like a bunny.

"Can you pause it on her—it?"

Loane did as asked, and they both leaned close to the screen. The figure resembled something from an impressionist painting, the undetailed suggestion of a human.

"Is this the highest resolution you have?" Jul asked.

"Unfortunately, yes," she said. "What is it? A fish? Could be walking on pectoral fins."

"In my professional opinion as a physical oceanographer, it's a 'deep-sea weirdo.'"

There were windows along every wall of the computer station, which was on the second deck of the R/V. Jul noticed a flurry of activity outside. Crew and scientists, all wearing bright orange helmets and protective gloves and vests, were preparing equipment. The omnipresent *chg chg chg* of the ship motor decreased in volume and then stopped. That meant one thing: "I think we just reached the Abyssal Pit," she said.

"Jul?" Loane asked.

"Hmm?"

"Who were you talking to earlier? Is that boy your son?"

"My nephew," Jul explained. "He was in an accident and needs surgery tomorrow, so . . ." She hesitated. Although she and Loane had shared a closet-sized cabin for several days, crammed together like sardines in a can, they hadn't really talked. "I'm just very worried."

Loane smiled, brushing away the negative energy with a swipe of her hand. "Oh, he'll be fine," she said. "Surgery is nothing these days. Before this cruise, they took my tonsils." She opened her mouth and stuck out her tongue.

"Glad you recovered," Jul said.

The computer station door swung open, and Boris peeked in. "Ah, there you are! They're going to deploy the CTD soon. Come down and watch, will you? Professor Milligan wants us to have first dibs on the deep-water samples."

In the liminal period between late night and early morning, every conscious scientist gathered on the lower deck, preparing to drop the oceanographic version of an all-purpose tool: the CTD rosette. Thirty 15-liter Niskin bottles—long, thin tanks for collecting seawater—were secured in a ring by a bright yellow metal frame. The device was taller, wider, and many times heavier than the biggest person Jul knew, her uncle Chuck. So it took four individuals and a prodigious system of cables, ropes, and pulleys to raise the rosette and dangle it over the side of the R/V.

It would be lowered four thousand meters, collecting water samples and data along the way. Then, as soon as the CTD rosette returned to the ship, like the starting pistol of a race, the real work would begin.

The CTD rosette plunged into the water, and the moment it was submerged, the surface ocean began to glow an eerie, gentle blue. Orbs of bioluminescent radiance swam within the water column. Some were dim with depth. Others pulsed. Were they squid? Balls of plankton? "Beautiful," Jul said, in awe of the moment's strangeness. She breathed the salt-spray air, trying to recapture the moment the ocean bewitched her. Instead, she remembered the bright yellow jungle gym in the park near home. How she and her sister used to play there when they were girls. Swinging, climbing, pretending to be surrounded by quicksand.

A voice called to her. Reggie. He sang, "Baby shark, baby shark, baby shark." Where was he? In the water? Playing on the yellow frame that encased the CTD rosette?

Jul tried to step forward, but Professor Milligan blocked her way. He was talking quickly. About what? Nitrates, oxygen, sampling. To Jul, his voice sounded as garbled and confusing as chatter filtered through bad internet reception. Why couldn't she concentrate?

"Julie!" Milligan said, grabbing her arm and squeezing tight enough to bruise. "Pay attention! This is important! Our research is important!"

She shoved him away, shocked into alertness by the pain above her elbow. "That hurt!"

Milligan seemed dazed, swaying with the rocking ship. "No," he said. "What? No, it didn't."

Jul looked up, surprised by the brightness of the sky, which was on the cusp of dawn. An hour had passed since the CTD dropped; how had she lost so much time? There were only a few people on the deck with her. Milligan. A couple chemists. A deckhand. The blue lights in the water were gone.

Suddenly, as if the world's biggest fish had swallowed the CTD rosette and pulled, the ship rolled to the starboard side, and the rosette cable strained against its pulley. Jul managed to grab a handle protruding from the wall behind her, but the professor fell and slid, pulled downslope toward the bulwark of the ship.

Something had to give. Either the ship would roll, or the cable would break.

Jul wasn't sure which scenario frightened her the most, as cables were serpentine guillotines.

CRACK.

The cable snapped and whipped back.

~

The pain in Jul's head, an intense ache that throbbed with every heartbeat, was migraine-level bad. She shifted, trying to unstick her face from the bumpy metal deck; she was glued by her cheek to the floor. Upon sitting up, she confirmed that the sticky substance was dried blood. Hers, judging by the ache in her head and the sharper pain that arced from her cheek to jawline. She removed her helmet and gingerly prodded her face, flinching as her fingers traced a fresh gouge left by the recoiling cable.

Could have been worse, Jul thought, rubbing her uninjured neck for reassurance. She stood, grimacing at a third layer of pain. One side of her body was badly sunburned, which meant she'd been lying outside for hours.

The sun was high, but was it morning or afternoon? Jul could not see anyone else outside, so she staggered to the nearest door, which led to one of the labs, and wrenched it open.

The interior was dim, lit only by natural light spilling through portholes and the artificial glow of a screen that was partially obscured by a huddle of five people. Their poses reminded Jul of a Renaissance painting. Loane sat on a plastic chair in the middle of the group, her hands playing across the ROV control panel. Boris and Milligan stood to Loane's right, while two biologists, a white woman with a long gray braid and a white man with a thick black mustache, stood to Loane's left: all four professors curled around the intern.

"Milligan," Jul said. He didn't seem to hear her. "Frank!" She took a step closer. "Please. I need a doctor."

"Are you watching?" Professor Milligan asked. He didn't look at Jul. Nobody turned. Their eyes were all trained on the screen. "We're streaming video from the pit!"

"I might be dying," Jul mumbled, but despite that, she was curious. What would they discover in that twisted, impossible place? The ROV was sinking quickly, and the water flowing past its camera was empty, except for flecks of white detritus that resembled snow.

"We're the first humans to witness this corner of the planet," the mustachioed biologist said.

Through a haze of pain and fascination, Jul recalled something important. "Why?" she asked. "Why is the robot ... why are you sending it down there? We can't disturb the site. How do you even know its shape?"

Boris shoved a piece of paper at Jul; because his eyes were still trained on the screen, the corner of the paper nearly poked the gored side of her face. Flinching back, she snatched it from the air and looked down.

He'd given her a hastily compiled rendering of the Abyssal Pit. It was sloppy but still more detailed than any previous image reconstructed from long-distance data. Boris and Professor Milligan had been busy while she lay bleeding on the deck.

The pit started as a straight drop from the sea floor. Then, it widened into a vast, egg-shaped chamber before narrowing again and veering to the right, left, right, left, and right again. Squiggling back and forth, its diameter decreasing.

Mouth. Esophagus. Stomach. Intestines.

A digestive system.

In unison, her colleagues went, "Ooooh!" Their voices were high with the rapture of discovery. The ROV had finally descended into the stomach-cavern, and its spotlight illuminated expansive structures of rock, plastic scraps, metal, and a white substance that resembled coral skeletons. The buildings protruded from the concave walls, floor, and ceiling of the stomach-cavern, like an impossible Escher town. Similar to swiss cheese, each building was filled with holes.

Immediately, a human-shaped thing with a flowing white dress and the suggestion of a head and arms swam toward the camera. It reached for the ROV, and in that moment, Jul could see the real animal beneath the mimicry. A large cephalopod-like creature that, to her untrained eye, resembled a fusion of *Thaumoctopus mimicus* and *Tremoctopus gelatus*, the mimic and the blanket, two very different types of octopi. As if able to read Jul's mind and no longer concerned about hiding its true nature, the creature changed color, erasing the chromatophore-painted image of a woman that had been splayed across its skin. Instead, it turned bright white. The sudden shift overwhelmed the ROV's camera, and before the machine could adjust, it was wrapped in four long arms and—

Two words flashed onto the screen: SIGNAL LOST

Everyone but Jul groaned. "Don't worry," Loane said. "There's a second ROV."

"Set it up!" the braid woman said.

Jul backed away. There was a little infirmary on the ship. She needed to get there and find painkillers and bandages. Then, she had to send an emergency signal to call outside help, because Dr. Milligan and the others were acting like they'd been hypnotized by a stage magician who commanded them to "Partake in bad science and otherwise be completely useless."

She made it to the area of the ship with the cabins before succumbing to an intense pulse of dizziness. Fainting, Jul managed to slide gently to the ground, using the wall—they called it a bulwark on a ship, didn't they?—for support.

Over the next few hours, slipping in and out of consciousness, she reached the infirmary by crawling on her belly, drank fresh water, wiped the blood from her face and tried to bandage her injury, and vomited at least twice. Jul saw no sign of the captain, first mate, or other crew. Where had they gone?

She remembered, then, feeling an illogical but powerful longing to jump into the ocean and find her singing nephew.

Jul briefly considered lashing herself to a mast with strips of bandages, like Odysseus had when his ship passed the island of the sirens. When they sang to him, enchanting him with the promise to share all the knowledge of the world, the restraints prevented him from swimming to his death.

But Odysseus had had a whole crew to help him. Jul was alone.

There was an emergency beacon on deck, near the inflatable life rafts. If she could reach it . . .

Jul looked out the single porthole in the infirmary and saw a calm sea and sunset-flushed horizon. She remembered the hauntingly beautiful blue lights that had swirled near the R/V. Many bioluminescent cephalopods were nocturnal, tucked away on the sea floor by day and making the vertical migration to the surface ocean by night. How long would it take for the sirens to ascend four thousand meters? Were they already coming? Would their call become louder as the distance between her feet and their song decreased? Could she shut them out by covering her ears, or did they speak a different way? Telepathically, maybe. Yes, that must be it. That's why everyone was acting so weird. But how was telepathy even possible? Jul wanted to understand. Maybe, if she returned to the lab . . .

Jul pressed a thumb into the cut across her cheek, using the pain to shock her into a clearheaded state. Enough questions.

Get the beacon. Call help. Hide. Return home.

More than anything, that's what she wanted: home.

In anticipation of the night, a vast dome emerged from the distant ocean. Big as an island. Its color and texture the consistency of dry magmatic rock. Jul witnessed it through the porthole. Were those monstrous eyespots hidden between sharp, jutting outcrops of rock? She screamed once, quickly, and then ran to the door.

The ship's rocking, once gentle enough to soothe an infant to sleep, intensified. Jul pinballed back and forth between the walls of the narrow corridor connecting the infirmary to the first-deck door. She absorbed the impact with her shoulders and made it outside. Scrambled to unlatch the thermos-shaped distress beacon from its cradle. She put her finger over the device's activation button.

No. She couldn't call more ships to the feeding frenzy. That would be too cruel! At the very least, Jul had to wait until daybreak to call for help.

"Jul!" Professor Milligan called. She glanced up and gasped.

"Professor, no!"

Milligan was climbing over the bulwark. Poised to jump. He pointed at the living island. "It's our abyss! You were right; it wasn't here twenty years ago. It can move! So sorry for doubting you."

"Apology accepted. Now, get down from there!"

211

He smiled. "It'll be fine. The abyss doesn't eat people; it coexists with us. Lives in a symbiotic relationship with us. We've been chosen." The surface of the living island writhed with cephalopod things. They swayed, as if dancing, capturing both the movement and appearance of humans almost perfectly. That "almost" cursed them with an uncanny-valley quality.

"They aren't people," she said. "Can't you see? They're octopi! You're being tricked!"

For the first time since they reached the Abyssal Pit, Professor Milligan looked Jul in the eyes. "It's a shame, Julie. So smart. But you've never had the right priorities to be a scientist."

With that, he fell backward into the ocean and was pulled into a writhing frenzy of glowing, gelatinous, long-limbed things. Screaming, Jul leaned over the bulwark—and then stumbled back when the creatures reached for her with beckoning arms. Her head! God, it hurt, but how much of that was the cable, and how much was *them*?

With her remaining strength, Jul carried the beacon back to the infirmary. After locking the door, she rifled through the medicine cabinets, casting aside rattling bottles of pills until she found the sedatives. She swallowed a strong dose and prayed to her ancestors that the ship would not sink as she slept. That when she woke, the sea would be calm, the island gone, and help could come.

As Jul slipped into unconsciousness, she saw—or perhaps dreamed—one of the cephalopod creatures climbing onto the deck outside her porthole. It was a little one, a baby or child, barely three feet tall. And it stood there with two of its little arms outstretched. With its delicate legs bent, as if broken. In Reggie's voice, he wondered, "When will you come home?"

Jul returned the hug.

JONATHAN MABERRY

The Orpheus Gate

Jonathan Maberry

-1-

Department of Quantum Physics
Harvard University

"Do you believe in faeries?"

Professor Jess Challenger leaned back in her chair. It was an old chair and it had several wonderful creaks, one in a precise A-flat. She cradled her coffee cup between her palms and waited for the punch line.

But the woman who sat on the other side of Jess's big desk merely waited, eyes blue and bright in a face that was a comprehensive mass of wrinkles.

"Not as a rule," said Jess dryly. "No."

"Do you believe in the larger world?" asked the visitor. Her name was Amelia Little. Small as a cricket, thin as a stick, and of incalculable age. She wore a dress patterned with sunflowers and a heavy scarf of a particularly shocking shade of bright yellow.

215

No makeup, no lipstick. Her jewelry was mostly silver, with freshwater pearls and a necklace of chunky stones the professor could not easily identify. Possibly amazonite and apophyllite. Her hands looked frail, the knuckles distorted by arthritis, and she hadn't offered one for a shake.

"'The larger world,'" echoed Jess, stalling a bit. She was quite familiar with the term. Her mother and grandmother were very much believers in a world that was bigger and more complex than the one the average person could see and measure. A world of ghosts and sprites, of divination and magic. "No," she said, "I don't."

"You're a lot like your great-grandfather in that," said Mrs. Little. "He didn't use to believe either."

Jess Challenger said nothing.

"Until he did," added Mrs. Little. A slow, knowing smile crept onto her lips. "And then he believed in everything."

"Great-grandfather is a ponderous label. My sisters and I just refer to him as G2."

"G2," echoed Little. "That's adorable."

"Not really." Jess drained her coffee cup and set it on the desk, then leaned her forearms on the blotter and gave the old lady a long, considering stare. "Yes," she said at last, "apparently later in life G2 went from being a serious scientist and natural skeptic to drinking enough of the Kool-Aid to develop a belief in the supernatural. That was also of the time, because theosophy was at its height, and his friend, Conan Doyle, had likewise become a fanatic on the subject. Doyle even wrote a rather fantastical—some might call it 'absurd'—novel about G2's so-called spiritual awakening."

"*The Land of Mist*," said Little. "That was published when, 1926?"

"Yes indeed," drawled Jess, making no attempt to hide her contempt. "It's a doozy of a story, but it's only a story."

"You regard that book as fiction, then?"

"I do."

"What about Professor Challenger's other adventures? The dinosaurs in the rainforests of Brazil? The one about the gas cloud? Or the—"

"Oh, those," Jess cut in. "Well, I suspect G2 was having some fun at Doyle's expense. After all, it's rather hilarious that the creator of Sherlock Holmes—fiction's most skeptical character—was so gullible when it came to matters of the fantastic."

"You're saying all of it was pure fiction?"

"Have you seen any dinosaurs at the zoo?"

"Well, no . . ."

Jess spread her hands.

"But that isn't really proof though," said Mrs. Little. "Is it?"

"I'm a scientist, ma'am. A physicist. Proof is what can be measured."

"As I understand it, Professor," said the old lady primly, "most of the universe is composed of dark matter. That can't be measured, and no one knows what it is."

That stopped Jess. "Well, that's true, but—"

"Scientists have no real answer for why people yawn," continued Mrs. Little. "No one knows why Saturn's north pole has a swirling, hexagon-shaped storm. There's no explanation for a whole forest of curved trees—the Dancing Forest—in Russia. Scientists understand *how* cats purr, but they're still not sure *why* they do. Medical science can't adequately explain the placebo effect. And as for consciousness . . . no one has been able to truly measure that."

Jess sat there, surprised and impressed. "Sure, but all that means," she said diffidently, "is the scientific community hasn't *yet* found explanations. It doesn't mean that there is anything supernatural about it."

"Oh, no, don't get me wrong, Professor," said Mrs. Little, "what I'm suggesting is that there's an arrogance among *some* scientists. They tend to dismiss things that they don't understand as woo-woo nonsense. After all, what we *do* know about the physical world

217

changes all the time. Look at the original 1980 Carl Sagan version of *Cosmos* and the Neil deGrasse Tyson version that launched in 2014. Our understanding of our own solar system has changed so radically. Our knowledge of evolution has changed since we've been able to sequence DNA from Cro-Magnon and Neanderthal. I bet if we went over to the university library, we'd find a lot of books whose 'facts' or, at very least accepted facts, are not current with what we know today."

Jess looked into her cup and wished there was something a bit stronger than medium blend. Conversations like this were best had three or four whiskeys in. She was also angry with herself for reacting to the old lady—a friend of Jess's late grandmother—in a deeply ageist way. Clearly the woman was alert and very sharp.

"I accept that," she said, and even to her own ears it sounded like she was having a molar pulled with rusty pliers. She got up and busied herself with refilling her coffee cup, offered more to the woman, got a head shake, and settled back down in the creaky chair. Now the A sounded even flatter.

Mrs. Little sat primly, her wise old eyes watching with amused interest.

"I agreed to this meeting because you were a friend of my grandmother," said Jess, "but I don't know you and I'm moderately slammed with work. I have to ask if there's a point to any of this? Or are we just making conversation?"

The woman did not appear ruffled. "Fair enough, Professor. I know I'm imposing on your time," she said mildly. "But may I ask you one more question?"

The woman really was a stranger. She'd made an appointment during office hours and had only gotten it because she dropped Grandma Enid's name. Enid, G2's only daughter, had been a doll. Eccentric and kooky but wonderful, and even fourteen years after her death Jess still grieved. Agreeing to the meeting was an entirely sentimental choice that she was now regretting. Jess's eyes flicked to the wall clock. She sighed and grunted something that more or less sounded like yes.

Amelia Little's eyes glittered like polished glass. "Do you believe in ghosts?"

"No."

"You answered that so quickly."

"It's not something I have to think long and hard about," said Jess with crumbling patience.

"Let me try it another way," said Amelia Little, "if ghosts *did* exist, what might they be? How might science explain them? After all, there is a great deal of scholarly and scientific research into the phenomenon. And there are so many kinds of ghost. Or spirit, or residual energy. There are poltergeists who can interact with physical objects but seem to lack a personality. There are ghosts that are like movie clips, endlessly repeating the same actions. Walking down a hall or sitting in a rocking chair. That sort of thing. There are places where people say they feel negative energy. There are interactive personalities that seem able to communicate with the living. There are orbs, wisps of lights, funnel ghosts, and cold spots. So many kinds. With so many sightings over so many centuries, with anomalous readings on various kinds of scientific equipment . . . what might ghosts be?"

"If they exist at all?" suggested Jess with poor grace. She was growing impatient with the old woman's rant. "Low frequency sound accounts for some of it, I expect. Humans can't hear sound below twenty hertz, but some people subconsciously respond to lower frequencies with feelings of fear or dread. Or some kinds of electromagnetic fields—EMFs. There was a neuroscientist, Michael Persinger, I believe, who tested a group of people wearing helmets through which a weak magnetic stimulation was channeled. Over eighty percent of them reported feeling an unexplained presence in the room. Carbon monoxide poisoning can cause hallucinations and sickness, and there are cases where repairs to gas furnaces in houses with reported hauntings resulted in families no longer seeing ghosts. Yes, Mrs. Little, I know the territory and the literature. After all, I am G2's great-granddaughter, and Enid Challenger's granddaughter."

Mrs. Little smiled. "I knew your great-grandfather. After his shift from absolute science to a more open spiritual belief, Professor Challenger had come to believe that there were veils between this world and an infinite number of others."

"The multiverse theory," said Jess. "I know. It's a theory in quantum physics, and to a degree it's even true. In super string theory, for example—"

"No, please, I know about those aspects of science," said Mrs. Little. "I'm old—older than I look, and I look ancient—but I am very much in step with science and scientific thought. I'm not referring to the Krull dimension of a commutative ring, or the Hausdorff dimension used for studying structurally complicated sets, especially fractals; or even Kaluza-Klein unified field theory postulating a fifth dimension beyond the standard 4-D space-time model. No, Professor, I'm talking about other *worlds*. Other versions of our own world. An infinite number of worlds. The omniverse, to use the pop culture phrase."

She had Jess's attention now.

"And, for the record, I also knew Theodor Kaluza *and* Oskar Klein."

"Wow . . . you, um, get around."

"Not as much as I'd like," said the woman, "but yes. Anyway, my point is that Professor Challenger knew those men too. He understood where they were going with what became quantum physics, and he was the very first person to believe that the quantum world and this world are parts of one much larger world. He believed that all Earths, every version of it, no matter how subtly different or extremely alien, were actually the same world. He described it to me once as phases of reality, like the phases of the moon. And that the only thing separating us from those other worlds are thin veils."

"If they're that thin, then how come we can't see those other worlds?" asked Jess, not even trying to keep the frank disbelief from her tone.

"Who says we can't?"

"What's that supposed to mean?"

"That we have been glimpsing those other worlds all along," said Mrs. Little. "Look back through history, to what's called mythology and superstition. Think about the phenomenon of extrasensory perception. Every major government has put great amounts of money into research on attempts to understand and quantify psychic ability. Your grandmother believed that the reason they have largely failed is that it's a talent from another version of Earth, and here it's much more rare and harder to use."

"Oookay . . ."

"And there are other clues to the larger world," continued Mrs. Little as if Jess hadn't spoken. "Professor Challenger believed that there were times some force, some release of energy from this or some other world, pushed against those veils and tore them open. Or, perhaps, brushed them temporarily aside. During those moments, things were able to pass through. Energies of different frequencies, images carried by psychic waves, and even people."

Jess smiled. "People from other dimensions?"

"Your great-grandfather theorized that Leonardo da Vinci may have been one such person. His absolute genius in so many areas—and the fact that his knowledge was so severely out of step with that of his contemporaries—suggested a man either out of time or out of place."

"Next you'll tell me Nikola Tesla was an alien."

"Not aliens," corrected Mrs. Little. "Not in the sense that they are from other planets. Just other versions of our world. But, no . . . the professor didn't think Tesla was from another Earth. He thought Tesla had *glimpsed* other Earths though. He also thought that the entire surrealism art movement—and much of what became the pulp fiction genre—was born in dreams had by people who caught glimpses of these other worlds. Writers like H. P. Lovecraft who wrote about Elder Gods and forgotten races and sights so beyond the understanding of humans from *this* Earth that their senses and reasoning crumbled when they were exposed."

"This is all rather fascinating," lied Jess, "but what does this have to do with me? G2 may have had dementia. He went from being a clearheaded scientist to—"

"—to someone with an open mind," cut in Mrs. Little, and there was a touch of frost there. Jess leaned back again, her coffee going cold.

"Agree to disagree," she said.

Little cocked her head to one side. "Do you know about the project he was working on before he died?"

"Ah," said Jess. "The project. Yes, by all means let's talk about the project. The Orpheus Gate."

"Did you know that he worked on that *with* Nikola Tesla?"

"That's an old rumor with no proof."

Instead of answering, Mrs. Little opened her large purse and removed a folder. From that she took a stack of photos and a sheaf of letters bound by a rubber band and laid these items on the desk blotter. Jess paused a long time before picking up the photos. They were mostly of two older men. One was big, broad-shouldered, fiercely bearded, and with a massive head. The other man was just as tall, though slimmer, with a receding hairline and a dark mustache gone gray.

Jess knew both faces. Everyone in most fields of science knew them.

The big man, although withered by age, was Professor George Edward Challenger.

The other man, without a doubt, was Nikola Tesla.

-2-

Jess leafed through the rest of the photos.

The top one was of the two of them standing outside of the old New Yorker Hotel, but the rest were taken in what was clearly a laboratory where they were at work building something—a machine so massive it filled the room, dwarfing them. On the bottom of one photo, written in black ballpoint, was a single notation:

The Orpheus Gate, 1934

"I . . . I . . . ," began Jess, but found that she could not actually finish the sentence.

"Your grandmother never told you about it," said Mrs. Little.

"No. Not a word."

"She planned to. But even as a little girl you were already set on your path. You never wanted to hear about the more outré adventures of Professor Challenger; you scoffed at the articles and stories Conan Doyle wrote that focused on anything *except* Sherlock Holmes. You used to make fun of your grandmother when she knocked wood, tossed spilled salt over her shoulder, or said that she believed in things like ghosts."

Jess said nothing.

"And so your grandmother decided not to give you these photos or the other things. She was afraid you'd just throw them out."

Jess licked her lips. "What . . . *other* things?"

Mrs. Little reached out and touched the letters. "Correspondence between the professor and Mr. Tesla. And . . . this." She took a much larger bundle of papers from her purse and placed them with a thump on the desk. She did not push them across to Jess, however, but instead sat with her palm placed flat on top.

"If you read the letters," she said, "you'll see that not only did your great-grandfather believe in a larger world—indeed in a true omniverse—but so did Mr. Tesla. They believed wholeheartedly.

Just as they believed that their device, the Orpheus Gate, could open the veils separating our reality from others in close proximity. It was their hope to create a stable gateway through which people or other beings could pass with ease."

Jess merely stared at her.

"And this project began when Professor Challenger met a ghost. You know that your grandmother was well-known for mediumistic abilities."

"Allegedly," said Jess, mostly to be pissy.

Little gave her a tolerant look despite the rude tone. "She was the conduit to introduce the skeptical professor to a number of people involved in what was then called spiritualism," said Amelia Little. "Ghost hunters, of a kind. Challenger introduced these same people to Tesla and sold him on the concept that they were not truly the spirits of dead people but were actually persons from other versions of Earth who'd come through the veils but were unable to return. They were trapped here, incorporeal because their essential substance did not belong *here*. They existed in a kind of limbo where their bodies did not decay or die. Imagine that, my dear Jess: Imagine what it would be like to be trapped on the other side of your own mirror—to be able to see, but not clearly; to not *be* seen properly. To never age, but yet feel the weight of the years as they gather into centuries. To never need to eat, but still feel the unending pangs of hunger. To never sleep again, but to be forever awake, forever helpless and lost. They are not *from* a lost world but have instead lost *their* world. Can you imagine what a horror that would be?"

Jess whispered a single word. "God . . ."

She picked up the letters, removed the rubber band, and began reading them. They were not, as she expected, hysterical rants by an old man with a failing mind. Nor did they proselytize a belief in the larger world. No. There was barely any of that. Instead they were a correspondence between two men who had come to accept the larger world—the concept of infinite worlds—as a truth. More importantly, as a *scientific* fact.

The old woman sat and waited while Jess read them all. When she set the last one down, Jess looked at her.

"Okay," said Jess, "so they were both clearly on the same page, but what does that prove? It doesn't even say here what they hoped to accomplish."

"Oh, I thought that was clear," said Mrs. Little. "They were convinced that ghosts were people or beings trapped here, just as people from our world might be trapped in other dimensions. And, possibly, some trapped in a limbo state *between* worlds."

"And . . . ?"

"And they believed that their Orpheus Gate could lift those veils and allow all of the ghosts to go home."

"Okay, let's say for the sake of argument that any of this is true and that this Orpheus Gate could open those doors . . . How would they ever calibrate it? How could they know which veils to open and which to avoid? How would they know how to return those, um, *beings*, to the correct dimensions?"

"They had help," said Mrs. Little. "They had guidance."

"From *whom*?"

"From people trapped between worlds, of course."

"*Ghosts* told them?"

"That's what they believed."

"And they—what?—just called the ghosts up on the phone? Or was there a seance?"

"Your grandmother was the medium for the communication."

"Ah. Of course she was."

Little drew in a breath through her nose. "You can mock, Jessica Challenger," she said with a great show of strained patience, "but your grandmother Enid was an exceptional spirit medium, and her skills got better every time she reached out. What Conan Doyle did not include in his *Land of Mist* novel was the most important thing that ever happened. The real reason your great-grandfather became one hundred percent convinced that spirits remain."

"And what was that? Did she channel Da Vinci?"

"She channeled a number of people. This is not the only world that has scientists. Or, rather, it's not the only version of Earth that has scientists. Enid was able to connect with great minds who are, themselves, trapped in the spirit world. Beings who want to be freed from torment." Mrs. Little paused. "And at Professor Challenger's request, she channeled your namesake. She channeled his dead wife, Jessica."

-3-

Jess stared at her. "You can't be serious."

The old woman nodded to the papers. "It's all in there."

Jess pulled the papers to her and began leafing through them. The pages were old, yellowed, curled at the edges, but everything written and drawn was clear and legible. She thumbed through them at first and then began spreading them out, pushing the items on her desk to the edges as she unfolded a series of design schematics.

"This is . . . this is . . . ," she began, and each time her words faltered.

"These are the plans for building an Orpheus Gate."

"No, that's not what I meant," said Jess, standing up so she could bend over the plans. "This is . . . *brilliant*."

She was silent for nearly an hour, during which sweat ran down her cheeks and her heart hammered in her chest. Mrs. Little sat watching, saying nothing.

Finally, Jess sagged back and collapsed into her chair. The A-flat squeak sounded like a cry of alarm. Jess picked up her coffee cup and tried to take a sip, but it was empty. She stared into the bottom of the cup for nearly three full minutes. The clock on the wall ticked very loudly into an otherwise absolute silence.

"My god," said Jess. She blinked her eyes until her vision cleared and then stared at the old woman. "The science of this . . . the engineering and formulae—they're decades ahead of where they should have been. This is deep quantum physics, particle physics, matrix mechanics. This is beyond Max Planck, beyond Max Born. This takes the Einstein-Podolsky-Rosen paradox and . . . and . . . it just tears it apart. I don't understand how they came up with this in the 1930s. We were nowhere near this back then. No one was. This is beyond . . . beyond . . ."

"Beyond anything from *this* world?" suggested Mrs. Little.

"I . . . I wouldn't necessarily say that . . ."

The old woman just smiled.

"Look," said Jess, "G2 sank most of his fortune into this. He nearly ruined the family. He drained his investments, cashed in most of his stocks, and he—I might add—used funds set aside for the education of his daughter and granddaughter. And you tell me that his end goal was to *free ghosts?*"

Mrs. Little's eyes flickered a bit, revealing an anger or perhaps disappointment. "Free your mind from the chains of old thinking," she said. "I use the word *ghost* because it's useful in conversation, but we are not really talking about the surviving personalities of dead people. Not entirely. Some of those spirits were once alive in this world, to be sure, but something happened, a veil opened near them, perhaps, and their consciousness— what psychics call the astral body—was knocked loose. With the spirit gone from the body, the body dies, and the spirit is caught *between* our world and some other. It's like being trapped in the walls of some old castle but never finding a doorway out."

"Spooky stories aren't my thing," said Jess.

"There are other kinds of trapped spirits too," said the woman. "I'm talking about living, sentient beings trapped in a timeless, endless hell of existence because they are trapped in a world that is not their own. Pause for a moment and think about that. With your heart, with empathy. If someone you loved was caught like that, trapped in an energetic form, unable to sleep or die or even dream, for year after year after year, what would you do? Or if they were trapped in another plane of existence, one where time runs differently, and all they could do was watch—as if through a window—as everyone they loved mourns their death and then grows old and dies. You, of all people, should want to do whatever is necessary to set that right."

"Why me? I'm a Challenger, yes, but I'm a lot more like G2 *before* he lost his marbles."

"Oh? What if we were talking about your own great-grand-mother—Jessica Challenger? What if her consciousness was one of those accidentally knocked free from her body and trapped forever? It might change how you think. After all, it was after her death that the great scientist and skeptic George Edwin Challenger opened his mind and heart to the possibilities of life beyond. To the realities of the larger world."

"Even if this Orpheus Gate worked," said Jess slowly, fighting for patience, "you said that once the spirit is separated from the flesh, the body dies. What good would it do to restore Jessica to this world if her body is dusty bones in a box?"

"Let me ask you this," said Mrs. Little, "if you were buried alive but trapped forever in the coffin with no chance of dying and no hope of ever being dug up, would you be content with that? No, of course not. But after all those years of torment of just being, without power, without contact, without light or release, wouldn't you rather have your existence ended rather than go on and on and on forever?"

"But I don't believe that's possible," said Jess, "and I don't think G2 and Nikola Tesla were anything but well-intentioned eccentrics frittering away the downside of their careers."

"You think there was no chance they were right? You can't budge one inch?"

"No," said Jess. "This is all pretty crazy. A machine to open dimensional doorways so ghosts could be freed? That's the plot of a *Ghostbusters* sequel. A bad one."

Mrs. Little studied her. "Because you only believe in science."

"Yes, because I can see that, feel it, touch it, measure it. *Know* it."

"If your great-grandfather was still alive and was working on a working model of the Orpheus Gate, would you try and talk him out of it?"

"To keep the family from being financially ruined? Sure."

"Wouldn't you have even the slightest interest in seeing the machine firsthand? To at least study it to determine for yourself if it would work?"

"Well, of course, as a scientist and his great-granddaughter I'd take a look."

The old woman's eyebrows rose. "And if you thought it would work?"

Jess shrugged. "I don't know. Maybe," she said, "but it's moot. According to the letters, the one G2 and Tesla built was at a warehouse in New Jersey and that burned down. Everything was destroyed. G2 recouped a little from insurance, but this is probably why Tesla was ruined. He died broke. No, it's gone and I'm certainly not going to build a new one. I'm not going to submit a grant for money to finance one either. I'd be laughed out of my department. I mean, the cost alone is absurd." She tapped the schematics. "There are precious metals and gemstones listed as crucial to the machine's functions. Trying to build one a century ago ruined the family. The cost in today's dollars would be . . . god . . . tens of millions."

The old woman nodded, then removed a piece of paper from her purse and placed it on the desk, paused to consider, then slid it across. She withdrew her hand and they both sat for a moment staring at the paper.

"What's that?"

"It's an address," said Mrs. Little.

As Jess reached for it the old woman snatched her hand back as if afraid to be touched. Her mind might be sharp as a scalpel, but her body was dreadfully frail.

Jess opened the paper and saw that it was the address for a warehouse on Windsor and Main in Cambridge, only a few miles away. There was a time—11:00 a.m. on the following day. A plastic keycard was taped to the page.

"What's there?" asked Jess suspiciously.

Mrs. Little smiled, stood, nodded, and walked out without answering. Jess got up and hurried over to the door, but the woman was already gone.

-4-

C-T Storage
Windsor and Main Streets
Cambridge, Massachusetts

Jess did not show up at the scheduled time.

She didn't show up for nearly three weeks.

There were no further unexpected visits from weird little old ladies. No calls or emails. There was nothing.

Except those letters, those photos, and the stack of finely detailed schematics.

For the first week, Jess dismissed it all, laughed it off, and went back to work on a design for a control system for CERN's new Future Circular Collider, which would be four times as long as the already massive twenty-seven-kilometer Large Hadron Collider. The LHC was currently the largest and most powerful of its kind, and the FCC would dwarf it, allowing a far greater range of testing. There were many secrets of the Big Bang to be discovered, and the FCC would be a giant standing on the shoulders of giants.

But day after day, each time she entered her office, she saw the stack of schematics on the corner of her desk. Each evening as she prepared to leave for the night, she felt their pull.

Early in the second week, Jess began leafing through the designs on her lunch break. Then she found herself lingering after work and coming in early.

By the third week she wasn't getting anything at all done on the FCC project and was spending fourteen hours a day going through the diagrams item by item. She had to admit that it was brilliant work. Inspired to an almost eerie level. Each day she would input information onto her laptop and upload it to the server farm in the air-cooled basement. There, in the frigid darkness, the seventeen-petaflop Titan supercomputers would run the numbers based on the calibration philosophies G2 and Tesla had concocted. In the absence of real computing power, they'd gotten only so far and then hit wall after wall. Their frustration was noted in their increasingly terse letters. They could build the machine, but they could not focus it, they could not tune it to access the worlds beyond this world.

Each night she would dream about the Orpheus Gate, and of G2—looking younger and more like a bull than in the photos on her desk. She dreamed of Nikola Tesla and the range of his genius. She dreamed of Jessica Challenger, who'd died years before Jess was born. And she dreamed of her own grandmother, Enid, also gone.

In each dream the Orpheus Gate seemed to grow in size and reality. It changed from the shadowy image in the black-and-white photos to something that gleamed with color and substance.

One morning, twenty-two days after Mrs. Little's visit, Jess did not go to work. Instead she climbed into her sturdy little Nissan Rogue and drove to the address on the paper. It was a Sunday and the sky was overcast with clouds thickening with the promise of heavy rain. The streets were nearly empty and there were no cars in the parking lot of C-T Storage. Jess got out—the schematics, letters, and photos in a laptop bag—and looked around. Nothing and no one.

She walked to a small door beside which was a keycard reader. The card worked perfectly, and the lock clicked. Jess took a breath and pushed the door open. When no alarms rang, she entered the building.

The door opened into a reception room that looked like it had been vacant for years. Some kind of animal had built a nest of sticks, rough twine, and old newspapers under the receptionist's desk. The calendar on the wall was for 2009 and there were mouse droppings on the floor.

"Swell," said Jess. She pushed through a swinging door into a hall, followed it past empty rooms, then down a long corridor of unlocked and disused storage bins. Even wearing sneakers her steps sounded too loud. Then she came to a set of very large steel doors that were firmly shut. Another key reader was beside them and once more the keycard disengaged the locks. Jess pushed one panel open and stepped in.

And froze.

The machine filled the entire cavernous main building. Cleary most of the storage unit had been demolished to make room for it.

It.

The Orpheus Gate.

The body of the machine was circular, like a wedding ring, but instead of a diamond there was a jewel of mechanical perfection. In front was a tall, round doorway ten feet in diameter. Jewels—real rubies and diamonds and other precious gems that had been cut into bizarre geometrical shapes—were inset in sheets of gold, platinum, silver, and copper. Coils of heavily insulated wire were wrapped around the body of the ring like the coils of a vast metal serpent. Switches and dials were arranged in clusters on either side of the Gate, and the "tongue" of the machine's mouth was a pad of scandium and yttrium composed in a kind of mosaic. The pattern on the mosaic was vague, more of a representation of something than an actual depiction. To Jess it looked like an octopus, but the proportions were strange and wrong.

The machine was big and beautiful in its way, but it was old, and there was a thick coating of dust over the metal and jewels. Jess walked around it, then stopped by the control panel and removed her cell phone from her pocket. She accessed a PDF file, opened it, and spent several minutes glancing from the notes she'd written to the physical controls and back. Everything synced up. Not just with what Tesla and G2 had painstakingly recorded, but with the extrapolations from the Titan computers. What had been impossible math for two of the twentieth century's greatest minds had taken Harvard's processors seconds to calculate.

Jess stepped back and studied the machine, her mind swirling with doubt and excitement.

"It's beautiful," said a voice, "isn't it?"

Jess jumped in surprise, dropping her phone as she whirled to see Amelia Little standing fifteen feet away. She'd moved without a sound.

"Christ," gasped Jess, "how long have you been there?"

Instead of answering, the woman nodded to the machine. "It's been here all these years. Enid made sure that it was hidden away. After all, the fire in New Jersey hadn't completely destroyed everything. And the insurance money allowed Professor Challenger to have it moved here, and to buy this building. Enid managed it, and your mother helped."

"They never said anything to me."

"No. I think they wanted me to be the one to reach out."

"Why you?"

Again the old woman didn't answer the question. "Enid and your mother made sure to encourage your love of science. Your passion for it. They nudged you ever so gently in the direction of particle physics and quantum science. Think back on it—they encouraged you, provided for your education, helped you prepare for tests, worked with you to draft scholarship applications. It was a long game, but they played it well."

"Why? Why would they do that?"

"Because they wanted you to be right here. Right where you are at this moment."

"But *why?* Why not just tell me?"

"Because they did not think you would listen. You have so much of George Challenger in you. The young George. The one who was so sure that science was the only power in the universe, and that he was its chief prophet." Mrs. Little shook her head. "You have no idea how certain he was. He was rude and crude, belittling and crass, but he was also almost always right. That was infuriating. When it came to science—virtually every field he touched—George was the most astute, the most insightful. He was an expert at being an expert."

"You've read all the Doyle books, that's for sure. You speak like you know him."

"Then he set out to debunk the spiritualists and mediums. It was his mission to expose them as frauds and prove without a splinter of uncertainty that there was no larger world." Amelia Little smiled. "And we know how that turned out."

"He was getting old."

"That wasn't it," said Little. "It was grief at the loss of his wife that lit the fire. He lost the person he loved the most and the one who loved him above all things. She was suddenly gone from the world and he was torn apart by it. Then to hear spiritualists claim they could talk to the dead made him furious. He hated that they were playing on the credulity and heartbreak of the grieving. In his rage he decided to drag them into the light of scientific immutability. But . . ."

Jess took a step toward her, but the old lady retreated.

"But he came to believe," continued Little, "and he discovered that his own daughter, lovely Enid, was a medium. A true one. A very, very powerful one. And Enid was able to facilitate conversations between George and several spirits."

Jess said nothing.

"And one of those spirits was Jessica. The lost Jessica." Mrs. Little wiped at a tear. "Imagine that moment. When a man whose entire life was built around two things—science and the love of his wife—found that science failed him and death stole from him. He was bereft until Enid reached through the veils and helped Jessica find her voice."

"I'm trying so hard to believe," Jess confessed. "But I've never believed in anything."

"Only science," said Little. "How like George you are. Not the same level of arrogance, not as rude, but the drive, the passion, the *faith* in science burns as bright in you as it did in him."

The old woman walked over to the machine and trailed withered fingers across it.

"Do you know what a poltergeist is?" she asked, apropos of nothing, then answered her own question. "It's a spirit who can touch the real world, but only just. They can lift things, throw things, but not people. Inorganic things only. Cups and plates, paper . . . They can touch those things but not people. Spirits can't really touch the living. Not in a world that isn't theirs. Instead they live for centuries in the spaces between worlds. Aging, feeling their bodies falter, knowing that at some point they'll lose even the power to knock over a saltshaker or flutter the pages of the morning paper. They fade, but never completely. No. Not completely. And they have no voice with which to even beg for mercy."

Jess said nothing.

"Unless a medium can find them. Someone like your grandmother. She could not only reach through the veils with her mind, she could give voice to the voiceless. That was how George spoke with those ghosts that Doyle wrote about. And it's how he spoke to his beloved Jessica."

As the woman's fingers moved over the dusty surfaces of the Orpheus Gate, Jess saw that they left no marks. They did not disturb the dust at all. Not a single mote.

Jess stared at Little. "Who . . . who *are* you?"

The old woman smiled a small, sad little smile. "Don't you know?"

Tears burned in Jess's eyes. One fell, scalding its way down her cheek.

"No," she whispered.

The old woman nodded. "Little was my maiden name. Amelia is my middle name. All of the books, the biographies of George, focused on his name but gave almost no information about the woman he married other than he loved her with his whole heart. And she loved him." There were tears in her eyes too. "She still does. She always will."

"I . . . I . . . ," began Jess, but she could not form any sentence that would make sense.

"I died young," said the old woman, "and time moves so differently where I am."

With a growl of anger, Jess rushed over to her and grabbed at the old woman's shoulders, needing to shake some sense into her. To shake the lies out.

But her hands did not close on cloth and muscle and bone. Instead they merely passed through Amelia Little.

Jess screamed and scrambled backward, slipping on the dusty floor, losing balance, falling. "It's impossible!" she screamed.

Jessica Amelia Little-Challenger stood looking down at her.

"That's what I've been trying to tell you, my dear," she said in a soft voice that was old as the world. "Nothing is impossible."

-5-

The Orpheus Gate

"But . . . you sat in a chair, touched my desk, handed me papers . . ."

The old woman bent and picked up Jess's cell phone, which was scuffed but undamaged. She held it out and Jess had to steel herself before snatching it away.

"Some spirits can touch inanimate *things*, remember?" said Jessica Challenger. "But not people. I can only talk to you because Enid gave me my voice back. And for all these years she kept in contact with my spirit. She allowed me to be as alive as possible. I got to watch her daughter grow up. I was there at your birth, even if you didn't see me. I've watched you your whole life, Jess. But now . . . with Enid gone . . . I can feel myself starting to fade. I'm going to fade completely soon and then I'll be beyond reach, even of the Orpheus Gate."

Jess stared past her at the machine.

"No," she said again. "It's impossible."

"Not for you," said her great-grandmother. "Not for someone as brilliant as you. You *are* like George. So smart. Smarter than anyone around you. And I know that you went over the schematics. I know you figured out how to calibrate the machine. After the fire, the machine was so badly damaged. George and Nikola brought it here and spent every last cent they had to repair it. But they were old by then, and the last bits of science they needed to understand were beyond their failing minds. You understood right away what their challenge was. They could build it, but they could not tune it so that it could do what they prayed and wished that it would. The science of their time wasn't enough. There were no supercomputers."

Jess Challenger began backing away.

"I can't," she whispered thickly. "This is madness, I can't!"

"Please," said her great-grandmother. She did not scream it.

237

She did not beg. She merely said that one word, and it jerked Jess to a weeping, trembling stop.

They stood like that, Jess with her face toward the door and her back to the old woman, and the machine looming above them both like a silent monster. Jess covered her face with her hands.

"My dear," said the woman, "my sweet. I know this is hard for you. It cracks your world open. I understand that. My world was cracked open and I fell. I was lost for so long. I'm not asking for pity and I don't even need you to believe."

"Then what do you want?" snarled Jess.

"I just want to go home," said Jessica Little-Challenger. "I just want to rest."

A sob broke in Jess's chest. Deep. Painful. Torn from deep inside her. She looked down at the cell phone. The screen had gone dark, but she thumbed it back. The PDF was still there. The numbers, the sequences. All there.

"I don't believe any of this . . . ," murmured Jess. "I can't."

"Tell me," said her great-grandmother, "if you calibrate the machine and I vanish, what will you have lost? It won't disprove science for you."

"It . . ."

"All it will do will be to suggest that the world you call science is much, much larger. That it embraces all of the many worlds. Versions of Earth you know and also lost worlds." She laughed softly. "You may even find that plateau with all the dinosaurs. You know it's not on *this* version of Earth, but it *is* somewhere."

"But you'll *die!*" wailed Jess.

Her great-grandmother smiled very gently. "I'm already dead, my dear. Long, long ago. If you turn on that machine, I'll be able to rest."

"You'll be gone," said Jess desperately. "There's nothing out there—"

"You don't know that," said Jessica Little-Challenger. "You don't. Enid didn't know what happens after true death. Not the fractured death I suffered, but true death. Those voices don't speak to the living. They've either fallen silent or have moved too far away. Maybe it's heaven, or maybe it's what you atheists think, that it's nothing at all. But I rather think there are many worlds beyond this one. Worlds where spirits can rest or fly or be reborn. I don't know, my girl. I don't. All I know is that I am so weary. More weary than you can know. I've been *awake* for a century. You can't even imagine it, and that's a mercy, because there may not be a heaven but there is surely a hell. I've been in that hell for all these years. Now . . . now I want to rest. To close these eyes and let the darkness and stillness take me. But, Jess . . . my sweet great-granddaughter, only you can give me that gift."

"What if it doesn't work?" asked Jess, her voice hollow and brittle.

"No . . . what if it *does* work?"

Jess covered her face with her hands and wept.

And then she set about calibrating the machine.

–6–

Jess turned the first of the dials.

She did every step exactly according to the descriptions left by G2 and Tesla. Her attention to detail and mania for exactitude fueled her precision. It took a long time. Hours? She wasn't sure. But she did everything right. When the meters were all at 50 percent, she watched them, looking for dips in power, not seeing any, counting the seconds. Then she began turning each dial up, listening to the change in the engine whine, seeing her great-grandmother's nod of approval, seeing the old woman's face grow brighter and almost feverish with anticipation. When the last dial was turned, Jess shifted to face the rows of gems that had been cut into their strange geometric shapes. Diamonds and rubies, sapphires and emeralds, garnets and topazes. So many of them.

The jewels began to glow.

The diamonds first. Flash-flash-flash.

Then the ruby.

The topaz.

The sapphires and the garnet together.

The diamond again.

All of them at once, then in sequences. It was not some slow progression but a wildness that flashed and dazzled the eye. Jess gasped as the patterns changed over and over and over again. Too fast for the eye to follow.

The diamond flashed twice and then the emerald, and she almost—almost—turned the dials. *No,* she scolded herself. *Don't. Trust the calculations. Wait. Wait.*

Jessica Challenger went over and stood inside the mouth of the machine. Patterns of light came and went, came and went. The whine of the engine rose in pitch. Inside the mouth of the Gate, the old woman stood with her arms outstretched, her head thrown back in ecstasy or agony. In extremis both emotions look exactly the same.

A ring of lights appeared inside the mouth of the machine, and Jess cried out. She had not installed lights and yet here they were, casting the old woman in a blue-white glow that was wholly unnatural.

Diamond, diamond, garnet.

The engine whine was a piercing shriek, rising, rising, becoming intolerable. Jess felt wet warmth in her ears and she knew, without question, that her ears were bleeding. The whole building trembled, shuddered. Brick dust dropped like falling ghosts from the ceiling. A jagged crack jigsawed across the floor and began climbing one of the walls.

Diamond, sapphire, sapphire, ruby.

Outside, the sky was forked with white lightning, and thunder exploded like cannon fire.

The world is going mad and I am falling with it, thought Jess, and she almost fled. She almost abandoned the old woman to this madness.

Almost.

Worlds turn on such moments.

Diamond, emerald, ruby, garnet.

"Let me sleep," cried the old woman, and now she seemed thinner, more frail, almost insubstantial.

Diamond, diamond, topaz.

Outside, the storm that had been growing came to life and the sky was split by thunder so loud it rattled the entire building. The Orpheus Gate trembled and shook. The gemstones all flared brighter and brighter and brighter until . . .

Darkness. Sudden and total.

There was a moment of nothing.

And then a whisper of a voice.

"Thank you."

It was not the voice of an old woman. It was younger. Full of energy. Alive.

Just those two words and then silence.

-7-

Jess Challenger took a month's sabbatical from Harvard.

She traveled the world.

She went to graveyards and castles, to battlefields and manor houses. To places that books and the internet insisted were haunted.

In each place she found nothing.

Not a whisper. Not a tossed plate or a cold spot or a moan in the night.

She found nothing.

Over the next two years all of the various ghost hunters' TV shows were canceled. Programs featuring mediums suffered a sharp drop in ratings.

There was nothing left to find. No one left to talk to on the other side.

There was . . . nothing.

Nothing went bump in the night after that.

Absolutely nothing.

DEXTER PALMER

Hotel Motel Holiday Inn

Dexter Palmer

I can tell from the way you're looking at me that you want to know *what I do*: why this suit jacket with its threadbare cuffs; why the beginnings of jowls ten years before they're due; why water in my glass instead of wine. You want to know *what I do*, for you think this will tell you *what I am*. But you fear that to force me to speak the answer would humiliate me, and I would see my own fallen station reflected in the quick instinctive flush of your cheeks, in your gaze flicking toward some other partygoer whose dress and demeanor suggest a more auspicious life.

It's no matter—no, stand still! I saw that half step backward: reverse it! Come close—I'll tell you what I do. I work in *sales*. I am a salesman, for a small liquor distributor located in North Carolina. I am a purveyor of modern rotgut. Not whiskeys or gins that a cultured man can respect, but libations designed in laboratories, blood red and neon blue, designed for irresponsible consumption by gentleman's-C college students and gaggles of bachelorettes.

It's bilge, plain and simple; it makes women throw punches and gives men nightmares.

I drive up and down the East Coast in a Chevrolet that rolled off the line in the first decade of the century, compensated forty-seven measly pennies per mile; on weekday afternoons, when bars in North Carolina and Delaware and New Jersey are cleared of all trade but the occasional pickled retiree regular, I walk in with a few bottles of Day-Glo swill, engage the idle staff in conversation, and suggest that my company has a brand-new product that would add some excitement and novelty to seven-ingredient spring and summer cocktails, perfect for women having a girls' night out who are up for some socially permissible naughtiness before getting home to their husbands and children by nine thirty. The bartenders will gather round, take polite, cautious sips, and try to repress their winces; occasionally a manager will come out from the back and join them. The best I can hope for from them is usually pity or, failing that, contempt not for myself but for my eyeless, tongueless masters; at worst I will be laughed out of the place and onto the street.

So this is *what I do*, but it is not *what I am*. What I am is an *explorer*; what I am is a *mapper of secret spaces*! What I *am* is—

You say you are going to get another drink? I will join you! My sparkling water is losing its effervescence: it could use some topping off.

~

It was nice to meet you too! Cheers. Now, as I was saying—wait: come back—I am a mapper of secret spaces.

I spend days at a time away from home, away from my wife, whom I dearly miss the second I step out the door; I spend night after night in hotels in Fayetteville and Newark and Swarthmore, in Motel 6s and Red Roof Inns and hotels run by immigrant families whose signs show the identities of their former proprietors stenciled in fading relief. (You are thinking to yourself, *He ought to use one of those newfangled electronic services that lets you rent a room for an evening from some random homeowner, desperate for money and coerced by circumstance into bowing and scraping,* but a man with pride does not use such services—ground down as I am by my myriad daily humiliations, I still cling to my pride.) If you have been in one hotel you have been in them all, I see you thinking—you're sure you know their odors and their sound-scapes. One smelly box is as good a place as another to lay your head for a few hours. Find the ice machine; ignore the television; sleep; leave; forget you were ever there.

Amateur! We restless journeymen make fine distinctions; we share a secret knowledge! At night, late on a weeknight, past one a.m., I will seek out a bar, to remind myself of what it was like to engage in the ritual of drinking without the fear of contempt from my server; perhaps, if I find myself in a city of sufficient size, the hotel itself will have a bar, well-appointed and dimly lit, which for my purposes is best. I will be sure to find my own kind there. I ask only for a glass of carbonated water, for I seek the simple cer-emony of chalice held to lip, without the consequence of a dulled mind; I sit in silence and I wait, and a wise bartender will exercise the gift his kind have, of making himself invisible unless eyes light upon him, for he knows I wait for others like myself.

And then, as if summoned by a signal only audible to those with nomads' ears, the others of my kind arrive: men in rumpled suits like my own, and shirts whose creases have gone soft after a day's wear; all of us with the same soft bodies, the same falling faces. We all sell different things out of the trunks of our cars, all of them going unwanted: dumb wooden toys in a world of micro-chips and plastic; leather-bound encyclopedias in a world where every fact and lie can reach you as fast as light. Can you imagine such a beautiful thing as a dozen men like myself all in a row, with matching bulging bellies, and shining pates crossed with a few last strands of a color we prefer to call silver, and faded gray suits, and faded red ties that were once bought with the intention of making a stranger's blood pulse, of reminding a potential customer of the pleasures of love and violence? You would have to see it for yourself; sadly, you never will. Such a gathering is *not for you*.

But I will do you this small favor: I will pretend that this water in my glass is something stronger that has loosed my tongue. I will tell you what we speak of after our curt, silent nods to each other, after we have pronounced our shibboleths and reassured ourselves that all of us are of the same small fraternity. To you, at this moment, I will relate some fragments of our unwritten lore traded only in whispers, of the secret contours and geographies of our temporary lodging spaces.

In the Sleepytime Inn in Harrington, Delaware, the blankets on the beds are made of some unpleasant synthetic stuff that's cheaply made and rough to the touch—they're so thin you can't get warm at night, even in summer, and the front desk will claim they've run out if you ask for more than two. Best to bring something warm to sleep in if you're staying there and you're a man alone. Socks for the toes; gloves wouldn't go amiss. (You didn't know that, did you? Now you know.)

Speaking of Delaware: the Wi-Fi of the Luxury Suites in Wilmington is mediocre *at best*. It frequently drops; I suspect it installs strange Chinese applications on laptops.

In the Hotel Marianne of New York City's Financial District, the taps behave oddly because of the terms of the lease from the property's original owner, a result of quirks in the city's antiquated real estate laws—they dispense only boiling-hot water in the morning, and only ice-cold water at night. Prepare for this. Your showers must be quick either way, for they will be scalding or freezing; the controls for the bathtub are labeled in hieroglyphs, but they are meaningless, perhaps one of Marianne's pranks, if she is real and not a fiction dreamed up by a businessman.

If you choose to lodge in the Dreamer's Den of Toms River, New Jersey, a single cookie, shrink-wrapped and sanitary, will appear on your pillow whenever you return to your room. If you leave and come back half a dozen times, you will receive half a dozen cookies. But there is a rule—you must leave the premises altogether, and stay gone for longer than forty-five minutes for the cookie to appear. This has been tested and verified by multiple people in our fraternity. The mechanism that generates the gift is unknown: surely a person enters and deposits the cookie on the pillow (I have checked for a hatch in the ceiling from which the treat might drop—there is no such thing), but how are the proprietors of the hotel tracking the coming and going of the residents and timing their absences? The keys to the rooms of the Dreamer's Den are mechanical, leftover technology from the twentieth century—therefore, there is no discernible electronic record of movement. Hidden cameras somewhere, perhaps? A dedicated "cookie runner" keeping watch on each door from a concealed location? This is a mystery. The cookies are of a variety called "black and white": chocolate frosting covering one half of the disc; vanilla, the other. Their analogs are available in grocery stores by the dozen, but are not as tasty—half the pleasure of eating them is in their inexplicable manifestation.

You didn't know that either, did you? Now you know!

It is possible to receive a discount at the Eternal Wanderer in Central Falls, Rhode Island, if when checking in you sing one of the tunes from the Cure's 1989 album *Disintegration*. Twenty percent off the bill if you complete the song with no errors in the lyrics; 40 percent if you perform an impression of Robert Smith that is judged by the clerk to be homage and not mockery. There is a way to get a 60 percent discount, but I cannot tell you what it is—now that I have given you the clues, you must stumble upon it on your own. When you do, you will understand why it must not be spoken of aloud.

There is excellent room service at the Forty-Ninth Knockout in Mooresville, North Carolina. If, between two and three a.m., you pick up the receiver of the old rotary phone beside your bed and whisper the word *beignet*, within three minutes you will receive a single beignet on a porcelain plate, hot out of the fryer, calling up a memory of New Orleans even if you have never visited the city. If you whisper the word *future*, a strip of paper will be slipped under your door shortly afterward with a five-digit number written on it: this will, without fail, be within ten points of the Dow Jones Industrial Average at the following day's close. You think I am lying, but my fraternity has tested this. Go to Mooresville and try it for yourself.

The vanity mirrors in the bathrooms of Morpheus's Conundrum in Sandy Springs, Georgia, have a feature that is strangely cruel—if you look in any other mirror in the bathroom you will see your face and body as it truly is, but in the vanity mirror, meant for shaving and primping, you will see not your reflection, but that of the room's previous guest. The face on the other side of the glass will nonetheless move as yours does—it is not a recording, but a mimicry. A middle-aged man trimming his mustache will see a twenty-three-year-old woman wielding the razor in his hand above a bare, cupid's-bow lip; that same woman who used the mirror to curl her lashes three days ago saw a sixty-year-old spinster doing the same. I drape a towel over that mirror when I stay there. Others may enjoy laughing or feeling shame; I do not.

If you find yourself in a city that has one of the three hundred hotels in the chain called the Republic of Pasiphae, you really ought to take the opportunity to stay the night. Well-appointed rooms for the price—thick, plentiful towels; free bottled water; plush bathrobes in the closets waiting for you. Also, some of the rooms have *portals*. You may find that the armchair in the room has an otherwise inexplicable safety belt, more appropriate for an automobile, and that a tiny crystal bottle on the nightstand contains a single sleeping pill—these are the signs. Take the pill, seat yourself in the chair—do not remove your clothes: this is important—and close your eyes. For three and a half hours you will drowse and dream of travel, aboard a World War II–era submarine or flying aloft with wings sprouting from your back, and at the end of that time you will find yourself in an identical room in another Republic of Pasiphae hotel, somewhere else in the world, randomly selected by whatever capricious power controls the ethereal transport device. Perhaps Paris; perhaps Peoria; you will arrive without your luggage and will have a slight queasiness of the stomach, but for those of the disposition to go on such an adventure, this is a small price to pay. In circumstances where arrival times are not urgent, companies will book their salesmen for nights in the Pasiphae hotels in the place of purchasing plane tickets, calculating that the possible cost savings when compared with the expense of a business-class international flight is worth the risk. I myself visited the Vatican that way.

Lastly, heed this: *beware all Holiday Inns.* Beware them especially if, as many salesmen do, you find that your mind wanders when you are away for long periods from the one you love, that you find yourself longing for the shape of a woman's body that is either far enough away from hers for novelty, or close enough to let you fool yourself that she is the genuine article. For if you woo such a woman in a bar or restaurant or library, and coax her back to your hotel room for a tryst that you hope will offer some feeble temporary pleasure and go unrecorded in history's ledger, then there is a chance that in several weeks you will receive a forest-green envelope in the mail with only your address on it, and none for a return. You will be certain of its origin, though, for when you open it, on matching green paper there will be written a rhyme that originated in the Bronx nightclubs of the 1970s:

HOTEL MOTEL HOLIDAY INN
I WON'T TELL IF YOU WON'T TELL
BUT I KNOW WHERE YOU'VE BEEN

Once, perhaps twice, I have returned from one of my voyages to find my wife waiting for me, a dutiful Penelope, gesturing toward the pile of mail that accumulated in my absence—solicitations to apply for reverse mortgages; advertisements for magazines I have neither the time nor the inclination to read; coupons for donuts and massages and sushi restaurants (why my wife saves all this junk I do not know—perhaps out of an excessive fastidiousness, or a misplaced desire to account for every single thing that happened while I was away). Once, perhaps twice, I have sifted through this dross to find an envelope with my name embossed upon it, forest green. I have opened it before her, holding my face still, let my eyes slide over the page inside (keeping it out of her view—she is short, and must look up at me), dismissed it with a grunt that brooks no further curiosity, and crumpled the paper in my hand. I toss it in the trash with the rest of the mail; later, when I am sure she is not looking, I retrieve it, light an eye on the kitchen stove, and burn it. A brief whiff of sulfur and it's gone.

~

You didn't know that, did you. Now you know.

SEANAN MCGUIRE

On the Cold Hill Side

Seanan McGuire

The ringing of the phone was like a fire alarm, shattering the pleasant shell of warmth and silence that I had pulled around myself. I fumbled for it, hoping I could make the noise stop before it woke Jinny. No such luck: by the time I had the phone in my hand and was sliding the little green icon to *answer*, she was sitting up in the bed, glaring at me with the sort of censorious judgment that meant I, and my phone, would probably be sleeping on the couch for the next week.

Jinny was in many ways the perfect wife. Patient with my foibles, tolerant of the fact that my work alternately left me underfoot for months at a time and dragged me away in the middle of dinner, and always willing to feed the cat when I went jetting off to some foreign country to do things I would never be able to tell her about. But she was very, *very* protective of her sleep.

"Hello?" I said, raising the phone to my ear as Jinny went stomping off toward the kitchen, presumably to put on a pot of coffee. According to the clock on her side of the bed, which I could read if I squinted, it was a little after five in the morning. No point in either of us going back to sleep, then. We'd just be getting up in an hour.

Oh, Jinny was going to *kill* me.

"Professor Benson, are you in a secure location?"

"I'm in my bedroom." I felt around on my bedside table until I found my glasses. "I *was* asleep. This better be a matter of national security, because I'm not getting out of this bed for anything less. We're talking full-scale incursion into our reality from some creepy-ass temple frozen in the Arctic until global climate change decided we needed the Old Ones to come back. We're talking a confirmed plesiosaur in Lake Michigan. We're talking—"

"Professor Benson, the island of Harbor's Hope has reappeared off the coast of Maine. We have verified satellite images, complete with infrared and seismic mapping. It's there. It's really there."

I managed, somehow, not to drop my phone.

"Professor?"

"When . . ." My voice came out as a croak. I licked my lips to moisten them, swallowed, and tried again. "When will my ride be here?"

"You have fifteen minutes."

"I'll be ready." I hung up the phone, dropping it on my pillow as I surged to my feet and toward the dresser. By the time Jinny came back to the bedroom with a mug of coffee cupped between her hands—only one, since I hadn't done anything to earn pre-sunrise coffee—I was shoving clothes into my duffel bag, piling them on top of and using them to pad my field gear.

She stopped in the doorway, taking a long, deliberate sip of coffee before she asked, in a dangerous tone, "Going somewhere?"

"I am." There was no way of knowing how long this would take. I grabbed a double handful of underwear and shoved it into the bag.

"Allowed to tell me where?"

I hesitated.

The government is not good at keeping secrets, full stop. But they *are* good at covering up and classifying things, and even if something is all over the internet, it's technically treason for me to talk about something that's already been put behind an official veil of secrecy. And yet. There's "we caught the Mothman and it turns out it wasn't a hoax" and then there's "a literal island has appeared in the Atlantic, within sight of American soil, and people are probably already taking pictures."

"I'm going to an island that doesn't exist," I said.

Jinny blinked. "Oh," she said, and took another sip of coffee. "Is that all?"

—

There is no official government organization dedicated to weaponized folklore. That would be silly, and a drain on the budget. The United States government is disturbingly willing to be silly, but they *hate* budgetary waste. Unless it's going to something with immediate military applications. The government *loves* budgetary waste that might lead to things blowing up in a new and interesting way.

There's no official government organization, but there are several unofficial ones, little departments tucked into the bodies of bigger, more profitable orgs, where they can feed off the blood of governmental funding without showing themselves. We're parasitic, in other words, and whenever we're ferreted out, we tend to be shut down loudly, publicly, and with prejudice, usually by some junior congressman who wants to make a big deal of being tough on waste and overspending.

And then someone gets devoured by a corn maze that was cut using a hex pattern someone's granny remembered seeing on the side of a barn when she was a girl, and we wind up reassembled and buried in someone else's budget, getting back to work before the cracks in the world of the probable can open wide enough to swallow anybody else.

I was recruited right out of college, when we were part of the FDA for some reason, and people used to crack jokes about us being the poison apple police. Then we got shut down and reestablished under the National Park Service, and then as part of the Treasury. Right now, we're part of the Fish and Wildlife Service, which I guess is as close as anything. It's just that we're more likely to be dealing with dragons than with dogs.

Because, see, most urban legends and folktales and campfire stories grew up around a seed of truth. Sometimes that truth looks nothing like the fiction, thanks to the multigenerational game of telephone that carries history into rumor into legend. But it's always there, and sometimes it finds its way back to the beginning. Sometimes it remembers how to be true.

Harbor's Hope was one of those stories. A folktale, an urban legend, a myth. Not as well-known as the Roanoke colony, possibly because the place where it had supposedly been was a lot more remote, and a lot less friendly toward outsiders. Neither the people nor the forest seemed to welcome search parties. After the death toll of "brave explorers" trying to find the island had exceeded the island's supposed population, people had consigned it to the scrap heap of stories that simply weren't worth chasing down. Humans can show a sense of self-preservation. Sometimes.

Supposedly, the island of Harbor's Hope was settled at the same time as the Popham Colony, in 1607. The island had possessed no native occupants, despite being rich with wildlife and fertile soil; it had seemed like the perfect place to establish a foothold without pissing anybody off. Surprisingly thoughtful for a bunch of colonists, really. Only they should probably have asked someone why, if the island was so perfect, no one lived there. One thing humans around the world have in common: we don't like to leave good things untouched. Harbor's Hope was a paradise. That should have been the first sign that something was wrong.

When the Popham Colony had failed, only a year later, the surviving colonists had asked the people who evacuated them whether anyone had heard from the residents of the island. They had lost track of their neighbors during the long Maine winter, and they feared that everyone in Harbor's Hope had died. Dead colonists were part of the cost of doing business, but losing a whole settlement smacked of sloppiness, and so ships had been dispatched to check on the island.

They came back empty-handed and confused. Their maps were very clear; their supply routes to Harbor's Hope were well-established, even if no one had sailed along them for months. But the island wasn't there.

More ships were sent. More maps were consulted. And still the island wasn't there. It had simply vanished sometime over the long winter, slipping away in the fog and disappearing. Fingers were pointed. Blame was cast. In the end, however, the only thing that made sense was that the island had sunk back down into the sea and been swallowed in its entirety, along with every living soul in the settlement. Tragic, yes. Unique, sure. But in those days, losing one settlement was considered part of the cost of exploration. See the world and conquer it, or die trying.

That would have been the end of things, Harbor's Hope being small and remote and not particularly shrouded in mystery, had a boat not come ashore in 1710, containing two teenagers with an assortment of trade goods and a strange, almost British accent. They made their way to the nearest settlement, a place too small to even properly be called a town, and proceeded to trade masterfully tanned furs and an assortment of dried meats for medicine, spices, and small tools. According to records of the time, they were ignorant of the fair value of things, and it was easy for the settlers to take advantage of them. Not that the pair seemed overly concerned: if anything, they were stunned by the generosity of the settlers, and indicated that they would be back the next day for more trading.

And they *did* come back, the next day, and the day after that, until the people they were trading with started to feel a little bad for taking advantage of them and asked where they were from. Or at least, that's the story. Maybe the people they were trading with actually wanted to follow them back to whatever trove of wonders they were sitting on and make one big, final, involuntary trade. "Trading" at knifepoint wasn't that uncommon in those days. Hell, it's not that uncommon now.

The teens replied, without a drop of guile, that they were from the town of Harbor's Hope, and that they just wanted to finish their trading before the tides shifted again. They were very clear about that: they needed to be home when the tides shifted.

Naturally, the locals didn't like this answer, and insisted on following them back to their boat, where the teens happily pointed out a large island, sitting too near to the shore to have been easily overlooked, and identified it—needlessly—as Harbor's Hope. The missing island had somehow returned, and brought its people with it . . . or their descendants. This was no tumble into fairyland. The people of Harbor's Hope had clearly expanded their settlement over the hundred and some years of their absence, and these teens had been chosen to bring home the things the island couldn't produce on its own.

I want to say that things went smoothly after that, that the settlers stopped taking advantage of the teens from Harbor's Hope, that everyone went home satisfied. But that wouldn't be much of a story, and it had to be a story if it was going to survive. The settlers seized the two teens, accusing them of witchcraft. They confiscated the remaining trade goods. They locked the pair in the basement of the church and set sail for the island, intending to catch its occupants unawares.

They were halfway there when the tides changed. A cold wind blew off the Atlantic, and a fog rolled in, faster than any fog they had seen before. One of the boats began to paddle faster, intending to make landing on the island and wait out the oncoming storm. The other boat returned to shore.

There was no storm. When the fog cleared, the lead boat was gone, never to be seen again. And so was the island.

The teens were convicted of witchcraft. What happened to them after that is less clear. It seems likely they were put to death. Only the method is missing from the records. If they were allowed to live, they never went home. Harbor's Hope wouldn't make another appearance until 1821—twenty years too early for there to be any photographic evidence. Lots of people went to see the impossible island. So far as we're aware, no one tried to sail out and pay the island a visit, and there are no reports of trading parties being sent by the islanders. They had not forgotten the theft of their children.

The island stayed for a month that time, silent and somehow ominous. There are records from the time of people on the shore and smoke curling up through the trees, which seemed to have been cultivated to provide cover for the town. Over the past hundred years, the people of Harbor's Hope had learned both subterfuge and caution. When the fog rolled in, exactly as it had the last time the island disappeared, the overwhelming feeling was of relief. "It was as if we had been tempted, and had managed, through our faith in Christ our Savior, to set temptation aside," wrote one of the witnesses. Accounts like that one are why scholars have been able to say with relative conviction that the 1821 manifestation really happened, unlike the "oh, I saw it on the sea" urban legends that were already starting to crop up.

I don't blame the bored teenagers who needed an excuse for skipping out on their chores to feel each other up somewhere out in the woods, far from prying parental eyes. I wish they could have done it without muddying the historical narratives surrounding Harbor's Hope, but it's not like hormones have ever cared much about history. Hormones care about the here and now. Everything else can wait.

The island appeared again in 1918. We have pictures from that occurrence, although without GPS tagging to authenticate, they could be pictures of any small island off the coast of New England. The shape of the shore—as much as can be determined—matches the old survey maps taken before the colony was established there. The trees surround the island's interior in a manner consistent with descriptions of the 1821 appearance, as long as the viewer allows for a century's additional growth. Smoke curls from somewhere inside those trees. It's the only sign of habitation in the 1918 pictures: no one saw boats either leaving or approaching the island while it was there, although local townships reported strangers with unusual accents and a keen interest in trading for medicine and tools. It seems likely, looking back at the occurrence, that the people of Harbor's Hope figured out how to do their trading without being caught. And then, of course, the Spanish Flu swept the country, and people became a bit less interested in disappearing, reappearing islands than they were in staying alive.

That occurrence lasted for six months before some locals got the bright idea to flee from the flu by rowing out to Harbor's Hope and asking for asylum. The fog rolled in when they were halfway across the bay; when the fog cleared, the island was gone. So were the people. There are no records of them ever being seen again.

But the island has been seen again. Here and now, today. After a hundred years of absence, Harbor's Hope was back, and this time, the government was going to get involved. This time, we were going to find out exactly what was going on. Or we were all going to die trying.

Folklore is a lot more exciting than my professors ever told me it was going to be.

~

One thing I will absolutely give to the United States government: they can be efficient when they want to be. By the time I arrived at the airport, I had a boarding pass on my phone, guaranteeing me a first-class seat on a direct flight to Portland, Maine, leaving in slightly under ninety minutes. That same pass had some encoded flags that caused the TSA employees manning the various checkpoints to go pale and wave me through without even the usual mockery of security. Apparently, once you have enough security clearance, you're no longer going to bring down a plane with that scary, scary bottle of water you forgot in the bottom of your purse.

In what felt like the blinking of an eye, I was settled in my remarkably comfortable seat, a glass of orange juice in my hand, scrolling through the news and waiting for the first sensationalist article about the mysterious island off the coast of Maine. It popped up just as the cabin crew was closing the doors for takeoff. A group of surprisingly social media–savvy fishermen had been on their way to a favorite fishing spot when they saw the island, rising out of a clearing fog like an iceberg appearing in the middle of the open sea. Their video was accompanied by a lot of cries of "Do you see that?" and "Holy shit, Carl! Holy shit!" I wasn't sure which of the voices was Carl, but as they all sounded pretty damn impressed, I was willing to say that he'd been as holy-shit-excited as the rest of them.

By the time we reached cruising altitude and the airplane Wi-Fi came online, a dozen more videos had joined the first one. The last one I found showed what looked like a detachment from the Coast Guard moving our would-be cinematographers out of the area, while they continued to film and shouted about freedom of the press. I was pleased to note that the guards looked unimpressed by these claims of journalistic integrity. There are things that need to be broadcast to the world, and then there are things that don't.

There are stories of disappearing, reappearing places all over the world. Towns are most common—who doesn't remember *Brigadoon?*—but valleys and islands aren't unheard-of. Like most recurring stories, they're easily explained as a quirk in the human psyche, some attempt to explain away tragedy or natural disaster. And maybe that works well enough for the places like the original village of Hamelin, which disappear and then never come back. Places like Harbor's Hope though . . .

They screwed everything up, because they refused to stay gone. It was easy to explain a place that simply disappeared as being swallowed by an earthquake or wiped out by a fever. It was a lot harder to explain them when they came *back*.

I spent the rest of the trip reading files on Harbor's Hope, interspersing them with firsthand accounts from the people who'd been able to reach the shore before the government shut them out, and when the captain announced that we were making our initial descent, I was sure of precisely two things. First, that either this was the real deal or somebody had managed to construct the most realistic papier-mâché model of all time, and second, that this was the opportunity of a lifetime, because unlike the fictional Brigadoon, the people of Harbor's Hope weren't slipping outside the ordinary flow of time. The settlement had visibly grown between the first appearance and the second, when the locals had abducted two of the island's teens and caused them to plant the tree wall between themselves and the shore. Every subsequent appearance had shown additional growth and density in the tree wall. They were living the same number of days that we were. They were just living the majority of them somewhere . . . else.

Did they go to another dimension, some parallel North America? Or did they float surrounded by the fog that heralded their appearances and disappearances, trapped in an endless wall of gray until the next time the fog parted and let them see the shore? It couldn't be too miserable, or the traders we'd seen across the centuries would have been looking for more than medicine and simple tools—the kind of things a settled, technologically unsophisticated island would have been unable to make for themselves.

We had so much to ask them, and so much to learn, and so little time to do any of it.

The government's thoughts clearly paralleled my own. Three agents in black suits were waiting for me on the jetway. One of them took my roller bag. The other two fell into step alongside me, whisking me away before the rest of the passengers could do more than line up and gawk. I gave the woman to my left a narrow-eyed look.

"You know they're all going to think I was some sort of terrorist or something who managed to get past airport security," I said. "That wasn't kind."

She smirked. "Maybe they'll complain a little less about the way we spend their tax dollars," she said. "Did you check a bag?"

It was a pointless question, the sort of small civility that extended all the way down to the roots of our daily interactions. I managed, barely, not to snort in derision.

"As if I would."

"Good, because I would have told you to come back and get it from the lost luggage office. The car's waiting at the curb."

"I assume in a no-waiting zone?"

Her smirk grew. "Honestly, do you even need to ask?"

Sometimes government goons really went out of their way to earn the title. I rolled my eyes and kept walking, not even bothering to ask whether we could stop at the bathroom. They'd be happier visiting an unsecured rest stop than letting me out of their sight at this stage. I'd never been able to understand why, but after as many trips as I'd taken in their company, I was willing to go along with the airport extraction. In what seemed like an unrealistic amount of time, I was in an unmarked black sedan with two more uniformed agents, and the three who'd escorted me this far were climbing into their own matching car.

It was normally an hour's drive to the city of Phippsburg, built on the site of the old Popham Colony, and a forty-five-minute walk along the shore from there to the vantage point which gave the best view of Harbor's Hope. That assumed speed limits. Even with a stop to buy a cup of coffee and use the coffee shop's bathroom, we were pulling into the lot commandeered for government use forty-five minutes after I'd stepped off the plane. My handling team from the airport apparently had even less respect for traffic laws than my driver: they were already there when I got out of the car. The lead agent made a show of checking her watch.

"Is this how you run all your operations?" she asked. "Sloppy, Professor Benson. Very sloppy."

"Sloppy is as sloppy does," I replied, and looked around the lot, focusing on the trail that had been blocked off by portable aluminum gates. In case that wasn't indication enough, armed soldiers stood to either side, preventing any casual tourism. "Isn't this a little bit extreme?"

"No," she said, and started toward the trailhead.

I followed. That's what I was here for, after all.

The walk took forty-five minutes, as projected. The government might be able to ignore speed limits, but they couldn't bend distance—not yet, anyway. I breathed in deeply, enjoying the fresh, bright scents of the Maine woods. It was the perfect time of year for a hike, not yet in the sweltering depths of summer, but far enough from the frozen winter to be hospitable and welcoming. Most Maine tourism probably happened around this time of year.

And then we came around the bend in the trail, and I saw the island, and nothing else mattered anymore.

It was clearly the island from the pictures of the 1918 incursion, although its core was hidden behind a thicker, denser wall of trees. Time had done its job, tucking the population away from easy observation. Smoke curled up from beyond the wall. There were people there. Harbor's Hope was still occupied.

I glanced to my escort. She nodded.

"We have satellite images for you to review. We're looking at a population of about eight hundred people."

Large, for an island of this size, but not unreasonably so, not as long as everyone was willing to work together and keep the peace. There would still be plenty of room for farming and forest, if the original survey maps were accurate.

"How many buildings?" I asked.

"Difficult to say."

I frowned. "How is that hard? It's simple math."

"They build vertically more than we expect from this sort of settlement. We have shots of what we assume are a sort of primitive apartment complex; individual homes don't seem to be a priority."

"Meaning they could be stacking themselves like cordwood. Got it. Have we made any attempts to contact the islanders?"

"Not yet. We were waiting for the specialists."

"Me, and . . . ?"

"Professor Helm. Lieutenant Milton."

I nodded approvingly. Professor Helm was a historian; our fields overlapped with surprising frequency, as his discoveries could feed into my own, while my scraps of semi-credible information could sometimes lead him to things the rest of the scientific establishment had long dismissed. Lieutenant Milton was an army linguist. If these people had drifted away from anything we'd recognize as "English," she would be able to steer them back, or at least chart her own course to their destination. Between the three of us, we'd be able to make this work. We

267

had to make this work. Because if we didn't, it was going to be another hundred years before we got our next chance.

"They're both here," said the agent. "We'll be lighting bonfires on the beach to try and signal our presence. We don't want to approach the island without giving them the chance to approach us."

I nodded again. Given their past interactions with the mainland, it would be perfectly understandable if the people of Harbor's Hope didn't want us coming anywhere near their homes—and their children. Silently, I cursed those long-dead New Englanders for their detention and persecution of two innocent teens. How much could we have learned from our dimensionally unmoored cousins if we hadn't reintroduced ourselves by stealing their children? So many opportunities, wasted.

Together, we walked the rest of the way down to the encampment on the shore, arriving there just as the bonfires were lit. Three of them, loaded down with accelerant and freshly cut branches still oozing sap. The green wood caught slowly and billowed smoke, great white gouts of it, like we were waving a flag of peace against the chalky morning sky.

I stopped next to the bonfires, my eyes on the distant island shore. A woman in a subdued brown uniform emerged from one of the hastily assembled tents and came to stand next to me, offering a polite nod.

"Lieutenant," I said.

"Professor," she replied, with a sliver of a smile. We both understood, far too well, what it was like to be a woman in a male-dominated profession. Sometimes a proper title was the greatest sign of respect there was. "How's the wife?"

"Oh, pissed, but she'll get over it when I come home with a gallon of real maple syrup. They have to call you off deployment?"

"Yes," she said. "Location's classified, but we've found some fascinating regional linguistic quirks that should make trade easier."

Meaning she'd only come here because she thought this was

somehow more important. Fascinating. "Any sign of movement from the island?"

"Yes." Her eyes widened. "There."

I turned.

Two wooden boats had appeared on the shore, each of them pushed by four people in what looked, from this distance, like homespun linen. They kept pushing, until the boats were floating, and then they climbed in and began to paddle their way across the water toward us.

"Well," I said. "I guess we're actually going to earn our paychecks this time."

There was a dull ache in my chest, somewhere between excitement and dread. The people of Harbor's Hope were making contact. What amazing secrets were we going to learn today? What truths did the island have to tell us?

Were we ready to learn?

⁓

It took about half an hour for the boats to row their way to shore. We were all lined up and waiting for their arrival by the time their passengers pulled them up onto the sand and turned to face us.

Two boats; four people in each, a number that made sense since, as they grew closer, we had been able to see that two people rowed while the other two held weapons at the ready, prepared to defend themselves. Two had bows, clearly handcrafted, made with a skill and artistry that made my fingers ache to hold them. The other two had guns, one a flintlock from the 1700s, the other a more modern 1900s pistol. There was nothing in the stories about the people from Harbor's Hope trading for guns, but we didn't have all the information. They could have done trades with smaller groups, or they could have stolen things from the locals. We had no way of knowing, and the guns were certainly real.

All four of them looked reasonably well-fed, although their

complexions were spotty and their teeth were interspersed with the kind of gaps I'd expect from people living in a society with limited access to dentistry. I silently added books on home tooth care to the list of things we had to offer them. Toothpaste wouldn't last the hundred years before their next appearance, but they had the technology to make charcoal and floss, and that might make a genuine difference in their quality of life.

Or maybe they didn't want to improve their quality of life. They were doing pretty well for themselves, as far as I could tell. Their clothing was handmade and well-worn but fit them well and looked both comfortable and warm. Their posture was straight, and their bodies showed no real signs of malnutrition.

"You come in peace?" asked one of the men. His accent was ... challenging, a mixture of what I would call deep Southern drawl and something swifter, more staccato. His vowels had drifted over the centuries in isolation. Not as far as I would have expected them to. They must have been making a concerted effort, on the island, to keep their speech in line with their societal memories of the mainland.

Pronunciation is a part of the oral tradition, the same as anything else, but this was the first time I'd ever been so close to a living example. Lieutenant Milton was staring at the eight of them like they were the most magical things she'd ever seen.

"We do," said Professor Helm. All of us had agreed that he was the best equipped to represent us. He had the historical training, he had the credentials, and he was an older white man, which would hopefully resonate with the population of Harbor's Hope. We had no idea what their society had done with gender roles, closed off from the rest of the world as they were. There were women among their party, which made me hope that they hadn't stayed with a purely colonial model, but there was really no way of being sure until we'd talked to them more.

"Not always so, when the shore appears," said the man.

"We have gifts for you, to show our sincerity," said Helm. "We brought things you've sought in the past, medicines and spices and simple tools. We also brought some books about the changes that have happened since Harbor's Hope was settled."

"We represent the United States government," said one of the agents, apparently unwilling to be left out of the conversation. "On behalf of the president, welcome home."

The people from Harbor's Hope exchanged a complicated glance before starting to laugh.

"Claim us now, would you?" asked one of the women. "Like we're for staying? We're not for staying. Tide will turn. Tide always turns."

"That's what we hoped to discuss with you," said the agent.

"Parlay perhaps," said one of the men. "Shall begin?"

"Shall," said Milton, and smiled.

～

According to the people from Harbor's Hope, they knew when the tide was going to turn. Little signs popped up all over the island, as if it was getting itself ready to shift to wherever it went when it wasn't here. It would move faster if its occupants were in danger, which explained the varying lengths of the island's appearances—and how it had stayed long enough to be settled in the first place. No one had lived there then. It hadn't had anyone to protect.

With at least three weeks to go before tide turn, and with so many questions in need of answering, an agreement had tentatively been reached: we would send one group of people to the island, to be called back at the first signs of fog rolling across the water. In the end, it was myself, Milton, Helm, and two agents who climbed into a small boat and followed the Harbor's Hope residents across the water.

The air changed when we were halfway there, turning sweeter, like it had yet to fully mingle with the outside pollution. The trees were clearly cedar, but there were small morphological differences in their branches, making me suspect that they might be a new subspecies. I took pictures, as many as I dared while we were on the water. I was no botanist, but the ones I knew would be enthralled.

An island. An American island that shut itself off for a century at a time, following its own path. There was so much here to learn, so much to document and know. I kept my eyes on the shore, waiting for the moment when we would run aground.

Back on the mainland, four of the Harbor's Hope residents were sitting down to discuss further trade with the government agents who hadn't elected to come with us. In an interesting quirk, we never saw the same people twice: they came over, loaded their boats, and then returned to the island, to be replaced by someone new. Maybe it was because they all wanted a chance to see the strangers. Maybe it was because they were afraid of cultural contamination. They had to be fairly insular by now, for all that they were friendly, openhanded and smiling.

There was so much here to learn, and so little time to learn it.

When our boat struck the shore, it was a gentle bump. The agent who had been steering killed the engine, and we all set foot on Harbor's Hope for the first time.

The experience was sadly anticlimactic. It felt like any other isolated, slightly rocky shore. Our guides moved ahead of us, beckoning for us to follow, and so follow we did, through the tree wall to a well-trodden path that cut through less dense but still towering forest. The trees gave way to small, well-tended beds of vegetables and herbs, some of which I recognized, some of which I had never seen before.

And then we were through, and I saw the settlement of Harbor's Hope.

It was built in a natural depression that seemed unlikely, for an island, where the water table had to be so close to the surface. Every inch of space had been used, and when there was no more space, they had found methods of inventing it, stacking their homes higher and higher, until they towered in a way that would have been quaint with modern construction materials, but seemed oddly anachronistic here. Bridges and skyways connected the upper floors, and primitive "elevators" had been constructed with ropes and pulleys, allowing people who couldn't make the climb to have full access to their own homes.

And the people! There were people everywhere, thronging in the streets, making their way from place to place. They were close-packed but not overly so; someone, somewhere, must have found a method of population control. It was my job to ask after that, along with so much else. I didn't want to. So many of the answers I would get might be horrifying ones.

"Mayor's expecting you," said one of our guides. "Hurry on, then. Meal's to be set."

The guides walked faster. I glanced to Milton.

"Am I concerned?"

She shook her head. "I'm still getting a handle on their grammar, but I don't think we've discovered a secret society of dimension-hopping cannibals. I'm fairly sure 'meal's to be set' just means that they're getting ready to put food on the table, and they want the guests of honor to be on time."

"Good. Jinny would be pissed if I got myself eaten before our anniversary."

Milton laughed. We all kept walking.

The people of Harbor's Hope were consistent with the ones we'd seen away from the island: well-fed and reasonably healthy, with some signs of poor access to medical and dental care. They had clearly constructed their settlement with the needs of all its people in mind. Their separation from the mainland had happened before the invention of the personal wheelchair, but I saw individuals in little carts, almost like wagons, being pulled by hearty-looking goats. They had simply adapted the chariot to suit their needs. Some people used crutches; one man walked on what was very clearly a prosthetic leg made from carved and fitted wood.

More interesting, from a sociological perspective, were the same-gender couples. Men walked hand in hand with other men; women walked hand in hand with other women. I nodded toward one of those couples.

"Look at that," I said.

Helm followed my gaze. "It's not uncommon for isolated societies to establish their own societal mores. I wouldn't be surprised if acceptance of other sexualities arose out of a need for population control. They don't have access to much in the way of contraception, and space is limited."

"And lesbians need help to make babies," I said flatly.

His cheeks reddened. "I didn't say—"

"It makes sense," I said. "We don't know that they have anywhere off the island to go." While the people of Harbor's Hope had been happy to talk about their trade needs, insisting on paying with furs, dried meat, preserved fruit, and dried herbs, they had been oddly reticent to talk about the place the island went between appearances. Time passed. Their small society thrived, despite all the odds the universe could stack against them. They were happy—or if not, they were faking it remarkably well. No one had mentioned wanting to seek asylum in the United States, something I was sure our government friends were relieved about. Were they citizens or weren't they? Their ancestors had been in North America before the founding of the United States, which technically would have granted *them* full citizenship, but were their descendants, who had been born somewhere . . . else . . . included?

That was a question above my paygrade. I was here to document folklore becoming historical fact, and I had more than enough to keep myself occupied.

We followed our guides through the settlement and into the woods on the other side, where a large clearing had been outfitted as an outdoor feasting area. Teens and older children brought out trays and platters, loading the tables with a surprising amount of food. We must have looked confused. One of our guides laughed.

"Good tidings, this, when visitors come to us and are not afraid," he said. "Sit. Eat. Enjoy."

The meat was rich and savory, seasoned according to flavor profiles that had fallen out of favor centuries ago. There was mead, and ale, although no wine or beer; they didn't have the space to grow either grapes or hops. Helm asked questions about the food while Milton drank everything in—words and alcohol alike.

Maybe that was why she lost consciousness first.

I blinked eyelids that suddenly felt too heavy and slightly removed, like they belonged to someone else, as I watched her slump to the table in a dead sleep. Helm collapsed next, while I was still trying to find the words to formulate a warning. I turned to the nearest local.

"You drugged us," I said accusingly.

"Yes," he agreed.

"Why?"

"Seemed better to have you live," he said, and then my head hit the table, and everything was silence.

~

I woke in a lumpy bed, under a pile of furs. My head ached. That seemed to be the only reminder of my experience at dinner. I sat bolt upright, and froze as I saw the window next to me.

Outside it was a world remade in fog.

"Can't go out," said a weary voice. I turned. There was a woman sitting guard by the door. She had a gun in her hand that I recognized from our camp. "Tide's turning, fog's up; out's not for us, not right now. When it settles, you'll see."

"You—why did you—"

"Need new bodies, time to time. Keeps the babies strong, keeps the minds open. When the need gets bad enough, the fog carries us to where we started, and we send out traders. Did it open at first. Now we do it hidden, because people don't take kindly to the truth."

"You could have asked."

"Couldn't." She looked at me calmly. "There's more than us on the island. We don't only carry furs when we go shoring. Wanted you to live, so we put you down long enough to tell your bodies how to breathe through the sickness."

It all came together with a snap. The weakness in my limbs; the strange, sickly odor in the room. The dates. The years.

1918.

"The Spanish Flu," I said, in a small, horrified voice.

"Don't know that, but know the sickness," she said. "Caught it before we went away the first time. We have ways to treat and cajole it away, but it always comes back. Went into the birds, we think. Went into the pigs. Need them both, and so we kept them. Found herbs, found simples, found mushrooms on the mainland. We can break the sickness when it comes for us. Can break it on the mainland too by now, can't you?"

We'd all been exposed as soon as the people from Harbor's Hope had come ashore. No one had been symptomatic, but that didn't matter. Viruses move on their own timetable.

There were so many gaps in the records. There were so many places where things simply weren't written down. When there's a gap in history, it's so often because something has been killing the people who would have kept the records before they could reach for a pen.

1918. The Spanish Flu. It had killed so many people. The numbers were still in flux, but I'd heard a hundred million, and it hadn't felt like an exaggeration. And that had been before the rise of the anti-vaccination movement, before the rise of cheap air travel. It was going to go even farther this time. It was going to damage even more.

Jinny, I'm sorry, I thought.

The woman rose from her chair, smiling encouragingly at me. Outside the window, the fog was thinning.

"Come to, you," she said. "It's time to see the mainland."

"The tide—"

"A hundred years, poppet. Same for you as for the rest of us. Come along now. Come along."

She moved toward the door. I got out of the bed and followed her. There was nothing else to do; the island had moved, and my world was lost to me, forever.

The rest of the story I'd come chasing was waiting for me outside.

She opened the door.

I stepped through.

JEFFREY FORD

The Return of Grace Malfrey

Jeffrey Ford

Lynn was away on business, and I was sitting out in my rocker on the porch, having a few drinks and smoking a joint. There was a cool September wind that rattled the dry leaves, the crickets rehearsed their winter song, and from out of the night a bent figure teetered into view. I jumped in my chair, if such a thing is possible, and said, "You scared the shit out of me." He gave a phlegmy laugh and came up the steps one at a time. Shuffling past me, now nothing but shadow in the perfect dark of the porch, he took Lynn's usual seat, and I handed him a beer.

He was primarily there to drink my beer, but that was okay. I wasn't really sure what he looked like, having only encountered him at night after drinking and smoking. There had been five or six other incidents when he'd shown up in the same manner, staggering out of the night. On all of these occasions, Lynn was away. He'd complain of insomnia, carry on about how the past was waiting for him in his dreams. That was followed by a steady stream of inconsequential bullshit that lasted through his second beer. By the time he cracked the third, his memory would somehow become like the beacon of a lighthouse and his disjointed utterances coalesced into the shape of a memory.

He said, "Did I ever tell you about Grace Malfrey?"

"No."

"She was a girl, eleven years old, who lived up a few farms toward Plain City on the other side of Route 42."

"When are we talking?" I asked.

"Oh, right. Would have been the '70s. If I remember, earlier rather than later. It was a lot different here than it is now. Just as much corn but more winter wheat. Way more isolated by a long shot. No computers, no cell phones. I was well out of high school when this happened. The girl, Grace Malfrey, went across the giant field behind her mother's farmhouse toward the woods. She carried a basket to gather pine cones and acorns and autumn leaves in order to make a place setting for Thanksgiving dinner. The family had been around here for a long time and in that very farmhouse for at least eighty years. That day, though, a few before the holiday, was when she went missing."

"Took off or was abducted?"

The slouching silhouette of the old man shook its head. "No, I mean went out like a candle at a birthday party." He gave his fingers a dry snap. "There one second and then not. Two people saw her disappear. One was her mother, standing at the kitchen sink and peering out the large window above it. The other was the paperboy who happened to be riding by out on the road, and saw her from a distance. He told them that she never made it to the tree line. Her mother corroborated the boy's statement. 'Vanished like a dream in daylight,' was how she put it.

"Oh, they looked everywhere for her. The police took the paperboy and the girl's mother seriously. They came up with a theory that perhaps she fell through a sinkhole in the field. A sudden plunge into the earth might have given the impression of her vanishing. They dug for days. There were also organized search parties to scour the woods. I was part of more than one. The loneliness of winter and the newly born myths of the girl's disappearance made the woods biblical.

"When no trace was found, suspicion turned on the mother and the paperboy. There was a theory that went around that the paperboy and Mrs. Malfrey had something between them. As the gossip went, young Grace caught them making the beast with two backs and so they clipped her wick and did a good job of disposing of the body."

"Hold up," I said. "How old was this paperboy? I was picturing the kid as about the same age as Grace."

"He was five years older, sixteen."

"How old was the mother?"

"Near forty, give or take . . ."

"Well, I guess that's more likely than her just going out like a light," I said. "But still . . ." I lit the citronella candle that hadn't been used for weeks and dug through the bag for more beers. When I handed the old man another, I caught a glimpse of a half-assed gray beard, like a seven o'clock shadow, and white hair that appeared to have been combed with a spoon. He was a pasty vision, à la Madame Tussauds. His bottom jaw hung open and his tongue was way too busy. He reached for a pack of cigarettes in his shirt pocket with a shaking hand. Lighting one on the candle, he scratched the middle of his forehead with a long yellow thumbnail and told me that when Grace Malfrey was gone for three years, a group of kids playing in a dried-out stream bed found a scarf that two of the girls identified as one often worn by Grace. When her mother was questioned as to whether the girl was wearing it the day of the disappearance, she cried and said she couldn't remember.

"Eventually the case went cold, although it was never officially closed. A year further on saw Mrs. Malfrey take her own life with a straight razor. Straight across the windpipe, in the toilet, wearing a pink nightgown. Mr. Malfrey had been gone from before Grace went away. In her suicide letter, Grace's mother confessed that she'd always thought that her husband had walked out on her because he didn't love her anymore. But now she'd begun to wonder if he hadn't been claimed by the same alternate dimension, space hole, time slip, pocket of god, that had enveloped her daughter. The last thing she mentioned in the letter, and something she was ever adamant about in life, was that Grace had most certainly *vanished*.

"In the years that followed, around Halloween time, capitalizing on the creepiness of the affair, the local paper would run a story about the missing girl. Kids drinking in the woods at night scared each other with sightings of Grace Malfrey back from the beyond to exact revenge. For what, though, nobody really knew. The old-timers like my grandpa, believed hex magic was at play, the old Pow-wow. Almost ten years after the incident occurred, I remember when it was because I'd gone away and tried to be a salesman in Cincinnati, and had just returned and rejoined my pa and, old as I am now, grandpa, working the farm here.

"The week after I come back, the story was all over the news—Grace Malfrey appeared in the parking lot of Der Dutchman's restaurant, bare-ass naked, and pale as snow. Three different people saw her just sort of fall out of the day, like a slit was made in reality and Grace was pushed through from somewhere else. She landed headfirst next to the sidewalk with a thud and a groan. Those on their way into the restaurant for an after-church Sunday breakfast were stunned. A woman from the gift shop had seen the whole thing and run out to cover the young woman with a quilt that had hung on the wall for sale. Eventually the police were called. Grace was found to be conscious and was escorted to one of the rocking chairs that lined the walkway to the entrance.

"The cops showed up, and by that night, on the local news, it was reported that Grace Malfrey had returned. There was footage of Malfrey, sitting in the rocker, stuttering uncontrollably at the questions put to her by the local press. Also, one of the women who'd witnessed Grace's arrival went on camera to say, 'She fell out of absolutely nothing. And she was followed by a distinct odor of smoke.' Reports soon followed that she was being held for observation. A doctor appeared on the news one night and told the public that Ms. Malfrey was traumatized and needed time to understand that she was safe. The reporters yelled out, 'So where's she been?' and 'How was she traumatized?'"

The old man put out his cigarette and leaned back in his chair.

"Then what happened?" I asked.

"I can't remember," he said. "I know there was more of it, but by then my life was in high gear. I was married, had two kids, and was trying to help keep the farm running. I didn't have time for it. Grace Malfrey wasn't going to help me get things done. I was glad she'd returned and to know the universe could be merciful in the way it handed her back over. But that was as far as my interest went."

"That's it?" I said. "Four beers and you're leaving me hanging?"

"Let's make it five," he suggested.

"What have you got left to tell me about Grace?"

"She's still local. She lives out a ways from town. I'm in my late seventies so she must be in her early sixties. She lives alone. I see her in town all the time. You have to go to this site online called *Grace Malfrey Testimony*. It's a video, a long one, and it's a camera on Grace, back from wherever, looking to be about thirty-something—long dark hair, black turtle neck sweater, smoking like a chimney. The camera work is bad, but it's definitely her and she's talking about where she'd been."

~

The next day, since it was an empty season, and I couldn't get anything cooking between my ears, I went online and looked for the *Grace Malfrey Testimony*. I found it just like the old man predicted. Beneath the video was a counter of how many views it had had since being posted in 1997, and the number was twelve. While turning up the sound, I saw Grace appear out of the static. There was somebody there, off camera, who was asking her questions—a male voice. She smoked nervously, her expression dull, her gaze distant.

The back-and-forth went on for some time, and I took notes on what transpired. Basically, she said that she traveled somewhere when she disappeared. The ground opened up as in a fairy tale to rectify an evil deed, she fell in and was swept away by a silver stream whose waters she could breathe while rushing underground. She passed through caverns teeming with giant toadstools, past the hidden violet ocean, through Hell, and across the flaming red sun at the center of the world. The next thing she knew, she was sixteen, living in a city called Adaleen. She had a factory job at night, sorting the pieces of severed human hands into buckets of thumbs, pointers, pinkies, ring fingers, wrists, and palms. Every evening she rode a rickety old bike out of town along a straight cracked road, which the dusty wind blew across in waves. There was the Spethzer Factory, a mile or more long and ten stories tall with smokestacks every thirty yards. It belched black smoke without interruption—morning, noon, and night. The soot fell in squalls like early spring snow, and a sturdy parasol came in handy.

One day at work she asked where the hand parts came from and her supervisor told her, "Hands." She rode to work in the near dark and returned in the pitch dark. Every few nights one of the young women who worked at the factory went missing from

286

somewhere along the bike path that connected Adaleen to Speth-zer's. There were glowing signs along the route that warned not to slow down or to stop for more than a minute. The sign actually claimed that "Nightmarish Beasts roamed the area." Grace attested that she laughed when she read the sign, even though she was "deathly afraid."

In her small apartment, the only entertainment that she had was a hand-cranked Victrola and two records. One was a symphony piece called "Mountain Snow Trance," a pretty tune that wandered, not in any hurry, and eventually left her staring out the window at an early morning's black snow falling across the city. The other record was a jolly tune with harpsichord and glockenspiel and a male voice saying more than singing, "Larf, larf, larf." She found the tune, "Larf a Larf," terrifying. Whenever it played, she said she remembered having caught her mother and the paperboy going at it when she was eleven. She said this straight up in the online testimony. Go check it out. The interviewer who must have at one point heard the old gossip inquired if the paperboy and her mother had tried to do her harm.

"You mean beyond my mother trying, with her endless blather about my faithless father, to make me a psycho, and the paperboy trying to get me to pull my pants down in the woods? No. They had nothing to do with my journey to Adaleen."

She told that her life at night was bathed in deep shadows with a rare bright light and surrounding fields of gray. On their one night off from the factory, she and the other workers scrabbled through the dilapidated remains of a once-fine city. It was empty, with plenty of places to hide from whoever was running the show in Adaleen. There was an illicitly made and secretly sold liquor known as Pistol Witch, that after a dozen or more unremarkable swigs eventually hit you with a knockout punch behind the eyes. Grace drank it and more than once had been left among the ruins to stagger home at dawn with all eyes upon her.

This strange life she'd fallen into went on for years, and yet she never lost the belief that she belonged somewhere else, in another reality. When she felt she was losing herself to the world of Adaleen, she said she would remember the harvest season back home, the autumn, the activity, all relying on each other. That worked well until she met Hasp. He was an escapee from the factory routine, choosing to live on whatever scraps he might find in the old city. The powers that were hunted the likes of Hasp. Grace met him in the abandoned reading room of the municipal library. The divans were layered with dust, the wooden lions crouched above each of the voluminous chairs, made to be like clouds one could fold one's legs up into and hide with a book.

She talked about how exciting his plans of escape were to her, how alive he was. They spoke in whispers, hoping no one would hear, of what they each remembered from their lives before Adaleen. At this juncture, she held up her hand to the interviewer as if intuiting his next question, and said, "Yeah, we did it. And he was a damn sight better than the paperboy." She laughed raucously until she got caught up in a cough that choked her. She took another hit of her cigarette, choked some more and then continued, saying that Hasp came home with her to her small apartment. Somehow, they both fit in the slender bed, they lived on her meager rations, danced slow and close to "Mountain Snow Trance." She continued going to work, and he went out thieving at night for whatever he could get.

The long and short of it was that she got pregnant. She stayed with her job as long as she could, even though the work disgusted her more now than ever before. The ride home from the factory became yet more dangerous in that she didn't have the energy to make the trip without at least one rest midway. Then Hasp took ill, seriously. He couldn't get treatment because he was no longer covered by the "Adaleen Workers Consideration." Grace had to carry on, getting to work and taking care of Hasp when she returned in the early morning in addition to being pregnant.

Whatever disease it was that Hasp had, it was changing him, transforming him into something different. At times she could hear his bones pop and crack in order to fuse into some other formation. He screamed every time, and she would have to cover his face with the pillow so none of the other tenants in her building could hear. It was against the law for the factory women to have male visitors. Once she was late to catch his scream in the pillow and it escaped to echo through the cabbage soup mist of the hallways. She covered his face as quickly as she could, but when she removed the pillow, she found that he had become her.

Grace reared back away from her own gaze. Herself, in the bed, said in her voice, "You are going to give birth to yourself. You will perish when your child is born." That said, the form that had been Hasp and then was Grace, all at once turned to salt. She had to remove the sheet from the bed and shake it out the window to get it clean. At that point of the story, on the videotape, she said, "I stayed pregnant for years. And carried the burden through all my shifts, even battled and killed a nightmarish beast along the road out to Spethzer's with a handheld crossbow I found in the ruins."

Grace wiped a tear from her eye with a knuckle and said, "And then it all came to pass in a day, and I was thrown into a violent labor. The little creature struggled to free itself, to escape back to Ohio. The slit in the day that people saw me fall out of in the restaurant parking lot was my vagina from a different dimension, if you know what I mean. I died in Adaleen, no doubt left another pile of salt on the sheets back in that hellhole."

That was pretty much that as to the disappearance and return of Grace Malfrey. But I didn't want to let it go and scoured the internet for other cases of people slipping out of reality. There are literally a million stories of people getting in their cars and heading for work or home and later the car is found but the person is missing. That's not the same thing. In these cases, it's pretty obvious the person in question met with foul play somewhere along their journey. That can't be said in the case of Grace Malfrey. In her situation there was neither time nor space for reality to intercede. She was simply, suddenly, *away*. It amazes me that it never became a national story, considering its inexplicable nature. An impossibility revealed. God, playing dice with the universe. The conclusion I came to is that most people don't want the impossible in their lives; it's hard enough dealing with what *is* possible. If the rules of the universe were found to operate merely upon whim, how terrifying life would be.

I wanted to discuss with the old man the "testimony" I'd watched. I was busy at the time, working on a deadline, so there wasn't a chance to stay up late and drink. Whenever I was out on the porch in those days Lynn was with me. And the old man seemed allergic to her presence. Finally, around the third week in October, during the harvest, I saw the ambulance across the road one evening at dinnertime. The red light swept through my living room. Sure enough, Lynn heard the next day through the old man's daughter-in-law that he'd "slipped away." The first thing I thought upon hearing that phrase was how the journey of Grace Malfrey was like death. But for her there was a destination beyond the dirt and her eventual return. I thought that if the old man ever came back and visited me on the porch, I'd shit my pants.

That winter came on strong and the long dim days led me by the hand into the dark halls of depression. Lynn was traveling extensively. I was really struggling to stay afloat and get some writing done. Grim business, but I'd been there before and I'd learned how to put my head down and push forward against the gale. One gray afternoon, on a return trip ten miles from town over the straight-as-an-arrow farmland road, unplowed and dotted with child-sized snow dunes, I spotted a beat-up, blue Dodge Dart pulled over at a weird angle in the deep snow. There was an older woman digging with a snow shovel around her tires. She wore a black winter hat down over her ears, long gray hair frayed out from beneath it. A black cape covered her coat and her hands were in black leather gloves.

A quick comparison of her small bent stature and the brutal winter, spread across the empty road and fields for as far as the eye could see, told me to slow down. I checked my mirror—with the exception of us, the road was empty. I hit the window button, and when the glass cleared on the passenger side, I yelled, "Hey, you need a hand?"

The woman looked up suddenly, wearing an expression of guilt. She hobbled over to me. "Will you help me dig out my car?" she said in a near whisper and a cloud of steam. She was trembling all over, barely able to hold the shovel.

"Look, you've got to get out of the cold. Throw that shovel in my back seat, lock your car, and I'll drive you home. Once you're there you can call the tow truck. It doesn't pay to be on the road in the snow. Somebody else'll come by and clip you. You never know."

"How do I know you're trustworthy?" she asked.

"How do I know *you* are?" I asked.

She shook her head.

"You're on the verge of freezing out there."

She acquiesced with a change of face, and her new look allowed me to see immediately that it was Grace Malfrey, only much older than on the video. I was instantly positive it was her. She put her shovel in the back seat and then scooted in on the other side. She was in no hurry, and all the time I wondered if I was going to ask her if she had been to Adaleen.

Instead, I asked her where she lived.

"Go along here for a while," she said.

I looked in the rearview mirror and caught her watching me. "You know who I am, don't you?" she said.

"Are you Grace Malfrey?"

"I am."

"Just this past autumn, I watched your videotaped testimony."

"I don't know why they called it a 'testimony,'" she said. "Why should I be on trial?"

"You've got a fantastic story."

"There was nothing fantastic about it; the whole thing was horrible. I was taken. My life has been a jumble since. I am my lover and my daughter. I don't know why this happened to me."

She seemed to be getting upset, so I laid off the questions and asked if we were getting close to the turn for her house. I was driving slowly. Still, no other vehicles had passed us going toward town, and the snow was picking up again. She said it was a mile or so farther and then a right. We went on in silence, and I shook my head slightly, unable to believe that Malfrey had found her way to the back seat of my car. What weird synchronicity that mere months earlier, before going the way of all old men, the old man unwound her tale on my porch.

I turned on the radio to cure the silence, and a meditative tune seeped into the car. I said nothing, but, of course, I knew it was "Mountain Snow Trance." What else could it be? "This is your music from Adaleen, isn't it?" I asked.

"Right, here." She screamed.

I hit the brakes and we skidded on the turn but managed to stay within the boundaries of the road or driveway we entered. I couldn't tell which because the storm had gotten worse, and all I could see was snow. Then the car wouldn't go forward anymore. "We're stuck," I told her.

"Close enough," I heard her say. "Keep the shovel." The back door opened and I turned to see her hop out and put up a pink parasol that emerged from thin air. When she started away into the white, I got out of the car and hurdled snow dunes to try to catch up with her. I was sure she would trip and end up dying of exposure. I had just about gotten to within an arm's length, when my knee gave out and I almost fell. A good thing, as I was way out of breath. There was an extra-strong gale that whipped the snow into a twister, the tail of which snapped her out of existence before my eyes. I was alone in the blizzard. Couldn't see more than a foot in front of me. I headed in the direction I thought my car was in, and walked for what seemed miles in knee-high powder late into the afternoon. When the storm suddenly stopped some indeterminate time later, I woke in my car to the tapping of the tow truck driver's flashlight on my side window.

What was I to make of Grace Malfrey? I pondered it that night, wrapped in two coats, on the porch with a bottle and a pack of cigarettes. (I hadn't had one in years, but if anything called for one it was another dimension where young girls were captured and made to work in an infernal factory, sorting pieces of human hands.) I lit the butts using the citronella candle. Its aroma was strange in winter. I spoke my conclusion aloud into the cold night, "It might have all happened but none of it makes any damn sense."

There was a rustling, then, in the dead bushes leading to the porch garden, a shadow shuffling into shadows, and a laugh as light as snow on the wind.

BECKY CHAMBERS

The Tomb Ship

Becky Chambers

If you wanted to mine space rocks, there were two territories for it. Neither of them were good.

The most popular option was the Urlis asteroid belt, a great place to go if you wanted to lose your life, your empathy, or both. Urlis was only two weeks' travel from Anlan soil. The flying was easy, and the pickings were plentiful. Inevitably, this meant every desperate digger had turned the place into a hellscape of booby traps, proximity mines, and ship-welded weapons built for anything but a warning shot. Urlis was nothing more than a cosmic cage-match, a carcass eternally fought over by feral dogs. The ancestral loathing between the five factions was as bitter there as it was on the ground, but it wasn't unheard-of for people from the same island to turn on each other, abandoning allegiance for the sake of a good haul. Colors were flown when it suited, but when it came down to it, things were always a matter of us versus them, you versus me. That was the Anlan way.

If a lawless arena didn't appeal, you could instead take your mineship into the Cetac Wastes, the poorly mapped region of interplanetary space that hugged the sun. Asteroids there were less plentiful, and the intense heat and radiation meant you needed special shielding to make it through alive. The edges of the Wastes were littered with picked-over corpses of ships that had thought they were up to snuff—victims of knockoff shielding and bad DIY jobs, in most cases. Others had just had a bad day.

Laym's ship, the *Winter Tide*, was the real deal. She'd paid out the nose for it, having done six miserable years in Urlis to save enough chips for a quality retrofit. The protection wasn't perfect. The interior was always sweltering, as evidenced by the circuits—which were in constant danger of frying—and Laym's bedsheets, perpetually kicked to the floor. Not that she'd have slept much better in a cooler climate anyway. The asteroid belt was, by the map, millions of miles away, but no matter where she went, Urlis was just out of the corner of her eye, reminding her in a hissing whisper of the things she'd seen. The things she'd done.

Laym hated killing, but she hated hunger more, and even here, in what should have been a blissfully silent region of off-grid space, someone else had arrived to stake a claim. For a brief, foolish moment after the Marthen ship appeared on her scanners, she hoped that maybe—just *maybe*—they'd turn a blind eye to each other and keep the day quiet. But the scanners were also guiding her toward a choice-looking target about an hour away—a tremendous concentration of precious metals, so big Laym wondered if maybe her equipment was finally failing. The presence of the Marthen meant that someone else had picked up the same thing. A fellow Elden ship from Laym's home island might—*might*—have been talked into splitting the find, but a Marthen? Never. They'd have been locked into this brawl even if the prize had been nothing more than a crust of bread.

Everything about a mineship fight was ludicrous, and Laym

had always thought so. This was not the dance of fighter craft, a heady mix of adrenaline and acrobatics, a display that might be beautiful if it weren't so macabre. A mineship, by contrast, was essentially one big cargo hold—a clunky belly waiting to be filled. These were ships that possessed neither speed nor grace, and attempting to engage each other in a dogfight would've been akin to trying to wrestle with a boulder strapped to your back. So when Laym and the Marthen encountered one another, they did what mineship pilots always did: they stopped their engines and deployed their attack bots. The little brainless fighters spilled from both ships like wasps from kicked nests, clouds of hundreds swarming toward each respective vessel. The mineships, in turn, sat still as the barrage began, able to do nothing but hope they would outlast the other. This was not a test of skill, but of money. Who had the better shields, the better bots? Who would be the first to die of a thousand automated cuts?

Stupid, Laym thought. It was all so painfully stupid. She did not bother putting on her helmet or strapping into an escape pod, as she had diligently done in her first years. There was no point. She'd blasted enough careening escape pods to know that some last-ditch attempts were not worth taking. She got up and made a cup of tea instead, ignoring the din of gunfire and drill bits attempting to breach her hull.

She blew across the surface of the steaming drink to cool it. This was enough to trigger a coughing fit. "Dammit," she choked. She scowled and took a hit from her inhaler. The plastic-tasting mist punched her airways open, and she pressed hard against the wall while the dizziness passed. Her throat was always raw from the stuff. She was up to twelve doses a day now, more than the last doctor she'd bothered with had been happy about. But a childhood spent breathing the fumes from the ore-processing plant had poisoned her lungs irreparably, and now it was either the inhaler or going the way her sister had gone: purple-faced and gasping on the factory floor. Laym had decided that very day that dying on your own terms was preferable.

A cheerful chime played from her control station, a playful tune cooked up by some console engineer with either a sociopathic sense of humor or no connection whatsoever to what life in minespace was like. The battle had been won, the music meant, as if it were a finished load of laundry or a fully heated meal.

The noise echoing through the walls ended abruptly as the attack bots deactivated in the absence of a functioning command ship. Laym sat back down at her console and took stock of the damage—superficial, all of it. Her earnings had served her well. She called her bots back, and continued on for the target. She did not relish her victories as some miners did. There had been two ships; now there was one, and that one was hers, and that was what mattered. Whoever had been flying the Marthen ship did not matter. Their life back on Anla did not matter. Their corpse, which Laym could see drifting with rag-doll clumsiness away from the twisted wreckage, did not matter. This is what Urlis had taught her. This is what she reminded herself while lying in the dark on a coverless bed.

In another scenario, Laym would've deployed the scrappers next, stripping the Marthen ship down and filling her own with its spoils. But if her scanners were correct, the rock that lay ahead would bring her a market haul like no other, and she wanted to greet that with an empty hold. She set in her course, drank her tea, and let an hour slip by.

Another chime woke her from an unexpected doze. Her mug lay empty in her lap, the last remaining drips spilled onto her patched trousers. She recovered her wits, looked out the window . . . and wondered if she might still be dreaming.

She'd reached the target, her charts read, but what lay outside was no rock. It was a joke, a trap. It had to be. There was no way it could be real.

Another ship hung outside, lifeless but whole. Its hull was an ethereal white, and the sunlight scattering off it would've blinded Laym instantly were it not for her windows' protective coating. The ship's form was decadent, ornate, a perfect egg etched with expert filigree, the farthest possible thing from the *Winter Tide*'s soulless utility. Laym had never seen a ship like it, but she knew it instantly. Anyone would know it, even though nobody had seen one for a thousand years.

It had to be a trap.

Laym ran scan after scan after scan, looking for bombs, holograms, cleverly scattered signals that cloaked ambushers lying in wait. But in scan after scan after scan, she found no life signs, no smoke, no mirrors. She sat back dumbly in her chair, knuckles against her mouth. Only one option remained, but she felt like a child for entertaining it. She focused the scanners on the side of the strange ship's hull, zooming in on a patch of symbols. No, not symbols—runes. Temran runes. Shaking her head at the absurdity, she ran the image through a translation matrix. Small Temran artifacts popped up in Urlis from time to time—fuel barrels, dead bots, and the like. Nothing big, nothing that would fetch a good price. Still, knowing if something read EXPLOSIVE! or DANGER! was always wise, thus being able to translate was handy.

The runes on the other ship did not read EXPLOSIVE! or DANGER! The translation came back:

DEATH AWAITS YOU, CHALLENGER
BEHOLD
THE WRATH OF KIMAT

"No," Laym breathed. She shook her head. She laughed, almost, though nothing about this was funny. There was no question now. This was a tomb ship. This was *the* tomb ship, the lost tomb ship. The one that had shattered a truce. The one that had broken the world. The final resting place of the final queen. The denied, the erased. Kimat the Calculating, holy empress of the Elden Provinces.

Laym continued to sit and stare. What the hell was someone supposed to do with something like this?

After ten minutes, she stood up, put on her spacesuit, and got in her shuttle. Scans weren't enough. She had to see this for herself.

~

The hatch opened, and Laym shielded her eyes. For a second, she thought this was it, that the solar shields were damaged and the sun itself was greeting her for one glorious moment before swallowing her in flame. But nothing burned. Nothing boiled. She lowered her arm from her faceplate, and gaped in silent wonder.

Gold.

She knew its glint from circuit boards and satellite panels. Gold was a practical metal, a special occasion metal, something you used as little of as possible when you couldn't use anything else. But within the ancient ship, it seemed that there had been no other thought *but* gold. The ceilings were gold, scalloped and angled to create seemingly endless geometric cascades of light. The walls were gold. Even the *floor* was gold. It glared haughtily from beneath her grubby boots.

Beneath her boots, she noted. This place still had gravity. It still had *power*. She had expected ruins, but if you'd told Laym this place had been abandoned five minutes prior, she would've believed it.

She considered that possibility and rested a hand on her holstered gun.

Once Laym had, with effort, accepted the fact that such a place existed, she assumed that *this* could be the only room like it, that this foyer was designed to stall the heart of anyone who entered. Surely it would give way to more reasonable decor. But as she walked the ship's labyrinthine corridors, the gold continued with her, unyielding and unending. How many mountains had been emptied for this ship? How many rocks split, how many rivers scoured? Laym could not imagine. She could think of nothing at all. Her mind was too dazzled by the light, too entranced by the warmth. She felt as though she were walking through the core of a star, flowing through the heart of a god.

There were other colors corralled within strict strips of the walls—mosaics of many-hued metals that told tales of conquest, glory, folly, might. They were only abstract figures, boxy shorthands for real flesh and blood, but they were enough for Laym to recognize the stories they told. Here were the fictional gods the ancients believed in, anointing their chosen on Anla. Here were the seven monarchs, dividing the world like a cake. Here were the people—so numerous the mosaics presented them as nothing more than identical square tiles, faceless ants that peppered the lands beneath the beautiful rulers—building the tomb ships that would rule from the skies. This had been the way of things for hundreds of years: untouchable rulers circling above, reminding you that they were always watching, that they were not of your world. They had been ruthless, the stories said. The sight of a tomb ship cresting the horizon was enough to make villagers drop to all fours in the dirt, sobbing their fealty and praying for blessings. The Temran-age monarchs were the conduit between human and divine, the flesh that controlled an ephemeral universe.

They were also, Laym had always thought, completely insane. This ship was doing little to change her mind on that.

The hallway rounded a corner, and there, Laym found a room. In the room was a bed, and in the bed, there were bones. Laym did not need to be told who they belonged to.

The queen.

The conqueror.

Kimat.

Laym approached the bones cautiously, as if she might startle them back into life. She did not believe in the supernatural, but she also had never seen a gilded spaceship before. Anything was possible, in that moment. She looked into the empty eye sockets, so deep and dark they reminded her of the vacuum outside. She felt as though they might suck her in.

Every hair on Laym's limbs stood upright. Every heartbeat lasted a hundred years. She had seen plenty of bodies before. She herself had broken bodies, hidden bodies, pushed the buttons that made bodies fly. Those bodies had been strangers, and so, too, was this body, technically. Except that it wasn't. This was the most famous body in history.

Laym was still making a valiant attempt to take this all in when a voice boomed from the walls. **"You must satisfy the protocol."**

Laym cried out and leapt back, gun in hand, trigger waiting.

"That is an inappropriate weapon," the voice said. Where was the speaker? The voice was everywhere, every age, every gender, at once both alive and dead. **"The protocol is specific. The knives. Look."**

Laym looked. *Where* she was supposed to look, she had no idea, no more than she knew what was happening. "Where are you?" she shouted. "Show yourself."

"I am here."

Laym frowned, holding her gun steady. The little metal figures from the walls marched through her mind, telling stories she'd been taught but had never before needed. "Are you . . . the computer?"

"I am guidance. I am servitude. I am . . . the Vizier."

Laym took that as a yes. She felt drunk, or fevered. This was magic, or something so close that the distinction was immaterial. She remembered childhood tales of computers that could think, and had been assured such things were real once, but how could anyone believe in that which no longer existed? "What do you want?" she asked.

"The protocol must be satisfied. I cannot hold other thoughts until it is."

"What is the protocol?"

"That which must be followed."

Laym wasn't sure if a computer would react badly to an eye roll, so she managed to resist the urge. She lowered her gun, but did not holster it. "You said something about knives?"

"The knives. The wall."

Laym looked to the walls. She saw art, trophies, a dry fountainhead that hung over an enormous bath. At last—*there.* An inlaid frame, containing two vicious-looking hunting knives. Their edges were jagged, their hilts as gilded as the ship. She walked up to the frame and ran her pocket scanner across it, making sure there wasn't anything connected to it that might blow up. The scanner came back green. If there were any surprises waiting, they weren't making themselves known.

"Please," the Vizier wailed, its voice inescapable. **"End it."**

"I don't understand!" Laym shouted back. "Also, why are we yelling?"

"Take the knives."

With a last glance at her scanner, Laym grabbed one of the knives. Nothing happened. It was simply a knife. A harmless object until someone decided otherwise.

"Good. This knife is yours. Take the other for her."

Laym startled, thinking perhaps someone else had entered the room. But no, there was only herself, and the voice, and the bones.

"You mean . . . ?" Laym pointed at the remains lying snug in their ancient bed.

"Yes."

She had less idea of what was going on than when she'd entered the ship, but Laym took the second knife and walked back to the bed. "Now what?"

"Arm her."

Laym blinked, stared, blinked again. Seeing no other option, she pulled back the embroidered covers and placed a knife in the skeleton's hand. "And now?"

"End her."

"She's . . . already dead."

"Follow the protocol."

What else could a person do when talking to a fairy-tale being? With the feeling that she was letting a bit of her mind slip forever, Laym slammed her knife through the cage where a heart once beat. The dry bone crunched like the shell of a crab. Laym wished that the sound bothered her more.

"It is done," the Vizier cried, its voice anguished and overjoyed. **"The queen is dead."**

"She was *already dead*," Laym repeated.

"The queen lives."

"What?"

"Hail, queen of stars, queen of void, she who has come and conquered. Hail, hail, hail! Give me your name, my queen, that I may guide your holy ascension."

Laym felt like she'd forgotten to study for a test she hadn't known she'd be taking. "I'm sorry, do you . . ." She shook her head. "Do you mean . . . me?"

"You wielded the knife. You satisfied the protocol. Give me your name, my queen."

"Uh. Laym. My name is Laym."

Something was happening within the ship. Laym didn't know what, but she could hear whirring and clicking and beeping all through the gilded walls, as if the entire machine were remaking itself. The Vizier roared triumphantly, its voice a thousand crowds: **"All hail Queen Laym!"**

There was a chair near the bed. Laym sat down in it and folded her hands together. "I'm going to need you to explain this to me."

"A queen's reign must end in one of two ways. Her ship may be boarded by a rival, and if the rival is victorious, she will die in the rite of succession. Or, the grasp of time will claim her, and her ship will carry her to the sun, where her soul will live for all remaining days, immortal, undying, bringing life to Anla as she adds her light to that of the victorious dead."

The figures marched. "Kimat died of old age, right?" Laym said, dusting off the memories.

"Two hundred and eight years of age. Two hundred and eight years of glory."

"But she never made it to the sun, obviously."

"Correct."

"Because of the Judde Collective."

"They were known to us as the Jeran. That is incorrect."

Laym frowned. "What do you mean, 'incorrect'?"

"That statement is not accurate."

"I know what fucking—" She shut her eyes in frustration. The stories never said anything about computers being this obtuse. "I understand what *incorrect* means. What did I say that's incorrect? The Judde sabotaged the ship—*this* ship—and prevented Kimat from her . . . her sun burial."

"Incorrect. The Jeran have never breached these walls. The Jeran have never defiled this vessel."

Laym's frown deepened. If this continued, Laym was sure her face would stick this way. "But that's . . . that's what happened. That's why the Three-Century War broke out. That's why . . ." That was why everything was the way it was. The denial of Kimat's immortality, the condemnation of a victorious queen to

307

an ordinary, *common* death without afterlife—that had been the sledgehammer swing that brought the whole cliff falling. It was the war that built Laym's world.

"**Incorrect,**" the Vizier said. "**The great ship of Kimat suffered a systems failure. Propulsion was lost, as was the homing signal. I failed to restore either. The protocol was unsatisfied. I have waited for rival or repair ever since.**"

"But . . ." Laym racked her brain, digging up what little schooling she'd received. The exact details of the disappearance of Queen Kimat's tomb ship were a mystery, she knew. Some stories claimed the order of sabotage came directly from the Judde monarch himself, others blamed trouble sowers from Myan Ra. Nowhere in any of it was there the possibility of an *accident*. You didn't start wars because of *accidents*.

And yet, there was the body, lying in unperturbed repose, no signs of murder or mischief anywhere—aside from a newly placed knife sticking out of a dusty rib cage. "If she didn't make it to the sun," Laym said slowly, "then she had to be defeated in combat. Those were the only options given to you."

"**Yes,**" the Vizier said.

"Even though she was already very, very dead?"

"**You challenged her with the knives of succession. You waited until she was armed, yet she failed to defend herself. The protocol is satisfied.**"

"That sounds like a technicality."

"**Logic is rooted in technicalities.**" The Vizier sounded pleased with itself, and Laym didn't blame it. If she understood correctly, the computer had found a loophole in the rules that shackled it. After centuries of being stuck, it deserved to feel smug about that.

"And by those technicalities, I . . . I'm . . ." Laym tapped her chin with her folded hands. "I'm . . . queen . . . now."

"**Now until your day of death. Until victory or defeat.**"

"Okay." Laym exhaled, trying to ease the tightness in her chest. She really didn't want to use her inhaler again for another two hours at least, but everything was going so *fast*. "But we don't have queens anymore. You know a lot has changed, right?"

"I have received all signals that have bled from your satellites. It is how I can speak your tongue. It is how I know your world has succumbed to madness and frailty." The Vizier's voice was angry now—scolding, even. **"Your leaders are no better than a jester's puppets, and yet you follow them dutifully, letting yourselves be cowed by cheap pretenders. You build slums where monuments once stood proud and fearsome. You scheme for scraps. You teach of heroes a thousand years gone, for you have none that come close to their splendor. Yours is a weak planet."**

"Thanks very much."

"Your people are lost without the ships that guide. In the absence of a crown, only chaos can reign. It is time, Queen Laym. It is time to reclaim the might of the holy line and restore order from the skies."

"Meaning . . . what?"

"Follow me, my queen. Your ascension awaits."

Having no better thought of what to do next, Laym followed the guide lights the Vizier activated through the halls. Open doorways stood to either side, and through them, Laym saw wealth beyond her most unabashed imaginings. A dining hall with crystal curtains hanging from the ceiling. A sculpture garden beneath a dome of stars. A music room filled with robotic instruments, ready to entertain an audience of one.

"She was alone here, right?" Laym asked.

"Of course," the Vizier replied. **"A queen must be untouchable. Unseen. Any who set foot in her presence must be either her conqueror or her prey, for there are none that can be her equal."**

At one point in her life, Laym would've found such an existence hellishly lonely, but no longer. She understood the appeal of such isolation. She felt safer within the cramped quarters of her mine-ship than she ever did in an orbiter or on the ground, surrounded by strangers who could put a bolt in your brain at any moment. And she was only a miner, not a queen with countless would-be usurpers slavering at the periphery. Laym imagined some would see the tomb ship as exactly what the name suggested—a coffin. A death that occurred long before you stopped breathing. But Laym saw it as what it must have been to Kimat: Sanctuary. Solace.

Maybe, a little voice within Laym began to think, *it could be mine too.*

~

The purpose of the room the Vizier led her to was evident. In the center of the circular space was a throne, set upon a dais. Ornate control panels were on either side, their buttons and switches set with gems. On the ceiling was a domed map of Anla, painted in stunning detail. Laym noted that the continent of Ebbre was present, not yet blasted to the bottom of the ocean in a seismic siege.

Where the ceiling attracted, the floor repelled. It was transparent, invisible except for the thin support beams that outlined the sheets of . . . glass? Was it glass? Laym instinctively hung close to the wall. Glass would've been an incredibly stupid thing to build a warship out of, but she had no idea what other material it could be. A secret of the ancients, made so that monarchs could view the planet below, never forgetting their place above it.

"Take your throne, my queen," the Vizier said. **"I will teach you."**

Laym took a tentative step. The glass—or whatever it was—held steady. Mildly reassured, she approached the throne, but did not sit. She eyed the jeweled panels, shaking her head. She'd never go hungry again with the price such riches would fetch, yet there they were, adorning *buttons.* "Does any of it work?" she asked.

"Aside from propulsion and long-range communications, all systems are operational. I have been maintaining them."

"How?" The Vizier didn't have a body, as far as Laym could tell. At least, she hoped not.

A panel opened on the wall, adjacent to the floor, and a small robot wheeled itself out. It, too, was gilded and jeweled.

Laym knelt down to examine the bot. The attentive machine was fitted with a wide variety of attachments, each affixed to a thin arm that folded neatly back. She noted something that looked like a screwdriver. "Repair drones?"

"Yes."

"I see. But they couldn't fix propulsion and comms?"

"The ship lacked the necessary materials. Our stores were low following the triumphant defeat of Pol Seg."

"Who was Pol Seg?"

"A fool."

Laym cocked an eyebrow. "A challenger?"

"Queen Kimat defeated him easily. He was dust in the storm of her might."

"But he got a few hits in, sounds like."

"Yes. The raw material stores were used to repair a hull breach and water storage. Damage to the other systems did not appear catastrophic. Queen Kimat had planned to replenish the stores, but before this could occur, she died victorious in sleep."

"And then your protocol kicked in. To take her to the sun."

"Yes."

Laym ran a hand along the edge of the control panel. The gold was smooth, so smooth. "Why couldn't you use the materials you have here?"

"I do not understand."

Laym gestured broadly at the room, the ship. "You could've stripped this down to fix the propulsion. You don't need a music room to get to the sun."

"I do not have this protocol. Such alterations to the vessel can only be performed at the queen's command."

Thoughts connected. "So, there are things you *could* do, but can't without the queen's say-so. You're bound by her orders."

"Yes."

"Are you . . . do *I* command you? Can I give you orders?"

"I exist to serve, my queen."

Well, that was interesting. She lay a hand on the arm of the throne, but still did not sit. Despite its sunny color, the metal was cold. "And everything else works?"

"Life support. Navigation. Weapons."

"Weapons," Laym repeated. Yes, she knew this part of the story too. That was what the Temran monarchs did, after all. They did not merely watch from the sky; they rained fire from it. She'd been to the township of Timmit, built in the crater that had once held an ancient town King Magen had deemed traitorous. She'd taken a barge down the Xerion River, cut by the orbital beams of Queen Savra. It was said Savra diverted the waters from the village of Kosh, which had displeased her for reasons Laym did not know. Campfire songs. Ghost stories. The sort of thing you intellectually knew had happened, but did not truly sink into your bones as something *possible*. It seemed even less possible now, almost, looking at the little buttons with their little jewels. One nudge of a fingertip to shape a planet. Laym's head spun at the notion.

She could end it, a creeping thought suggested. The bloodbath in the asteroid belt. The wars and riots on Anla. No amount of attack bot swarms could bring down a ship that could move rivers. She could go in, mop it all up, and keep everybody in check from above. Alone. Impenetrable.

"How many challengers did Kimat defeat?" Laym asked.

"Eight hundred and twenty-nine," the Vizier said with pride.

"And none even made it inside?"

"None."

Laym squeezed the arm of the throne. Sanctuary. Solace. She closed her eyes. This was insane. Insane. And yet, she found herself imagining life in a gold cocoon, eating fine meals from glass plates while robots played music to drown out the challengers dying unseen beyond her hull. Except there would *be* no real challengers, for there were none left with a ship like this. No one person controlled the resources needed to *build* a ship like this. The sky would be hers, and hers alone. She thought of sprawling out in that giant bed—she'd get some new sheets, after the bones were gone. She could sleep easy, study sculptures, swim in fountains as she circled the world. The world she shaped. The world she ruled.

She let go of the throne, opened her eyes, and walked out of the room.

"Where are you going, my queen?"

Laym walked briskly down the halls, finding her way back. "I need to think about it," she said. "Just let me . . . let me think about it."

~

The *Winter Tide*'s shabby interior greeted her, and its familiarity prompted a sigh of relief. A coughing fit followed, doubling her over and erasing all thought. She tried to steady herself, but her airways shuddered inward. She scrambled to get her helmet off, dropping it on the floor as she rushed toward the control room. Spots were dancing in her eyes by the time she grabbed her inhaler. It was too soon since the last dose, but she didn't have a choice. She got the dispenser to her mouth, the medicine to her lungs. She slid down the wall as the drug did its work, coughing turning to gasping, gasping turning, at last, to quiet breath. She tasted blood at the back of her tongue, the cost of trading one injury for another.

Laym leaned her head back against the bulkhead, looking out the window as she panted. The tomb ship waited beyond her scuffed window, her un-jeweled control panels, her worn chair with a busted seam. The taste of living copper lingered.

Unbidden, unwanted, Laym thought of her sister. She hadn't coughed blood at the end, but foam. She'd been thirteen years old. She'd died in a dirty factory, in pain and afraid. Laym had dropped her lunch bun in a puddle earlier that day; her sister had split her own in half so they could share. She'd been grouchy about it, but she'd done it all the same.

And then there was Kimat, two hundred and eight, slipping away peacefully in her lavish nest among the stars, mind untroubled by the fiery death of her eight hundred and whatever-th rival. Laym imagined the queen had eaten well that day.

She crossed her legs, and she thought. She thought for hours, even after her calves went numb and the bolts in the wall made her back ache. Unbidden, unwanted, she thought of the body she'd seen drifting free of the Marthen mineship—her own rival. What would have happened if the Marthen had won, if they'd entered that ancient hatch? The Vizier would have treated them no differently. They'd be Kimat's successor now.

What would they have done with that?

Laym ground her teeth at the thought of such weaponry in the hands of the Marthen—but then, her rival would've felt the same about her. And Kimat felt the same, given how the Vizier had reacted to mention of the Judde. Us versus them, me versus you. The Anlan way, as it had been in Kimat's time, and a thousand years before, and a thousand years after.

She looked out at the tomb ship, its apocalyptic weaponry lying hidden beneath deceptive polish.

She could end it.

Laym got into her chair. The grooves in the seat cushion fit her and no one else. She pressed a button, flicked a switch, entered coordinates. A metallic clanking echoed as the outer panels opened.

Her speakers switched on, a short-wave comm forcing itself through. **"My queen,"** the Vizier said. Its voice sounded utterly wrong within the *Winter Tide*, an unwanted guest. **"What are you doing?"**

Laym said nothing. A button, a switch, a flick. She got up to make a cup of tea.

Alarms blared, and she whipped back toward the window. The tomb ship was opening panels of its own, revealing its daggers at last. Laym felt the blood race out of her cheeks as she saw rows upon layered rows of sleek firing barrels locking into place. She didn't know how they worked. She didn't need to.

"My queen, you must return," the Vizier said. **"A saboteur has taken control of the mineship. Return quickly, and we shall end them."**

Deep within the firing barrels, something began to glow white-hot.

Laym scrambled for her transmitter. "You will not fire on my ship," she said.

The Vizier was silent for a moment. **"You would not,"** it said. **"You cannot."**

"Power your weapons down," Laym said. She licked her lips, taking out a new set of words and trying them on. "Obey your queen!"

The glow died. The firing barrels retracted. The Vizier obeyed.

Laym allowed herself a small smile. She gave the control panel one more flick and deployed the scrappers.

The Vizier howled as the hungry bots sailed toward their target. **"Why, my queen?"**

She got up and filled her mug. "Because my weak planet is what your monarchs made it. Everything you are, they stole. I'm glad they're all dead. I'm glad Kimat never made it to the sun. I don't want so much as an *atom* of her shining back at me. Rotting in the void is more than she deserved. I wish that had happened to all of them."

"You dare!"

"Yeah," Laym said. She sat back in her weary chair. "I guess I dare."

"Defiler!" the Vizier shrieked. **"Betrayer!"** Its syllables fractured with electronic anguish, the spaces between writhing.

"That's me," Laym said. She took a sip of tea.

"May you perish in flame and oil! May your soul be shattered before the stars!"

"Okay."

"May you be cast into the screaming pit, friendless and forgotten, a clot of refuse forever decaying, never granted the mercy of an end!"

Laym took stock of her breath, then blew across the surface of her steaming drink. "Okay."

The Vizier continued to curse her as the scrappers chomped through the ship's hardware, its insults descending into meaningless babble as the tireless machines stripped the tomb ship to the bone. Laym thought, after a while, that the computer had finally been destroyed, but for hours onward, a ghostly moan of static would ooze through the speakers for a moment or two, the last gasps of a slow death in the circuits. When silence finally reigned, Laym wasn't sure she trusted it.

～

She consumed a lot more tea in the time it took for the scrappers to fill the cargo hold, plus a bowl of rehydrated porridge. She added a spice packet to that, which she usually only did on her birthday. It felt like a special occasion. Wasn't often you got yourself crowned and deposed in a matter of hours.

When the scrappers had all come home, Laym climbed the ladder down to the cargo hold and looked over the edge of the catwalk at the dizzying stacks of shining metal. The *Winter Tide* was unrecognizable with such riches in it. This wasn't a storage

316

compartment. This was a dragon's hoard. She studied the haul for a long time, cupping her empty mug between her palms. She could retrofit a whole island with the profit from this. She could *buy* a whole island with this. She could buy dry homes and good medicine and big guns for everybody she knew.

"Okay," she said. She picked up the transmitter hanging from a cord along the catwalk rail. "Scrapper control, listen."

The bots perked up, responding to her command. "Scrapper control listening," their program replied through the speakers. It was so good to know that they couldn't think.

"Three commands. First command: Calculate the amount of each material harvested. Second command: Divide each material store into five equal lots." She paused. Was she really doing this? "Third command: Deliver one lot to . . ." She paused again, the hairs on her neck standing up once more. She was doing this. "All lots to government headquarters. One to the Elden Provinces, one to Arien, one to Myan Ra, one to the Republic of Marth, and one to the Judde Collective."

"Commands confirmed," the program said. "Price set?"

Laym stared up at the ceiling. She could retire—a luxury so unheard-of, the thought nearly made her giggle. She'd never be hungry. She'd never be cold. She could spend her days in a temperature-controlled palatial bunker, the threats outside so distant she could forget them entirely. A pampered life of soft things and pretty things and sex whenever she wanted. An absence of uncertainty. A life without fear. Sanctuary. Solace.

"Price set?" the program repeated.

Laym took a breath, a good breath. "Price set: zero." She nodded with surety. "Oh, and, two commands, to take place after the first three. First command: Remove standard sender ID from shipping labels. Second command: Replace standard sender ID."

"Replacement text?"

"'From Kimat, to make amends.'" She nodded again. The

world didn't need a queen. The world needed its stuff back. What they did with it was up to them. Maybe they'd kill each other over it, but maybe they'd understand the gift for what it was, do the right thing, split the lunch bun in half. That wasn't for Laym to decide. People had to choose for themselves.

"Commands confirmed." The scrappers got to work.

"Wait," Laym said. "One more command, to come after the first five. Command: Set aside a sixth lot of one—no, two kilos of gemstones. Any mix you find." She was getting herself new lungs, at least.

The scrappers did as instructed. A day later, they handed their wares over to the *Winter Tide*'s shipment drones, which departed the cargo hold for Anla, each with a different heading.

Laym was unaware of their leaving. She was too deeply asleep.

THEODORA GOSS

Pellargonia: A Letter to the *Journal of Imaginary Anthropology*

Theodora Goss

Dear Colleagues:

We think that's the right way to start, because Julia's dad always started his letters that way. [Starts, not started. He's missing, not dead. —Julia] Starts. Anyway.

We [Julia, David, and me, Madison] [That should be I, not me. —David] are writing to you because we need your help. Professor Jorge Escobar is missing, and it's all our fault. We hope we're not going to get in trouble for what we're about to write. [But we're pretty sure we are. —David] See, we were the ones who created Pellargonia. We know it says Professor Escobar on the article ("A Brief History of Pellargonia," *Journal of Imaginary Anthropology* vol. 12, no. 2, Fall 2018). But we were the ones who wrote it and sent it in. He didn't even know about it, which is why Julia was so surprised when the letter came. [Surprised is an understatement. —Julia] It was on heavy cream-colored paper, with a crown and a coat of arms on top, all in gold. [Embossed. —David] The address was The Royal Society of Pellargonia, 12 Santa Eugenia Stras, Bellagua del Mar 1024. It came to his office at the university, and he brought it home to read to Julia's mom before dinner while Julia was doing her math homework at the kitchen table. He said, "Honey, I've been invited to give this year's keynote at their annual conference, and they want to make me a Fellow of the society. What do you think?" [Did I get that right? —Madison] [Mostly. But my dad speaks Spanish at home. —Julia] [Well, I don't know Spanish, and some of our readers might not either. —Madison] That's the weirdest part of this whole thing—even he thought, I mean thinks, that he wrote the article. But it was us. [We. —David]

In case you don't believe us, I'm going to send photocopies of the maps and all our notes. [I drew the maps. —David] They're pretty messy—at least my handwriting is. David's is pretty neat, and Julia types everything anyway. But I think you can be more creative when you write by hand—you can sketch and doodle and stuff, and it sort of sets your brain free. [Great, if you can read it afterward! —Julia] And I'll tell you the whole story, how we created Pellargonia and lost Julia's dad.

At first it was just a game we played between classes. The country didn't even have a name yet—we just called it Country X. In Honors Bio it was David's turn.

> The rebels are closing in on the capital. Cesar Fuentes has set up his headquarters in the old Estrella Ceilo estate. They have AK-47s that they bought from the Russians, plus some rogue American military advisors.

He is really into military history. And weapons. [But not in a school lockdown kind of way. My interest is purely theoretical. The only thing I've ever shot is a Nerf gun. —David] Then Julia and I had Algebra II while David went off to Honors Math. That was Julia's turn, because she doesn't really need to pay attention in math. Her brain does that stuff automatically. She could be in Honors Math if she wanted to, but she says it's too much work, and her parents let her take pretty much whatever she wants. I wish my mom was that way!

> Zoraida Delacorte, the mistress of King Leopold IV, is about to assassinate him. She has the poison ready. She will put it in the glass of whiskey he drinks every evening before going to bed, so he won't even taste it. After he drinks it, she will flee through the secret passage to join Cesar Fuentes in the forest.

Then we split up: me to French, Julia to Latin, and David to Spanish. He wanted to take Latin too, but his dad didn't understand why he would want to take a language no one else speaks. His dad manages the main bank here in Lewiston. He wants David to become an accountant. [Over my dead, decrepit, and decaying body. —David] No one wrote anything then, because you have to pay attention in language classes. Anyway, we were all working on a language for Country X that would be sort of like French and sort of like Spanish, but with some weird Latin stuff mixed in. Like declensions. Julia really likes declensions. But in AP World History it would be my turn.

> Princess Stefania, who has never trusted Zoraida Delacorte, switches his whiskey glass with that of the Prime Minister, who wants her to marry Baron Alfonse el Cerdo, who is at least twice her age. She thinks with longing about her school friend, Clotilde, and that kiss they shared on the day they graduated. Will she ever see Clotilde again?

And then we had electives: art for Julia, cello for me, and programming for David, not because he needed it—he's really good with computers—but because his dad thought it would be useful.

After school, we would go to the library to study and hang out. The lady who runs the YA and kids section, Doris, who's known me pretty much my whole life, would say, "Here come the Three Musketeers!" Which is a pretty lame joke, but I kind of get why she says it. David and I have known each other since we were kids and he lived next door. He moved after his parents got divorced—now he lives with his mom on the other side of town, and his dad lives with his stepmom in a big house close to the reservoir. Mom and I still live in Grandma's house, which is close to the library, so she doesn't have to walk that far to work. We couldn't afford to move even if we wanted to, and anyway, my mom says it's the perfect house, with an office for her by the kitchen and a bedroom for me up in the attic. I could have moved down to the second floor after Grandma died, but I like it up there. It's like a nest. And I wanted to keep her bedroom the way she left it, with her celluloid brush and nail buffer on the dressing table. I never knew my dad—I was just a baby when he died in Afghanistan—but at least I had a long time with Grandma.

Anyway, I've known David for most of my life, and Julia moved to Lewiston the year after he moved across town, when her dad started teaching at the university. In ninth grade she was behind me in homeroom, and we got along right away—Julia's the sort of person who can be friends with almost anybody. She's naturally curious about people. At first David was kind of standoffish with her, but then they discovered they both liked graphic novels and tabletop RPGs, and that sort of made them non-enemies, even though David liked World War I reenactments and Julia was into classic D&D. And then they discovered they liked a lot of the same books, and also disliked a lot of the same books, including everything we were assigned in school, from *The Catcher in the Rye* to *The Great Gatsby*. I actually like *The Great Gatsby* myself, and that's where I got the idea for Fitzgerald G. Scott, the American who bought up that land on Mount Floria and built a casino resort, which Cesar Fuentes took for his headquarters when the revolution started. [OMG you are so rambling. —Julia]

Anyway, I wasn't really into all the stuff David and Julia were into—you know, games and fantasy and sci-fi. I prefer history and romance, which is why I know who the Three Musketeers are. But when Julia got the idea for Country X, it was like, okay, let's try it. It had war for David, and lots of drama for Julia, and we were going to write it down, not just make it up, which is what got me interested. I want to be a writer and create books, not just sort and catalog them like Mom.

So Julia and I biked over to David's house, because he has a game room in the basement, and we planned it all out. I mean the basics—how Country X had been founded by one of the Gaelish tribes [Gaelic. —David], and then the Romans came, and then it was part of Spain for a while, and then part of France, and it sort of went back and forth until finally it became its own country. We decided it had to be on an ocean, so we could have lots of trade and immigrants. We wanted it to look like us—you know, diverse. Like David being African American, and me being mostly just white but part Polish, which I guess counts for something, and Julia being a mixture of lots of different things, including Native, which is the way she says people are in Argentina. And all different religions too, although the three of us aren't very diverse that way. David's family is Methodist, and my mom isn't really religious— she says she's spiritual and goes around smudging things when there's bad energy around. Julia goes to Mass every Sunday with her parents, which I guess is sort of different, at least for Lewiston. Anyway, we wanted it to be as different from Lewiston as possible. Mom once said that living in Maine is sort of like eating Wonder Bread for lunch every day, which isn't totally true—we have some kids in school from Somalia and Bangladesh, and we have a girl in homeroom from Thailand. I don't know her that well because she's a cheerleader, and they tend to hang out together. But it's still pretty boring here. I mean, people go bowling or to miniature golf on dates, and the biggest social event of the year is homecoming, although Pride Day is getting bigger every year. [Hello, my dad is still missing. Can we get back to talking about Pellargonia? —Julia]

On the earliest map [I labeled it Figure 1. —Julia] you can tell we didn't even know which ocean it was on. The wavy bit is just labeled "Ocean." That was last fall. We were still getting used to tenth grade, and taking an AP class, and our parents starting to talk about college. We were taking PSAT prep tests and comparing our results. [I'm the one in Honors Math, and Julia still gets the highest math scores. —David] [The PSAT is just another way high school indoctrinates us, so we can become cogs in the industrial machine of late capitalism. —Julia] [Okay, but you still have to take it. Your mom said so. —Madison]

It was Julia who first told us about the *Journal of Imaginary Anthropology*. I think it was around Columbus Day [Indigenous Peoples Day. —Julia], because that was the last long weekend before Thanksgiving. Her parents live in the university dorms—I mean, they have a regular apartment, but it's in a dormitory on campus, and her mom and dad do a lot of advising and stuff, like when students are sick [You mean drunk. —Julia] or have problems with their classes. So the university is sort of like her neighborhood—she knows all the buildings and a lot of the people who work in them, and everyone knows she's Professor Escobar's daughter. One day she was in her dad's office in the anthropology department, waiting to talk to him about a problem from school [The bio teacher said she would fail me if I didn't dissect a fetal pig. —Julia] [Julia is vegan and eats those weird fake burgers. —David] [You eat chicken embryos. How is that less weird? —Julia] and she saw a copy on his desk. She was leafing through it and when he came in, with his hair all rumpled from teaching [He always runs his fingers through it, so you can't tell if it's gray or just chalk. —Julia], she asked him what it was.

"Nonsense," he said. "A bunch of nonsense. Written by a group of grad students who should know better. This is what happens when you take postmodern literary theory too seriously. You start thinking that if you can *write* reality, you can *create* it. Bullcrap." [He was going to say bullshit, but he tries not to swear in front of me, even in Spanish. —Julia] "Now, what's this about bio, and did you really call Mrs. Ellerton a carnivorous fascist?"

The next day, we went to the university library. I mean, wouldn't you, after what Julia's dad said? If it was bullcrap, we wanted to find out what kind of bullcrap it was—we wanted to know what imaginary anthropology was, and if it was as interesting as the real kind. Julia had her own UMaine-Lewiston library card, but you can't take journals out, so we sat on the floor of the stacks, with the bookshelves all around us, reading the back issues. There weren't that many, since it was a new journal. We spent the next couple of hours sitting on the cold floor—I don't know why they have don't rugs, like in the regular library—telling each other about the different countries, their customs, the people who lived there. It was as good as reading a history book. And some of the articles talked about theoretical stuff too, although we didn't understand all of it. But that's how we learned about the Tlön hypothesis, and Cimmeria, and Hyperborea, and Zothique.

It was David who said, "We should make Country X real. It deserves to be real. Mount Zamorna, and Cabo del Alexandrion, and Santa Petra Bay."

"And that little town where Hemerosa first met Alonzo Lorca," said Julia. "The one in the poem he wrote. I mean that Madison wrote for him. And Karolus Ludvig University, and the Bellagua Botanical Gardens."

"And the Berengaria Mental Hospital where they locked up Zofia Montague until she agreed to marry her cousin, King Leopold II. And the Livia Sagrada School for Noble Ladies, where Princess Stefania met Clotilde." I wanted that school to be real.

I wanted Stefania and Clotilde to be real. It was going to be the greatest romance in the history of Pellargonia. [Greater than Hemerosa and Alonzo? —Julia] [Oh, definitely. —Madison]

But how were we going to make it real?

"We have to start writing about it," said David. "Like on Wikipedia and stuff. We need to write an entry for . . ." That's when we realized our country didn't have a name.

It was Julia who came up with it. I don't think even she knows exactly where it came from. [No clue. —Julia] But later, when I was looking it up online to see how many entries it had, I noticed there's a flower called pelargonium. So maybe that had something to do with it. [But I don't know anything about flowers. Anyway, "pelagic" means "of the sea," and Pellargonia is on the sea. —Julia] [There's also "archipelago." Like those islands off the coast where Federico the Red hid when Leopold II was trying to get rid of all the pirates. —David]

There were other names suggested—Mossimore was one. So was Elsivere. We made a list of names—you can see the list in our notes. At one point we started playing around with spelling. Dajuma, Jumada, Majuda. But we thought they all sounded fake, and we wanted Country X to be real.

Pellargonia was the one that stuck. And then we had to figure out where it was going to be. Because of the language, the obvious place to put it was between France and Spain. But it had to be on the ocean because of the pirates who pillaged around the Arroz Islands. That left only two choices: either on the Mediterranean or on the Bay of Biscay. I wanted the Bay of Biscay, because it sounded romantic, but Julia wanted the Mediterranean because of the *Odyssey*, and David said it was better for pirates. And on the map we found a little country called Andorra, right in the Pyrenees mountains. It was so much like Pellargonia that we figured someone else must have had the same idea we did and put it there. I mean, you can tell it's one of the imaginary countries, like Ruritania and Liechtenstein.

First we wrote the Wikipedia entry, with a history of Pellargonia back to the Stone Age. David wrote the ancient stuff about the tribes that had lived there, fishing and hunting, and the cave art they left in cliffs around the Ruata river basin. Julia wrote from the Roman occupation through the Middle Ages, when Ottaker converted to Catholicism, and made everyone else convert too so he could marry Princess Magdalena, the youngest daughter of the French king. He became Otto I, the first king of Pellargonia. David covered from the conquest by the Umayyad Caliphate to the Reconquista, and then Julia took over again, because she had learned about the war between Aragon and Castile in Spanish class, and Pellargonia became part of Aragon for a while. I took over from the Renaissance through the nineteenth century, including when Louis XIV claimed Pellargonia for France as part of the War of Spanish Succession. I also covered the Industrial Revolution and a bunch of other revolutions—real ones, I mean. The Pellargonians rebelled a lot, especially when Julia was bored in math class. We worked together on the War of Independence and the Treaty of Bellagua, when Pellargonia finally became its own kingdom again. Well, queendom, technically, under Queen Zofia, since Leopold II died in mysterious circumstances just after their wedding. Then David did the twentieth century, because he really likes the World Wars. [I don't *like* wars. I like studying wars. That's totally different. —David] He did the modern stuff, like Pellargonia being in the EU and Schengen and all that.

We made Wikipedia pages for all the important figures, from Amalia Croce, who started the 1883 Women's Revolution and got the vote for women, way before we got it here in America, to Cesar Fuentes, the leader of the Pellargonian National Front,

who may be holding Professor Escobar captive. You can tell it
was us because we're listed as the earliest editors: JuliaE@lhs.edu,
Maddie@lhs.edu, and superyoda@gmail.com. Julia was worried
about the people who were there already. "What will happen to
them? I mean, some of them are French and some of them are
Spanish. Will they go on being French and Spanish, and just sort
of move to make room for Pellargonia?" To be honest, I hadn't
thought about that. She's more socially conscious than me and
David. [David and I. —David] She doesn't even wear leather shoes.

"They'll just become Pellargonian," said David. Anyway, that's
what we hoped would happen. Like, one day they would start
speaking Pellargonian, and their passports would turn into Pellargonian ones. It was still in the EU, so they would be fine, right? It's
not as though we would really be changing very much. Just, like,
the street signs, and they would have a new king, but Leopold IV
was a constitutional monarch. He was mostly there for opening
hospitals and riding a white horse down Santa Eugenia Stras on
Liberation Day. Pellargonia was still a representative democracy.
Finally even Julia decided it was all right, because the French and
Spanish had colonized so many other people, they deserved to be
colonized a little themselves. Anyway, we wouldn't actually be
hurting anyone. To be honest, we didn't think about it as carefully
as we should have. I mean, exams were coming up. And we only
half believed it would work. Could we really create a country just
by writing about it? Maybe it was bullcrap, after all.

After we put everything up on Wikipedia, we divided the
social media stuff. I posted on Facebook, because I still have an
account so I can share funny cartoons with my mom. Julia posted
on Instagram. She took photos around Lewiston and photo-
shopped them, putting in castles and villages from tourist agency
ads. She had to add a lot of sunlight because Lewiston isn't exactly
on the Mediterranean. She painted a bunch of historical figures
herself. [Sort of. Digital painting on top of older stuff. Like, Queen

Magdalena is really Leonardo da Vinci's *Lady with an Ermine,* but I changed it to a dog, because who keeps an ermine as a pet? That's as bad as wearing fur. —Julia] And David did whatever you do on Reddit, because he's the only one of us who's actually been on Reddit. I don't even know what it is, to be honest. [Because you're not a nerd. —David]

We filled the internet with Pellargonia. It took a lot of time, because we still had to study and eat and sleep and stuff. And Julia had soccer. Lewiston High was as close as it had ever gotten to the state championship, so she had to go to a bunch of away games. [We came in second, after one of the big Portland high schools. —Julia] Just when David and I thought we'd done enough, Julia said, "You know, we need to write an article. For the *Journal of Imaginary Anthropology.* It won't be real without that."

Of course, none of us knew how to write an academic article, so we spent most of Thanksgiving break in the university library. We looked at all those articles from the *Journal of Imaginary Anthropology* again and wrote down sentences we could use. Not to plagiarize, we know that's wrong, but so we could sound like professors. We learned words like "industrial capacity" and "agricultural sector" and "balance of payments." [Those are phrases, not words. —David] We realized that we'd thought a lot about the history of Pellargonia, but we hadn't really thought about how it would fit into the modern world. We knew it used euros, that was easy. But was it a member of NATO? [Yes, it joined at the same time as Spain. —Julia] And we wrote a lot of footnotes—we noticed journal articles had a lot of footnotes. David was especially good at those. He sort of talks like a footnote anyway. [There's nothing wrong with being articulate. —David] [See what I mean? I would never have used the word "articulate." —Madison]

I wrote the first draft, except for the footnotes. Then Julia revised it and added a lot more. Then David revised it, because he sounds the most professory, and then I revised it again to take out some of the professoryness, because we wanted it to be read-able. [It *was* readable. And what's wrong with saying "articulate"? Just because you have a limited vocabulary doesn't mean the rest of us have to. —David] [I don't have a "limited vocabulary." I just happen to talk like a normal person. —Madison] We also added a bunch of maps and charts [Those are Figures 2-12. I drew all the maps. —David] [You already said that. —Madison], including the dates of the different kings and queens, since women can be head of state in Pellargonia [Damn straight. —Julia], ever since Saint Eugenia, the youngest daughter of King Ludovic I, became queen in 1306, after her two older brothers were assassinated. The Pellargonians were out of possible kings, so they just went ahead and made her queen—plus she had a divine vision that she was chosen by the Virgin Mary herself. [I put that in. Maybe it was a real divine vision, maybe not. We'll never know! —Julia] Then we formatted it all correctly for submission to the journal, the way it said on the website.

The last step was putting "Jorge Escobar, PhD," on the first page, right below the title. I remember at the time we all thought it was pretty funny—and harmless, because Julia's father would never find out. I mean, how could he? He doesn't have a sub-scription to the *Journal of Imaginary Anthropology*—remember, he thinks it's bullcrap. And even if he did, no one actually reads academic journals. They just download the articles from JSTOR. We figured only a few people would ever see the article, but with all the other stuff we were doing, it would make Pellargonia real. Then we decided we should add his name to the Wikipedia page, as an expert on Pellargonian history—after all, he had written the definitive article on Pellargonia, right? Of course, now we wish we hadn't done it. But if wishes were horses, beggars would ride, as my grandma used to say. [What does that even mean? —Julia] [It's a proverb. —David] [That doesn't mean it makes sense. —Julia]

We got a reply back only a month later. I mean, Professor Escobar got it, but Julia was checking his departmental mailbox, and she took it before he noticed. We opened it together, not really expecting anything. Julia handed the letter to David, who read it out loud—our article had been accepted![1]

After that, things got really busy for us. There was Christmas break [Winter break, technically. —David], and then studying for the AP exam. Our AP World History teacher wanted all of us to take the exam that year because he said it didn't really count. Since no college gives AP World History credit anyway, he thought it would be good practice. So as soon as school started again, we started taking practice tests. Julia was working on an online graphic novel in Spanish, posting a chapter a week. David was practicing for the jazz ensemble (he plays the trombone, but he said he was getting tired of marching band). [Too many football games. —David] I had decided to join the girls' basketball

---

1   This is, of course, an extraordinarily short period of time for acceptance to a peer-reviewed academic journal. Although the writers of this letter could not have realized it, we were at the time receiving very few submissions—the situation in Gondal was at its most tense, and there were some voices calling for an end to the imaginary sciences, saying that imaginary anthropology, archaeology, geology, and the nascent field of imaginary astrophysics imperiled us all. Others pointed out that some respectable fields—xenobiology, for example—had always been at least partly imaginary, and that reality was not more relative and conditional now than it had ever been. The history of cartography, for example, consists entirely of imaginary maps that can never accurately depict the territory. I remember when this article first crossed my desk. I shared it with my office mate (also an adjunct at Southern Arizona State, teaching a 4/4 schedule with one class per semester in the anthropology department, the other three freshman comp). It had some mistakes that I put down to hasty composition and corrected in proofs, but I had no reason to believe it was not by Professor Escobar. Reviewer 1, my office mate's ex-girlfriend who had also gotten her PhD in our department and who was now an assistant professor at Mary Margaret Wentworth College in Virginia, said it was fine. Reviewer 2, who had been my thesis director, said it should refer to his seminal work, *Imaginary Anthropology: Theory and Practice*, which he says in every review, and which I felt was not applicable in this particular case. So the article was published as it was sent to me, with only minor alterations. —Ed.

team. I'm not great at basketball, but I'm tall, and that counts for a lot. We still worked on Pellargonia when we could—I mean, we didn't want to leave Zoraida Delacorte in trouble, and there was a whole revolution going on. [As usual. —Julia] Plus I really wanted Princess Stefania to meet up with Clotilde again. There was a girl on the basketball team who looked a little like Clotilde, and I wondered if she might like to go to the mall, to get bubble tea or something. But there wasn't much time.

One day, Julia grabbed me in the hall as I was heading to lunch. (That quarter, she was in a different lunch period, so David and I ate together.) She was all jumpy, the way she is when she gets excited, like a jack-in-the-box. "I got a Google Alert!" she said. "Look at *this*! And tell David."

This was an Air France flight to Pellargonia. "CDG to BDM," it said: Charles de Gaulle Airport to Bellagua del Mar. On sale for 80 euros in economy.

When I got to the cafeteria, David was already sitting there, with tater tots on his tray. He has tater tots every single day, with ketchup. That's it, just two servings of tater tots. [It's the only edible thing in the cafeteria. —David] I got a rectangular pizza and the obligatory vegetable, probably spinach because it was green and slimy, like seaweed. [You should get tater tots. They count as a vegetable. —David] If Julia had been there, she would have brought something from home, like a tofu ham sandwich or one of those rolled-up nori things.

When I showed David what Julia had shown me, he took out his cell phone and said, "Siri, how can I get to Pellargonia?" He's the only one of us with an iPhone, which his dad bought him. I just have my mom's old Android with a dented case, and Julia has an ancient BlackBerry. [Didn't the dinosaurs use those? —David]

"There are two ways to get to Pellargonia," said a mechanical female voice. "Would you like to go by plane or by train?"

My phone doesn't have a fancy voice, but while David asked

about flights, I looked up train routes on Google Maps. There were trains to Bellagua del Mar from Barcelona and Montpellier. The one from Barcelona stopped in Girona and Figueres. The one from Montpellier stopped in Perpignan. Once you arrived in Bellagua del Mar, it looked like you could get around Pellargonia pretty easily. There was a highway from Bellagua to Magdalena, in the northern mountains, which is sort of a resort town. That's where Fitzgerald G. Scott built his casino. It's also the center of the revolution. There were a lot of smaller roads to towns we had named, and towns I had never heard of. Who had created them? And there was a dotted line from Mallorca to the Arroz Islands.

"That's a ferry service," said David. "It runs three times a day." He showed me his phone, which had all the times, 40 euros round trip. He swiped to show me the train tables, and then the Air France website. "Would you like to book a flight?" asked Siri.

Pellargonia was real.

David said, "And look at this." He swiped again, and there was YouTube, with PTV-1, the Pellargonian state TV channel, broadcasting the news in Pellargonian. I could sort of understand it, a little. We had made up the basic stuff, like verb tenses, words for things like sun, moon, cat, dog, trees, flowers, traitor, king, succession, assassination. Conjunctions and prepositions. But this was a real language! We just sat there staring at each other, until Ms. Patel told us to hurry up and put our trays in the rack, because lunch was almost over. She's usually the gym teacher, but she was monitoring lunch that day. Lunch only lasts twenty minutes— I don't know who can eat in twenty minutes, even if it's just rectangular pizza. David shoved the rest of his tater tots into his mouth. Then we heard the bell, and we had to rush to AP World History. At least the three of us had that class together. We were talking about Europe during the Cold War—we had just gotten to the "Modern World Order" chapter in our history textbook.

"Yes, David?" said Mr. Delacorte. We named Zoraida Delacorte after him, although she's a former ballet dancer and spy, while Mr. Delacorte is a short man with a halo of white hair who's been teaching history at Lewiston High since my mom went there. To be honest, I wasn't really paying attention. I mean, there was the whole Pellargonia thing, but also I had a basketball tournament that week, and I was visualizing my jump shot. Ms. Patel, who is also our coach, has us do a lot of visualizing—she says that's how players in the WNBA get so good. First they visualize, and then they practice what they visualized over and over. It helps with cello too. [That is so not important right now. —Julia]

"What about the little countries?" said David. "Like Luxembourg and Montenegro and stuff. What happened to them during the Cold War? Or like Pellargonia, just for example."

I sat up in my seat and looked back at him. He had such an innocent expression on his face, like he had just happened to think of Pellargonia right then. David can do that—he never looks guilty, no matter what he does. That time he cut my hair and then swore he didn't do it, my mom believed him, even though he was standing right there, holding the scissors. I got sent to my room, and it took a year for my hair to grow back. [We were *five*. You've got to let that go. —David]

I was ready for Mr. Delacorte to ask him what he was talking about, to say there was no country called Pellargonia. But instead he said, "Well, these little countries, David, tend to be heavily influenced by the larger countries around them. Luxembourg, surrounded by Belgium, France, and Germany, became a wealthy banking center. Montenegro is not really that small. It was part of Yugoslavia, which we covered last week, so I'll refer you to your notes from back then. It's still dealing with the effects of ethnic conflict. And Pellargonia, which borders on the Catalan-speaking part of Spain, is in the middle of a civil war between those who want to remain part of the EU, speaking New Pellargonian, and the nationalistic Euroskeptic Old Pellargonian speakers. Evidently, it's going rather badly for the central government, and there's talk of deposing the king. Not that he has much power anyway, but fighting in the north has created a refugee problem on the French border from people trying to escape the fighting, and they're looking for someone, anyone, to blame."

A civil war? We had thought of it as one more romantic revolution—I mean, Pellargonia had a history of revolutions. It had been about Cesar Fuentes, and Zoraida Delacorte, and King Leopold IV, and Princess Stefania. We hadn't really thought about the political consequences. Or, you know, people dying. All that stuff about Old Pellargonian was just a footnote. David wrote it because we thought there should be some kind of history about how Pellargonian had changed over the centuries, like from Old English to regular English. Julia and I thought it was a cool idea at the time. [We were kind of dumb. —Julia] [We didn't really believe in it. I mean, it was like a game, like when you're the Dungeon Master in D&D. I thought it would be interesting to have a different language for the northern part, around Mount Zamorna. I never thought anyone would have a war about it. —David] [We're not making excuses for ourselves, just trying to explain. —Madison]

But what were we supposed to do? We were just three kids [Young adults. —Julia] living in Lewiston. We weren't politicians, or anything like that. And the Tlön hypothesis says that once you create a country, it takes on a life of its own, and then it's not yours anymore. That's supposed to be the coolest thing about it. Except I guess it's not cool if people are fighting and dying, for real.[2]

---

2 This is, of course, the problem with imaginary anthropology. People and the political systems they create are inherently unpredictable. You never know what they will do. The situation in Ruritania is a case in point. You can't really blame David Ignatious and his group at Harvard for the autocratic regime of General Szarkov. I mean, you can, and this journal issued a very stern warning for all imaginary anthropologists to be particularly careful when creating former Soviet bloc countries. That configuration seems to have inherent instabilities. The Harvard group was out of its depth, but what do you expect from a bunch of

We stopped playing at Pellargonia after that. It wasn't a game anymore. Anyway, school ended and the summer vacation began. David went off to math camp [Which was like math class all day, every day. I started having nightmares about being chased by quadratic equations. —David], and Julia went to her grandmother's in Los Angeles. I was left by myself in Lewiston. Well, not exactly by myself, because I was volunteering at the library, so I got to spend time with Mom. But you know what I mean. Every once in a while, we texted each other:

> Did you see that there's a truce between the Pellargonia National Front and the Social Democrats? —Julia

> There's a story in *El Mund* saying the Prime Minister might have been poisoned. Do you think they'll figure out it was Zoraida Delacorte? —Madison

> Fighting has broken out again around Magdalena. I saw it on PTV-1. —David

> They just announced that Princess Stefania is going to assume the throne. King Leopold is stepping down on Friday. —Madison

> The referendum was 57% remain in the EU. But that still means a lot of people want to leave, and they're mostly in the north. —Julia

> They found Cesar Fuentes' headquarters at the casino, but he had already fled. I hope Zoraida is with him. —Madison

---

Ivy League grad students? They're convinced they can walk on water. Each of them wants to, individually, be God. What I have learned in the imaginary sciences is that reality has its own imagination, and we are all only a small part of its creative power. I will be expanding on this hypothesis, with Pellargonia as one of my examples, in a paper to be given at the Imaginary Anthropology Symposium at the University of Glasgow next summer. —Ed.

Hey Mad, did you see the cover of *Vogue France*?
There's a blonde woman with Princess Stefania. Is that
Clotilde? —Julia

OMG can someone send me Oreos? The only cookies
here are these weird chewy things with flax seed,
because they say it's brain food. I'm going to die of
starvation. Oh and BTW someone tried to bring a
bomb into the Catedral dela Santa Eugenia during
the coronation. It was hidden in a camera—he was
pretending to be a journalist for *El País*. I'm glad they
caught him. —David

Queen Stefania made a statement on PTV-1. She's
going to try to negotiate with the PNF. I hope it works.
—Julia

But mostly we focused on other things. We couldn't think
about Pellargonia all the time. And we figured, now that it was
real—now that it was part of the world—there wasn't much more
we could do. It was like we'd created Frankenstein, and now it
was going to go off by itself, doing whatever it did. [Frankenstein
is the scientist. The monster doesn't have a name. —David] [The
scientist *is* the monster. —Julia]

Until the letter came for Julia's dad.

It came just before school started, after David got back from
camp [Six weeks of math and mosquitoes! I thought I was going
to die. —David] and Julia got back from the art program she had
gone to after Los Angeles. [We painted from a nude model. A *male*
nude model. My mom kind of freaked out when I told her. —Julia]
It was all we could talk about, even though we were going to start
eleventh grade and there was so much to catch up on. This year we
were going to be taking the SAT, and all our teachers had decided
to assign summer reading—before the first class! I was thinking
about asking my friend Audrey [the one on the basketball team]
out on a real date. David had a crush on a girl from math camp

[I wouldn't call it a crush. It was a mutual attraction. —David], and Julia had started selling some of her art on Redbubble, on mugs and things. [I'm JuliArt. —Julia] But all we could talk about was Julia's dad and the letter.

We'd thought about visiting Pellargonia ourselves some-day. Like when we were in college backpacking around Europe together, staying in hostels and stuff. Julia's mom had done that with some of her friends, when she was young—I mean younger, since she's not really old, although she has gray hair. [Most hair dyes have chemicals that can give you cancer. —Julia] Anyway, it sounded pretty cool. But now Julia's dad was actually going!

Why had they invited him? Because he was an expert on Pellargonian history, of course. After all, he had written the definitive article—it said so on Wikipedia. [I told you no one ever reads the actual journals. —Julia] How was he going to get there? Air France. Where was he going to stay in Bellagua del Mar? The university had a guesthouse at the Estrella Ceilo estate. Would he meet Queen Stefania herself? He had no idea, and Julia was asking so many questions that he told her to please stop pestering him, because he had a keynote address to write.

Of course we were a little worried, because we knew that Queen Stefania's offer of amnesty had been rejected, and the PNF was still active in the mountains around Magdalena. "He'll be fine," Julia said. "He's just going for a week to some academic con-ference. He goes to conferences all the time."

But it wasn't fine. You know that—I'm sure you've seen the footage on PTV-1, and it was even on CNN. Just as Queen Stefania started her welcome address, the rebels burst into the auditorium. They had Kalashnikovs, flash grenades, and tear gas, and David says he even saw a rocket launcher. [The video was blurry, but I'm pretty sure that's what it was. —David] They wanted the queen, of course. Well, they didn't get her, but after all the smoke cleared, three of the people who had been sitting beside her on the dais were gone: Dr. Otto Lenker, the president of the Royal Society; Dr. Amélie Beaulieu of the University of Lyon, and Julia's dad.

It's been three months. The PNF made a deal with the French government, and Dr. Beaulieu was released. Dr. Lenker and Julia's dad are still being held captive. There was an offer to exchange them for two of the rebel leaders being held in prison, but the Pellargonian government said it didn't deal with terrorists. We think he's still alive—I mean, we know he is. [He is. —Julia] Julia's mom got in touch with Senator Mitchner as soon as she heard the news, and he says the U.S. government is doing all it can. She's pretty frantic, and she keeps talking about flying to Pellargonia, just so she can be there. I mean, she needs to be here to take care of Julia, but she's asked for a leave of absence from the clinic she works for, and she thinks another therapist can cover for her, for a while. [Sometimes I can hear her crying at night. —Julia]

So we've started a GoFundMe to get her and Julia to Pellargonia. I mean, we *made* Pellargonia. Maybe there's something Julia can do, and maybe David and I can help, even from Lewiston? But we're just three kids. [Young adults. —Julia] You were probably in high school yourself at some point. [Everyone has to go through high school at some point. It's like the common cold. —David] So you must know what it feels like—everyone tells you that you're almost an adult, so you're supposed to be responsible, but no one *treats* you like an adult or takes you seriously. When I tried to talk to Mom about what had happened, she said, "Sweetheart, you can't make up a country. Pellargonia has been around for a long time. You can look it up on Wikipedia."

The GoFundMe has about $700, mostly from David's stepmom and his band friends. We thought, maybe the *Journal of Imaginary Anthropology* could send an email to its members, or post something on the website? We need money, but also, we need someone to go with Julia and her mom—someone who really understands imaginary anthropology, and might be able to fix things? Like one of the authors who wrote those theoretical articles. If there's someone like that out there, who can actually help us find Julia's dad and maybe stop the civil war, please contact us at Professor Escobar's university address with a letter of intent, your CV, and two references. [Does that sound right, Jules? —Madison] [Yes, that's the way it's usually done. —Julia] We look forward to hearing from you.

Sincerely,

Madison Kowalski, David Lewis, and Julia Escobar

~

Editor's Note:

I have published this letter in full, exactly as I received it, from Madison, David, and Julia, whom I have since communicated with by email. I am convinced that they did, in fact, create Pellargonia— a remarkable feat for a group of high school students, considering that the Stanford group failed to create any country whatsoever after two years of trying. This supports a pet theory of mine that creating a country is not, finally, about expertise but *imagination* and the *capacity to believe*, or at least not *dis*believe. Davidson et al. started out as skeptics. No wonder it didn't work. More importantly, I'm including this letter in the current issue instead of my usual introduction in the hope that our readers will support the Save Professor Escobar fund. I intend to travel with Julia and Dr. Gabriela Escobar myself. I don't know if there's anything I can do, but as editor of this journal, I feel a sense of responsibility.

Since I received the above letter, conditions have improved in Pellargonia. Queen Stefania is considerably more popular than her father, and her economic policies are expected to help the poorer northern districts, including Floria and Zamorna. Her personal appeal to Zoraida Delacorte on PTV-2, the fashion and lifestyle channel, was both an effective political move and good PR. Hopefully the current cease-fire and the resumption of negotiations between the government and the PNF will help us free Professor Escobar. Whatever happens, I hope to document our trip and my observations in a future article in this journal. I will call it "Pellargonia: A Case Study in the Problematics of Imaginary Anthropology."

CADWELL TURNBULL

There, She Didn't Need Air to Fill Her Lungs

Cadwell Turnbull

She returned with an impossible story: There was a tree on top of Fishtail Peak. The roots of the tree clung to the ice, she told us, growing right out of the stone, sending deep cracks along the face of the mountain. The tree leaves were vibrant green and blue ice-fruit hung heavy on branches, plump and ready to burst. Fur-covered rhesus macaques reached for the fruit, gliding on patagia wings flecked with frost.

Fishtail Peak was too high, we wanted to say. It would be growing above the tree line. No vegetation could survive there. But it was the way she said the impossible thing, the quiet intensity of every word, each spaced like a marker along something sacred; it made us doubt ourselves. We could feel the cold on our fingers, the sticky spray as we cracked open the ice-fruit, the delicate sweet flurries on our tongues. But we were women of science. We were divided, split in two.

A year later, when she said she was going back to Nepal, we all jumped to go with her, wound to action by some toymaker's hand.

"Why are you so excited?" she asked.

The Tree, we said.

"What tree?"

We could see the lost expression on her face, loss and the vague awareness of that loss. Never mind, we said. Take us with you. Take us to Fishtail Peak.

She smiled, nodding. How long had she wanted to take us home with her, show us the pieces of herself always left behind, those shiny parts of her being that had never made their way to America? She could never explain. There are certain things that can't be said. The words aren't there. She would have to show us.

"Fishtail Peak is sacred," she said. "No one goes there. But we can see it from the top of Poon Hill, though it is a very long way up. Are you sure?"

Yes, we said.

～

We all got a flight together, stopping in Helsinki and then Dubai before arriving in Kathmandu. It took thirty-two hours and we were a sticky mess by the end of it, all greasy skin and oily hair and body odor. Maya's mom and dad picked us up from the airport and we spent four days with them, eating Nepali food and sitting on the rooftop of Maya's family home, baking in the sun and staring out at Kathmandu, its edges hazy with dust and city smog. We played card games and received impromptu language lessons in Nepali and Newari, the latter of which was Maya's ethnic language, which had atrophied less over the years living abroad. Between lessons we talked about the trek up to Poon Hill.

"How high is it?" we asked.

"About ten thousand five hundred feet," Maya said.

"And that's a *hill?*" Caroline said, incredulous. Caroline was from an island called St. Croix, whose highest point was only

1,100 feet. Low by most people's standards, but even Laura, who did treks all the time in New England, seemed impressed by the height and surprised by its designation as a hill.

"It is in the hill region," Maya explained. "Up there we will be able to see Fishtail Peak, which is almost twenty-three thousand feet."

This we knew. Machapuchare wasn't as large as Everest, but still a monster of a thing. Ileana whistled; her eyes glazed over in awe. She'd done some minor hiking in her native Mexico, but nothing like this.

Maya shrugged and said, "I think we should take a bus some of the way up."

"I agree," Ileana said.

"No way—we should climb it all," said Laura.

"We should get to The Tree as soon as possible," Margot said. She'd grown up in Washington State and was just as equipped for a long trek as Laura, but was more excited about the reason they'd come in the first place.

Maya watched us again, confused. "What tree?"

The rest of us looked at Margot, communicating with our eyes.

"I'm sorry," Margot said. "I don't know why I said that."

~

Maya's friend came early in the morning on the fifth day and we packed his car with our suitcases and bags. The drive out of Kathmandu was quiet. Rain drizzled on the windshield of the SUV as we drove over dusty streets quickly turning to mud. On one road heading out of the city we hit a bit of traffic but it cleared by the time we reached the first roadside town. We drove through winding hillside roads, along river valleys connected by simple suspension bridges, with troops of rhesus macaques playing on the roadside.

Six hours and we were in Pokhara, the beginning point of our trek, and we spent the rest of the evening stopping into stores clearly meant for tourists and walking along the lake and eating appetizers at local restaurants. Looking out at the night-time lights of houses reflecting into the lake, Caroline remarked that it reminded her of her own home, the tourist-economy and restaurants near the water and the way the lake shimmered. The evening was cool and we all were wearing hoodies and drinking cocktails, anxious and tipsy and feeling so alive.

"I'm so glad you're all here," Maya said. "This place is in my heart, in my blood. And now I feel closer to all of you."

Ileana laughed, her face red with cold and alcohol, and said, "Next stop, Mexico," and we all cheered and clinked our glasses together. We were all graduate students, all plant scientists of one sort or another. Ileana and Margot studied macro plant systems, climatology and ecosystem stress, and the rest of us studied plant-level systems, leaves and roots, stomata in leaves, tree rings. Which was why the tree captivated us. A tree growing at twenty-three thousand feet? With blue fruit? And rumors of flying rhesus macaques? A story, surely. And yet, we'd come all this way.

Maya was staring into the fire, her amber pupils reflecting the flames so that it looked like her eyes were tiny infernos. "You ever feel like there's a part of you somewhere else? That you lost it so long ago you can't remember and now you just keep looking for it everywhere and it's become your whole life, looking, looking and never finding?"

We didn't know what to say to this. We knew what she meant, but at the same time we didn't. The truth of it was speeding toward us all and we could hear it coming, the blare faint but ringing in our ears. That feeling though—we'd all known it and yet never put name to it.

"Up there," Maya said, and her face looked up toward the hills.

"Up there," she said again, and then looked around at us as if she had said something more, searching for our comprehension.

"Up there," we repeated.

~

Maya's friend dropped us off at the bus stop and then we took the bus out of the city, along paved roads lined by anonymous homes. Beautiful and living. Clothes on lines. People in their yards. Construction trucks and their workers. Entire lives and histories stretching before us, yet the barest glimpse revealed.

Farther out, the roads turned to dirt and then became steep, winding and thin, the tail of a large serpent wrapped around hills long buried. We encountered homes here too, though more spread out, and then guesthouses once we made it to the area the trek would normally begin, one every few miles along a river of clean trembling water. Single- or two-story structures offering beds to rest in, showers, and food. We passed them by, noting each one out of our windows.

Before long we were so far up that below us lay the peaks of smaller hills staring up at us, rice paddies and small villages we had no idea how to get to, everything a dark, rich green.

The road was only a whip of a thing now, the bus rocking along, driving over boulders and uneven dirt. Every now and then a vehicle in descent would force us to the edge of the road where we could look down into steep ravines with anxiously held breath, the earth disturbed by the bus tires falling to new resting places. Margot had to look away, her blue eyes wide, an openmouthed smile, both joyous and horror-struck.

We all thought of other timelines where the driver had miscalculated or the road had given way, plunging us to our deaths, each turn, each effort to make way for another vehicle, feeling like dice rolling on forever.

We stopped at a small village with storefronts on each side of the bus. The driver got out and began loading supplies to drop off higher up in the hills: eggs, rice, oil, and flour mostly but also tanks of gas and containers with their own secrets inside. A half hour there and we were off again, climbing even higher. Now all we could see for miles in every direction were rolling hills, the smallest signs of civilization. The air was cool. Teenagers in the back of the bus played their guitars and sang Nepali and Hindi songs.

By midafternoon we made it to Ghandruk. We got out of the bus and stretched our legs, looked around. The village was laid out on the incline above, single-story and two-story houses and stone steps leading up through it all.

We stood around for a time, admiring the view, readying ourselves. We needed to start soon if we would make it to the next village on our schedule before nightfall made the passage difficult. The air was thin and even after a few steps Caroline could feel her lungs working to give her body the oxygen it needed. With each step Caroline felt her muscles working and her joints straining, the gravity different somehow, weighing her down. Ileana also felt the beginning signs of what might become trouble later on. Laura was ahead, powering through any discomfort she felt, Margot close behind, but looking back in concern. Maya was third in line, feeling a slight struggle for breath, but nothing yet to worry about.

Before long, we were at the upper edge of the village. The path ahead was made of flat stone laid out like puzzle pieces, just like the steps that led through Ghandruk. On the trail heading out of the village a dog sat waiting for us, black fur with brown spots above its eyes and a patch of brown along its chest. A Tibetan mastiff, Maya guessed, or a mutt with the breed mixed in. We had no clue who the dog belonged to, or if indeed he belonged to anyone. He stared at us, calm and completely at home so far up in the hills. No collar, waiting expectantly, tail curled up over his back. No threat in him, but not much excitement either. He felt like a sage who'd transformed into a dog. We walked on and he let us pass before following, staying close.

"What should we name him?" Laura asked.

"Ghandruff," Ileana said, and we all agreed.

Ghandruff soon got bored with our slow pace and went ahead of us, sniffing the shrubbery along the path, going off-path a little to look around, until we caught up. The forest we entered was silent except for the distant sound of birds we couldn't see.

Caroline was already lagging behind, the breath coming out hot and fast. At inclines where the path turned to steps again, she had to ready herself for the climb before attempting it. Ileana was a little ahead but vocally expressing her discomfort. Maya kept calling back to Caroline. "I'm fine," she responded, obviously winded. After a while, Maya let her lag behind but quietly kept an eye out for her. When it began to hail, Caroline screamed out in delight, the forest carrying her voice.

"Are you seeing this?" Caroline yelled. "Oh my god!" Even after a few years living in Boston, Caroline still got excited about hail and snow. These things did not exist on St. Croix.

We came across a part of the forest where the branches of the trees reminded us all of the bronchial tubes of a lung. We were all captivated, but Caroline even more so than the rest of us. When we moved on, she stayed behind. She stood in a copse of trees empty of sound except for the soft crackle of hail hitting fallen leaves.

The chirp of a bird broke the silence, and Caroline looked in its direction. The creature watched her and then with a flourish, spread its wings, revealing feathers too much like leaves. It opened its beak, the color and texture of bark, and screeched, as if in warning, before taking off into the air.

～

It was near dark when we reached Tadapani, the next village up from Ghandruk and where we'd spend the night. The hail had turned to snow, which had stuck but not in terrifying amounts. Ghandruff the dog followed us quietly, and then, once we had chosen the guesthouse we'd be staying at, he continued onward through the village and disappeared.

We went inside the dining room, which was a small room with a furnace at its center. One by one we went to the bathroom for our ablutions and then returned to order food from the menu: Nepali momos, fried dough served with a fried egg on top, and hot lemon tea for everyone.

Laura looked tired but was otherwise in good spirits. Ileana was sore but the warmth of the room had improved her mood greatly. Maya wasn't quite at ease until the food arrived, and Margot was only happy when the whole group was happy.

We spent the time before bed playing a word game called Mind Meld, where two players would shout out words and then do it again using the previous set to get closer to a common word. As we played, Maya spared a few glances at a group of European trekkers talking quietly at another table. Maya didn't know the language, but guessed it had a German root by its vague similarity to English. The language itself wasn't the interesting thing. It was their smiling faces, serene and odd in an unnamable way. Beautiful too. One of them turned her attention to Maya and smiled with pure joy. Maya smiled back.

"Tomorrow will be a full day," said Laura. "About seven hours to Ghorepani."

"I've packed a ton of candy bars in my bag," Margot said, "in case we need energy on the way."

All the talk about the next day made Ileana suddenly tired. "We should go to bed then."

Maya agreed. After Margot drank the last of her tea, we all went to find a room. All the rooms were the same: beds to sleep in, a dim light bulb, and hooks in the walls to hang clothes. There was no more than that, but it was enough. We chose a room with five beds and got changed and pulled out our sleeping bags from our backpacks.

The night was difficult. The room had no heating so we covered ourselves with the bed comforters as well, which smelled fine but their questionable hygiene made Margot and Laura a bit nervous. Through the night we alternated between smothering ourselves with the sleeping bags and comforters and then freezing when, half-asleep, we'd kick our way free from our cocoons. Morning came too quickly and none of us were well-rested, so we idled a bit too long at breakfast.

Ghandruff had been waiting for us outside our door, but seemed to lose interest in us and eventually followed the European trekkers back down the hill.

We ate egg and fried dough and drank tea and embarked again. None of us had showered since there was no heating at our guesthouse. This affected our mood more than we'd expected, but we were determined to continue on.

The early morning trek slipped by mostly in silence. The little bit of snow that had fallen the previous day had turned to ice and more snow fell as we climbed, which made the way treacherous. Laura had trekking poles and let Ileana borrow one. Everyone else used discarded bamboo sticks they'd found, a cheap alternative commonly used along the trail. We passed mossy streams, waterfalls that were more icicle than water, men with donkeys carrying loads of flat stone, and a herd of water buffalo so calm they barely paid any attention to us at all. These sights warmed us, and we were much more talkative in the afternoon, engaging in enthusiastic conversation about the plant life we were seeing on our journey. The trees and shrubbery were familiar—we could tell what sort of plants they were, their family and lineage to a degree—but we were utterly lost when it came to specifics.

"Fuck," Laura kept saying. "Some kind of oak?" or "Rhododendron?" or "Hell, who knows?"

Ileana found an old tree, a native maple by the look of it, with a hole in its center that looked like the back of a human mouth, the uvula hanging at the entrance of a pitch-black pit. She called out to get our attention, but Laura was far ahead and Margot and Maya were looking at a shrub, trying to figure out what it was by its leaves. Unable to resist, Ileana leaned forward just a bit and looked inside.

~

When we finally stopped for a break and a quick bite it was around noon by Laura's watch. We found a very small guesthouse with only a couple rooms. We wouldn't be staying so we got some fried rice to split between us and some hot lemon tea and we nestled together next to the furnace, poking at the burning wood inside.

Maya got to talking to the woman running the place. The exchange was in Nepali and afterward we asked her what the conversation was about.

"She said the way up is icy and they weren't expecting this much snow."

"That'll slow us down," Laura said with some concern.

"It'll be okay," Margot said. "We have flashlights if it gets too dark."

"But even with lights, it'll be hard to travel at night," Laura said. "We have to speed up."

"And be careful," Margot added.

Laura smiled thinly. "Of course."

"She also said that this place is the boundary between worlds, that we should be careful where we wander."

We didn't know what to say to that so we just nodded.

After our meal, we resumed our trek up the trail. The way was indeed treacherous, and as we went, climbing ice-slick stone and descending slippery paths, we passed other people on their descent. At one point we helped a Kenyan couple—Maya remembered the accented English from friends in undergrad—descend a dangerous area covered with ice.

They were very grateful. "We cleared some of the ice up above," said one of the men, "but our magic is weak on this side—"

The other man put his hand on the man's shoulder. "Safe travels," he said and with a final smile and wave carried on down the hill.

After that the ice continued on for another half hour before disappearing, leaving only snow and ice on the sides of the path.

We stopped near an icy stream to eat candy bars. There we found a collection of structures made of flat stones stacked on top of each other. There were hundreds of them, some with stacks of over a dozen stones, all small enough to be carried by human hands.

We collected some of these flat stones from along the stream and left a few of ours.

"How long do you think people have been doing this?" Margot asked.

"Years," Maya said. "Decades, maybe." We listened to the stream. It was the only sound we could hear. The sky was overcast and growing darker.

We went on, the steep trails giving way to more level paths, wider and covered in soft snow that hadn't turned to ice. Laura went ahead of us. We kept a good pace but let the distance between us spread out, enjoying the dense forest and making new trails of our own in the fresh snow.

"What do you think we will see when we get to the top?" Margot asked.

"If the sky is clear, we should be able to see Fishtail Peak with no problems," Maya said.

Margot knew better than to mention the tree. "Oh, that's nice," she said.

"I've been feeling strange. Haven't you?" Maya asked.

"A little, but I think we will feel better when we reach the top of Poon Hill," said Caroline and Ileana in perfect unison, their voices whistling like a gust through a cracked window.

Maya nodded in agreement. "Yes, that makes sense."

Without realizing at first, we had passed into a deep fog that made it difficult to see more than a few feet ahead. Laura had wandered quite far by this point and we had lost sight of her, and she, of us. She was standing next to a shrine of some kind, words written in Nepali script she couldn't read. She was on the crest of a hill, the tree line falling away to a field with yellowed grass. Patches of snow lay everywhere, here and there, but much of it had melted without the cover of trees.

In front of her the fog was very dense and the ground and sky seemed to disappear altogether into a uniform gray that blurred and concealed everything. Laura figured it would be a while before the rest of us caught up. Her knees were aching, her back in knots. She closed her eyes to stave off a headache that had been building since lunchtime.

"Not far now," she heard her own voice say. Startled, she opened her eyes.

~

When the rest of us reached the shrine we took a few photos, smiling and sweating in our layers. We ate a couple candy bars, sharing them between us. The way was easy and we arrived at our destination by late afternoon, a canopy of many-colored flags and an archway signaling the entrance to Ghorepani. It was near sunset by then, but we'd made good time.

A great many guesthouses lay before us, peppered throughout the village, along winding paths of stone steps. Despite its size, Ghorepani was empty. Our laughter and excitement carried in the quiet dusk. We found one of the only open shops and bought T-shirts to commemorate the trek, the owner of the shop smiling at us with pure joy. Then we climbed several rows of steps to a guesthouse that loomed over the others, resting at the highest point in the village and quite near to the trail leading to the summit. A woman greeted us at the door, and as we entered we sighed with collective relief at the warmth of the place.

We ordered a round of tea for everyone and sipped them in front of the furnace, hanging up our sweat-drenched clothes on lines around it. We ordered momos and fried dough with fried eggs and shared the meal, looking at the photos from the day on Maya's phone.

Maya was still feeling strange but the food and the heat helped. Outside, the snow fell steadily as she flipped through picture after picture.

"I don't know what it is," Maya said. "Up here I feel like I've been split in half. I mean, I always feel like that, but—" She lost track of the thought; it just floated away, right out of her head. There were other people in the guesthouse dining room. They were smiling at her. Something about it made her uncomfortable so she looked back at the pictures. She stopped at one of the photos at the shrine, staring at all our smiling faces. She didn't like the picture but didn't know why.

"It's special here," Margot said.

"The boundary is thin in the high places," the guesthouse woman said in Nepali, placing a tray of tea on the table near us. "You can see yourself clearly," she added and walked away.

"What did she say?" Margot asked.

Maya shook her head and wrinkled her nose. "This picture looks funny," she said, showing us.

In lockstep, Caroline, Ileana, and Laura shook their heads. "No it doesn't."

~

We were told it was best to see Fishtail Peak at sunrise so we got up when it was still dark to make the journey to the top. The air was so thin now that Maya had to breathe a full long breath with every step. The bamboo stick she still carried helped steady her somewhat, but in the dark it was hard to tell the difference between ice and snow, which made the climb require so much more effort just to keep from slipping. Other people passed Maya on the way up, their grinning faces filling her with rage. Margot was a little ahead, panting with effort herself. She kept looking back at Maya, shining her light in her face.

"Go on ahead," Maya said. "I just need to take my time."

"Please take care of her," Margot said, to which Caroline, Ileana, and Laura smiled and said, "Yes, sure, absolutely," and Margot continued on.

Maya wasn't going very fast but each step felt like she had run a mile. Her stomach hurt, her head was spinning, her lungs felt like they were ready to burst.

Something else was happening too. As she climbed, she was feeling the fog in her mind clear. She hadn't realized the fog was there, but up here so close to the summit of Poon Hill, she was recovering so much—memories rushing back to her from the last time she'd made the trek and she remembered that it was the same then too, the fog clearing and then finally she could see herself, her whole self and those forgotten memories of the life she had lived on the other side.

There, the air wasn't so thin.

There, she had magic to fill her lungs.

There, her knees didn't hurt.

There, the stone toads would carry her, the forest birds would sing to her, the ice would part for her, the earth would cushion her.

How could she have forgotten? Still, these recovered memories were only fragments, but they carried with them the knowledge that she didn't belong here. There was no magic here, no sense.

Maya lost track of time as she climbed, lost track of her body too, until she was nothing more than a roaming consciousness, her pain and failing breath distant as a faint dream after waking. The sun was coming up and then in a blink it was over the mountain where it had slept. Maya's legs picked up the pace, independent of her mind. She saw only the path ahead, the slow climb, the scenes changing like spliced images before her eyes. A few times she thought she had made it to the summit only for the path to turn sharply and reveal even more steps, an infinity of flat stone stretching ever upward. Maya retched, but nothing came out. She groaned like a dead thing reanimated, stuck in a purgatory of involuntary movement.

When at last she saw the open sky, she could barely believe it. Her mind simply could not compute. On the top of Poon Hill was a small observation tower already filled with several people, smiling and looking over the hillsides and mountain peaks that were mostly hidden behind cloud and fog. In her exhausted state, Maya could not make it up the tower and so she collapsed on a bench near the steps she'd just climbed. She bent over and vomited, a stream of fluorescent green fluid spilling from her lips, expelling the last of her magic from her gut. It pooled there on the ground beside her feet making its own light, and she watched it, stupefied, her mouth tasting of bile.

We didn't know what to do so we stood around her, so she would know she was not alone.

"*I can go back down this side,*" a voice offered—her own.

Maya could barely lift her head so she lobbed to one side and flicked her eyes in the direction of the voice. A woman stood there, her long hair blowing into her face, casting it in shadow. But she knew the hair and the face even if she couldn't see it clearly.

She took a few long breaths, filling her lungs. "I forgot my whole life," Maya said.

"*Me too.*"

"I lost my magic," she said.

"*I found mine. It will be a shame to lose it again.*"

"What is it like?" Maya asked. "On the other side."

Above them, for a moment, the two Fishtail Peaks revealed themselves in the glare of the sun, one upright and the other inverted, the life tree's frosted fruit glistening and dripping rain down and up into both worlds. Flying rhesus macaques swirled around the tree like dancers.

"Much the same," said her other half, in Newari. "Easier in some ways. In some ways, harder. You'll see."

Maya looked up at the rest of us, a complete being now, not two half-selves yearning for something more. Ten bodies. Five souls. Together now, but not forever. Nothing ever is.

Thank you for bringing us here, we said, smiling down at her, sharing our warmth, our magic. *Rest now. There's a long way to go from here.*

Acknowledgments

My most heartfelt thanks and appreciation go out to Shawn Speakman (for his insight and, of course, for publishing the book) and the rest of the team at Grim Oak Press. To my agent, Seth Fishman, for being, as always, awesome and supportive. To Gordon Van Gelder and Ellen Datlow, for being great mentors and friends. To my wife, Christie; my stepdaughters, Grace and Lotte; and my sister, Becky—for all their love and support. To my intern, Alex Puncekar. To all of the writers who had stories included in this anthology, and in all of my other projects. And last but not least, to everyone who bought this book, or any of my other anthologies (or subscribed to the magazines I publish: *Lightspeed*, *Fantasy*, and *Nightmare*)—you're the ones who make this dream possible.

About the Contributors

Called "violent, poetic, and compulsively readable" by *Maclean's*, science fiction author **Tobias S. Buckell** is a *New York Times* best-selling writer born in the Caribbean. He grew up in Grenada and spent time in the British and U.S. Virgin Islands, and the islands he lived on influence much of his work. His Xenowealth series begins with *Crystal Rain*. Along with other stand-alone novels and his more than fifty stories, his works have been translated into eighteen different languages. He has been nominated for awards like the Hugo, Nebula, Prometheus, and Astounding Award for Best New Writer. He currently lives in Bluffton, Ohio, with his wife, twin daughters, and a pair of dogs. He can be found online at tobiasbuckell.com.

Originally from New Orleans, **James L. Cambias** was educated at the University of Chicago and lives in western Massachusetts. His first novel, *A Darkling Sea*, was published by Tor in 2014, followed by *Corsair* in 2015. Baen released his novel *Arkad's World* in 2019, and *The Initiate* in 2020. His short fiction has appeared in *The Magazine of Fantasy & Science Fiction, Shimmer, Nature*, and several original anthologies; most recently in the collection *Retellings of the Inland Seas*. In March 2020, his story "Treatment Option" was adapted for audio by DUST Studios, with Danny Trejo.

Cambias has written for Steve Jackson Games, Hero Games, and other role-playing publishers and co-founded Zygote Games. He is a member of the XPrize Foundation's Science Fiction Advisory Board. He blogs at jamescambias.com.

Becky Chambers is the author of the Hugo Award–winning Wayfarers series, which currently includes *The Long Way to a Small, Angry Planet*; *A Closed and Common Orbit*; and *Record of a Spaceborn Few*. Her books have also been nominated for the Arthur C. Clarke Award, the Locus Award, and the Women's Prize for Fiction, among others. Her most recent work is *To Be Taught, If Fortunate*, a stand-alone novella. She lives with her wife in Northern California and hopes to see Earth from orbit one day. She can be found online at otherscribbles.com.

Kate Elliott's most recent novel is *Unconquerable Sun*, a gender-swapped Alexander the Great in space. She is also known for her Crown of Stars epic fantasy series, the Afro-Celtic post-Roman alt-history fantasy (with lawyer dinosaurs) *Cold Magic* and sequels, the science fiction Novels of the Jaran, the YA fantasy *Court of Fives*, and the epic fantasy Crossroads trilogy (with giant justice eagles). She lives in Hawaii, where she paddles outrigger canoes and spoils her schnauzer. You can find her online at kate elliott.substack.com and @KateElliottSFF on Twitter.

C.C. Finlay is the author of the Traitor to the Crown historical fantasy trilogy, which began with *The Patriot Witch*, as well as a stand-alone fantasy novel, *The Prodigal Troll*. He's published more than forty stories since 2001, many of which have been reprinted in volumes of the Year's Best Fantasy, Year's Best Science Fiction, Best New Horror, and other anthologies. Some of his short stories have been finalists for the Hugo, Nebula, Sidewise, and Sturgeon

Awards and have been translated into more than a dozen languages. Fourteen early stories were collected in *Wild Things*. Between 2014 and 2021, Finlay also edited *The Magazine of Fantasy & Science Fiction*. He lives in Arizona with his wife, young adult novelist Rae Carson. You can find him online at ccfinlay.com.

Jeffrey Ford is the author of the novels *The Physiognomy, Memoranda, The Beyond, The Portrait of Mrs. Charbuque, The Girl in the Glass, The Cosmology of the Wider World, The Shadow Year, The Twilight Pariah, Ahab's Return*, and *Out of Body*. His short story collections are *The Fantasy Writer's Assistant, The Empire of Ice Cream, The Drowned Life, Crackpot Palace, A Natural History of Hell*, and *The Best of Jeffrey Ford*. Ford's fiction has appeared in numerous magazines and anthologies and has been widely translated. It has garnered World Fantasy, Edgar Allan Poe, Shirley Jackson, Nebula, and other awards. Learn more at well-builtcity.com.

Theodora Goss was born in Hungary and spent her childhood in various European countries before her family moved to the United States, where she completed a PhD in English literature. She is the World Fantasy, Locus, and Mythopoeic Award–winning author of the short story and poetry collections *In the Forest of Forgetting* (2006), *Songs for Ophelia* (2014), and *Snow White Learns Witchcraft* (2019), as well as novella *The Thorn and the Blossom* (2012), debut novel *The Strange Case of the Alchemist's Daughter* (2017), and sequels *European Travel for the Monstrous Gentlewoman* (2018) and *The Sinister Mystery of the Mesmerizing Girl* (2019). She has been a finalist for the Nebula, Crawford, and Shirley Jackson Awards, as well as on the Tiptree Award Honor List. Her work has been translated into fifteen languages. She teaches literature and writing at Boston University and in the Stonecoast MFA Program. Visit her at theodoragoss.com.

Darcie Little Badger is a Lipan Apache scientist, writer, and friendly goth. After studying gene expression in toxin-producing phytoplankton, she received a PhD from Texas A&M University. Her short fiction has appeared in several publications, including *Fantasy Magazine* and *Strange Horizons* and the anthologies *The New Voices of Science Fiction*; *New Suns*; and *Love Beyond Body, Space, and Time*. Her debut novel, *Elatsoe*, came out from Levine Querido in 2020. Darcie tweets as @ShiningComic. To learn more, visit darcielittlebadger.wordpress.com.

Jonathan Maberry is a *New York Times* bestselling author, five-time Bram Stoker Award–winner, and comic book writer. His vampire apocalypse book series, V-WARS, was a Netflix original series. He writes in multiple genres, including suspense, thriller, horror, science fiction, fantasy, and action, for adults, teens, and middle grade. He is the editor of many anthologies, including *The X-Files, Aliens: Bug Hunt, Don't Turn Out the Lights, Nights of the Living Dead*, and others. His comics include *Black Panther: Doom-War, Captain America, Pandemica, Highway to Hell, The Punisher*, and *Bad Blood*. He is a board member of the Horror Writers Association and president of the International Association of Media Tie-in Writers. Visit him online at jonathanmaberry.com.

Seanan McGuire was born and raised in Northern California, resulting in a love of rattlesnakes and an absolute terror of weather. She shares a crumbling old farmhouse with a variety of cats, far too many books, and enough horror movies to be considered a problem. She publishes about three books a year, and is widely rumored not to actually sleep. When bored, McGuire tends to wander into swamps and cornfields, which has not yet managed to get her killed (although not for lack of trying). She also writes as Mira Grant, filling the role of her own evil twin, and tends to talk about horrible diseases at the dinner table.

An (pronounce it "On") **Owomoyela** is a neutrois author with a background in web development, linguistics, and weaving chain mail out of stainless steel fencing wire, whose fiction has appeared in a number of venues, including *Clarkesworld, Asimov's Science Fiction, Lightspeed,* and a handful of best-of-the-year anthologies. Owomoyela's interests range from pulsars and Cepheid variables to gender studies and nonstandard pronouns, with a plethora of stops in between. Se can be found online at an.owomoyela.net.

Dexter Palmer is the author of *Mary Toft; or, The Rabbit Queen,* which was shortlisted for the 2020 Joyce Carol Oates Prize and longlisted for the 2021 Dublin Literary Award; *Version Control,* which was selected as one of the best novels of 2016 by *GQ,* the *San Francisco Chronicle,* and other publications; and *The Dream of Perpetual Motion,* which was selected as one of the best debuts of 2010 by *Kirkus Reviews.* He lives in Princeton, New Jersey. Learn more at dexterpalmer.com.

Cadwell Turnbull is the author of the novels *The Lesson* and *No Gods, No Monsters.* He is a graduate of North Carolina State University's Creative Writing MFA in Fiction and English MA in Linguistics. Turnbull is also a graduate of Clarion West 2016. His short fiction has appeared in *The Verge, Lightspeed, Nightmare, Asimov's Science Fiction,* and a number of anthologies. His *Nightmare* story "Loneliness Is in Your Blood" was selected for *The Best American Science Fiction and Fantasy 2018.* His *Lightspeed* story "Jump" was selected for *The Year's Best Science Fiction and Fantasy 2019* and was featured on the podcast *LeVar Burton Reads.* His novel *The Lesson* made several "Best of 2019" lists, including *Publisher's Weekly, Library Journal,* and *Kirkus Reviews.* Turnbull teaches creative writing at North Carolina State University. Learn more at cadwellturnbull.com.

Genevieve Valentine is the author of *Mechanique: A Tale of the Circus Tresaulti* (2012 Crawford Award), *The Girls at the Kingfisher Club*, *Persona*, and *Icon*. She has written *Catwoman* for DC Comics and *Xena: Warrior Princess* for Dynamite. Her short stories have appeared in over a dozen best-of-the-year anthologies, including several years of Best American Science Fiction and Fantasy. Her cultural criticism has appeared at NPR.org, *The AV Club*, *LA Review of Books*, Vice, Vox, and the *New York Times*, among others. Learn more at genevievevalentine.com.

Carrie Vaughn's work includes the Philip K. Dick Award–winning novel *Bannerless*, the *New York Times* bestselling Kitty Norville urban fantasy series, over twenty novels, and upward of one hundred short stories, two of which have been finalists for the Hugo Award. Her most recent work includes a Kitty spin-off collection, *The Immortal Conquistador*; a pair of novellas about Robin Hood's children, *The Ghosts of Sherwood* and *The Heirs of Locksley*; and a new novel called *Questland*. She's a contributor to the Wild Cards series of shared-world superhero books edited by George R. R. Martin and a graduate of the Odyssey Fantasy Writing Workshop. An Air Force brat, she survived her nomadic childhood and managed to put down roots in Boulder, Colorado. Visit her online at carrievaughn.com.

Charles Yu is the author of four books, including his latest novel, *Interior Chinatown*. He has received the National Book Foundation's 5 Under 35 award and has been nominated for two Writers Guild of America Awards for his work in television. He has written for shows on several networks, including HBO, FX, AMC, and Adult Swim. His fiction and nonfiction have appeared in *The New Yorker*, the *New York Times*, *The Atlantic*, and *Time* magazine, among other publications.

E. Lily Yu is the author of *On Fragile Waves*, published in 2021, which the *New York Times* described as "devastating and perfect." She received the Artist Trust's LaSalle Storyteller Award in 2017 and the Astounding Award for Best New Writer in 2012, and has been a finalist for the Hugo, Nebula, Locus, Sturgeon, and World Fantasy Awards. More than thirty of her short stories have appeared in venues from *McSweeney's* to *Boston Review* to *Tor.com*, as well as twelve best-of-the-year anthologies.

About the Editor

John Joseph Adams is the series editor of Best American Science Fiction and Fantasy, as well as the bestselling editor of more than thirty anthologies, including *Wastelands: Stories of the Apocalypse* and *The Living Dead*. Recent books include The Dystopia Triptych, *A People's Future of the United States*, and *Wastelands: The New Apocalypse*. Called "the reigning king of the anthology world" by Barnes & Noble, Adams is a two-time winner of the Hugo Award (for which he has been a finalist twelve times) and an eight-time World Fantasy Award finalist. Adams is also the editor and publisher of the digital magazine *Lightspeed* and publisher of its sister magazines *Fantasy* and *Nightmare*. In addition to his work in short fiction, Adams also ran the John Joseph Adams Books novel imprint for Houghton Mifflin Harcourt for five years, for which he acquired books by Veronica Roth, Hugh Howey, Carrie Vaughn, Greg Bear, and many others. Learn more about him online at johnjosephadams.com and on Twitter @johnjosephadams.